Caron Freeborn was born into a ~~~~~~~~~~~~ ~~~~~~~~~~~~
no academic qualifications wen~~~~~~~~~~~~~~~~~~~~~~~~~~late
twenties. She is now a senior member of Lucy Cavendish
College, Cambridge, teaching English for several colleges in
the university. She is thirty-six. This is her first novel.

Three Blind Mice

By
Caron Freeborn

An *Abacus* Book

First published in Great Britain in 2001
by Abacus
This edition published in 2002
by Abacus

A CIP catalogue record for this book
is available from the British Library.

ISBN 0 349 11382 3

Typeset in Rotis Serif by Palimpsest Book Production Limited,
Polmont, Stirlingshire
Printed and bound in Great Britain by
Bookmarque Ltd, Croydon, Surrey

Abacus
An Imprint of
Time Warner Books UK
Brettenham House
Lancaster Place
London WC2E 7EN

www.TimeWarnerBooks.co.uk

To Bobbie and Tony, for learning me my language

Chapter One

'. . . just sit with your back to the wall.'

'I might just do that.'

'And don't ask for anything poncy.'

'Is lager hard enough?'

'Long as you chase it.'

And chasing never hurt a man, although some chases were longer than others.

Ben might not of clocked them coming in, if he weren't watching the door. Marvellous. Who was Rosie up to now? Don't show her face in weeks, and now she turns up with some big geezer two steps behind. TR6 towing a Transit. Never looked like a client neither, and most definite weren't from the manor. She looked brilliant, more'n even what she usually did, but it never looked like work. Dress so tight you could see what she'd had for breakfast, shoes up to her armpits. Better suss it out, get the score fore Spence got here. If Spence thought Ben'd let some tosser get his mitts on her . . . Ben picked up his pint, and moved to the darkest corner of the pub, settling hisself in the big leather chair. Rosie and the geezer had gone round the pool table and dumped their gear, and was stood right over at the other side of the bar. What's the matter with him – she have to hold his hand or what?

Weren't all that surprising she never see him, way she kept her eyes on the bloke. Ben never hardly remembered seeing her do that, not since that flash bastard she'd gone with first come down here with her, and never with that last one. But for the life of him, he couldn't see what she thought she was looking up at. Weren't all that. Walked like a fucking cripple. Nose had taken a pop at some point, tell her that much for nothing. He'd never even had a shave tonight, far as Ben could tell. You go out with a woman like Rosie Spence, you make the effort. Looked like he never knew what she was. Ben run his hand over his own chin. Smooth as a baby's arse. Weren't doing him no good, was it? Never had done. He could paint hisself in gold, and his spunk could be Glenmorangie, but it wouldn't never be good enough. So why this one? Geezer looked like he'd been down the jumble and all, and what's he have that Sainsbury's carrier for? She was a diamond, and look at him. How the fuck had that happened?

When a butterfly in Africa flaps its wings, Asian mountains tumble.

No way, man. No. Not Alex with that Rosie Spence. Not him with her. Sam could've cried, except for that would be miles over the top. But if Alex was going about with her, the world weren't like Sam'd thought it was. The world weren't right no more. *Asian mountains tumble. Asian mountains tumble. Asian mountains tumble.*

Should've got off at Stepney, gone down Globe Road and home that way. But something'd kept him stuck to his seat on the tube and, shit man, nearly missed the next stop as well. Come out the station, looked over at the hospital – felt like the dark was cos of some massive shadow from that instead of half the street lights being out. Too many bad ones in there. Too many times of being pumped out like one of their bags of blood, like you didn't have no feelings. His family always said he had too many feelings.

Hated it round here, specially at night. Sam turned left and straight away see the green Jag, smiling at him like in that crocodile poem at school. One of them mad brothers' motors – yeah, belonged to the mega-mad one. But it weren't stopping, just slowing down as it passed the pub. Sam's heart was too quick. Never had no trouble with them, but he couldn't handle being on the end of their smiles, neither. Only ever been in that pub once. Except for the dirty old sign, what had mice on it with rat faces and what squeaked like the rats was about to leap down on you, it looked fine. Nice even, done up with flower lights and shit like something Up West, but Jags was nice too, and they could still hold things you didn't want to be too close to.

Then he see Alex with his hand on that lady brief's back, going after her through the pub door. Going. In. There. Shit, she was a freaky lady, spite being small. All . . . lines, as if God'd sharpened her up. Even from the back she looked hard, like an upside-down triangle, weren't no softness nowhere. No crocodile would dare touch her, man.

Alex. Last see him a couple or three month back at the Centre. Gave him the horrors that place too, always had done. Could call it a Centre instead of a Drugs Unit all they liked, but didn't change what it was. Words, that's all – didn't mean nothing. Still full of poor little birds with sores over their faces, like it was the latest fashion. Even the frigging concrete had cancer.

'Sam Patterson, boomerang boy. Would say it's nice to see you here again, but it isn't . . .' Alex. He was safe, guy. Sorted. Put on a bit a weight over the last three year, but he'd always been able to pick you up off the floor if you needed it. Safe. Alex'd pulled a bit of paint off his door, and showed Sam into his office. Different one from before. Window nearly too high to see out of, and way too filthy. First off, Sam'd thought that poster cheered the place up a bit – butterfly, loads of colour, sort of thing girls stick on their bedroom walls. But that was when he'd noticed the words. *When a butterfly in Africa flaps its wings, Asian mountains tumble.* One of them things meant nothing. More words to mess with your head, trying to make sense out of something made no sense. With words. Had to get some jellies later, words whizzing about in his head.

Alex made sense. Not always what you wanted to hear, but
you could hear it all right.

'Look, we both know that's all bollocks.' Sorted it for you.
Bollocks. Yeah. Some bird told Sam that Alex was a mentalist
what lived on his own, and he must be as old as her dad. Said
he was a sad old git. No way, guy. Never used to live on his
own, Sam could remember that. And he never used to be a
mentalist.

But now, with the door of the pub swallowing Alex up, Sam
weren't sure what to believe. If Rosie Spence could make out
Alex, Sam must've got him all wrong. Better go get a 'script.

'How am I doing?' Alex said in her ear. Rosie shivered and
sipped her wine.

'No one much is in yet.' What on earth was Alex making
of all this? Perfectly ordinary brewery make-over: a middle-
aged dive given a veneer of respectability, an allusion to class,
with its tulip lamps and green leather, even horse brasses, for
Christ's sake. No wonder tourists wandered in here, fooled into
thinking it was a half of Best and tuna sandwich kind of place.
Alex must have thought she'd been exaggerating. 'Give us a
cigarette, will you?' she said.

'So when do the lions arrive?' Alex lit two cigarettes, passed
one to Rosie. She drew deeply, looking intently at him through
the smoke. The way he was pulling on his pint was a good
move: steady, not rushing it, not sipping. Clearly, he'd listened
to her.

'Any time. There's one of my major clients now, sitting over
at the bar. With his wife, the ones with their bums pointing
out at the world, look. Can't have seen us.'

'Right.' Alex glanced over, uninterested. 'You look gorgeous
tonight.' He stared down at the table, then suddenly looked
back at her.

'I do?' They'd better not mess this up for her. And he'd better
not mess it up, either.

'You know you do.' He took her hand, rubbing the knuckles

with his thumb. 'Sorry,' he said, letting it go. She searched the pub with a quick look, nodded at a couple of punters. Four weeks of dinners, coffees, bars; just that, and she was bringing him here. Precipitate. It wasn't as though she knew yet where else they were going. 'Rosie, stop fidgeting, it'll either be fine or it won't. Worrying about it won't change anything.'

'Yeah, I know that, thanks.' Good job they were already sitting down; Rosie didn't want Alex's heavy-footed, uneven walk to be the first thing people noticed about him. Looked as though he'd only recently reacquired the skill after an accident. And why did he always have that carrier bag full of his papers? Even a briefcase would be more acceptable. 'Did you get a chance to look at that book?'

'God, woman, that wasn't a novel, that was mental masturbation. I showed it to someone I work with, and she couldn't believe it.'

'Yeah, well you hate novels, bloody Philistine.' She rolled her shoulders. And then the circus finally arrived right in the town square. 'Here comes my pet lion cub, anyway,' she said, downing the rest of her wine.

'All right, Rosie love?'

'Ben!' She offered her cheek to be kissed. 'This is Alex. Ben's an old friend of the family.' Rosie had to laugh at herself. Bloody middle-class concept. Made it sound as though Ben was regularly invited to their estate, rather than having eaten chips at their house at least as often as at his own when they were growing up.

'I was just going to get them in,' said Alex, rising to his feet, looming over Ben: stone blunts scissors. Sorry, Ben, you haven't got a prayer next to him. More chance of being Pope.

'No, mate – my pub, my shout.' Sounded more like a whine. 'What're you chasing?'

'Vodka. And Rosie's on red. Merlot.' Nice one, Alex, letting him know the score but softly, gently. Rosie pushed her glass across the table.

'Vino? Sure you don't you want a . . .' Ben held his thumb and forefinger an inch apart.

'Not yet, I'll drink with the big boys later.' She hadn't meant it to come out like that. Oh well, tough. Ben let it go, but she could see he was hurt. 'You can get us some crisps, though. Ready salted.' Rosie watched Ben snake his lean frame through the pub; she gestured pointedly to his back, wanting Alex somehow to see that the walk, the sartorial etiquette, the nuances of agreed behaviour, were the tools of the guild. That individuality was suspect. But to explain would be to break ranks. Why the hell wasn't Alex either less sexy or more convenient?

Good, there was Ben mooching across from Rosie's table. Sue was itching to know. Weren't exactly packed yet, but she didn't think Freddy had even seen that his brief was in with a new fella. You could say Ben not coming over to discuss it, before going to see Rosie, showed a lack of respect. Course if Sue'd said they was in, Freddy'd have told her nicely to keep her nose out.

'. . . and a packet of plain crisps. What about the missus, Freddy – what's she having?'

Sue wished Ben'd talk direct to her, not just to the old man. Blimey, the skinny-arse had worked for Freddy on and off for years, doing whatever his boys did, think he'd have the decency to use her name. Freddy'd say she wanted Barcardi and Coke. Pity – she could've fancied a white wine.

'Spence's Rosie's about, with some geezer,' said Ben, holding a note over the bar. 'See him? There, table behind the boys.'

Freddy straightened his cuffs, sort of like he weren't doing nothing particular, and slowly turned round. Blow that, trying to be subtle. Sue shifted her bum on the bar-stool and leaned over to have a proper butcher's this time. Rosie always did have right good taste. Late thirties, early forties? Older than Rosie anyway, though plenty of dark in his hair still. He caught her staring and flashed her a big smile, looking away then right at her again, with another smile. Sue felt herself go all red. Cheeky so-and-so. But she couldn't help smiling back.

Lovely eyes, that kind of grey what looks clear but then you
see it goes on too deep to get to the bottom of him. She pulled
at her neckline, so's it definitely covered the top of her bra.
Not a problem poor Rosie'd ever have. Though fair's fair, Sue'd
love to be able to get into that little dress – definitely designer,
something trendy like Lacroix. But then Rosie didn't have kids
of course. Probably didn't want to spoil her figure, what little
there was of it. Felt sorry for her, in a way – weren't natural
for a woman to be so career minded. There weren't any side
to her, but she was a hard one to make out.

'I'd better have a word with madam,' Freddy said. 'The man
looks kosher enough, but we'd all prefer to be sure. What you
reckon, Ben? Weights or the measure?'

'You be careful, love,' Sue said, trying not to sound like a
nag. 'We can't afford to get her back up. I don't want to be
stuck.' Women and children first? That's a joke. Faces and their
briefs, more like.

'Rosie'd never let that happen – don't come no sharper.
Worth too much to her, ain't I?'

Ben scratched the end of his nose.

'Some cunts think they can come down The Three Blind
Mice and just shoot off with the fucking prize,' he said, under
his breath. To Freddy.

They was so busy moaning on at each other like a couple
of old women scared the new granny'll push in at the post
office, they missed the best bit. Spence strolled in, looked round
the pub in that squinty way, and – what's the word? – *saun-
tered* over to Rosie's table. Stood next to her, eyeballing her
fella, pulled his knife out of his jacket, started cleaning his
nails with it. How casual was that supposed to look? Might as
well be watching a spaghetti western. Not that Spence was
exactly Clint Eastwood, unless Clint had lost a few inches from
his height and found them round his waist. Sue wanted to
laugh. She couldn't see the fella's face, Spence's arm was in
the way, but she'd bet he never found it as funny.

*   *   *

Internally, Rosie cringed. They needn't think she hadn't noticed Freddy's missus having a good old nose. Sometimes, being Rosie Spence wasn't all they thought it was. And did he *have* to behave like a five-year-old, showing off his toys?

'Think you better introduce me,' he said. After a careful space. Oh for Christ's sake, where was he playing at being, Sicily? Rosie shook her head at him.

'Don't you bother with *hello*, these days?' She stood, and planted a showy and probably unwelcome kiss near his lips. He returned the kiss, his eyes firmly on The Stranger. 'Alex, this is my brother, Darren. Just to confuse you, most people call him Spence. Darren, Alex. And no, I haven't known him long.' Ben came over carrying their drinks. Rosie sat down again. 'Sorry, Daz, Ben's beaten you to it.' Bugger, knowing Daz, he'd mind that she'd immediately used that nickname in front of an outsider.

'Turn it in.' Daz examined his nails, and closed his knife. Slowly. Of course. He started to put out his hand for Alex to shake, then appeared to change his mind. Luckily, Alex hadn't begun to respond. 'Ben, get them in for us.' He reached into his jacket, extracted the inevitable large wad of notes, threw it on the table. Had to be a grand there.

'Prices gone up, have they?' asked Rosie. Risky, but she couldn't let Daz get the upper hand, not this early in the game. Alex looked at the money, then at Rosie. His expression barely changed, but there was just a hint of contempt in his eyes. Careful, Alex, don't blow it. Ben peeled off one of the notes and went back to the bar. Daz pulled out a chair; he leaned on it for a couple of seconds, displaying to advantage those scarred hands and his Rolex. Protection in broker's clothing.

'So what you doing here?' Blurred around the consonants, as usual.

'Same as you. We've come for a drink.'

'Likes a drink, does he?'

'Yeah, and he takes sugar and all. Come on, give us a break.' Rosie reached across the table, lightly touching his hand. 'And

give us a cigarette, angel.' She looked into his eyes, giving him
the full treatment. He returned her stare, his eyes still, then he
grabbed her wrist and pinched her cheek (not hard enough to
hurt), his voice low.

'You little tart – what've I told you bout wearing nail
varnish?'

Alex sat up straighter. Don't say anything, babe.

'It's only the clear stuff,' Rosie pointed out, irritation chafing
the inside of the wrist he held.

'Here,' said Alex firmly, handing her a lit cigarette. Would
Daz hack that? Rosie eased out from her brother's grasp.

'So what do you do, mate? Same line as Rosie?'

'No, I work in drug rehab.'

Shit.

Shit.

Shit.

So much for being clued; why hadn't she told him? It was
such an obvious one, it was always going to come up. And
with Daz in the mood he was in. Daz gave a wry smile. He
looked . . . well, like he'd just been told her new boyfriend
worked in rehab.

'Here, mate – see him?' he said at last, nodding at a big
tattooed bloke by the toilets. 'No, don't look. He's a nutter.
Axed his brother.'

'Least he kept it in the family.'

'Everything's kept in the family round here, pal.' In full rent-
a-villain mode, Daz easily beat himself trying to be funny.
Rosie smiled.

'Careful, you'll have Alex thinking we're all inbreds.
Motherfucker.' She'd made him laugh. Good. If he relaxed, he'd
look less like he'd had a personality bypass, and Alex would
know more what he had to work with.

'I'm in the metal game meself,' Daz told Alex, softly.

Elbow room was getting a bit hard to come by, and every cunt
had sent over a drink. They was lined up, and Ben watched

close, see if the geezer was bottling it. Couldn't be sure. Might
be a different story if the boys decided to bring the pints over
theirselves, stead of standing just near enough to clock the
action. Even though Rosie was off jawing to that client's missus
on the far settee, Ben could feel her keeping Alex on the end
of her sight-line, like she could see through them elbows. But
he couldn't of said how he knew. Or if Spence did.

'Play pool, do you?' Ben nodded over at the table.

'A bit.' Alex eyed up the cloth. 'Why, d'you want a game?'

Spence'd make trifle of the bloke. Ben looked forward to
seeing that.

'Maybe lateron.' Spence said, making Alex turn his head to
him as if he was watching Wimbledon. 'See anything else you
fancy?' Opening his arms like a yid on a stall, nearly belting
the old boy behind him. 'Talent's okay here – not much of it,
but the quality ain't bad.'

'I'm pretty fussy usually about the company I keep,' Alex
said.

'Keeping the best tonight.' Spence picked a bit of skin off
his lip.

'I think so.'

'She's our little diamond,' said Ben. 'Place'd be empty, weren't
for what she does.' Don't know what he'd said wrong, but
Spence never liked it.

'Thing is, best company don't come cheap – d'you understand me? Price's got to be right.' Giving Alex the meaningfuls.

'What about the currency?' Holding Spence's stare. Ben had
to give the geezer that – he had balls.

'Well . . . yeah.' A load of lines come across Spence's forehead. 'Scuse us, mate. Only be five. Shift it, Ben – we got to
go sort something.'

With the reptile away, the cat has full extension. Rosie eased
through the scrutiny and came back over to her chair, resting
her shoe on Alex's thigh, under the table. He brushed her cheek
with the back of his hand. Brave, considering. Rosie pressed

her spiked heel into the top of his leg, making him flinch, and then took her foot away. She looked at his mouth, up into his eyes.

'Behave yourself.' But he did lean across the table to kiss her, softly, briefly, on the lips. Automatically, she glanced around the pub, catching at the stares before they could get free.

'Daz's a nice bloke, really. Just . . . I don't think he can get his head around the fact that I'm all grown up.'

'Rosie, anyone with half an eye can see you're all grown up. Definitely all the blokes in here, even him.' He scratched the hairy back of his hand. 'Feels like they're checking if I'm fit to be one of the drones. *And* you can protect them from the one thing they're really scared of. That's powerful, you must know that.'

That's the point, baby. Look up, and see how they run.

'Don't think any of them know what to make of you.' She laughed. 'By the way, my Daz would've been a candidate for the Centre in the old days, in another universe.'

'Oh, that's great, thanks for telling me. So he's in the metal game? What was that, a reference to his knife?'

'Scrap metal.' Admittedly, that was a point of view. 'He's got a yard at St Pancras.'

'I was joking, Rosie.' He picked up his pint, then replaced it without drinking. 'No sense in giving an advantage.'

But in this place, no one waited for advantages to be offered, they just had them away on the quiet. And suddenly, it all seemed too much: the constant watchfulness, the trial-by-cliché. All the flies circling, the web clinging to her feet. Yeah, Alex did something serious to her, but was it worth it, after all? To be judged by default from both sides, to have to say to each one that she wasn't what they claimed for her. Rosie lit yet another cigarette. Alex couldn't have failed to notice that she didn't offer him one. On the wall, above his head, was a print of some eighteenth-century cartoon personifying Justice as a crabbed old woman; should be a bloody narky villain.

'You've gone right in on yourself, haven't you?' He stroked her arm. 'We can get through this, you know. I think it's worth it, myself.' Just when she'd thought it wasn't, he'd chosen to read her mind and to change it. Dangerous bastard. Rosie picked up one of his drinks; he took it from her, shaking his head. Jesus, it was going to be a long evening.

The pub was getting too warm as well now, smoky; Rosie blew Freddy Boyd a kiss, and raised her glass to Sue. Alex chased another vodka. Daz and Ben exchanged little glances, two big kids with a secret. Rosie breathed in the familiar smell of deep whiskey-soaked pile, thick and expensive, of new leather and cigars. If she were to close her eyes and stop her ears, she'd be hard pressed to know whether she was here or in her club. Her colleagues would be horrified by the comparison; they really believed East End pubs were all Knees Up Mother Brown and slapping a badly dressed cellulite thigh. And they actually thought their own game was complicated. What if Alex decided he couldn't handle being a player? Well, he'd never be that, but he'd have to fake it, holding up with no chance of Kalouki, even with both lurkers. God, she wanted to get him where she wanted him. Never actually had to persuade a man to come on to her before. It better had be worth it.

'Lipstick, girl.' Daz indicated the direction of the toilets.

'I'm not a kid, I can decide for myself whether my make-up needs doing.' But she went anyway and, sod him, he was right, her lipstick had been left behind on her glass and cigarette ends. Alex had probably never even heard of Kalouki. She sharpened her lip-pencil, determined not to rush; for one thing, it would look too much like he needed her protection, and for another, she had to make sure she looked good around here.

Alex's ball was close over the bottom pocket, but the other yellow was too tight on the bottom cushion. Not easy to guess what he'd play, whether he'd go for limited risk. If he managed to come in accurately down the table, he should be able to disturb the tricky one off the cushion and still get his pot, but if he messed up, Daz would clear both his reds no danger. Rosie's hands were clammy with empathy or excitement; it was a tight game, Daz wasn't getting it all his own way, though Alex needed to win this one. Okay, he'd lost the first on the black and won the second with three balls, but Daz had got too cocky and thrown it a bit there. There was a ton on the table; Alex hadn't had much choice, placing his four tens, a five, four pound coins and some change on top of Daz's note with a steady hand. Not that fifty quid was the biggest stake here. Ben had his arm around a girl who must have once been told she had a beautiful laugh: every time Alex sized up, she screeched like she'd been shot. Rosie pressed her hands together. The glare hurt her eyes; even tulip lamps weren't giving a soft enough light. Come on, babe, you have to do this.

Ben didn't think the geezer could do it – but be fair, he'd played it sweet as. Spence had made a wrong call – the bloke was still upright, and getting the balls. It was quite a naughty angle, not one Ben would've liked to been forced to play in them conditions. Sort of shot you'd look a right cunt for missing, but what was easy enough to balls up. His reach was long though – had a good few inches on Spence. Rosie couldn't take her eyes off him. Seemed like the scruffy bastard must be getting it. But how? What's his story?

Rosie caught Alex's eye. Briefly, they stared at each other, then Alex bent to take his shot. His body curved into the table. The white went soft on the easy ball, which clipped the awkward one as it went down. Alex straightened, moved heavily, almost stumbling, around the table, eyed the ball. Rosie flushed; couldn't he move normally? Daz turned to her, red-rimmed lids unblinking.

'Who do you fancy?' Hardly moving his lips. Rosie pulled her hair back out of her face.

'Wouldn't you like to know, Daz?' But Alex was now out of her line of vision; some prat had positioned himself in front of the table. Slowly, she went over, reached up to put her hand, still holding her cigarette, on his shoulder. 'Better move I think, don't you?' she said. 'There's a good boy.' Looked like he'd love to say something, but Rosie was buggered if she was going to give the chancer an opening. 'Quicker to train a chimp,' she added. He shifted. Rosie felt everyone watching her. What was she, the interval entertainment? Alex lined up the shot, took it; it curved a bit too much, but it went down. Although the black was behind a red, it wasn't too difficult a ball.

'Yours, mate,' said Daz, handing him the ton. He even grinned. Rosie wouldn't have expected that. 'And your shout, if I ain't mistaken.'

Hemmed in. Head throbbing, desperately needing to stretch. Freddy Boyd came over, followed by other clients, a junta parade of silver jackets and coloured shirts. All prepared to pay the price. Rosie began to refuse drinks, although Alex, God help him, hadn't wimped out. Buzz, buzz, buzz. The pinkish lights seeming slowly to be darkening; Rosie staring into her lap, the brothel tint creeping over her black dress; soundtrack looping, a reel-to-reel never upgraded.

Notebook, seen him?
        So what's that involve, then?
She played a blinder today – you'd have . . .
        You known her long?
                . . . proud.
Long black curly teeth, walks with a lisp.
        He's a fucking lucky bastard – how'd he do it?
                Walked away. Lovely.
Ben reckons he's . . .   My Sue bought one.
        In his dreams.
                        . . . her.
Got hollow legs.

      Tuesday.   *Won't touch me with a . . .*
   Paper bag job, mate.
               Better not let her hear . . .
What's he got that I haven't?
   A dick?

                      . . . say that.

'You coming back with me, tonight?' Rosie bit her lip. Alex looked her over, slowly.

'No, not tonight, I'll get the cab to drop you again.' As he reached for the ashtray to put out his cigarette, his hand shook slightly. What *was* his game? Did he get off on watching her practically beg? She was sure it wasn't this place that had scared him off. 'I'm getting used to these now,' he said, tapping her cigarette packet against his glass. 'I couldn't see why you smoked them at first. Thought the name was bang on, being as they tasted like the dung of camels or something.' Oh no you don't, boy.

'Fine. But you don't have to drop me, I'm sure one of the blokes would take me.'

'I'm sure they would . . . but I wouldn't be too happy with that.' He stared at her. Of all the bloody nerve. She leaned forward, letting her hair fall in front of her eyes, so she could sweep it back and look hard at him.

'Okay.' What? Just occasionally, her mouth engaged before her brain. Which he'd know about, if ever he had the bottle to come home with her.

Rosie drank some water from the fountain and repaired her face; she was okay, now she had some room to move. Alex would just have to carry on taking his chances. Not that he seemed to want to take them with her. And yet, he was definitely a bit more than interested: she'd seen, and seen to, that.

'He's a doll.' Sue had come in, and was piling on the lippy, although not quite on her lips, it had to be said. Alex could make that into a wicked little drawing.

'I know. What's Freddy think?'

'You know him, darling – but him and you have got so much history . . .'

'Don't worry, Sue, I've always seen Freddy all right.'

'I know you have, love. Here, is he as good as he looks?'

I don't doubt it.

'Sorry, client confidentiality.' Funnily enough, that was one of the first things she'd said to Alex. He'd been furious on the 'phone, ranting at her perfectly reasonable inquiry. For Christ's sake, she'd been prepared to pay, and that place certainly needed the money. She'd thought he must be Mr PC, all bezzy mates with the poor disadvantaged junkies. And her client had a real chance of time without the Centre's help, crucially needed that referral. But Alex had kept on, implying her dishonesty, demanding why and what. Client confidentiality, she'd told him coldly. To which he'd replied, *Bollocks.*

Something in the way he'd said it made her ask him to come in to see her. He'd lurched through her office door the next evening, wearing an ancient quilted jacket that swelled his already considerable bulk to bouncer proportions; immediately, she'd realized her interest had been misapplied. She'd begun, systematically, to refute his accusations of buying rehab as a soft alternative to prison; abruptly, he'd stopped her. He hadn't eaten all day, he was *hungry*, couldn't they discuss it over a curry? She must be able to get one on expenses. Rosie had been about to refuse when he'd smiled. Bollocks.

'See you again, mate,' the Governor said to Alex as they left The Mice.

'Really?' said Rosie, quietly. Instinctively, she sniffed the air. Still missed the hops, the treacle smell of her childhood, replaced now by the petrol of the new Sainsbury's garage. Nothing remains the same.

In the cab, Alex leaned over Rosie and kissed her, his carrier bag pressed against her leg, but he moved away as she started to kiss him back, and put the bag on his lap. She could have pulled a trick, but she'd need to have some idea first of why he was so able to resist doing what she wanted. Otherwise, she'd just come off as incompetent.

'You did all right tonight, considering.'

'Considering what? No, don't think I let you down.'

'That pool turned out to be a good move.'

'Loved it, didn't you?' he said, rubbing her thigh. Bastard. 'See you tomorrow?'

Assuming or asking?

'Ring me first, in case something comes up.'

But the way he shook his head, with that twisted-mouthed, right up to the eyes grin of his, suggested he was sure of his ground. One little triumph, and he thought he had it made. Though what he thought he had made was another question. He was a cocky git, but he'd better watch himself; there were only so many chances on offer here, and he'd used up most of them.

He kissed her again as the cab drew up outside her building. She caught the soapy smell of his neck before pulling quickly away.

And she was alone.

She stretched out on the bed, fully clothed. Lifting one leg, she flexed her foot. Her most expensive shoes, the softest, the hardest. Bloody Alex. Sod him. He could just kiss her bloody shoes. Looking at them again, Rosie nodded. Now there was an idea: actually, yes, maybe he could. She tugged her dress up to her hips, and smiled.

Chapter Two

Rosie sat on the middle bench of the three by the round flowerbed; just last week, it had looked stunning, but now (except for some fat purple things that might or might not be chrysanthemums) it was all green and brown, starting to die of its own accord before winter could get in there and finish it off. Didn't blame it. October is the stroppiest month, making its presence felt before September has properly finished its turn. Rosie really didn't have time to come all the way back down here for lunch, but after the morning she'd had, she needed to be well away from the office. Sod it, she'd left *The Times* there, though, and the new Margaret Atwood. She had the period from hell too; had ruined her knickers and they weren't even period pants. Forgetting to put up her *Carpe Diem* on that call just put the lid on it. Not that she ever had any trouble making her six hours, but it had been an uncharacteristic mistake. Of course Alex wasn't married; he might refuse to sleep with Rosie for all kinds of reasons, but Miranda was well wide there. How come Rosie could ring him at home, then? Daz would love that one, if it were true. And since when did being married mean a bloke would turn down a sure thing?

Without enthusiasm, Rosie unwrapped her bagel; smoked salmon flapped out of the sides like generous fins. Her dad used to maintain that fewer than three slices was an insult to your mouth. Probably still did claim that. She opened her bottle of water, and washed down half a Diazepam. *Zara*. Bloody stupid name. She carried it off somehow, though, just like she carried off that outrageous hair, and the reddest of lipsticks, and the suede trousers. Like she carried off the look in her eyes that said she had it and she knew it. Like she carried off their dad. Sometimes, Rosie thought she missed him, but that wasn't it, not really; it was more that her brother couldn't seem to realize she didn't need fathering anymore, and maybe a real father would know that instinctively. From that point of view, Dad was a superstar: he'd anticipated it, and taken it away before she'd had time to want it gone.

'Nice day, ain't it?' An old bloke sat himself heavily beside her on the bench.

'Bit nip. But it's nice to see the sun. Cheers you up, don't it?'

'What you need cheering up for, young girl like you?'

'I think we all need it sometimes, don't we?' She rubbed at her crow's feet, and looked down at her uneaten bagel. 'Listen, I'm not being funny or anything, but you don't want this, do you? It's just, I'm on a diet and I shouldn't be having it.'

'Not charity?' He gave her an appraising stare.

'No, I don't do charity, mate.'

'You girls starving yourselves – ain't natural. Men like a few curves.'

'I'm not exactly wasting away, am I?'

'There's nothing of you! Well, I'll eat it if you're only going to chuck it in the bin.' He took the roll and opened it, nodding approval at the amount of fish. 'Here, you're Mrs Spence's girl, ain't you? Tell her old Herb said all the best. You don't favour her much, sept for being so dark – more a look of your daddy.'

'So they tell me.' Better get a move on, that poncy Counsel was expecting her at his chambers. Pompous git still said Hilary term, as though he were making constant Clinton gags. Have to go straight there; Rosie never allowed herself to be late. She got to her feet.

'And don't forget now – men like a few curves. Don't go silly with it.'

Nan had always tried to get Grandad to come down Barmy Park, but he'd invariably said he wasn't going to sit with all

them old buggers. He'd been over eighty by then. Always wore
a suit, never put his deaf aid on for the street. Would never
have accepted a bagel from a strange woman: *What d'you
think it is here?* Maybe she should have thrown the bloody
thing away.

Who the hell was at the door this time of night? Rosie hadn't
got home until after nine, and had barely had time to take
three Nurofen before someone was trying to muscle in on her
headache. Ought to go over the pleading before relinquishing
it to their outdoor clerk for issue tomorrow, as well. She looked
through the spyhole, not convinced she was going to answer.
Oh, might have known. Through the distorting lens, his face
lengthened and his hair further receded, making his usual pallor
a clown mask. Resisting the urge to put on the chain, she flung
open the door.

   'What're you doing here?'
   'Mum sent me to say you ain't been round in three week.'
He coughed. 'I got to freeze me knackers off on your doorstep,
or what?'
   She eyed him. Daz'd probably told Mum about Alex, to force
her orders. Rosie couldn't decide where to lay her money: on
Daz staying with the importance of family routine, or going
with the Alex inquisition. But at least he'd have dope.
   'Come in, then,' she said. Now she'd have to get up at six
to look at her file.

Darren liked Rosie's little place. It had class, specially the leather
suite and now that new carpet in the same sort of red. Too
many books around, though – and she was allergic to dusting,
dirty cow. When she had a cleaner it was all right, but she
never at the minute and it showed. He watched her take off
her jacket and kick off her shoes. She must of been dying to
do that – how she walked in them, he couldn't never make
out. That blouse was a bit see-through, for work. And he
couldn't chill with her standing there like his brief.

'Do us a favour – stick on a pair a jeans and a tee-shirt, will you?'

'Thought you liked my work clothes.' One of them smiles she done on her face.

'I do, but I feel like a client.' Fuck her, staring him out – he needed to chill right bad, what with Charlie Boyd being on his case all day.

'Oh, all right. Won't be a sec.'

Darren stuck a CD on, from the top of a big wobbly pile. Some black bird on the box. Motown shit. Nice little system, though – he done all right there. Most probably her video could do with a change next off. He took a wander over to check it out, but the row of photos on the shelf behind the telly catched his eye. Bleeding hell, forgot she had that one – him and her and Nana at Southend, when Rosie must of been bout fifteen. Darren leaned over, picked it up by the frame. Flash, that frame, gold coloured. Rosie looked out of it at him, laughing, right skinny and bandy in her black swimming costume, long hair all over the show. He was pretty skinny in it hisself. Why's she have that out? The one of her finishing at college, in the old cap and that, he could understand. And the blurry little one of the old man – well, her choice. But this? She looked a right state, and him and Nan never looked no better. Like the Munsters. He put the picture down, and sat on the settee. Papers all across the nice glass coffee table, most probably from her work. Look at this gaff. Stockings over the radiator . . . spose it weren't just him what come round? They was the sort with the lacy tops, and all. Give a right good pression, that would – cross between an office and a knocking shop.

Rosie sort of danced back in. Jesus, girl – never meant paint your arse blue and put on a tee-shirt must of shrunk in the wash. Mum'd love that.

'All right to skin up?' he said.

'Since when did you ask? I'll put the kettle on.' She chucked one of them big Indian cushions on the floor. It landed by his feet, and she went off to the kitchen.

Bit of a job getting the Rizlas to stick. Cack-handed sod. Must be all the grief. Things round Charlie Boyd was always dodgy, but this one was going to be worser than usual, he could feel it, sick in his stomach. Geezer'd always thought he could be what his brother was, and every now and then had to have a go at it. But he wouldn't never be no Freddy, not if he took out every face tween here and Basildon. And Darren weren't bout to chase no so-called debts to Bow for him, no matter how much the ante went up. But Charlie had to keep on – he was possessed over it. Didn't give a toss that if it went wrong, all The Mice could be in schtuck, here. They was seen as a sort of family firm, and families stick together. Wonderful. Darren shook down the spliff, sparked it up. How Charlie could offer some miles-off pub protection out of nowhere, then after they'd laughed him out the place, get sterical saying they owed him a monkey . . . stroll on. Cost him that to get it sorted without Freddy's direct say-so. Brain cell get lonely in there? Bow weren't their business, never had been. Freddy treated his brother like he was a kid you sometimes had to let play with the grown-ups. Said it'd blow over, he'd have a quiet word. Might just as well of said he'd send Charlie to bed with no tea. Darren licked his finger, wetted the end of the joint where it was burning uneven. Could do without having to check up on Rosie and all. When he thought of them white hands on his Rosie's body, felt even sicker to his gut. But it wouldn't never last, spite Mum saying drugs was a good job. Darren most probably wouldn't even have to keep an eye when it come to it.

Rosie hadn't been stoned in ages. She drew the smoke into her lungs, held it there, like he'd taught her when she was fourteen. Daz was sipping his tea, watching her.

'So how's Mum?' She breathed out. Buggered if she'd cough.

'None too thrilled with you, girl.'

'I'll go next Sunday. Here.' She reached up to his chair from the floor-cushion.

'Cheers, darling.' He took two consecutive tokes without exhaling. 'Enjoy yourself Friday, did you?' he said, his eyes half-lidded. Lizard eyes. Right, we know where we are, now.

'I did, as it goes. You?' She tried a flippant look; he caught it in his pale glutinous stare.

'What's the score – he think he could do it, or didn't he know?'

'Be truthful, I don't think he really realized.' Rosie laughed, and took a mouthful of tea. 'But Alex's no idiot, Daz, he could handle himself most places.' Stop it, don't make excuses for him. Her stomach clenched with a mixture of embarrassment, protectiveness, pride; Christ, it was too soon to feel this involved. Especially with someone that foreign.

'Not sactly in your division, is he, darling?' Daz shrugged. 'With his carrier bag and that. Bet he earns buttons, doing that wanky job. Beer money – that's bout his lot. Can't see him handling you, somehow.'

Rosie could, all too easily, but she thought she'd better not get into that.

'I don't need handling, I'm not a dog.' She pulled her legs into the lotus position.

'My point sactly, sweetheart. You could have anyone.'

Unfortunately, it appeared not.

Why couldn't she never sit up proper? And why she always have to fidget bout so much? *Ants in her pants*, Mum used to say when they was kids. Darren membered when he got his first decent Ben Sherman, more whiter than anything else in Mum's wash. Button-down collar, stiff cuffs, smashing bit of work. Mum was down Auntie Mim's for the day, so he'd had a go at ironing it hisself – took him hours. Laid it over the chair after, not to get it creased fore going out, then Rosie'd come in from school. Sat her little bum right down on the shirt, wiggled to get comfy, and opened a bottle of bleeding nail varnish. *Get your arse off there.* She looked all surprised. *I'll only be a minute. What's your problem?* Wouldn't of put

it past her to of curled right up on it. Shit – he was smoking
roach. Got his stash off the papers on the table, put a nother
one together.

Felt a bit out-of-it. He give Rosie the joint, touching her
fingers when he passed it. Cold fingers. *Cold hands, warm heart*
– that was a nother thing Mum said. Too warm sometimes,
like with that Alex geezer, least for the minute. But no whiter
than white social worker'd never be enough for her. She'd
always move, sooner or later. Doubted she even knew what
she wanted in a bloke, but Darren could see it – she wanted
them to match up, like when she spent four year looking for
a lamp same as the old one Nana give her. She give that up
in the finish. Rosie put her hand on his knee, stroked it. Darren's
heart was going. He wanted, bad, to tell her bout the strife. It
most likely weren't a good idea, though – what she never knew
couldn't hurt her. Charlie boy never knew the rules, that was
the trouble – couldn't see the difference between doing the
business for the needful, and getting your hands dirty for no
reason. All their hands, by sociation. Rosie stroked more firm,
like as if she could feel his concerns, without him saying
nothing. Could well be seeing this Alex purposely, she could
be such a wind-up merchant. He been round here yet, or what?
Seen her stockings and her personal bits and bobs, had a pop
at that horrible photo? Her fingers never felt cold to Darren
now, through his Calvins.

'Yeah all right, enough of the schmaltz. Put one together,
girl – got to be your turn.'

She give him ABH of the ankle with her bare foot, and held
up her free hand, what still had half his spliff in it. Laughing
at him.

But for some reason, took him a nother hour to leave.

Alex had said he liked to eat anything except beetroot and
horseradish. In what universe would anyone serve a guest beetroot? Rosie didn't even know if they did it in Marks's. Waiting
for him, she took ages to choose a CD (Otis or George Michael?

Morcheeba? No, Otis) and drank a glass of wine too fast. Better watch it; didn't want to be half-cut before he got here. Ridiculous. She wasn't the type to get like this over a bloke. Even if he did have improbable dimples and dockers' arms and . . . well, whatever it was that sometimes made her wet just thinking about him. But she couldn't work out how to make him come to heel, and she wasn't sure she liked that. Rosie glanced round her flat; what did it say about her? Not quite what it usually did: she'd dusted a bit, hoovered, tidied away her files. Being a man, he probably wouldn't notice. She went to the bathroom, saw her Canesten on the cistern and put it at the back of the cabinet, checked her make-up. Added more mascara, an extra coat of lippy. Felt her hipbones through her leather skirt, ran her hand over the curve of her stomach. Was it sticking out? Leather might come over a bit much for indoors, especially with the shoes, but Rosie was going with a hunch. Besides, a few more years and she might have to live in trousers.

'Hello.' Alex kissed her on the cheek, as though he were her brother.

'Hi. Come in.' She showed him into the living-room. 'Red wine okay?'

'Fine, thanks.' He sat on the settee, pulled out his cigarettes, apparently only so he could play with the packet. 'Nice flat.' Was he nervous? He ought to be. 'You look good,' he added. Good. Standing here in a four-hundred-quid skirt, with a two-hundred-quid haircut, half a ton of Clinique, and he says she looks good. She could have looked good for fifty. Rosie sat on the armchair; attempting to sit on the floor in this skirt would be awkward, and she didn't feel like placing herself at a dis-advantage. 'You like Art Nouveau, then.' Alex still sounded edgy. 'I love that one. Egon Schiele, isn't it?' Pointing at the print next to the bookcase.

'Yeah, an ex gave it to me. Didn't know anything about art, but he knew what I liked.'

Alex laughed. Yeah, he always got the point. She never

would have thought she'd glance twice at a man in such urgent need of a barber and a new pair of trainers. But when he looked at her, she felt he could see what no one else had: that Rosie Spence was a code. That was a start. Whether he'd ever have the key was another matter.

'So what have you been up to this week?' he said, then behaved as though she'd asked the question. 'Can you believe we've had more of the same about our funding? You know they closed half our residential last year? Same idiot from Oxford has been sniffing around, with all that liberal bleating about methadone, the stupid regional woman still wants my blood . . .' Seemed like he was about to go into one of his half-hour rants, but he bit his thumb and shook his head. 'We've got a ten-year-old at the moment. *Ten.* Mother's a pro, no dad. A little girl, Rosie. Jade, she's called. We draw teddies and things together, and she loves it. God.' He reached across the table for her hand, squeezed it, dropped it abruptly. When he spoke about his work, the passion was barely contained. And it was access to that fire Rosie wanted. 'Anyway,' he said, 'you must have done something since we saw each other?' She drew breath to answer, but so did Alex. 'Yeah, and that's another thing . . .' He grinned. 'Sorry, I'll shut up.'

'Just as well it's endearing.' Careful to get a sarky tone, so he wouldn't know she was serious. 'I did get a new client at the beginning of the week. Freddy Boyd's recommendation. You met Freddy, he's kind of . . . important. Flash sod, diamond cufflinks, attractive wife.'

'*Important.*' He shook his head. 'Yeah, think I know who you mean. Wife's a blonde, bit plump, lots of cleavage.' Typical bloke. And if he was a breast man, she was in trouble.

'That's the one. Sod it, I left some bits in the oven.'

She brought through a plate of only slightly charred snacks. Alex grabbed a handful of bhajis and tandoori chicken strips, eating them almost before Rosie had got back to her seat. The

CD finished; better leave it a bit, or she'd look like a jack-in-the-box.

'Are you allowed to tell me what Freddy's recommendation wanted?'

'I don't do *allowed*, I make calls on whether I can trust people.' She eyed him.

'You don't trust me, then?' He leaned forward to help himself to more food.

'Jury's out.' Rosie crossed her legs, watching his face. Alex nodded, laughed under his breath. He glanced down, then stared straight at her.

'Suppose you're going to tell me he didn't do it. This mysterious thing.'

'He wasn't after defence, just advice. Anway, none of my clients ever *do* it. I couldn't take them on if they did.' Truth or Dare.

'Fair enough.' But he hadn't looked away. He held out his glass, then downed his fresh drink in two. 'Law's really specialized, isn't it? I know that from when I was in probation.' Was that a nasty tone in his voice? He picked up the bottle, scratched his stubbled chin, not letting her out of his gaze. It was like being pinned to a board.

'Well, you can't have your cake and eat it,' she said, as lightly as she could.

'Yes you can. You can't eat your cake and have it. People always get that wrong.'

'Eat your . . .' He was right. 'Pedant. All I know is, there wouldn't be much cake either way if I hadn't been realistic.' What did he think she could have done, gone into Med. Neg. or Human Rights? How could she have explained that at home? Literally incomprehensible.

'So what you're really saying is, you can't have principles and money, the one with the other?' Alex laughed. 'No, can't say that's not true.'

'Come on, who's going to give the people I look after a real go, if I don't? People who won't get legal aid because

they don't want to have to deal with the forms about their
income . . .'

'And there was me thinking you were just a materialist.' Alex
rubbed his thigh, still not taking his eyes from hers.

'Sod off.' Thank God he'd interrupted her; she'd been about
to say too much. Why did she feel the need to defend herself?
'Okay, you make a difference, Alex, but so do I, in a way.'

'Mm. I'm sure.' He was eating macadamia nuts now, noisily,
dropping the odd one on to the carpet, carefully retrieving the
strays. His fingers big in the delicate green bowl as he searched
out the remaining nuts, his eyes on the task in hand. Rosie
picked up a fish ball, bit into it, dropped the other half into
the ashtray. She had trouble swallowing her mouthful. Alex
was so present in the room: huge, shaggy, hungry. Rosie wanted
to stroke him.

They needed more wine. Coming back through, Rosie handed
the open bottle to Alex. She wanted to be nearer. Her chair
could do with being that bit closer, pulled over a fraction.
Better. She sat, nudged aside the bhajis with her foot, and
rested her legs on the little table, crossing them at the ankle.
Her shoe scraped the glass surface as she wriggled to get
comfortable, a faint scratch setting her teeth on edge. Alex
flinched. She smiled and shrugged. Without taking his eyes off
Rosie, Alex went for the last of the food: reaching around her,
narrowly avoiding her heel scratching along his arm. Briefly,
he caressed her ankle with his free hand before drawing back.
She made herself stay silent, giving him her most intense stare,
forcing him to look away, to return her look. She could wait.
There was all the time in the world. She ran a nail hard over
her lips, still watching, still waiting. Alex hadn't moved. Then,

'Can I put some music on?' Bastard was grinning.

Rosie cleared the table, took the poached salmon out of the
fridge. He should have been sitting up to beg by now. She
tossed some salad in a bowl, poured olive oil over it, squeezed

in some lemon juice. Ought to give him bloody beetroot. Serve him right. Yet she'd had an effect, she was certain. When he'd got up to check out her CDs, he was definitely pushing down a hard-on. And Rosie wouldn't let any man fuck with her mind; that was one part of her she'd never willingly open.

'Can you come in here a minute?' Alex called, as though he could hear her thoughts through the thin partition wall. 'I think in fairness I'd better tell you something.'

Something always came of something; nobody ever said they wanted to tell you something you'd like to hear. Great. Just what she'd wanted from her Saturday night. Apprehensively, she came through, considered sitting next to him on the settee, but went back to her chair. Alex bit the side of his thumb, cleared his throat, turning it into a laugh. Almost.

'Wish I hadn't made a big thing of this now,' he said, tracing patterns on his jeans with his forefinger. 'What it is, you must think I'm . . . Sorry, I'm making a mess of this.' He did another version of a laugh. 'Look, I've had my head messed with a bit too recently. And the truth is, this is difficult territory for me. I'm not too sure what it is I can deal with.'

Rosie examined her fingers. The truth was, his uncertainty was her own difficult terrain.

'All I'm saying,' he added, 'is bear with me. I'll try not to let you down.'

'Right.' What else could she say? Yet it felt wrong. Alex shook a cigarette from the packet, and sprawled back across the settee, watching her through the smoke. He gestured for her to come closer. She moved across the room, slid onto the settee, perched near his crotch, but warily. He bent over her, resting his forehead against hers, just for a second. She took the cigarette from him, drew on it, handed it back. He smiled. Pulled her into him. Kissed her. She bit his lip. Dug her nail deep into the soft flesh of his back. He groaned.

And actually pushed her away.

* * *

'Rosie!' Ben couldn't hardly believe his luck – ten o'clock of
a Saturday, and here she was. No big geezer in tow, and Spence
off seeing Freddy about what the score was. Sweet as. Smiling.
He kissed her on the cheek – she smelt spicy, of ginger and
leather. Signalling to the Governor, he dug in his pocket for
his wallet. 'Here are, Tom. Go sit down, darling – I'll bring
them over. Scotch?' Then she give him that look he sometimes see her give other blokes, like she was wondering what
you could do. He might just be in here. Fucking Rosie Spence
– or he would be, given half a chance. Just have to hope she
never heard the word on The Red Lion. Like Spence said, that
was well beyond naughty, torching the joint. And if it did
have something to do with Charlie Boyd . . . But Rosie was
here, and some burnt-out pub in Bow weren't Ben's first
concern, not unless it messed up that half-chance. 'What you
reckon, Tom?' He nodded to where Rosie was taking off her
jacket.

'With your eyes closed and your right hand, maybe.
Dreaming, mate. Wonder what happened to that bloke she was
schtupping?' Yeah, Ben was wondering that hisself.

'What you doing on your own?' He stuck her drink on the
table.

'I'm not on my own, am I? I'm with you.' She put her hand
over his. Obvious she'd not heard about The Lion yet, anyway.

'We . . . um, got the kid to give the yard a bit of a tidy
round, today. Some of the metal was so old, had fatigue.' Shut
up, you doughnut. Looking round the boozer now, she was.
'Spence ain't coming in tonight – think he's seeing some bird.'
Yeah, a right hot date.

'Mm? Sorry, Ben. Who's that bloke talking to the Governor?'

Ben glanced over. Flash git carrying half hundredweight of
gold. Bit familiar. *Sorry, Ben.* Typical of her to say that right
before she went and done whatever it was she was sorry for.

'Introduce me,' she carried on, fore he could answer.

'Why?' You got to be joking. *Sorry, Ben.*

'Because he looks interesting. I don't know, just do it, okay?'

Sometimes, this woman was too much like her brother. Right dark where he was light, ribby where he was well covered, big eyed where he was small, but no one could think their mum had played away from home. Same blood in them veins. Rosie stood up, pushing her hair back off out her face. Then marvellous, one of the boys spotted them.

'You hear, Ben?' he said, quiet. 'That landlord's sister was in there.' Ben shot a look at Rosie – it was okay, never thought she heard that. In the pub, when it happened? She hurt? But he weren't about to ask out loud at the minute. Be like wrapping up his night in red ribbon and giving it this bloke for a present.

'Catch you later,' said Ben, meaningful. 'I'm a bit tied up.'

'You're Rosie Spence, ain't you?' More loud, this time.

'Why?' She picked up her bag, all impatient.

'Nothing, it's just that . . .'

'If it's nothing, then I'm sure you'll excuse us. Coming, Ben?'

First time in years he'd had some sort of chance, and it weren't no chance at all. If he was truthful with hisself, weren't never going to be. Been a nice dream, while it lasted. Now this geezer was getting the treatment – from a social worker to muscle by the pound. She had her foot on the low rail, was pressing herself into him. And he was loving it. Could hang your hat on that. Ben found hisself staring at her back. Have to tell Spence about this. Course he'd have worries about Bow, they all did, but he'd still want to know what was going on with his Rosie.

He looked like too many of Rosie's clients: a shark in a suit. But he was attractive, if you liked that kind of thing. And after what had happened this evening, Rosie liked anything that wasn't Alex bloody Tolliver. How could she *bear with* Alex, when obviously he couldn't bear to touch her? His angst was rewriting her as undesirable; she'd had no choice but to ask him to go, and he'd instantly complied, therefore proving her point. This other bloke was easy: one scent of the blood, he went in on the attack. He took her version of Rosie Spence as read. True, she was bored senseless, felt more like telling him to fuck himself than to fuck her.

'. . . anyway, so I got the brief . . .'

'Evidently.' But he was there.

'What?'

'Nothing.' Give me strength. 'Sorry, go on.' Unfortunately, he took her at her word.

For what seemed like hours, she drank scotch as though The Mice had laid it on as bait irresistible to the predator, turning the hunter into the hunted. If she could get enough down her without falling over, she might even go through with it. The gyre widened. He had his arm around her; she could feel his hand damp on her bare shoulder. Ben, or someone, was standing too close, forcing her forward. She fixed her attention on the bar, sticky with scotch.

In amongst his monologue came shouted greetings. *All right Rose, my love?* She knew that too many eyes were on her; the bar crowded with familiar stares, waiting to see what Rosie Spence was going to do. He was no slouch, but she could feel their surprise boring into her exposed back. Someone squeezed past, bumping into the shark, jogging his arm.

'Sorry, mate – accident. You all right, Rosie? Seen Spence, have you?' Her brother was her bloody keeper. One more drink, then she'd decide. After all, there'd been eighteen years (barring some sweet exceptions) of foregone disappointments. And even bad sex couldn't be as bad as the sexual humiliation of offering yourself and being found wanting.

'How come you're not with anyone, beautiful? Or should I watch myself?'

She looked up. He was smiling, white teeth capping a tannin face. Why wasn't she with anyone? Because that bastard had shoved her away, so pushed her into coming here alone. But on the other hand, what the hell was she pretending to do? If this one here tried for the rest of his life, he wouldn't be what she could begin to desire. She was thirty-two years old, not twenty-two; Alex might be wasting her time, but she knew too much to waste it on her own account.·

'Sorry, sweetheart. Any other time . . . but I'm sort of seeing someone. And at the minute, I don't think he'd be too pleased with me.' As it turned out, she was right.

Chapter Three

'Scotch, straight up, please.'
   'Right you are, Ms Spence.'
   'Has Mr Johnson been in today?'
   'You might try the lounge.'

William Johnson saw his partner arrive, obviously straight from court; the alleged difficulty of any case was to be judged by the severity of her suit. Given the amount of time she spent before the bench, she really should have gone to the bar. William waved at her, and took a mouthful of his gin; he knew that Rosie wanted to talk money, and he was aware too that he wouldn't be in a good position to refuse. And his eyes ached; he really should see about getting reading glasses. He ought to have had years yet before it came to that. Wearily, he stood to kiss her.

   'Conditional discharge,' she said, before he could ask. 'I was hoping for something a bit less damning, but obviously we had the Merry Widows, so . . .'

   'So you did well. Can I get you a drink?'

   She indicated her full glass, and sank into the big armchair, placing her briefcase carefully at her feet.

   'Did you get my message?'

   'I did. Rosie, there's simply no way we can justify . . .'

   'Oh come on, William, we can afford it. And believe me, new furniture'll bring in more business. We need to keep looking like a class act. I know we *are* a class act, but it has to show.' She unwrapped a packet of cigarettes, watched him. Brazen.

That's what William's mother would call her. Among other things. He brushed his hair out of his eyes, letting it flop back over his forehead. 'Great effect,' Rosie said, laughing. 'Michelangelo dressed as David.'

'Even supposing we can afford it, and I'm not saying we can, don't you think the money would be better spent employing another junior? Harry certainly thinks so.'

'No, frankly I don't. There's the office space to consider, for one thing. We can think about more employees when the new chairs bring in more clients.' She laughed again. 'Not that we need more, but I'd like the opportunity to be particular. More big cases, fewer petty thefts.'

'We're not exactly inundated with small crime, not at two fifty now.'

'Well, quite. Although three for you, and for Harry.' Her eyebrows raised. 'Our reception should reflect your client base.' Increasingly, William was glad this woman was on his side.

'How much?' He might just as well get down to it; he should have to in the end, anyway. He could almost hear the practice accounts whimper as their flesh was threatened to the bone. And his own bones ached almost as much as his eyes.

'Sixteen hundred per chair. Four thousand for each sofa. Very cheap, I assure you.'

What exactly did she mean? Approving Rosie had entailed approval of pluralism.

'Ah . . . Rosie . . . I don't quite know how to put this, but are they . . .'

'Good quality leather? Of course.' She smiled and drained her glass. Damn her eyes. Which no doubt worked perfectly.

'All right. You'd better order them, I'll get it past the others. And I think we'd better have another drink.'

She inclined her head in assent, and pushed her empty glass towards him.

William was conscious that by Rosie's standards, his capitulation had been painless.

*   *   *

'Lovely, looks like I'm just in time. G and T, please.'

William stood to kiss Elizabeth, then returned to his chair, hitching his trousers at the knee as he sat. Rosie jumped up and hugged the other woman.

'Haven't seen you for ages!' she exclaimed. William crossed his legs. Rosie Spence was enough of a job of work, without one of her cronies. Elizabeth was attractive, though. Elegant. The sort of woman his mother would have wanted for him, had things been different. The sort he used to try to want for himself.

'With Jack getting scarlet, and having to cram in my CPD hours, I've been rushed off my feet,' Elizabeth said. She didn't sound as though she'd rushed anywhere since childhood. 'Lovely suit, is it Nicole Farhi?' She leaned over to feel the fabric.

'Spot on. You look pretty gorgeous yourself.'

Spare him. William signed for the drinks, and silently cursed. He'd forgotten to ask Rosie what was happening with that extortion case. Perhaps it was better if he simply left it to her. At this rate, his role would be confined to going over the post in the mornings.

'Darling, is it true that you've got a new man in hand? I saw Randa at Clowns . . .'

'Jesus, is nothing private?' Rosie sighed, theatrically. 'Okay, yes, I was seeing someone. Until a couple of weeks ago, anyway.'

'Do you want to talk about it? William won't mind.'

'Nothing to tell.' She put out her cigarette, picked up her drink. 'I met him, we liked each other, things got too difficult. How much did Randa give you?'

Miranda had been saying to all and sundry that she rather suspected this character of being a yob, but William didn't think Elizabeth was fool enough to repeat that.

'Only that he didn't seem to be your usual type, whatever that means.'

'I nearly married my usual type, Lisbeth,' Rosie said, archly. 'Like all the best tragic heroines, I don't have one anymore.'

She actually winked. 'I'm going for a stroll into the bar. Anyone coming?'

William broke one of his rules, and started on his third cigar of the day. The practice's bank balance needed the nicotine. Elizabeth nibbled at an olive, coughing as he lit up.

'Sorry, how rude. Darling, did Rosie look rattled when I mentioned the new inamorata?'

'I don't think she's used to men leaving her. I got the impression that's what had happened, didn't you?'

'I did, a bit. This is going to sound terribly bitchy, but I've never quite understood why some men fall over themselves to get to her. Even Jack. I'm not sure whether he disapproves of her, or if he's excited by her. I'm certainly never encouraged to ask her to dinner, but she's always first on his list for parties. I mean, she's not even very pretty, is she?'

William shook his head. Not pretty, no. Not beautiful.

'She doesn't need to be,' he said.

Had to know, man. Wouldn't get out of his head. Sam knew it wouldn't hurt to cut down on the whiz anyway. But . . . the frigging Centre. Weren't no better on the inside – thinner, darker, every time you come. No point in having lights if you was going to cover them.

Alex smiled, always had smiled at Sam. Nearly always. Sam couldn't never help smiling back, no matter what. But needed to keep his head together, make sure he remembered why he was here, remembered the plan. Needed to know if the world was still in place, man. Kept seeing that picture of Alex Going In There with that lady . . . that . . . that geezers' brief. Couldn't handle it if Alex weren't what Sam'd thought, if the way he cared about stuff, tough but knowing what it was like, was a lie. Most of them give him respect, guy. They said he was real. But maybe they was all wrong.

'Right, we get to the important part *again*,' Alex said, laughing a bit. 'Do you want to stop using?' His over-to-you expression, like he was interviewing some politician off the telly.

'Had to come here, man. Might need a lawyer.' Forgot to think of a reason why. Shit. Alex looked at him, sort of gentle, despite that battered face. Despite being a mentalist.

'I'm not about to let you use our time and our resources when it's not what you want.' Did what he used to call his quote-unquote voice. 'You know we can't force you to pack it in, we can only support you.' He smiled again. 'If you change your mind, then come back and we'll try to get you a referral. I don't have a problem with you doing that, at all.'

'But I might need a *brief*. I thought . . . Rosie Spence. Aren't you, like . . . seeing her?'

Alex drummed out a rhythm on his desk, like he had a tape on what Sam couldn't hear. Then Sam's head got in with it. Had to find out. Had to find out. Had to find out.

'Why, do you know her?' Never looked gentle now, eyes gone all dark. Not safe. Not.

Sam stared at the poster. Didn't mean nothing.

The 'phone rang just as Rosie's cab arrived. Always the way. The machine would have to take it, but she'd listen in case it was Alex, calling to cancel. If it were, he'd had it; he was lucky to have been given this chance after leaving it so long before asking to see her again. She was even standing up Daz for him. God, she hated that: some idiot refusing to leave a message. 1471. *You were called, today, at nineteen fifty-six hours. The caller withheld their number.* Great. Very useful. The cab hooted again. Keep your hair on. She picked up the wine, strolled out of the flat, slowly locked the doors.

'All right? John Stuart Mill House, please, on the Bridgemore Estate. Stepney.'

'Quicker to walk it, love.'

'Cheaper, too.' She tapped the no-smoking sign on the window. 'All right if I smoke?'

'Go on then – get me shot, you will.'

Ten past eight, the cab pulled up beside a big, ugly block. But it wasn't as bad as she'd expected: not much graffiti, not too many kids drinking cider and smoking dope. Quite quiet.

'There you go, mate. Keep the change.'

'Thanks, princess. Have a good evening – off to see the boyfriend, are you?'

She made herself flash him a smile.

'Something like that.' If someone who rejected you and then didn't make contact for two weeks, could be said to have any status other than bastard.

No, it wasn't too bad a place, but still she wasn't going to chance the lift.

'Excuse me.' She stepped carefully around some wino with his can of Brew, poor beggar, and made a guess about how far up to go. Typical Alex. Just expected her to know.

'You found it, then?' He was smiling one of his cocky little smiles, but there was something else going on behind his eyes, something that looked out at her, asking her to read it.

'Evidently.' She handed him the bottle. Years. It was time staring out at her, decaying the smile. She kissed him on the cheek; hadn't meant to do that. His arms began to go around her, but she side-stepped into the flat.

It was so bloody tidy; if her mother could see this, Alex would get several squillion Brownie points. Smelt of polish, maybe it was all a bit recent. The living room was small, not much furniture, but everything was clearly set up for someone who knew what they wanted: little table by the armchair which pointed at the telly, second chair by a bookcase, tapes neatly arranged on a shelf above the machine. She'd lay money they were in alphabetical order. The only extravagant touch was the number of sketches, mostly unframed and pinned to the wall. A violin, a factory, an old man, an unpeopled bar, charcoal, pastels. Rough, hurried, but pretty good. Especially the violin. It looked as though someone had just put it down after playing, its strings barely having stopped vibrating.

She slipped off her jacket and handed it to him. It was a bit chilly in the flat; Rosie wished she'd worn a jumper, but the day had promised a warmer evening that it had delivered. He lumbered off into another room with the wine. Amazing how specific people are: Rosie might not have guessed from the obsessive order, but the Mayfair cigarette packet, the Sainsbury's vodka on the shelf, the telephone-pad pencil chewed down to the middle, the drawings, would have told her this was Alex's place. She'd met him only seven or eight weeks ago, and already she recognized him. Would he be able to pick her out from so few clues?

Alex returned with the open bottle and two glasses. Rosie sat on an armchair; he hesitated, then sat on the floor opposite her, poured the wine.

'How have you been?' he said.

'Okay, very busy at work. William's a real technophobe, can't accept he has to put draft orders on disc now, and we're trying to drum it into him.' *Don't ramble.* 'You?'

'I've missed you.' He held her gaze, looked away. One of his little tricks. He'd missed her? Why hadn't he rung her then, had he been mute for a fortnight? 'Quite a lot, as it happens,' he added. 'Kept thinking about 'phoning you, but I wasn't sure there was any point. Didn't know if I could make it any different. If I'm honest, I wasn't sure it was even worth trying.' He watched her face. She protected it with a veil of smoke. So he didn't think she was worth it. That's that, then. She wasn't going to stick around to be humiliated. But as she calmly uncrossed her legs, about to stand, he held up one hand, stopping her. What did he think he was, a traffic cop? 'But things kept reminding me of you,' he said. 'Me and my friend Connie went to see a film I thought you'd quite like. And at the dentist, I came across something about Queen Mary and Westfield in a magazine. And so on and so on. Lots of little things really, but . . .'

Rosie took a gulp of her drink. She couldn't see where this was going, but she understood about absent presence. *Christiane F* on telly one night; a piece in the *Sunday Times* about living alone; a song on the radio claiming you didn't have to be in love to miss someone. Specifically.

Who the hell was Connie?

'What made you ring now?' Deigning to decide she was *worth it*.

'A client, in a funny sort of way. I realized we might bump into each other from time to time, one way or another. So I thought we better get things sorted.'

'One way or another. Can I have a top-up? I think I'm going to need it.'

'Course.' He looked surprised, almost instantly recovering and getting to his feet. 'And I'll sort the dinner out. You could put on a tape, if you like.'

Rosie could smell garlic and sweet onions, could hear pots thumping, competing with the bass of 'Brown Sugar'. She felt that Alex had needed her to say something, to make it, whatever the hell it was, easier for him. But that would be to leave herself open, vulnerable. Yet she didn't like the years in those bloody eyes: the temptation was too great to reach out, to try to make it better. Metaphorically, to kiss the eyes. Foreign, schlocky temptation. And what had he done to earn it? Messed her about. If she went on like this, she'd undo her own long years.

You couldn't let a man get to you. It was proven through history. *Slag* in the playground after a party, *selfish bitch* when studying took precedence over sex, *stupid piece of cunt* if commitments clashed. Rosie didn't understand how a married woman could take her husband's name: letting a man in meant *a priori* losing your own name, without that collusion. She'd spent those long years learning to put herself first; if she was going to be called a selfish bitch, she wanted to have earned it. Just because Alex wasn't from a world she recognized, didn't mean he operated outside the rules of the worlds she knew. She had to be careful. A soulful expression of past damage, and cooking her a meal, needn't suggest he'd allow her to be Rosie.

*   *   *

The food was good. Spaghetti, tomato and olive sauce, salad, warm bread. Despite herself, Rosie was impressed. They balanced plates on their knees; she was glad she'd gone with jeans.

'I like that colour on you.'

'This?' She looked down at her shirt.

'Someone I knew at Art School told me it's the colour of the deepest oceans in the world, that's why it's called navy blue. She was Japanese.'

'Yeah?' Was her nationality relevant? Couldn't possibly be relevant to the reason Rosie had schlepped all the way over here. The clever money says the Japanese girl was his first love; bet she broke his heart, and he still gets a tremor whenever he sees a young Japanese woman. Like Daz with Pre-Raphaelite type redheads. 'This is great, I was starving.' Suppose she must have been: lunch with that skinny cow Randa meant serious competitive under-eating. But how did any adult woman gauge her own hunger? 'Don't exactly believe in modest portions, do you.'

'No harm in eating properly, Rosie.' He nodded as he spoke, agreeing with himself, and wound a huge knot of spaghetti round his fork. She was actually quite touched. What was it about this man, that he got to her with things she'd never let anyone else get away with?

'Hang on, it's a bit awkward. Hold this a sec.' She passed him her plate, and unlaced her boots, tucking them behind her chair. She slid down on to the floor; now she could sit cross-legged. It was still tricky not to get it over his carpet, but that was his problem, not hers. Might even improve the colour; no ocean in the universe was this desperate sludgy blue. 'Who taught you to cook? Daz can barely do beans on toast.'

'No one, but I had a reason to learn.' He grinned and waved his fork at her. 'See, my mother preferred bridge to frying fish-fingers. When she did do them, they were all burned on one side, soggy on the other side, and frozen in the middle. Not just fish-fingers either, even things that weren't frozen to start with, like sausages. Think she used Spry Crisp 'n' Dry 'n' Icy.'

'Even better at it than me, then.' Tread a bit carefully here, girl. 'From the bits you've told me, she doesn't sound exactly maternal.' Rosie dipped a fragment of bread in her sauce.

'No, but I had a great aunt. Not a *great* aunt as in old, a brilliant one. Much younger than my mum, as it happens. She used to draw cartoons for us, suppose there's where the interest started.' He gestured vaguely to his sketches. 'Perfect she was, lovely long hair, tiny little feet with her toenails always painted, you know? Fantastic smile. I was in trouble there for a while, when I was a teenager.' He was speaking with his mouth full. 'Tried to kiss her once, properly kiss her. And God, I put my hand on her breast. I was about fifteen, she must have been twenty-five. More, maybe.'

Rosie picked up a lettuce leaf with her fingers, waiting for him to go on.

'What happened?' she asked, after a few seconds.

'Nothing. She laughed it off. She was a total star with me.' He spoke absently, clearly having expected her to be shocked. Jesus, if that was the worst he had to offer, a sin gathering nearly thirty years of dust, she'd been seeing a saint. Was that what she'd come over to hear?

'I think it's sweet, in a way,' she said.

'*Sweet?* I felt big-time guilty about it, until I managed to tell someone in my . . . second year? . . . at The Slade. Had wet dreams about her 'til I was nearly twenty. About my aunt.'

'So?' He'd been a teenage boy, for God's sake. To go by Daz and Ben, even The Wombles would turn on a boy at fifteen, the memory lingering furtively for years. Alex laughed uneasily as he stuffed another forkful of food into his mouth, turning the laugh into a cough. 'Careful, babe,' she said. 'I'm hardly likely to know the Heilick manoeuvre, am I?'

'What?' He wiped his hand across his mouth.

'Alexander technique or whatever it is. First Aid.' She licked her fingers.

'Heimlich. God, I had really comforting words from that first person I told.'

'Maybe she took it more seriously.' Had to be a she. Probably the profound Japanese, with sentiments deeper than the deepest oceans. This was bloody cosy: a nice little chat about his past loves.

'Good thing, I really needed that. Not that she made a huge issue out of it, she wouldn't.' For Christ's sake, Alex, why not rave on a bit more about how fantastic she was? But mopping up his sauce methodically with the last of his bread, he lowered his voice and spoke to his plate. 'Rosie, why did you run?'

Shit. *She* nearly choked on her mouthful. She was still way too sober for this. Say more about the understanding Geisha, say any damn thing, but don't ask that.

'Come off it, you know why.' She put her plate on the floor and fumbled with her cigarettes. 'And it was worse because you initiated it, you know you did. I can't get my head round it. You pitch up in my life, then, I don't know. Just blow me out, just like that.'

'You shouldn't have run away. You don't give anyone a chance.'

'I gave you plenty of chances. Anyway, I didn't run, I asked you to leave.' The circus is a bad place, Alex Tolliver; you get to be the lion or the tamer, and in my position, if the lion lashes out, and you can't break it with its own confusion, you find another lion.

'I was going to write you a letter,' Alex said. 'To explain.' He put his empty plate underneath hers, and poured some more wine. 'But I couldn't get the negotiations sorted out.'

'Jesus, you'll be training for my job next. What bloody negotiations?'

He reached down, took her hand.

'What it is . . . I'm married, Rosie.'

Bastard.

Miranda was right. That explained the tidiness of the flat, it explained, well, everything. Rosie snatched her hand away. Just walk out, girl.

'Okay, fine.' But those boots, just lying there, out of view and out of reach. Slowly, she got to her feet. Alex jumped up, put his hand on her arm.

'That came out all wrong. Please, Rosie. I knew you'd think I meant it like that. I'm just not divorced, that's all. We've lived apart for over two years. For God's sake, I didn't mean I'd been having you on. It's complicated.'

Rosie's heart was banging hard against her chest, tormenting her into a corner. She had to make a serious call here: was she going to hear him? This was no crush on an aunt from centuries ago, no sweet-memoried early girlfriend. Alex dropped his arms to his sides and looked down at her. She had to call now.

'Okay. I'll listen.' She sat, screwed her cigarette into the ashtray and lit another. Alex pulled over the other chair, so that it was next to hers. He drained his glass. Abruptly, the tape clicked off, offering a respectful silence. Rosie wished she could bear to turn it over.

'My wife . . . had problems. Still has, probably. She didn't when we got married, not big time, so the obvious conclusion . . .

'Anyway, I was always having to collect her from strange addresses where she'd disappeared for days on end. I got great at clearing up sick, and worse, where she didn't take care of herself. She hated me, and I'm sorry, but I hated her too. Even though I still loved her . . .

'When I met her, she was the most beautiful woman I'd ever seen. Like someone you'd see in a film. Last time I saw her, she weighed six stone and looked ten years older than she was. More maybe. Right till the end, I thought I could save her . . . but the truth is, she didn't want to be saved . . .

'I nearly went mad myself with it : . .

'And for a long time, I thought I needed to be punished, but there was no one who could do that except for her. There wasn't any absolution . . .

'She didn't want me, sexually, for the last two or three years we were together, but I still wanted her. I thought, if I could make love to this . . . thing I'd created, it would be the sort of humiliation I deserved. Especially because she didn't want me. But I didn't . . .

'And in the end, she left me, and I was glad. I was fucking glad, Rosie. She wasn't my responsibility anymore. We're only not divorced because I don't know where she is . . .

'If you still want me after that . . .'

Rosie got up, looked behind her chair. Her hand closed over the thin black laces: allies turned traitors. Alex watched her as she pulled them tense, knotting herself in. Brushing at the knees of her jeans, she tried to absorb the information. It was like starting a book in the middle, trying to get a hold on the story and realizing you'd missed out the chapters giving you clues as to who was the villain.

She looked at Alex.

And went to sit on the arm of his chair. She put her hand on his shoulder, but applied no pressure. There was too much pressure crushing into her to give any away. Her heart felt squeezed; the long years had reached right in there, and wouldn't let go.

'So you see?' he said.

'Yeah, I see.' Rosie scratched her calf with her toe. Gently, carefully, she moved her hand to the nape of his neck, stroking where his greying hair met his skin. 'You should have told me before.'

'You'd have been happy with that, would you? Before you knew anything about me?' He had a point. She continued softly to stroke his neck, his unkempt hair. Maybe she should leave; for all she knew, those early chapters might say that Alex was a nutter who really had screwed with his wife's head. She could hardly believe that she couldn't believe that. And he should have told her, two weeks ago. Although, no, probably not before.

'I was so angry with you that night, Alex.' She pushed her

fingers harder into his hair. 'I nearly made a really basic mistake in the pub because of it.' One that wouldn't have been her style. A twenty-four carat mistake, most of it worn by the mistake himself. Alex twisted his neck, trying to see her face. Then he laughed, in a way that made it clear nothing was funny.

'Right, I get it, a bloke. God, did you have to? It's obvious how I feel about you. Couldn't you have given me the benefit?' Shrugging off her hand. 'You must have known how hard I'd find that to cope with.' He breathed heavily into the silence. 'No,' he said at last, 'maybe you were right to go off. Wouldn't blame you if you thought so now, anyway.'

I'm sorry.

Where had that come from? Thank God she hadn't said it aloud.

'I said *nearly*. Didn't do it in the end, did I? You ought to be pleased. Anyway, thought you said you didn't know if it was worth getting in contact? If you're so sure it's obvious how you feel, what's that about?'

'You misunderstand on purpose, you must do.' Alex pressed his thumb into his temple. 'I don't know, Rosie. What am I going to do with you?'

'That's what I keep asking myself.'

'Are we going to keep seeing each other?' He turned to look at her.

'I'd think so, wouldn't you?' she said.

Darren sent Ben to get a nother couple of large ones. Anything less looked like a damp glass. That bitch – he'd swing for her. If she was off tarting around, he'd do his nut. Fucked if he was ringing her mobile. Sat here like a lemon while she . . . If he'd of done it to her, she'd of done her pieces. That was Rosie all over – one rule for her, a nother for the rest of the world.

'Not turned up yet, then?' Ben put the drinks on the table.

'Yeah, but she's gone invisible – right handy, that. Freddy could use her to go out with the boys. What's the matter with you?' Stroll on. Yeah, that's what she always done, come to think of it. Like that time she come round Darren's first flat to a party, and was hardly through the door when she walked straight over some hairy bastard's biker jacket.

'She could be at work still.'

'Either you stop being a cunt, or I'll stop you.' Darren would of been well into one if it'd been his gear. Even at that age, she didn't sactly wear the sort of shoes what wouldn't do some right old damage. Weren't like she was invited, neither.

'All right, no need for . . . I've got a few lines, if you're up for it. Not here, indoors.'

'What?' But end of any day, Darren was more bothered bout what the geezer might do to Rosie than bout what she done to the geezer's leathers.

'We could ask that Mel and Sharon back, make a night of it.'

Darren didn't want coke and he didn't want tarts. Too much hassle. He wanted to go home, put one together, listen to some sounds. Ben was getting right on his wick.

'No, not tonight. I've had enough, mate.' Any more of it, he'd have him.

'Of a Saturday? You must be losing it,' Ben said. Yeah, pretty nearly, boy.

'Be told. I just want to crash out. If my Rosie shows, do us a favour and look after her, will you?' Darren swallowed his drink and stood up. Slut. Right spoiled his night, she had.

Pub was heaving, rows of squared-off shoulders, and what was worser, some of them turned round and had mouths on top, what opened to let out a load of old shit. Slapping them shoulders, he shoved his way out, nodding but trying not to have to talk to no one else more'n 'Later'. Then there was only some big fat cunt blocking the door.

'You Rosie Spence's brother?' This one spoke, and all.

'What the fuck's it got to do with you?' Could well do without this.

'I've got a message for her. Tell her The Lion won't lay down for no roast lamb.'

Message for Rosie? What fucking lamb? But there was only one Lion what could be meant. Geezer was from Bow, had to be. That was more'n a fortnight ago now – Darren'd really started to think Charlie must of got away with it. This weren't pretty. Roast lamb . . . landlord's sister, that got stuck in the pub when it went up? What'd it have to do with Ro?

'Listen, pal.' Darren felt for his blade, obvious, so's the geezer could see. 'She won't be getting that message. Tell whoever sent it from me it ain't a good idea to try again. Okay?'

'Fair play, mate.' The bloke nodded. 'Just following orders.'

'Maybe we should go for a little stroll – discuss it? I like a nice chat.'

'I don't know nothing, mate – bit of a thicko, me. All I know's the Governor's sister's had it.' He looked Darren right in the eyeballs. 'Interesting, about families, the way what happens to one person affects the others. But like I said, I don't know nothing about it.' He patted his jacket. Darren could see the bulge of what could well be a shooter. He fronted him, but had to let the bastard walk away. Fuck, fuck, fuck. *Had it* – she must of died in the London. Hung on the two weeks and all she had, with third degree burns, and now the stupid slag goes and gives up. Better find Freddy, and quick. Just have to hope he had his mobile on.

It weren't going to be Darren what took the rap – if that was the score, they'd of had him by now. Even had a nalibi. But why couldn't that pub of just stumped up the dough? Come to that, why was Charlie's warning bout it so far past what was reasonable? Even though the girl was . . . Darren never believed The Lion wanted a war, and he knew The Mice never. But what was that bloke saying – Rosie was in the pot? Not that they'd dare when it come down to it, spite of everything. But them saying bout her meant the stake was miles too high not to find a solution soon as. A real one. An hard call, to know how much to tell her – she wouldn't do the sensible, his Ro, and get away for a bit. Might just try find her own solutions.

When they was kids, they'd always had them play fights. And just when they was getting started, she'd say *No pinching, no punching, no pulling of hair, no biting, no kicking – but I can.* Every time, in the same order. He'd always wanted to kill her – she got it in so quick. She hated being tickled, though, and somehow, that'd never made the list. If it had, he'd of been fucked. Bitch. *But I can.*

Chapter Four

'Give us a bit.'

'Here are.' Ben broke the other end off his Crunchie, like some fussy old woman. What one of them'd he think'd got the clap? Small bit and all, greedy sod.

'Dying for a slash.' Darren slowed, looking out the window. He chucked a left and pulled over next to a big dirty building. 'Here, ain't this where that Alex works?' Maybe he should just take a chance on him being there, have a little word. Hadn't been any use talking to Rosie. What's she mean, what's he mean, *Keep a little look out*? Not that he told her bout the fat cunt, but she should of picked up there was something going down. Even while he was there, she had two blank calls on her machine. She come over on a banana boat? In twenty-odd year, Darren'd only known, what, four or five stiffs. It'd be sorted, no danger – but you'd be a mug to take no odds. Last few days, since the warning, Darren'd been on pins. Skin on his forehead so stretched, felt like that'd been pinned back, and all. If Alex was going to be hanging around, he should know to watch her. 'Ought to pop in, see him.'

'And say what?' Ben got a Mars out. Unwrapped it slow, more than what was natural.

'Ain't going to say nothing bout Charlie's big day out, am I? I ain't thick. Just that she needs a bit of an eye keeping.' He leaned over to grab the Mars, bit it, and give it back.

'Want me to wait here?' said Ben.

* * *

'Through there, down the corridor, second on the left. Says
Alex Tolliver on the door.'

Second on the left. Second on the left.

'Cheers, babe.' He winked – might as well make her day.
Second on the left. Them places was all the same – sept for
the farm, that was all right. But the others. All long stinking
corridors, and closed doors, and the people behind them doors
screwing with your head. Second on the left. Shit – she mean
the first door there, or what?

'Come in.' Sorted – that was his voice.

Alex looked like one of them cartoons, where someone's jaw
hits the deck, and their eyes bulge out their head. But he recovered quick, give him that. Made tea, like Darren was a pukka
visitor. Darren brung out his B&H packet, matching them
manners. Paki shop never had no Marlboros this morning. Still
needed a piss, that tea weren't going to help. Alex squeezed
hisself back behind the desk – obvious they couldn't afford to
give him a decent office, one at the yard was bigger'n this.
Darren swigged his tea. Just have to tie a knot in it. He waited.
Alex shifted bout in his seat, but never looked away.

'So what can I do for you?' Like he knew Darren'd come
for something off him. Was going to be well difficult sounding
like he was just giving him something he ought to know.

'Look, mate – I've come bout my Rosie.'

'Oh yeah?' Alex said, lifting his eyebrows, and had a
mouthful of his tea. Thinks he's being warned off, don't he?
Not that Darren weren't tempted, but Rosie'd never talk to him
again, stubborn little mare. Anyway, weren't that simple.

'It's nothing pacific sactly . . .'

'No.' Sarky laugh.

'What?'

Well spooky, way that Alex kept staring right at Darren.
Something funny bout them eyes, like they was X-raying your
head. The Man with the X-Ray Eyes. Minded him . . . fuck,
minded him of Rosie. Darren looked up at the wall behind
Alex's head – butterfly picture, only bit of colour in the room.

How to get Alex to see without them eyes making him spell it out? An eye for an eye, that'd be the plication, if they didn't box clever. Had a bit of minding courtesy of Freddy's regular boys last few days, but if she knew, she never said. Could hear her, at three year old, *I can do it by my own.* Still wanted to do it by her own – but she couldn't always be let. Couldn't never tell her that, though. *When she was good, she was very, very good, but . . .*

'All right, Nan?'

'Which one are you?'

Jesus Christ.

'You been dreaming again, Nana. It's Darren – Pat's boy.'

'Haven't you grown?' She give him a kiss, and grabbed at the bottle of Harvey's and the box of Quality Street. 'I spect Black Magic was a bit too dear?' In some ways, she'd never changed at all.

'No, Nan, they never had none. Got a nice cup of tea for us, have you then?'

'No point in giving you a nasty one. You coming in?'

This place was worser'n Rosie's, least her joint never reeked. Mum come over here every week to clean and that, but no one couldn't stop Nan from leaving old bits of grub everywhere, and the cat from pissing where it weren't let out. Where was the bleeding thing, anyway? That's what Grandad had used to call it – *That bleeding thing.*

'Did you pass your exams, then?'

'Yeah, got all top marks.' What exams? 'What bout you?' Made her laugh.

'I'd pass if you got exams in making tea! Do you fancy a biscuit?'

'Yeah, go on then. Got any chocolate ones?'

'You always did love chocolate, pair of you. Greedy little beggars, hands always in the tin. Where's Rosie today? Too busy with her dancing to come see her old nan?'

'Nana – Rosie don't dance, I told you that. Not for a living,

like. She's a lawyer, member? In a flash office. She's the one
got all the exams.'

'Mm, she works very hard. Not that I approve of her showing
her tummy like that. But still, things are different from when
I was young. Do you fancy a biscuit?'

Nana was getting more and more of a worry. Mum said she
never knew how much longer she could be let to live on her
own, specially with that fall going the Baths, even holding on
to the pram. Right old performance. Just recent, she'd got this
in her head bout Rosie being a belly dancer – but she was
good, evidently. On telly and everything. Darren couldn't never
see how Rosie went along with it like she done. One time,
she'd give Nan a demo of her dancing, wiggling and clicking
her fingers like that bird they'd see at that Ali Baba place.
Barking – Darren didn't know who was worst. Mum'd told him
bout when her and Rosie went to buy Nana a new armchair,
and she'd said for Rosie to pretend to be Nan, see if she could
get in and out of it. So Rosie sits down, and starts drooling
and thrashing around. Wicked little . . . Mum'd been creasing
up when she come to tell Darren, but she said she'd give Rosie
a slap round the legs for it. *You're not too big to go over my
knee, my girl* – Rosie must of heard that a million times. Weren't
true – Mum was a bit of a midge though she had the weight
– but it never stopped her meaning it. Never stopped Rosie
doing things to deserve it, neither. Darren wished he could risk
telling her bout the situation, and that it least deserved an
handle with care.

She'd better freshen up, shave her legs, get changed, and her
hair was still damp from the rain. But she kept running the
possibilities when she should have been running a bath. Trying
to read her notes on the train back from Colchester, she'd been
a bit distracted by what Alex might make of this; now she was
home, the problem was more imminent. Minders, subtle as drag
queens at a tea dance. Did Daz really think she wouldn't notice?
More to the point, what if Alex noticed? It'd be like when she'd

slept on a camp-bed in Mum's room for the best part of a year, having a teenage brother with cocaine eyes, books torn from her hands in derision: normal, until you thought about telling someone who hadn't lived like that. Context. The hardest thing in the world to explain. Alex was the most interesting possibility to have occurred in a long time; it'd be typical of her brother to wreck that with his own interests. All those complex minor cases, with strict rulings: The Mice-v-lending; The Mice-v-protection; The Mice-v-fencing. Something must have been breached; patently, Daz was concerned that what he'd done or failed to do might affect her. Hardly the first time. Those blank calls . . . Rosie had a hunch it was all connected with Bow, there was such a buzz of interest in it, but that didn't make total sense: that far east wasn't anything to do with Freddy and his boys. And The Mice never touched arson, it was against the rules, a mug's game. That would be a breach well too far. Whatever the truth, Rosie wasn't scared, just edgy, but she could easily see how it might look to an outsider. To Alex.

Just let it go for now, girl. Could wear that jade shirt she'd picked up in Jigsaw, with her charcoal trousers. It was so time consuming, being a woman; Alex would probably come straight from work. Randa had once told her that as a little girl, she'd watched her mother putting on make-up, and thought: *When I'm grown up, I'll have to do that, every day. Think I'll stay little for ever.* Wore more slap than anybody going, now. Rosie had been desperate to have her own exciting tubes and gold compacts and slippery lipsticks, rather than having to pinch them when Mum wasn't looking. But it did mean you could never choose to go back, to leave off the lipstick, powder and paint; it would be easier to walk down the Waste wearing a short skirt and no knickers. Which Rosie might well have done fifteen years ago, if only to send her brother into one. But not these days. Anyway, she didn't have the legs she'd had fifteen years ago. She dragged herself up from the floor; only time for a quick shower now.

*   *   *

'So what's on TV?' Alex was flicking through her *Radio Times*.

'You've got the thing.' Rosie licked her fingers. 'Shit, got blood all over my hands.' She caught Alex's frown. 'Ketchup, moron. From your fish and chips,' she said.

'Got anything on video?'

'*The Lost Weekend*?'

'Let's just say that ought to be my mother's favourite film.' Alex shook his head. Rosie waited, but he changed the subject. An alkie? Maybe that's why he was such a do-gooder. But it wasn't as though he railed against the demon drink. 'Did I tell you,' he said, 'I used to make little ten minute films?' He mimed a camera action. 'Not many, only six or seven over about fifteen years, but I just got them transferred onto video. Pretentious rubbish, mostly.'

'You'll have to bring them over sometime.' Rosie had never had a hobby in her life, unless you counted reading. Alex would be telling her next he grew prize-winning marrows; that couldn't be any more alien. 'Ian McKellen's *Richard III*? Or is your dad deformed?'

'No he's not, as it happens. Not much of anything interesting. But that'd be great, I've been meaning to see it.' Relaxed, stretching. Good sign. 'Did you know,' he told her, grinning, 'it was probably polio Richard had?'

'You're just a mine of useless information, aren't you?'

'We had a big set of history books at home. Richard three, Henry seven, Henry eight, Edward six . . .'

'Jesus, spare me.' She pinched his arm, and he laughed. 'Bet you know the workings of the internal combustion engine, too. I bet you do.'

'We had encyclopaedias, as well.'

'Great. Loads to look forward to, then.' Rosie picked her way through her papers to the telly, rummaged in the cupboard underneath the set. Christ, she had some junk in here; in what universe would she watch *Terminator* again? Come to that, why had she watched it in the first place? With Scottie, probably. She found the right tape, switched on the little lamp,

turned off the overhead light. Alex had taken off his shoes
and socks, was half lying along the cushions. He reached out
his hand, pulled her on to the settee, so she was leaning against
his chest, could feel the swell of his stomach against her rib-
cage. Then he encircled her with his arm, as though making
sure she wouldn't move. Not planning to go anywhere, babe.
For a second, she closed her eyes, quickly opening them when
she realized she was in severe danger of falling asleep. Prison
visits were always knackering, especially those to one of
Freddy's best boys. And the rain against the window, still
audible underneath the film, seemed to reinforce the soporific
warmth in here. The ache was leaving her shoulders, she could
breathe more freely, but her head was fuzzier. Well, that was
okay. Going to sleep was to go that bit too far, though.

'All right?'

'Yeah, fine.' More than fine, in fact.

In fact . . .

She *must not* go to sleep. Concentrate on the film.

'I don't mean to be cagey about my family,' he said, against
the first soliloquy. 'I know I'm a bit messed up about it, but
there's nothing more to say than that, really. My mum just
didn't like being a mum and we all knew it, me, my dad and
my brother.' He laughed. 'Tragic story, make myself cry in a
minute. No, I do go back to Billericay sometimes, but not often
and I never stay over. They're just not a big part of my life.'
Alex shifted Rosie's weight against him. 'I think that's why I
find it so hard to work out you and Darren, you know? I don't
even see Drew now, and it's not because we fell out or anything.
We just don't.'

'Don't you miss him?' Rosie put her hand on his chest. Didn't
see his brother? How the hell did he manage that? If she moved
to Australia, her family would somehow still be there, a chain
of paper dolls crossing the Atlantic, the Pacific.

'No. I don't feel anything about it, either way. That's what
I mean, it's hard for me to see how your relationship works.'
He pulled her in even closer, kissed her ear through her hair.

'What about the sexy aunt? Do you still see her?'

'Occasionally. She's married now, got a grown-up son who frames pictures. I don't fancy her any more, if that's what you're getting at. But I still think my cousin's lucky.' Stroking her face. 'Rosie . . . could I stay, tonight?'

Suddenly, she was wide awake. What exactly did he mean by *stay*? Sleep on the couch? Sleep with her, make love to her? It was on the tip of her tongue to say *Depends what you mean*, but she realized that it didn't. She'd prefer it if he slept with her, of course she would, but the way she was feeling tonight even his presence in the living room would seem, what? Good. Safe. Yet that was scary; she hadn't let herself get cosy with a man for an age. But just maybe it would be okay. Perhaps safety didn't have to be terminal.

'Sure you want to?'

He kissed her again. She turned her head, knowing he would kiss her properly. His lips felt soft against her own. Gently, she pushed her tongue into his mouth. There was no question tonight of an audition, none of the scent of greasepaint. For one night only, Rosie was prepared to surrender the power to closeness. She hadn't been kissed like this since she was a teenager: where kissing seemed to be for its own sake, not necessarily as a kind of preview. And yet it wasn't at all like the fumblings of the distant past, with eyes desperately closed against the danger of witnessing a reaction; this grown-up version was about looking as much as kissing, each trying to see beyond the public face to the person who lived inside the other's eyes. For once, Rosie couldn't call what was likely to happen, and as the kissing went on, she stopped thinking about it.

The 'phone.

Shit.

'Leave it,' Alex said against her mouth.

She tried, she really did. But she tensed as she heard her own voice suggest the caller leave their name and number, and she pulled away to listen to the message. There wasn't one. Five today, two more than yesterday. What *had* Daz done, this time?

'I'm sorry Alex, I'm going to have to do 1471.'

'What for? It's just some idiot with a phobia about answerphones.' Way too loud. Practically shouting. He sat up, leaned forward, fiddled with the magazine; Rosie noticed that his hand was shaking. Just barely, but shaking nonetheless. Why was he wound up? Maybe he was so turned on that the interruption left him disoriented . . . but it didn't feel like that to Rosie.

You were called, today, at . . . What a surprise, the caller withheld their number. Out of the corner of her ear, she heard McKellen's voice:

I pray you all, tell me what they deserve
That do conspire my death with devilish plots
Of damnèd witchcraft, and that have prevailed
Upon my body with their hellish charms.

'Number withheld?' Casually. Too casually. First shouting, now feigned nonchalance.

'What makes you say that?'

'It's what I was saying before. You know, your work life spilling over into your private life.' There wasn't quite a question mark at the end, but it was the bloody ghost behind the arras.

'Don't play me for a mug, babe.'

'What are you going on about?'

'Leave off, Alex. You pitch up here, demand to stay the night, go all weird when some wanker doesn't leave a message . . .'

'I didn't go *all weird.* You're the one over-reacting.' He pushed his wine glass across the table, pulled it towards him again. Then she saw absolutely. Oh, that bastard.

'You've been co-opted into the "A team", haven't you?'

'What's that supposed to mean?'

'Come off it, the innocence routine just doesn't wash. Jesus,

I see it every day at work. What happened? Did he come and see you, ask you to keep an eye on me? He did, didn't he?'

Alex picked up his wine, downed it.

The bastard, hypocritical, lying, bastard; what had he been intending to do, fuck her to keep her safe? A duty fuck. Or perhaps he just intended to kiss her all night, less hassle than actually having to fucking fuck her. Well, he'd had it now; no way was Rosie going to give him the time of day after this. Fair enough, he couldn't help it that Daz was an interfering moron, a wannabe pimp, but Alex could have told her. Bastard. That's what you get for letting your guard down. That's the price of comfort. Don't trust any fucker.

'He said you'd been getting blank calls, dropped hints about trouble . . .'

'Well, thanks but no thanks. You'd be about as much use as nothing. What were you planning to do if there was someone after me, rant them to death? Hit them with your qualifications? No, I know, you probably kept a windscreen wiper from when you were at Fords. Do me a favour.'

Alex rose. For a split second, Rosie thought he might go for her. She stood her ground.

'For God's sake, woman, feels like I'm in some B movie and I've not even got access to the script. It's all bollocks as far as I'm concerned.'

'You should have told me.'

'I *couldn't*.' Balling his fist, punching his leg. 'I just said, I don't even know the score here, Rosie.' He put his hand on her arm. 'Could you?' What the hell was he getting at, suggesting she should have told him this was par for the course? It'd be like telling Nana why Daz always had plenty of cash, like Alex explaining to him why he shouldn't smoke dope. Yeah, context. Nothing read without that.

'Just go home, Alex.'

'I'm sorry I didn't tell you, all right? But now you know, maybe you'd like to tell me exactly what the fucking score is.'

'I don't think so.' Even if she could. God, did Alex being

enlisted mean there really was something to worry about? No, Daz'd got Scottie involved once, and that was . . . Alex hit himself on the forehead. Amazing how frustration could look like bad theatre.

'I don't want to leave you now, not after that call,' he said.

'Thought it was just someone with an answerphone phobia? Besides, there's gorillas watching this place. Why don't you run down and meet them? You could all be bezzy mates, I'm sure they're right up your street.'

'For God's *sake*.'

'I want you to leave. I'm asking nicely. In two minutes I'm going to tell you to piss off.'

Alex sat down and began to put on his socks and shoes. Looked like he was going, then. Good riddance. If he couldn't be bothered to put it right, that was up to him.

'Rosie, I know this is probably the last thing you want to hear, but I do love you.'

Great. What was she supposed to say to that? Was that one of his tricks, to throw it in? In that tone of voice, he might as well have said he hated her. Alex all over. Opaque.

'Yeah, well.' Even to her own ears, that sounded harsh. But *love*; that was a facer. He might just mean he cared about her, that he valued her friendship. On the other hand . . .

'I'll ring you tomorrow,' he said, picking up his carrier.

'If you get the machine, remember to leave a message.'

He shook his head, touching his tongue to his top lip.

Yeah, well.

It'd been a cunt of a day, and it weren't over yet, not by miles. About eighty mile, to be sact. Last thing Darren wanted was to go right out near Thaxted, in all this weather. Least it seemed to be easing off – pointless driving that far if it kept raining, couldn't keep a fire going outdoors if it was too wet. But one good thing bout the burn part of his job – being out there let you be away from the shit here. When he'd first started at the scrap-yard, fore he put money in it, going out to a field on a burn was a laugh. Getting shot of all the coating off the metal just with your muscle and the fire – better'n any weights for keeping fit. But it was a young man's game. The hours was, anyway, and the risk. Wished burns was legal, then you wouldn't have to hit the countryside in the middle of the night. Darren weren't convinced they was that naughty, anyway – how was burning a bit of plastic and rubber off going to ruin that zone layer? Them weirdy-beardies most probably never had to graft for a living – didn't they realize you couldn't do nothing with metal what had shit still on it? He looked at his watch. Better make a move, go get the lorry. Picked up his pint, was bout to off it. Weren't that . . . yeah, it was. What was that Alex doing here? Thought he was meant to be at Rosie's tonight? Don't do this to me, pal. Darren stood up. Alex shook his head.

'No, she's at her flat, she's fine. But she worked out you'd seen me, went mental . . .'

'And slung you out on your ear. Nice one, mate.' He sat back down. See what happens when you give a job to an Essex boy. They was all the same – plenty of front, nothing to back it up. But least he had the bottle to walk in and hold his hands up.

'Wasn't like I could explain to her, was it?' Said cold. 'Anyway, what now?'

'Wait for her to calm down – I fucking much know. She'll be well pissed off with me, and all.' But maybe it was what Mum called *a blessing in disguise* – maybe Rosie'd come to her senses after this, kick the geezer into touch. 'Ain't all that as a minder, are you?'

'Doesn't look like it.' Alex sat and all, but he was still giving Darren the evils.

'D'you want a drink?' Most probably shouldn't be drinking with him, but Rosie might just stick to him out of stubbornness, then Darren'd be the one stood out in the cold. Sometimes, having Rosie for a sister was like having a full-time job. Mum always said that's why she never went out to work – Rosie. Weren't never any time off, neither.

'All right, Spence?'

'Not too bad, Windy – yourself?' Lovely – that nose ointment Windy Miller must of heard bout Rosie being placated. That pointy, poxy face was after info, for definite.

'Fair to middling. Not seen your Rosie lately. You're the boyfriend, ain't you?'

'Am I?' Alex said. Not bad, old son. You got a lot to make up, but it's a start.

'Right, well, I'd better get back up the bar – me brother's just turned up from over the river, and it ain't easy for him. He's got Parkinson's disease.'

'Christ, sorry about that, mate.'

'Yeah, it's tragic. Can't stop interviewing people.'

'Cunt!' Darren slapped his fist into his hand. Windy laughed and went off up to some geezer . . . and the bloke was shaking all over, like he was plugged into an electric socket. 'Here, check that out – he weren't fucking joking.'

'Some people are beyond a joke.' Alex weren't laughing.

'Wicked git.' Darren stood up to go the bar. Then Alex's bleeper thing went off.

Rosie was halfway down the second bottle of wine. Alex wasn't coming back, not now. Sod him, then. His loss. Couldn't see why she'd got involved with him in the first place, sanctimonious git. Yeah, he was sexy, and sometimes they really began to connect, but at the end of the day he just didn't get it. She'd called him wrong, thought here was someone who'd see all the rules, maybe even make up a few of his own. Instead, he was bowling when she was trying to serve, which was no use at all. Perhaps that's why he hadn't come back. And what was really getting to her was the way Daz had created a role for Alex in her life, well before she'd decided for herself what she wanted. It was like Alex was going out with both of them. Daz had been taken from the start by that bridge being built to connect the two sides of the Mile End Park; must have captured his imagination more than she'd thought. But all bridges were vulnerable structures, even the sturdiest. She'd

nearly lost it back there as well, all that kissing. *Love.* What
was he trying to do, lull her into a false sense of security?
And it would be false, it always was. Wished she had dope;
the curtains were drawn, but she knew how dark it was out
there, how cold. Didn't even have any Valium left. *I can't
manage.* She never wanted to hear herself say that again, not
ever. It had been like having serious 'flu, with thoughts that
had shivered and sweated and frozen, her brain streaming
mucus. Never, ever again. And it's no good relying on anyone
else to help, you have to be able to tell yourself that you'll be
all right. Even someone as big and comforting as Alex, someone
who'd kiss you and kiss you and kiss you, would let you down
in the end. No, he definitely wasn't coming back tonight. Shit.
Music. Put some music on, that's it.

There was a dusty tape apart from the others on the high
shelf, a compilation she'd made ages ago, long before Alex
was around. That would do. She couldn't remember much about
what she'd put on it but she was at least sure she'd like it all,
and that's what she needed at the moment. She stuck it in the
machine. Oh, terrific.

A high-pitched male voice, slightly off-key, told her about
a woman who stayed in every night alone, running her terrors
around in her head, fearing for her sanity as she downed yet
another beer. Rosie couldn't even remember who the song was
by, it was something obscure she'd borrowed from bloody
Scottie's collection, but every word was horribly familiar. And
if those weren't minor chords, she'd eat her own head. Trapped
in the middle of yet another melodrama, and even the soundtrack was a player. It was almost funny. Trouble was, Alex
was the only person she knew who'd see the gag, although
he'd probably say the song had a point, self-righteous sod.
Always offering his opinions like tablets. Men. All offered stuff
that was supposed to be about you, but was really about them.
Daz and his gorillas. The old man and his terrible jokes. Ben
and his admiration.

Scottie had offered her words, little gifts against his character.

Sure, he was articulate, but he wasn't exactly a literary type. Yet, infrequently, he'd brought her a scrap of paper with a single word written on it. She would stick it on the fridge with a magnet, got quite a collection in the finish. But one night, Daz took them off and binned them. Said he thought he was helping tidy round. Yeah, right. Christ, she hadn't thought about that for a very long time. *Behemoth, Luminiferous, Rebus, Barquentine.* Scottie hadn't often bothered to discover what the word meant; it was better, he said, to imagine. And he'd refused to tell her why he did it. Perhaps he didn't know. Alex would have looked them all up, would have used them in sentences to see how they worked, taken them apart as though they were inventions from his Boys' Own Annual. But he wasn't here. Scottie wasn't here, and Alex wasn't here, even Daz wasn't here. Rosie poured herself another glass of wine.

Chapter Five

'She's only gone and had her leg off.'

'*What?*'

'Your Auntie Mim. You know what she's been and gone and done? Had her leg off, without telling me. A year ago, evidently. I was really hurt.'

Darren stared at Mum, gobsmacked. She going like Nana, all of a sudden? Rosie was falling bout laughing, and he was having a job hisself, keeping it in. This was better than the programme blaring out the telly, where everyone was killing theirselves.

'She always said she wanted to do a bit of weight.' Rosie was half choking.

'Rosie Violet Spence!' said Mum. 'Where d'you get it from? You wasn't brought up to take the mick out of other people's misfortunes. Bad though, isn't it, not telling me?'

'Come on, Mum, you know what that lot's like. Don't worry about it.' She curled her legs under herself on the chair. Not a good move, girl – you still got them stupid shoes on.

'Oy – feet!'

'Sorry.' She reached underneath her, and pulled off her shoes like one of them magic acts getting a rabbit out of a hat.

'She's right, Mum – don't let them get to you. I weren't never too fond anyway – stuck up cow, thought she was everybody cos of Benfleet. Always had too much mouth, and all.'

'Not this time she never. Not half enough, if you ask me. Choked me, it did. Anyway, her Bert was only on the dust. I couldn't be doing with that, what with the stink. Tell you what, how about a nice little glass of sherry? Cheer us all up.'

Mum might like a nice little glass of sherry, but it was hard to think of anything more worser, sept a big glass. Rosie was acting like she'd had a personality transplant – bought the sherry without Mum having to say nothing else. Just when you thought you knew what she'd do, she'd go and do the sact opposite. Nan had used to call her Mary, Mary, but that was previous to Rosie being a belly dancer. Come to think of it, Rosie never liked sherry, neither – and that was three glasses she had there. Truth was, both of them'd lie bout liking it cos of what else they wouldn't tell Mum. Rosie bunged the tray on the coffee table, and flung herself on the floor near Mum's feet.

'I've brought in your nuts and raisins, and all. Good for your blood sugar level.'

'My what? We don't want none of your lectures, madam. Anyway, you're still in trouble with me – when am I going to get a look at your young man?'

Rosie's charm bracelet jangled round her stick of an arm as she shook the nuts and raisins into the little bowl. Never hardly wore that bracelet no more, most probably cos it sounded her mood too much. Week since they'd fucked her off between them, but Darren weren't sactly back onside with Rosie hisself yet, so it weren't all that likely Alex was, what put her in a bit of an awkward one. Jangled.

'He's not young,' she said, 'he's over ten years older than me.' Started sorting through the bowl, picking out the raisins what she loved, like she always done – for Ron. Lateron.

'I'm glad about that – it wouldn't do to go courting with some boy, not at your age.'

'Blimey, Mum, I'm not exactly past it!'

'I'm not saying you are, lamb, but you're going to have to get your skates on.'

'What, this won't get the baby a new bonnet?'

Good girl. Just this side of taking a liberty. She was wound

up, he could notice that, but she was acting cool, looking Mum
right in the eyeballs.

'She ain't sactly desperate, Mother. When've you known her
go without a bloke when she wanted one?'

'That's enough of that sort of talk – you know I don't like
it.'

'And I can speak for myself, thanks very much.'

Stroll on – couldn't never win. Try and be nice, all you got
was GBH of the earholes. Check Rosie now, pulling all her hair
away from her face, making out she didn't know it made them
big eyes even more obvious. All right, girl – can see you're
giving me the evils. Careful, your nose makes you look like a
four-by when you do that. Darren just wanted a bit of recognition. But all he ever got was *Piss off and leave me alone*.
Mum ought to wash Rosie's mouth out with soap.

'Suppose she's ashamed of us,' said Mum. 'Or is there something wrong with him?'

Had to give it one last try.

'He's okay,' Darren made hisself say. Rosie turned to look at
him. She nodded, all slow.

'Yeah, he is, isn't he?'

He got out the motor, to watch her indoors. She come round
his side. He held his breath. She weren't smiling. But she put
her hands on his shoulders and her cheek on his.

Then she kissed him.

Every time the doorbell went, Rosie's stomach clenched, her
mouth drying out as though she had an instant hangover.
Ridiculous. Didn't help that the local kids had been letting off
fireworks for the past week, rehearsing for the big bang. Penny
for your nerves, Missus? Despite the cold, she'd forced herself
to go to Barmy Park after work, to drink her Diet Coke there,
to prove she didn't feel at risk. Certainly didn't allow herself
a Diazepam. Indoors, she'd even started imagining doorbells,
jumping up to check on Mr Nobody. Victim mentality, and

she'd always despised victims. But Daz still hadn't called the minders off; his concern was beginning to affect her, particularly since neither he nor Freddy had told her the minders were there. Whenever they were this evasive, it meant someone had slipped up. Rosie knew the rules, knew when not to keep on: knowing more than they did meant that sometimes she had to know less. But lack of knowledge equalled a weakening of control. And when you were frightened, you couldn't think about anything else; your head was stuffed with it, smothering rational thought. And when the caller *was* real and turned out to be Postie or bloody Daz, the adrenaline had nowhere to go, and you shook and hyper-ventilated and hated yourself. Which was okay if it *were* her brother, because she could shout at him, but even she could hardly freak out at the postman for delivering her Folio Society selection.

She was fairly sure this time. Oh, Christ. Putting down her book, she crossed the room.

Peered through the spy-hole.

Alex.

A rush of relief. But couldn't he have 'phoned first? Okay, perhaps she should have taken his calls. Quickly, she checked herself out in the hall mirror, standing on tiptoes to see her waistband. She'd bought this suit to impress any judge with her veracity rather than her sexuality. Was that skirt a bit tight? No lunch tomorrow. She untucked her shirt and opened the door, but stood between Alex and the hallway.

'We both know you're going to let me come in. It's freezing out here.'

'Tough.' How dare he make assumptions? She'd decide who she let into her flat.

'Don't be so childish. If you don't want to keep seeing me, the least you can do is let me in, give me a drink, and tell me properly. I've rung every day this week, Rosie.'

Good point. Rosie hadn't decided whether she was going to

see him again, but it was undignified to behave like this on
the doorstep. She stood aside. Alex took off his jacket, hanging
it on the peg like he lived there.

'Got any voddy?'

'Yeah. You can get it yourself, seeing as how you're so
familiar with the place.'

And he loped straight to the drinks cupboard, even though
she was sure he'd only ever drunk wine here. Did he have the
place under surveillance, or what? God, she wouldn't put it
past Daz to have sorted that, and given the tapes to the
Neighbourhood Watch. Alex went to *her* kitchen, crashed
around, came back with lemon slices in the bowl that was
meant for nuts. Don't know the place that well then, do you?
He put his drink next to hers on the table, sat on the settee,
lit a cigarette. Rosie perched on the edge of the armchair,
adjusting her skirt as it rode up. Bloody Italian cuts.

'Well?'

'I should be asking you that.' Alex scratched the bulge of
his stomach.

'Didn't my brother tell you? Never thought you'd be the
type to do what someone else said without an explicit contract.'

'I'm not a *puppet*,' he said, picking up his vodka, fat with
lemon slices, then he replaced it without drinking, shook his
head. 'On paper, it'd look like one kind of thing, but . . .'

'I really don't know any more than you do. It's boys' stuff.'
Don't give away the fear. Not when he's got that sceptical look
on his face.

'And I'm meant to be satisfied with that, am I?'

'There's nothing else to give on this one.' Crossing her legs
and tasting her drink.

'Blatantly.' Controlled. Bastard must be dying to go into a
rant. 'This is getting very familiar territory. Feels like I'm doing
the hokey cokey half the time, with you.'

'That's what it's all about.' She poked at her book with her
toe.

'Does anyone ever get beyond that?' He was half laughing.

'No one has for a good while, no.' Rosie flexed her foot, making little circles in the air from her ankle. He seemed to be waiting for her to elaborate, but she wasn't going to.

'I just need to know if I'm ever going to get beyond that.' He reached out as though intending to touch her, but picked up his drink again instead. Thick fingers, dark with hair; they could probably crush the glass and barely feel it.

'It's not an easy line to cross, Alex.'

'No, I realize that. But I don't think you meet too many people like me, do you?' Arrogant git. He might be smiling at his own presumption, but it was a smile that said he was standing by it. 'I'll be straight with you. I think you're worth a hell of a lot.' He returned her impassive look with one of exasperation, and exhaled through his teeth. 'But most of the time, I'm so furious with you . . . Then I start to think that's not going to be enough.'

'You came back.'

'And you knew I would. But I promise you, it doesn't mean I always will. I've about had it, as you might say. There's you being so contemptuous every time you're not second guessed just right, and your brother expecting me to play Cowboys and Indians in the dark, and me having to worry all the time about what's going to happen to you when someone isn't there looking out for you . . .'

'Someone always is.' Yeah, and in the act of being watched, you were being changed.

'For God's sake, do you want to see me or not?'

'You sound like you don't want to see me.'

'I'm not saying that. But no, not if you're going to keep blowing hot and cold. Christ!' He rubbed his hand furiously across his forehead. 'You're the most difficult woman I've ever met.'

'And your point is what, exactly?'

'You're something, you know that?' He played with his crushed cigarette butt for a couple of seconds, making patterns from the ash. She watched him, knowing she didn't have to

say anything. 'The trouble is,' he said, slowly, 'I've got this
. . . I really like strong women, you know? It's . . . I've just
sort of got this thing about . . . being beaten, I suppose.'

Rosie's heart jumped. *Beaten?* What the hell was he saying
that he set himself up to lose? But he, oh my God, he couldn't
mean *beaten*, surely? As in, what? Chains and stuff? Was that
what his problem was, sexually: he couldn't get off unless you
produced a whip? She wasn't sure how she felt about that;
could she literally beat this man? He looked up, the loose skin
around his eyes crinkling with a smile that didn't show on his
lips, and then she realized what he meant; he wanted the battle,
but he didn't want to win. Not too easily, anyway. Come to
the right place then, hadn't he.

'I don't like feeling policed,' she said.

'It goes with the job, doesn't it?' His voice neutral.

'I guess.' Only with the job of being her brother's sister. 'Do
you want another drink?'

'I'll get them. You look really stressed out, Rosie. Why don't
you sit back and relax.' What happened to the moral high-
ground? She reached for her big cushion, put it in front of
her, and dropped into it, leaning her back against the chair.
'Then you can tell me what you've decided,' he added. 'Okay
to put a CD on?'

What was he planning to do, sing her into submission? The
Kinks. Apparently, she really got them so they don't know
what they're doing. Oh, yeah.

Rosie watched him pour the drinks. Despite the sermon, it
felt good to have Alex in the flat; almost imperceptibly, it was
warmer, more inhabitable. There was a faint smell coming from
his clothes, sawdusty, constantly re-announcing his physical
presence. And he took up so much space, not intrusively, but
you could never forget he was in the room. He passed Rosie
her scotch, and looked at her, drilling right through her skull.
She returned the look. So he'd known, before she did. *Cut off
your nose to spite your face, you do.* Not this time, Mum.

'I must like a challenge.'

'I think you probably do.' He lowered himself on to the floor beside her, awkwardly, squeezing between the table and the settee.

'I think you probably do, too.' She put down her glass, and pulled herself in one movement back on to the chair. Alex watched her for a second, then knelt on the cushion. Rosie shifted her legs so that Alex was kneeling between them. He put his hands on her thighs.

'Okay?'

'Yeah.' Aware of her legs, soft under his hard hands. 'Do you want to go to work from here in the morning?'

'I was hoping you'd say that. Only one problem . . .'

'How long?'

Ben was getting cold, hanging around like a cunt. He weren't muscle, anyway – Spence and Freddy knew that. But suppose if the payroll boys was needed elsewhere. Only a couple of hour, they said – been more'n that already. The boyfriend'd just left in a cab. Couldn't be getting any, weren't in there long enough. Meant that Rosie was on her tod, now. Tempting to knock up at hers, ask for a cup of tea – he'd be just as much use in her flat, surely – but he'd been told to stay here, and the moody Spence had on him, Ben weren't going to cross him. It was an hard one to pass on. But he'd nearly stuffed up already today. He'd been getting earache off that Sam Patterson kid about who was Rosie going out with, nosy bugger, when she nearly give him the slip, into Barmy Park. That was barmy – swanning around like she never suspected the score. Spence'd said the big geezer'd be bound to get back onside, what would help, but Ben never see how – soon as he did show, he fucked off. Why Spence rated him at all was one for Miss Marple. Specially when he'd messed up once and all. And . . .

Fuck!

Steel at his

throat

must
not
move.

'The Lion never sleeps.'

'You was, though, mate. Benny, ain't it? Spence's little bum
chum. Well, Benny – you weren't never much of a looker, but
after tonight, no one's going to call you a pretty boy.'

How many? Two? More?

The steel travelled from his throat to his cheek.

So much . . .

pain . . .

The nerves kicked in, but there was none of the recent foolish
terror, no clawing in her guts, no loss of saliva. Alex had said
he'd get the cab to wait. If he'd been lucky with the traffic,
there was a slim chance it was him at the door. No, that was
seriously over-optimistic. Rosie looked through the spyhole:
Daz, half bent like he was a bloody coalman. Great, that's all
she needed, Daz pitching up with his own baggage when Alex
had gone to get his. She didn't believe this.

Oh, Christ.

That wasn't a sack. It was a person.

> *And I love to live so pleasantly*
> *Live this life of luxury*

Frantically, Rosie scrabbled to free the locks, and fled back
to the living room.

> *Lazing on a sunny afternoon*

Jesus, Jesus, Jesus. *In the summertime*

. . . what the hell had happened?

> *Sipping at my ice-cold beer*

Was Daz hurt, as well? *Help me, help me, help me, sail
away*

They half fell through the living room door, Daz supporting
(oh God, no) Ben, whose face seemed to be flapping open and
closed, blood pouring on to the carpet. *Give me two good*

reasons why I ought to stay He looked like a rubber toy, all bendy and flapping. Except for the blood. Rosie watched dispassionately for a fraction of a second, then she remembered to breathe out, and the words came too.

'What . . . is he all right?'

'Course he's not fucking all right! Here, help me put him on the settee. Does he look fucking well all right?' *In the summertime* He held Ben on the settee, tenderly stroking his shoulder. 'It's okay, old son – you'll be fine, mate.'

'Shall I call an ambulance?' She looked at Daz.

'No,' he said.

'Didn't think so.' No way would Ben get to go to Casualty, not for what was wrong with him. 'But at the very least, he needs serious stitches.'

'Babe – get Doc on the blower. You got the number?'

'Yeah.' She moved towards the telephone. Ben was hurt; she had to get help. Mustn't think about anything else, just about helping Ben. The doctor's voice sounded bland, efficient; Rosie had trouble concentrating. But it'd be okay: the doctor was coming. He must have seen much worse, but oh God, maybe less bad was all he could deal with. Barely conscious, Ben began to whimper. Rosie poured three brandies, and ran to the hall to grab a clean towel from the airing cupboard. 'Here, hold this to his face. Can he drink at all?' She put the glass against Ben's lips. Nothing. With her fingers, she managed to get a little brandy into his mouth. Don't look at the face, just don't look. Daz had the towel pressed to Ben's poor cheek, and was able, with a bit of obvious effort, to throw his drink down his own throat. 'You sure Doc's going to be enough?' Rosie coughed as she swallowed her brandy.

'D'you want to end up like this poor bastard? Cos I know I don't fucking want you to.'

Imagine losing your face. She bit her lip as hard as she could, to stop herself from crying. None of them needed an hysterical woman on their hands, least of all Rosie herself. Automatically, she refilled their glasses. She suddenly felt sick, sat down abruptly on the chair, turning her face away from the towel that was quickly being drenched in blood.

Breathing slowly, she forced herself to glance back at the settee; Daz was stroking Ben's hair. Now she was really close to losing it. She desperately, passionately, wanted a cigarette but she wasn't sure it'd do Ben any good. Why had Daz brought him here? Had Ben been out there, minding her? He wasn't a gorilla, just a little ferret with a lot of front. She'd known him all her life. *Mrs S – can Spence come out? Do we have to take your Rosie? Me mum says I can stay for me tea.* And then when Rosie finished college, he'd suddenly developed an interest in getting her knickers off. Almost wished she'd let him, now.

'How's he doing?'

'I don't fucking know! You all right, Benny boy? Yeah, course you are. That's it.'

'Daz . . . why . . .'

'Bad call. I'm a cunt.'

'Don't say that, sweetheart. You weren't to know it'd come to this.' Whatever it was.

'Why shouldn't it of?' He was right. In his world, it always could come to this. And it looked like it had come to this on her doorstep. Rosie sipped her drink.

'It was me they were getting at, wasn't it?' she said. The diamond in their crown.

'I'm really sorry, darling.' He looked across at her, nodded, slowly. 'Charlie Boyd . . . he was after collecting from that Lion, know what I'm saying? So when some cunt went mad with the petrol . . . they think someone from The Mice done it.'

God, she should have seen. Had to be something like that. Every pub from Bow to Aldgate East knew how important Rosie Spence was to The Mice. And every pub in a smaller radius knew how to attack Darren Spence: through her. If she hadn't been so preoccupied with Alex, Rosie would have put the pieces together weeks ago. But then,

'Did any of you do it?'

'I never had a bar of it, doll – promise you.' His eyes teared up; Rosie thought she believed him. But where did that leave them? 'Ain't as bad as it looks, Ro. They won't dare . . .'

The door.

Had to be Doc; Ben was a warning, not a prelude. But, shit, might be Alex. She forced herself to breathe as she rubbed a mark from the spyhole. Thank you, God.

'Where's your bathroom? I need to get myself this side of clean.'

'So what, you've both been on the fish and chips, have you?' Alex said. Made no sense to Darren, but Rosie seemed to get it.

'That's right.'

'I'm not an idiot. What happened?'

A nightmare, Alex just missing Doc taking Ben off, checking out the blood on the settee and all over Darren's best jacket. First off, he asks Rosie if she's all right, then he started. So Darren waded in then, to let his girl off the hook.

'Cut me hand, didn't I?' Sitting down on the settee, on top of Ben's blood.

Alex shook his head, and Rosie – bloody Rosie – give it up.

'It's Ben. Got his face slashed. Not badly, he'll be fine, but we had to bring him here.'

'Where is he now? In hospital?'

'No, he's back at his mum's. Our doctor says he'll be okay.'

Alex didn't say nothing straight off. Went over to the cupboard, got hisself a drink. He offed it in one, and stood in front of Rosie, put his hand on her arm.

'*Your* doctor, I get it. What's the matter with you? What if it was you? Would I be expected just to chance you'd be all right?'

'We can't have the Old Bill involved, babe, we just can't.'

'You got to see that, mate. D'you want Rosie to be next, or what?'

Rosie plonked herself on the chair, and Alex sat on its arm, a right black spression on his face. Few minutes dragged past, then cat let go of the geezer's tongue.

'So what's this about?' Weren't obvious who he was asking.

'It's really tricky, babe. You have to realize everything has to do with everything else.'

'Yeah, and when a butterfly flaps its wings another bloke gets carved up.' Looking between them at the telly, like as if it was turned on. What's he on about, fucking butterflies?

'Don't worry, mate – they ain't going to be let to get away with it.'

'That's not what I meant. Bollocks.'

No one said nothing again for a bit. That Alex was gnawing on his thumb like he'd never had no dinner, breathing all loud. But Darren thought it was more like he was wild than worried. Ro was picking at a catch in her tights. Make a ladder, she would. Slowly, an horrible thought come to Darren, but much as he tried to out it, it wouldn't go away. He caught Alex's eye.

'Might be best if she . . .' He really, really never wanted to do this '. . . stays with you for couple. Just for a caution, in case.' No, the bloke weren't no mug. He was doing one of them Rosie looks at him, and it was a tough call to know how shit-scared he was. But if Darren couldn't tell, no one else'd be able to, and that had to be a result. 'You always knew it would be spensive,' Darren kept on. 'Can't you afford it?'

'I hope I'm not the *it* in this.'

Yeah, nice one – just the right time to bring up all that feminine crap. Seemed to Darren that Rosie had all her priorities arse about tit. Some nutter'd be trying to kill her, and she'd be moaning on about birds' rights to work. Can't work if you're six feet under. Weren't that he thought it'd happen, nothing like, but it was starting to look that bit too real. And he weren't taking no chances with his Rosie. A sister for a sister – over a lot of dead bodies they'd get that.

'This ain't your call, girl.'

'Yeah, I can see that. Better leave it to you, then. You've made some right good calls lately, haven't you? Really spot on.'

Fucking mare. How far below the belt she think she had to go? It weren't like he wouldn't see that poor cunt's face for the rest of his natural, like something from an horror film, only the geezer making the film was Darren. Well, it was them bastards from The Lion, but Darren was there, holding their cameras. He might as well of torched the place hisself – couldn't of been no worser. Jesus Christ, darling – what you want, blood?

'I held me hands up to that.' Come out sort of mumbled.

'Maybe Alex better just go,' Rosie said.

'No way,' said Alex. He handed round a packet of fags. Cheap fags. Dark blue packet. 'No, no way. If you're staying here, so am I, or you can come with me. I think you're both being big time . . . well . . . But I'm not leaving you here on your own.'

'She's not on her own, cunt.'

Alex made his hand into a fist, gainst his leg. So quiet, his breath come like a slap.

'If you want to stay with me, that's fine,' he said eventual, to Rosie. Sounded well wound up, now. 'I don't have a problem, well, I do have a problem with that, but I've got more of a problem with you being where I can't at least do my best to keep an eye on you.'

'Right.' She rubbed at a mark on her skirt, what might've been blood. 'Sorry, I'll have to change first. What're you going to do, sweetheart?'

'Get meself round home. Have to let Mum know something about Ben – she'll want to see Cath and check with Doc, won't she? I'll keep you out of it.'

'Suppose someone ought to call Tricia. Get Mum to.'

'Still don't suppose anyone's going to tell *me* what's going on?' Alex said. 'Expect I'm better cannon fodder if—'

'I'm not listening to any more of this,' said Rosie. 'What about the gorillas, they coming to Alex's?'

'I'm not having you out there with no protection.' She knows she's being minded. Course she does. Weren't nothing else it could of been. Most probably she knew way before what happened to Ben.

'Yeah, he's got a point, Alex. You'll be safer as well, not just me.'

Weren't his point at all. Made no odds to him what happened to the bloke – so long as whatever happened never made it worst for Rosie. She was looking at that Alex now, with one of them little sad secret smiles what made you feel you and her was part of something no other person knew bout. Most probably just an act, but he was bound to fall for it, do whatever she said. Darren had a pain in his guts – must be all the grief over Ben. Holding her hand now Alex was, scratching her palm with his thumb. Darren didn't hardly know where to look. She lifted up one shoulder, much as to say she knew what she was, and was asking Alex to put up with it. Darren'd had that a million times. You had to feel sorry for the bloke – never knew what he was letting hisself in for. All them years of eating the bottom of the iced finger after she'd had the icing, and having to eat the worms off of worm cake cos she never liked them. The amount of times he'd ended up with a pocket full of coppers she never wanted in her purse, then her going on his earhole for a fiver to go the pictures. The favours he'd called in for her, the shit he'd had to put up with from other blokes. Couldn't see the social worker hacking all that. He'd most likely try to *reason* with her. Darren'd love to see that. His Rosie didn't do reason. Well, she never done reason herself, but she was right good at making you feel you was the one what never. Oh fuck – she was kissing Alex's cheek, all soft like as though he was a kid what'd just lost his mum. He was giving her his X-ray look, brushing her hair out of her eyes. Little tart'd let it fall over her face on purpose, he'd lay money on it.

On the other hand, that Alex wouldn't know how to love her. He'd think like he did, but knowing was a whole nother kettle of fish. Loving Rosie was bout lying down and taking it, even when you was in a right strop with her and showing it, even when you had to let her jump all over your feelings at the same time as you was having a real major go. Alex wouldn't cut it – no chance. Just cos she done them smiles, and seemed to give the people what they wanted, didn't mean to say she was really like that. And if certain people never realized that, there was bound to be trouble. Darren would tell the bloke he was sorry – be fair, he'd earned that one – but the end of the day, the result'd be the same. Goodnight Vienna. If Mum was waiting for their Ro to settle down, she'd be waiting a long old time.

Darren tried to think of something to say, something that wouldn't send Rosie into one, but he kept getting caught up in the little kisses and touches. And then Rosie did something so pushing it that Darren thought Alex might fuck off then and there. Most blokes would of done. She got hold of his hand and bit the fingers, dead hard. Darren could see the teeth marks. He flinched hisself, but Alex never – he just carried on looking at her. Then he smiled, sort of with the corner of his mouth, so's his face all screwed up. He said something to her, right quiet – sounded like *Bitch*, but it couldn't of been, Rosie'd never of worn that – and spite everything she laughed. That was more'n enough for Darren. He stood up.

'I'll ring you a cab. You get your gear together, right now. Just sitting here . . . Fucking deserve it, we would. Here, mate – you better help her, else she'll want to take seven suitcases. I know my girl. You ain't had thirty-two year of it, have you?'

Alex rubbed his bitten hand gainst his good'un.

'Not yet,' he said.

It was like they was all in a cage they couldn't find no way out of. There was a wheel Alex was on, and Rosie thought she had the run of a miles bigger place than what she did have, and Darren was the only one could notice how strong the bars was. Some decent cunt had give them food and water, but it was a cage, just the same. Darren felt like telling them, but he couldn't of. They might of laughed, taken the piss, even though he was in the right of it. Stead, he watched while Rosie brung in a great big bag, slung papers in her briefcase. You think that'll do it, girl – not a prayer. More chance of catching leprosy. And as for Alex – he never had a clue. Not a fucking clue.

Chapter Six

Rubbing his hand over his chin, he went over to the window and looked out, then closed the curtains. She sat on the armchair opposite the telly. Maybe they should put it on, might be a distraction. What a night. Rosie pressed her hands together. Suddenly, she felt shattered. Just to crown it, she had to stay here. She wanted to be with Alex, but she'd wanted him on her turf. Yet her place wasn't her refuge any more. And he was bound to rant on about not calling an ambulance, and she wouldn't have the option of sending him away. The only consolation was he could hardly tell her to leave, either.

'Put a shot of this in my tea, will you?' She rummaged in her bag for her hip-flask.

'You're such a walking, talking cliché at times.'

'Don't I know it.'

Alex pressed Play on the tape machine: halfway through a song by some woman whose voice insisted that life was inevitably tragic, even though the lyrics were perfectly cheerful. Then he went back over to the window, pulled aside the curtain and peered out into the night, before going into the kitchen. She wasn't about to ask if he could see the gorillas.

He was back suspiciously quickly; he better have boiled that kettle properly. Alex knelt on the floor in front of her, and held out a mug. She took it from him, burning her fingers, and gulped at the tea, burning her throat. He sat back, twisted and ungainly.

'Come on, get it over with, then,' she said.

'What?' He looked surprised. 'Do you mean . . .'

Bloody men.

'No of course I didn't mean that, you idiot. I meant don't you want to have a pop about my lifestyle or something?'

'How can I? I don't know what it is.' Calm disapproval looked out at her; it filled all the available space, damply surrounding them.

'Are you scared?' she said through the miasma, wanting that answered, badly: what was all this doing to him.

'Of course I'm scared, but I've made a choice, here. I could have walked away . . .'

'But you didn't.' Trying not to say *I'm scared, too, Alex. Even me.*

'No, I didn't. And I might not like it, well I'd have to be mad to like it, wouldn't I? But I like you, and I don't see how I can do anything different, really.'

Like? He'd said he loved her, recently. Bastard.

'I hope you realize what you might be letting yourself in for, here.' And it had to be here, didn't it, where she wasn't sure how to find things, and the only armoury she had was in one suitcase, and the soundtrack was that woman wailing on about love being just dandy.

'I'm not likely to be the world expert in gang warfare, am I?'

'Jesus, you've been reading the *Guardian* again.' Wanting to tell him she wasn't sure what would happen either, how serious it was. Was Ben more disposable than Rosie Spence? Could the repercussions of hurting her ever be worth the risk? No editorial would help them with that one. Alex offered his hand; she took it, but held it limply and he let go. When he spoke, it was as though she were a client at the Centre, as though he were observing the drama of someone else's life, both inter-ested and disinterested. And gentle.

'Tell you the truth, I've no idea what I'm getting into. What exactly happened, Rosie?'

'I don't want to think about it any more tonight.' In what universe would she tell him exactly? Like serving defence papers by e-mail: you could do it, but many of her older colleagues thought it an unwise mixing of *modi operandi*. 'There'll be enough fall-out tomorrow.'

'You brought it up.' The same compassionate professionalism. He drained his mug; must have an asbestos mouth. God, it couldn't be good for her legal rep either, to be that close to something. William would love this.

'He looked so terrible, Alex.' She watched for his reaction: he hardened back into knowing her again. Or perhaps she meant softened.

'Thought you didn't want to think about it.'

'I don't.' But it was so difficult. Rosie reached out to touch his face; it always felt this rough. She ran her fingers over the stubble, poked lightly at those dimples, traced his lips with her nail. He pressed his head into her hand. She put down her mug, and with her free hand wrote an invisible line from his eyelid down his cheek. What would Ben look like, once he'd healed? More like a polecat than a ferret, covered in stripes. She didn't want to think about it; didn't quite want to leave it alone. Taking her hands from Alex's face, she pushed them through her hair.

'Drink your tea,' he told her, too kindly.

'What are you, my mum?'

'Blatantly not.' He sounded irritated now. Jesus Christ, it was Rosie who was stuck here, it was she who'd seen Ben's face. Alex had it easy compared with that.

'Might have known we weren't going to have a good night. We never do.'

'No, inconsiderate of your friend, getting his face cut up.' Alex laughed, hitting a spiteful note.

'I *said* I didn't want to talk about it. Are you deaf?' Something was taking its course. Not that he'd get the allusion, bloody literalist.

Alex picked at the carpet, his face turned away from her.

'We're going to have to sort of put it on hold anyway, to get on with normality,' he said, after what felt like minutes.

'You know? I haven't got a clue what's going on, you're not ready to tell me and I have to make the decision to go with that.' Turning to face her again. 'So here we are.' He stretched out one of his legs. No way was he comfortable, sat there on the floor. Smug bastard, thinking he had all the answers as to how they could behave after what had happened. Yeah, here they were. She'd thought she felt okay at home, in control, but now it was as though she'd been thrown in a cell, had slashed Ben herself and was being punished. Or like Alex had held the blade, and it was all his fault. 'Funnily enough, you look fine,' he added.

'Bloody miracle, if I do. I feel like shit.'

Alex leaned forward and touched her foot, stroking the leather of her boots.

'Do you want to take these off?'

'No. Why, what's wrong with them?'

'Nothing, they're great,' he said. Did he think she could be flattered into a different life?

'I got them with Randa the other day.' But he was right, they were wonderful. 'Mind you, they want to be fabulous.'

'I bet. Nothing comes cheap with you, does it?' For a moment, she thought she saw something sharp in his eyes, a double-edged knife.

'Believe it,' she said. 'Risks bring rewards, babe, that's how come I always pay my own way. And I love having stuff.' Hearing her own words with interest, listening to a self who hadn't been present that evening. 'I like spending way too much on impractical boots. Couldn't handle being broke again.'

'I can't give you *stuff*, as you call it.' He was giving her that intense look of his, and that screwed-up-face smile, as though he thought he could offer something better.

'You want to start by giving yourself some stuff. Where do you shop, Alex, Oxfam?'

'Markets, mostly.'

'I got these trousers at a market. In Italy.'

'Silk, right?' He pinched the fabric between his thumb and

forefinger. 'It's all about currency with you, isn't it?' Alex rubbed the back of his neck.

'What the hell's that supposed to mean?'

'Thought you were meant to be bright.' They glared at each other; Rosie wanted to slap him, scratch his face, anything to make him drop his gaze. Anything to gain ground.

'Can I have a drink?' she said. Shit. Shit. Oh sod it, she was having to be a guest, let him be a host. He hesitated for a moment, then got to his feet. Good call: wine. More tea would be too much of a reminder that there'd been an accident. He put the ashtray within her reach. But he didn't smile.

Alex returned to the floor. She crossed her legs, tip of her heel just kissing his cheek. He took off his shoes and socks. She hated those shoes. Hated them.

'Look at you,' he murmured. 'There's no justice.'

'Yeah well, like you said before. I bet my boots came to way more than your entire wardrobe.' Scruffy *bastard*. She managed to hold it together after all that blood, and Alex sat there looking as though his mother had dressed him. And didn't like him very much. Which, evidently, she didn't. How dare he?

'I don't doubt it.'

'Look at it this way . . . if each of us took off anything we were wearing that cost less than fifty quid, who'd be the one to end up naked? What d'you reckon?'

'Just wish I knew how you felt,' he said, softly.

'Listen to what I'm saying, then.' Rage rattled around inside her, but she was buggered if she'd shake on the outside.

'Always say what you feel, don't you? Transparent.' Alex ran his hand over his eyes.

'You're right, it depends on the currency.' Would he do it? Rosie had too many unanswered questions about this man; this time, she wanted something concrete. She wasn't going to spend however many days in his flat, possibly in his bed, only to end up none the wiser. She was in the humour to win. He owed her one. 'For instance, do we really need that awful jumper?' she added.

'Is it that bad?' He plucked at the front of it and shrugged.

'Oh, yeah. And it cost you how much?'

'Fuck off, Rosie. I'm a pauper compared to you, that what you want me to say?' He pulled off the jumper and threw it on to the other chair. Scratching his head, he faced her; she could see his chest moving with every breath. Rosie touched her mouth-ulcer with her tongue. He was going to go for it, she was almost sure; whether this was about attraction or contempt or fear was less certain.

'And the tee-shirt? Fiver, was it?'

'Pay for it now, shall I? Or do you take plastic?' Heavy on the sarky tone. Gratuitous.

Rosie watched as he exposed his flesh: a great expanse of white, tempered with thick black-grey hair. Fattened-up muscle. Slight beer gut, but she'd known about that. Yeah, the body was a definite improvement on the faded tee-shirt. She reached for her wine, which she'd left on the table next to her chair.

'You didn't get yourself a drink.'

'No, I didn't think.'

She offered him the glass, but when he went to take it, instinctively she refused to let go; he swore under his breath but leaned forward to sip as she held it. Rosie wiped her thumb across his lips.

'Thank you.' Touch more irony there? 'Looks like I'm with the bank that likes to say yes.' He gave a laugh, which settled into a cocky grin. She had to put a stop to that. She wasn't sure why, but it seemed important. No, vital. Rosie uncrossed her legs, put down her glass, and beckoned him closer. Look at him, kneeling there, ever-so-slightly amused. She thought she might kiss his bare skin, until she didn't: she sank her teeth into his shoulder, biting as hard as she could. He groaned; she ran her tongue over the bite. Bet he wasn't grinning now.

But it was nothing like enough. Not that she could have said what she meant by that; *not enough* simply ran through her mind like a mantra. And every woman bites. She sat back in the chair, watching him. He was just looking back at her, as though she hadn't done anything at all.

'Give us a cigarette, babe.'

'*Please.*' But he lit one for her, taking several deep drags before passing it over. She inhaled, and gently kissed his top lip. He pulled away.

Mind fucker.

'Aren't you still a bit under budget?' She had to know what it would feel like, to have him naked before her, all for a six hundred quid price-tag. God, her mind needed a replacement for Ben's inside-out cheek. Alex was frowning. 'What's the matter, darling, can't you handle it?'

'I didn't say that.'

'Oh I get it, all bets off. Fair enough. Shall we put the telly on?' She could feel her heart filling her whole body.

'It's just, no man's going to find that bit easy. You know that.'

She did. Even given what had happened, a man would still have to worry about his cock.

'If it was easy there'd be no point in it. Come here.' She shifted to the edge of the chair, and Alex came closer. Rosie put her cigarette out and her hand over his heart. 'Don't panic,' she said. *Panic*, she thought. The buttons of his flies were stiff. 'New jeans?'

'Yeah. Not cheap.'

'No, and they're nice. But, Alex, I know exactly how much 501s cost. Just under.' Slowly, she undid them, running her nails lightly over his stomach. 'Take them off.'

'Just because you say so?'

'No, not just because of that.' Keeping the rage still.

'Wanted to run that one by, anyway.' He nodded. Awkwardly, he struggled out of his jeans. Rosie could see the outline of his erection through his underpants. His obvious fear gave her a rush of adrenaline; she brushed his cock, lightly, with the hard leather toe of her boot.

'You haven't got a prayer with these, have you?'

It was impossible to know whether he'd wear it; she could only find out by testing him. And she had to test herself, to see exactly what she was prepared to do. Not just because she told herself she had to, but to stop the blood bursting from her veins.

He watched her watching him.

Twenty, thirty seconds.

'Okay. Take them off, now.'

Briefly, he closed his eyes, then opened them to look back into hers. His breathing sounded loud, even over the music. Carefully, he inched the pants down until Rosie could see his cock. She smiled, couldn't help herself. He put the pants on top of his jeans.

'Well?' he said.

'Well what?' She knew what he meant.

'God, you don't want to make this easy at all, do you?'

It's a sexy cock, Alex, she said. But not aloud. Let him sweat. Bastard. All bloody bastards. Rosie reached down, intending to take his cock in her hand. The black lace sleeve of her shirt looked formal where it fell against his bare skin. She sat up straight again, and raised her eyebrows. Thought you were going to get something then, didn't you?

She placed her left foot high on his leg, then the right on his other thigh, encasing his balls. Any pressure, and her heels would pierce his flesh like thorns.

'Careful,' he said.

'Why?' All right, so she'd keep them there. He smiled.

Shit, she could really do him some damage here, stamp all over his cock, anything. Would he still kneel there, and smile? She leaned forward, her arm across her knees, bearing her weight down. The silk of her trousers brushed against his flesh, a gently mocking echo of the harder contact.

He flinched, but held his ground.

Rosie moved, catching his skin.

Alex breathed in through his teeth.

She saw two raised weals on his thighs as she lifted her legs from his.

He didn't even glance down.

What was he waiting for, kneeling so still and sure of himself? She was damned if she was going to concede anything. Oh God, she needed a reason to let out all the stuff inside her, to get some relief from the effort not to shake. Shifting back in the chair, she crossed her hands behind her neck; if he were concentrating, he'd know what she wanted.

He knew.

And moved.

Alex kissed her, pressing his body in hard, and unzipped her trousers. Her stomach tightened. He slipped his hand inside, and began to rub her, gently. Rosie watched that concentration on his face; was this about her, or him? She closed her eyes, shut out his intensity, tried to go with the feeling, to ignore everything else. Gradually, his face faded from the inside of her eyelids. Gradually, she let herself centre on his stroking fingers. Gradually. Gradually.

As she came, he murmured something. Perhaps it was her name.

'All right?'

She opened her eyes, sat up, shook off the new languor.

'Expecting *quid pro quo*, are you?' she said.

'Not with you, no.'

Rosie stretched out her leg, resting her foot against his chest; his hand came up to stroke her ankle. She tensed her calf, pushing at his chest, forcing him down by suggestion until he was lying on his back, naked. Did he really have the bottle to take anything she might throw at him? Christ. And how much was she prepared to throw. Her foot was still on him. She began to apply a little pressure.

And there was a knock at the door.

Three long, two short, one long.

Sod it. Now maybe she wouldn't find out, about either of them. Sod it, sod it.

'It's okay, definitely nothing to worry about. I'll get it,' she said.

Taking her foot from his chest. Standing.

Rosie! From outside. The knocks' signature.

'But it's my flat.'

God, two bloody men making demands of her; well, no way was she going to give in to both.

'I said, I'll get it.'

Still on his back, Alex looked up at her.

'Bollocks,' he said, gently, more kiss than curse. 'Why don't you just walk all over me?'

Rosie bent over him, her face inches from his. He bit his lip.

'What makes you think I wouldn't?' she whispered.

She straightened, and moved towards the door, but taking the long way, around him. He remained very still, one arm outstretched. Rosie could have stepped over that arm, but she didn't, she followed the map of his body. She brought her foot down hard, millimetres away from his nails. His fingers twitched, but he didn't clench his fist or move his hand away. Most people would have done, Rosie was sure. Come to that, most wouldn't have dared to be so exposed in the first place.

They was taking long enough to answer the door. What was they doing in there? They couldn't be at it, could they? Not with that poor cunt all stitched up at his mum's, and the boys watching the windows. No, they'd of waited til they went abed, at least. Even then, Rosie most probably wouldn't feel like it. And if that Alex did, there's no way she'd let herself be talked into nothing, not his Rosie.

Bout fucking time.

Look at this joint, well small. Darren'd knew Alex was boracic, but this was beyond-a-joke-ridiculous. He followed as Rosie marched down the hall to the living room, never even giving him a look, nothing. Alex was stood there with his tee-shirt all untucked, and nothing on his feet. Scruffy bleeder. Rosie sat on what some people might call a chair. Suppose it might of been, one time. Couldn't he even afford decent

furniture? Maybe Darren ought to get him a deal on some.
Rosie looked right out-of-place.

'So what the hell are you doing here, Daz? We're perfectly
capable of managing a few hours without you, you know.
Thought you was with Mum?'

'I was. She wanted me to check you was okay.' What was
with all them pictures on the walls? He done them, or what?
No, can't of done. Better'n the furniture though, give them
that.

'You told her? Brilliant. Nice one, Einstein.'

'No, I never. It's just, she found out it happened near you.'

'Just found out, just like that? She got second sight now?
Anyway, lost the use of your dialling finger, have you? Apart
from anything else, you scared the shit out of me.'

'I did our knock!'

'Yeah, you might well have done. So?'

But that'd always been their knock, ever since he'd first left
home to live with that Mandy bird. They both done it, always,
if there was a need to show who it was at the door. Three
long, two short, one long. He'd of knowed it if he'd of heard
it in his sleep.

'Now you *are* here, can I get you anything?'

He'd forgot about Alex, who was stood there like a spare
part, watching them.

'Got any tea?'

Darren'd have to pull that other chair over, be near enough
to talk proper to Rosie while Alex made the tea. Have to off
that tatty old jumper, and all. No wonder Rosie weren't doing
her usual sitting on the deck – don't know what she might
catch.

'What are you shifting the furniture about for? Going for a
job with Pickford's, are you?'

'Give us a break, girl – I was only doing what Mum said.'

'Yeah, you were only following orders. Don't I get a private
life any more, just because you got Ben slashed?'

'Yeah, he's not doing too bad, thanks for asking.' Hard-faced

cow. 'Still under. Best thing, really. Cath's going up the wall
– Mum's round there now, pouring sherry down her throat.'
That made her smile a bit. 'I want it sorted, Ro.'

'Don't start, Daz, not tonight. It's really late, I'm knackered,
and I just want to crash out.'

Me and all – but it ain't always that easy. If you think you
ain't going see that poor face every time you close your eyes,
you got another think coming.

Alex come in with three mugs of tea. Looked round, like
he's wondering where to sit. Know the feeling, mate. In the
finish, sat on the arm of Rosie's chair – must be well uncomfy.

'How's Ben?' he said.

'He'll be an ugly git – mind you, he always was. All right
to smoke?'

'Course.'

'He doesn't mean cigarettes, babe.'

Wonderful – Mr Social Worker most probably thinks draw's
the same as drugs.

'Right. Right. I'm sorry, I can't have smoke in here, this is
a tied flat.'

'You know what he does for a living, Daz, don't be a prat.'

'You like a bit of puff.' Get out of that one, girl.

'Fair dos.' She looked at him, straight. 'But I wouldn't smoke
around Alex, and I haven't bought any for years. I'm not
exactly a dope-head.'

Alex was eating this up with a fucking massive spoon, but
Darren didn't think he was too happy with Rosie. Bet he never
knew she had the odd spliff. Most likely hating it, even if he
was getting off on the aggro.

'It's up to Rosie what she does,' Alex said. 'I'm not about to
rush over to the Centre and bring either of you back a load
of leaflets about the evils of cannabis. I just don't want to be
unemployed.' Was he being funny? No, sounded on the level.

'Fair enough, mate. Got any booze to go with this tea?' Shit,
Rosie was right into one. She'd come first in a filthy look
competition with that, no danger. What more she want? It's

not like he ignored the boyfriend and skinned up. What's that word what always comes up, with her? Compromise, that's it. Seemed to him like it was never her what got compromised.

'There's some scotch left in Rosie's flask.'

'I might need that for myself.' But Alex weren't having that – give her a sort of *Yeah, right* look. Never thought he had it in him.

'Quick scotch in there, then I'll make a move.'

'Very quick scotch, Daz.'

'Thought he'd never go. He's got a guard-dog complex at the minute.'

'Can you blame him?' Alex sat in the chair that Darren had been on.

Rosie pulled back her hair and watched him. Sod brothers and blame. He scratched his stomach, not taking his hard stare from hers. She chewed her lip, listening to her pulse beating in her throat. It wasn't as simple as just wanting Alex; there was a gap here to be filled with more than a fuck. Would he dare? Or was he relieved to be off the hook, taking the opportunity to return them to the bloody scene, to its implications. Would she dare?

'Cast your mind back a bit differently, Alex.' Where had that come from?

'To what?' he said. So she was meant to lay it, and herself, on the line, was she? No chance, sweet thing. It was enough to have surprised herself like that.

'Before Al bloody Capone turned up, with his secret knock. Suppose he let you in on it, made it his and your little knock, so you'd always know it was your governor. I want you to say that to me again, what you said earlier.'

'*My* governor? Think you've got things the wrong way round there.' He scratched at his palm, but continued to look at her. 'It's not that I can't see why you're wound up, but you don't exactly make things easy, not for yourself or for anyone else.'

'That what you expect from me even now, to make it easy?

Want me to get some Laura Ashley, do you, and give you a nice massage? Is easy what you think you're getting here?'

'No,' said Alex. He bit the side of his thumb. Wasn't going to repeat it, was he? Rosie forced herself to speak.

'So you don't remember then, where we were?' The look on that face. Of course he knew. Set himself up, hadn't he? But it seemed as though he might try to slide out of it, snatch that hand away just in the nick of time, before she could ruin his gift. Did he think she wouldn't notice? 'Maybe I could remind you,' she added. And his grin returned. You'd better be able to deliver on it, Alex; you've gone way too far to turn back. Whatever happens.

He'd made some dangerously bad choices up to now, as though he'd been assuming Rosie could be messed around for ever. But now he seemed, just possibly, to be getting a handle on what exactly he was messing with. This was a whole different deal. Maybe he was beginning to count them: on top or underneath, no middle deck. Tough, on anyone who couldn't match the stakes. And if Alex was beginning to get a feel for it, and if he counted on following through the doors of her pub again, close enough for all the sharks to know for sure, then he'd better not be slow in following where she was taking him back to now.

Oh my God. Stark naked. Back on his knees, his cock hard. She gestured for him to kneel up straight. Better: she could reach his chest. She drew a nail along it, trying it out. His gaze was steady. Deeper. Still he didn't react. Only when the third time she came close to drawing blood, could she make the bastard blink. But he was still smiling. It was beginning to look as though he didn't expect her to play at this, at least not unless she was prepared to play seriously. To play with the big boys.

What the hell was it they were doing, here?

Here.

On his knees, but not quite like before. Easily remedied. Just on the one thigh, to start off with. Firm, though. Her own personal boot boy. And her call.

'Well, how's your memory, baby?' Then on the other thigh, too. She could see him swallowing. Suddenly, he looked at her square on. His eyes darkened.

'It's what you think you want, isn't it?' His voice steady. 'Why don't you do it, then.'

'You think I won't?' She leaned forward.

'I think you ought to see if you will. If you can.'

It must have taken real bottle for him to get that out. No way could that have been easy, although no difficulty expressed itself in his confidence. None. Why not? As though he understood what she'd needed from a man and never quite had realized. Sure, she could have taken anything she wanted from some craven sod, but that would have stopped her wanting it in the first place. Having it offered. No pretence. Don't blow it, girl, whatever it is. Get him down lower. Let him get the feel for it. If he really thinks he can cope, let him try. Let him have the chance. To give her the chance.

'What about . . . ?' Rosie prodded him, sharp, on both legs. 'You said how much you liked them. And I'm not stepping on anything round this place barefoot, or even in tights, not at twenty quid a pair.' Not this time. 'Not until you've got carpet that doesn't look like something out of a skip.' They locked stares, more fiercely than before.

'That's fucking irrelevant. If you really think you've got the right to walk all over people, then prove it. Now. Literally. Go on. It's not my decision any more, any of it. It's yours.' He looked at his thighs. Rosie eyed him. Then once more she lifted her legs from his. She reached for her cigarettes. She said nothing while she smoked. There he was, surer and surer of himself, secure in his victory. Did he think there was a time limit?

She crushed out the cigarette. And spoke to the ashtray, rather than to Alex's face.

'You'd better lie down, then.' Now she eyed him again. Oh yes, he'd got well ahead of himself. How high was the back of that chair? High enough. 'Behind the armchair, I think . . . or am I supposed to be performing some sort of balancing act?'

His look changed, instantly. The colour had gone out of his cheeks, if that wasn't just a trick of the mood or of the light. But his erection got harder.

And he moved.

He looked back at her still sitting there, wearing the arrogant look she'd taken right off his face. Some of his stuff was worth having, after all. Rosie only ever wore quality. But despite what she'd claimed, it turned out she wasn't always the one who paid.

He was on his back. Rosie stood, and went over to him. She stretched out to test the back of the chair. About right. At least, the chair was. She stabbed at the body on the floor, forcing cold leather under his flesh, under his ribs, up to her ankle.

'Still think I won't?' she said.

He was looking up at her. His face was down below her, looking up. She couldn't read his eyes; well he shouldn't have played then, should he, if he wasn't sure.

'I don't know. Do you?'

Suddenly, no, she wasn't so sure herself; it had sounded like an invitation, but in that moment she could see it wasn't. She'd asked; he'd simply passed on a test. Now she had to pass.

'Is this what you want?' she said.

'I don't know that yet, either.'

Let him find out.

'Not like that, then. Looking to the floor.' Lifting her foot. Rolling him over.

Like a dog. Obeying her. No muzzle, no stick. He must be fourteen stone; no way should she have been able to turn him so easily, not unless he'd in part colluded. Maybe he had. Accessory, before the fact. But now she could take him, all by her own. She'd got him. Face down, on the carpet, where his choices didn't matter anymore. God. Perhaps he still thought she wouldn't have the guts. Perhaps she wouldn't. Okay, well he'd wanted to gamble, had he? Everything, on one card? Go on, girl. Now. Literally. She'd learned the game over twenty years ago. Dealer pays Black Jack.

And she knew then that she couldn't stop herself, there was nothing that could stop her. Alex raised his head, trying to look at her, made an almost inaudible sound, buried his face in the carpet. She realized that he knew it, too.

His shoulder looked like it might be the best bet. No. Just below. Almost the small of his back. Then the first touch; she thought she could feel his warmth, through the sole. It was scratched, that sole. Marked. From a broken bottle, on the half-lit pavement outside Alex's block. But tougher than flesh. Oh Jesus. Hide on hide. What price both? And Rosie, pressing one into the other. Harder, harder. Barely touching the back of the chair with the tips of her fingers. Lifting herself right off the ground. But balancing, on her toes, like she'd promised herself she wouldn't. She needed to be forward more. Just four inches or so. Shit, she was doing it. Now she was right where she wanted to be. It was more relaxed, not such a strain on her calves. Those heels bit in, right in, deep.

She was doing it. She was there, in heels. Screwing her life into his back.

'What did it feel like?' Alex rolled over and sat up, rubbing his chest.

Like stepping out on to a stage, a space that made you higher than anyone else. You could keep your Lady Annes and even your Carmens; this was a buzz that no actress or singer could begin to imagine. This was the ultimate act: the real thing. Performer and audience both.

'What did it feel like to you, more to the point?' she said, and laughed. She fetched her glass; as he drank from it, his hand shook a little. But she didn't think it was from rage.

'It was . . . really, really important to me. Seriously. It was really painful at times, but not so as I couldn't cope with it.' He pulled her into him, and kissed her. 'It mattered because it was you. God, I can't believe you went for it.'

'Why not?'

He kissed her again, as though that were an answer.

'It was . . . well, yeah,' he added. 'God.' Then he ran his hands through his hair, ruffling the curls. 'Christ. You do my head in, but . . . I've never met anyone like you.' What did he mean, she did his head in? Alex grabbed his tee-shirt, drew it on, a curtain across her stage. Then pushing her hair out of the way, he stroked her cheek. 'That's a beautiful face.' And lifted her, effortlessly, on to his lap.

'Am I squashing you?' she said. Alex looked disbelieving, making her grin. That already seemed like hours ago; it felt almost unreal now. She yawned. 'How's your back? Sore?' He nodded. 'Good.' Yeah, it was. It was good. What the hell did that say about her?

'Are you happy?' he murmured.

'Happy?' Ben was cut to pieces and she could hardly feel it. She wasn't sure she knew how to do normal emotions any more. 'Don't know. But I'm happier than I've been in a while.'

'I'm glad.' He kissed her on the forehead. 'So am I.'

'Weird though, isn't it? We're here together because . . .'

'No we're *here*, as in my flat, because of that, but we'd only have been at yours.'

'Yeah, that's true.' Only too true.

'I've never done that before, you know.'

'What? Oh.' No, she'd just assumed he hadn't. She needed it to be about her.

'Yeah. I've thought about it, about things like that, a lot, but I've never met anyone before who I really believed . . . whatever. You know.'

'I haven't done it before, either,' she said, cuddling in closer. This man was turning her into a sentimental schmuck.

'Well, you haven't done it like that, anyway.' Cheeky sod. He squeezed her, hard. 'I don't find sex easy, I never have and then . . . But when I met you, I knew I wanted you. You know, I let myself know it. Couldn't help it really, even though I was scared.' He was speaking into her hair. Rosie let his voice seep into her, feeling as much as hearing the words. 'But it wasn't just that I wanted to sleep with you, although

I did. I do. It was like, I knew you were potentially dangerous for me, but . . . God, the buzz of you losing yourself like that.'

She closed her eyes. If she wasn't careful, she'd go to sleep right here, and they'd both wake up aching.

'Do you want to go to bed, Rosie?'

'Mm. Might be an idea.'

She hadn't even seen Alex's bedroom. In keeping with the rest of the flat, it was functional: a small double bed, a wardrobe, a chest of drawers, a mirror. No pictures in here, no rug, no ornaments, unless you counted the little alarm clock. Minimalist. The only personal touches were a half-drunk bottle of Coke by the side of the bed and an open copy of *Chaos* by someone called Gleick. Riveting bedtime reading, babe. The room was very clean; Rosie thought even she would have been able to keep so few possessions in order.

'You can have the cupboard in the hall, next to the airing-cupboard. You might have to shift the *Standards*.'

'Not recycling?'

'No, I keep them for the crossword. I've been too busy lately to get to many.'

He wasn't kidding; must have been thirty papers piled up at the bottom of the cupboard next to one of those big artist's folders, and paperbacks and albums on two of the three shelves. Shift them to where? She should have unpacked earlier. If her suit was creased, she'd be buggered for work tomorrow. Oh, sod it. She was too tired to care, leave it until the morning. Just run to the bathroom, have a quick wee, introduce her toothbrush to her teeth, crawl into bed.

He dropped the clothes he was carrying on to the floor and pulled off his tee-shirt, turning to put it carefully on the chest of drawers. Jesus. White and red tracks. All over, the imprint of tiny horseshoes. Her imprint. *Hers*. Modern art. His back was a bloody mess. She shivered. And on his shoulder, a perfect little wreath.

'What does it look like?' Twisting his neck, trying to see in the mirror.

'It's weird. I like it, though.'

'Do you? I mean, do you really like it?'

'Yeah. I've never seen anything so . . . exposed, if you know what I mean.'

'Right. Yeah, that makes sense.' He nodded, and felt the small of his back.

And then she realized she would have to get undressed. It wasn't that she minded being naked but it was deeply strange, to say the least, to take off your clothes in front of a man whom you'd seen completely undressed, who'd made you come, who you'd trampled over for God's sake, and yet who hadn't seen so much as your ankle. Then there were the faint scars on the tops of her thighs; most men didn't notice them, but Alex wasn't most men. She did have a tee-shirt in her case, but it felt wrong, somehow, to rush back off to the bathroom and come out wearing a massive top that declared John Smith's was the best. Too much of a statement, and not even a statement she wanted to make. She sat on the edge of the bed to take off her boots; the zips slid too easily under her fingers. Looking at the dark polish on her nails, visible through her tights, she felt as though she'd already been stripped of everything else.

Alex folded the rest of his clothes on top of his tee-shirt, and stood there naked, watching her. It wasn't too difficult to take off her trousers and tights, but then she hesitated. She got up and added her trousers to Alex's pile of clothes; his arms went round her, and they kissed.

'All right?'

'Yeah, just tired.' She felt the weals on his back, traced where he'd traced, and smiled. 'It's been a bitch of a night.'

'You can say that again.' Alex tugged at her shirt, lifting it over her head. That was miles easier than having to do it herself. He ran his hands across her body, lingering over her rib-cage. 'Soft skin.' He slipped off her briefs, before she had time to think about it. His fingers found the thin raised lines from the tops of her legs to her pubic hair; she tried not to flinch, and he didn't comment, unless to kneel and kiss them was a comment. He rested his head against her stomach for a second. Then he pulled back the duvet. 'Come on, you'll get cold standing there.'

They did make love, but briefly, messily, as though making a note for next time. He held her afterwards, and she knew she'd sleep better than she had a right to.

She'd invented Rosie Spence, switching between codes until she could work to her own, risking daily being despised by her colleagues, becoming a trophy for her past. Keep the hunger, girl. She was peerless, paying the price for her singularity. No pain, no gain. And what had happened tonight between her and Alex, she'd been waiting for all the time. In ignorance, in ability, and in longing. The currency thirty stitches and another man's devotion.

As she drifted into sleep, the 'phone rang.

Darren sat by Ben's bed. He couldn't hardly bear to look at him, with his face all sewed up. Looked like when Nan tried to teach Rosie to do embroidery, and she'd made a right pig's ear of it, thrown it cross the room. Never one for making things, their Rosie – always more preferred smashing them up. She'd wrecked Ben's bike, once. They was bout fifteen, so she'd of been ten, eleven. Took it and rolled it down that hill on holiday. Cath went mental at her, and Mum made her stay in for a week when they got back, but it never did no good. Poor sod never got a nother bike neither, not even when they used to go on the rob, and when Ben'd started at the yard, took him on as a bit of a favour as it happened, it'd worked out pretty good. They was both already doing bits and pieces for Freddy, so they knew how each other operated. Darren done all the sorting, Ben done what he was let. But he was all right with the paperwork and that, and it weren't long fore Darren couldn't hardly remember working without him. Scare the

punters now, he would. Couldn't see him doing much with the
birds, neither. Funny, Ben'd always done all right there. Sept
where he really wanted to, and that was never going to be a
goer. What did that lot think they was doing? Freddy talked
large, but there was this feeling it weren't going to be all that
clever any time soon. Specially cos Freddy'd never let his retard
brother hold his hands up. The Lion was a piss poor outfit,
and all. Dad had pissed off with that Zara tart, him and Ben'd
gone looking for him. They'd only been kids, but they'd got
hold of blades, and reckoned they was going to teach him a
lesson or three. Never found him. Don't know what they'd of
done, not really, if they had of. But that weren't the point –
Darren'd said what they was going to do, and Ben'd gone along
with it, same as always. Wonder how much that plastic surgery
stuff cost? They could do all sorts, these days. Miracles, they
could work. He'd see a programme on the telly bout it. Yeah,
miracles.

Ben shifted bout in his sleep.

Oh fuck – he weren't going to wake up now, was he? Not
with Cath spark out and Mum trying to get five minutes. No,
he was still soundo. There was a right peculiar feeling in
Darren's guts. He'd never had nothing to eat since dinner, come
to think bout it. Alex most likely had a good heart, but what
was he going to do when it come down to it? Maybe Darren
should of stayed there, and all. But he was needed here, and
he had to be with Freddy at the crack of. It was doing his
head in. Like, there was an answer to all this, but he couldn't
quite get an handle on it. Bit nip in here – he pulled the covers
up round Ben more. Always felt the cold, weedy git. Rosie
used to call him ferret features. Said he had a body like one
and all. Looked more like one of them other things, now –
them things what their next-door-neighbour'd kept at Wessex
Street. Rabbited with them, he did. Ugly little things. Poor cunt.
But they could work miracles, these days. Darren was sure he'd
see it on a programme on the telly.

Chapter Seven

'How come you've never done anything about getting a divorce?'

'I told you, I haven't got a clue where she is.'

'Bet you could find her. We use a couple of firms . . . don't look at me like that, Mr Holier-Than-Thou. I meant private detectives.'

Alex sat up in bed, raked his fingers through his hair. Why wasn't the bastard jumping at her offer? Maybe he wanted to stay married. Maybe he hoped his wife would come back, looking like she did when they'd first met. The most beautiful woman he'd ever seen. Bastard.

'Leave it, Rosie. Please.' He slipped his hand under the duvet, ran his nails along her rib-cage. 'What it is, you're the only woman I've slept with since . . . except once. A prostitute. And that was spectacularly unsuccessful.'

'You went to a *prostitute?*' She moved his arm away. Talk about sad. Hand-job for a can of Special Brew, down King's Cross. Bloody Gladstone. And if he thought he could compare Rosie with a tart . . . Bet he'd picked one with big tits. Probably managed to touch them, then; Rosie hated the fact that he'd never yet laid a hand on hers. Never.

'A couple of months after Louise,' he said at last. 'Suppose I was lonely without her.'

Louise. Beautiful, mad Louise. Rosie could just imagine her: waifish, blonde, massive watery blue eyes. Flowing cheesecloth and tiny gold sandals. Nose stud. Nice, middle class voice. Vegetarian, no, vegan. Bless the little fluffy bunnies. Degree in English. Probably took drugs in secret, to cope with the strain of the wicked world. Alex could be such a stupid sod.

'What did she do for a living? Before she went barking, that is.'

'Jesus.' Alex looked down at her. 'She was a musician, violin. And she taught it round schools, you know.'

Just marvellous. Talented, beautiful, mad Louise. What a myth to carry round in your heart for all time. That picture on his wall. *Her* violin. Her shrine.

Then gradually, he bloody admitted yes, he thought Louise had been brilliant; okay, Rosie suggested it, yet he agreed, not exactly aggressively but righteously on the verge. Rosie sat up, clutching the duvet round her. She knew how he felt about her, did she? He just wasn't ready to see Louise yet? Clever men had that way of turning a woman's legitimate concerns into unreasoned paranoia; to object to that was to reinforce it, and it could never then be struck from the record. Alex suddenly became solicitous, propping a pillow behind Rosie's back as though she were an invalid. Sod off, she wouldn't die of his having a wife. If he wanted to stay married, that was up to him. Told him, too: his call. Alex looked a bit panicked at that. Good.

'I didn't say I wanted to stay married, I said—'

'I heard what you said.' And she heard him sigh as well, loud and deliberate.

'Just because you've done what you've done to me, doesn't mean you can be allowed to dictate everything. Especially when it's this big.' He leaned over the bottom of the bed to retrieve her glass from the floor. The first set of marks was deepening in colour, turning to bruises; the others still looked fresh and clean. Even feeling like this, Rosie couldn't get over the wonder of them being hers.

Rosie took her wine and swallowed it. She held out the glass. Alex had to get out of bed to fetch the bottle from the top of the chest of drawers; you'd think he'd have a bedside table. He took the bare essentials philosophy that bit too far. Probably

Louise had sold all their furniture for drugs; either that, or her mind had been on higher things than physical comfort. Rosie pulled the duvet closer to her chest. How much longer was she going to have to stay in this pokey flat, trying to keep her office and court clothes smart without proper cupboard space, enduring two extra stops on the tube every weekday? A few miles could make that long difference. And the 'phone went at all hours, with no-hopers or their hopeful carers ringing for advice and comfort, and Saint Alex never, never let the machine take it if he were in. It had only been four days, and already Rosie felt besieged by the junkies. But most of all, this wasn't her place; the only marks she'd left were temporary, easily erased. Except for holidays, Rosie hadn't spent more than the odd night or two away from her own flat in years. Home was where the stuff was.

Alex sat on the edge of the bed. She could see his back reflected in the mirror on the far wall, as though he had, after all, decided to frame one of his pictures. *Still Life, With Pain*.

'Can you remind me,' he said, 'I ought to ring my friend Connie. I was supposed to be meeting her for a drink, and I'll have to let her know I can't.' Suppose he thought he was changing the subject. And why couldn't he take Rosie to meet this Connie?

'Who's Connie?'

'Psychologist at work. She won't mind, she's a total star with me, I'm always changing arrangements. I'd rather be with you.'

But not with me and your *friend* Connie. Did he fancy this friend or something, or was it that he didn't want his bleeding heart chums to know he was seeing a legal?

Or specifically that he was seeing Rosie Spence.

'Alex, I've been thinking. I ought to tell Daz it's about time I went home. The settee's been cleaned, and every time I've rung into my machine, all I've had are proper messages.'

'Connie's my age, Rosie. At least.' He sounded amused.

'So?' Women can't be attractive in their forties? Rosie would be washed up in ten years, would she? God, she wished she knew how old Louise was.

'Nothing. As soon as Darren thinks it's safe, he'll be round here to get you like a shot.'

But Daz wouldn't be able precisely to call it; safety was a movable feast, commensality turned to water and stones by human greed. What happened to Ben needn't mean necessarily that Rosie was part of some *film noir*: lovely heroine pursued through the streets of London by the underworld; casual violence made causal, by arrangement. Ben was one thing, Rosie quite another. The Lion might well want tokenism, to force someone's public accountability, maybe an arrest. Rosie had seen that one before, even amongst villains. And she wasn't convinced that being with Alex was safe: there were no gorillas watching to prevent her feeling too much, except those she created for herself.

'I should spend part of this weekend working,' she said. 'There's a problem with a trainee's seat in litigation. And I want to check my e-mail. I need my laptop.'

'So send him for it.' He put his hand around her neck, caressing her throat with his thumb. 'Or tell me what's going on, and I'll help you decide.' He increased the pressure.

'I need to be at home.'

'No you don't. Might want to be, but that's different. Surely you can think of ways to take out your frustration.' Alex pressed still more firmly into the base of her throat. She swallowed against his thumb. Bastard. Nearly . . . nearly choking her. Pushed harder. 'Or can't you?' Mocking her. She grabbed his wrist, sticking her nails in, deep. Forced out her voice.

'Have you got any rope?'

Silence that you could fall inside, let yourself be swallowed by. Silence that, for a while at least, you could let yourself believe in. Against traffic noise, against music, against desensitized pain, it pushed until it won. Inevitably. Rosie liked the idea of something that had victory built in. But more than this, it seemed to her that it was a silence big enough to hold even Alex, big enough to hold both of them. It didn't last long, this silence of theirs, but there was always the threat of a next time.

Rosie hadn't been near him. It'd been days now. She might of been told it weren't a good idea. Be nice to see her, though, and he might stand a chance, on the sympathy ticket. Birds loved feeling sorry for you. But then, Rosie weren't most birds. Never heard her say she wanted to be a nurse when she grew up. She knew from third year Juniors what she wanted. Homework always done, but not for the benefit of them teachers. Always making lists what she called *Life Plans*. But careful never to come over like a boffin, bit wild, getting off with more blokes than even her stupid little mates did. She weren't like that now, though – she was right fussy, and Ben couldn't see her wiping his forehead with no wet sponge. It was still hard to talk and all, with his face all tight – wouldn't want to sound like a cunt in front of her. But it was so boring, lying here looking at the ceiling. Middle ear infection now, Doc said. *Almost certainly related to the injuries.* No, go on, was it really? Like Spence said, they did come out with some strokes, them quacks. And he'd been told not to throw up if he could help it, cos his mouth couldn't open proper yet. Like he'd want to. So he couldn't get up, cos the room started round and he knew he'd spew his guts. Done him up like a kipper, they had. Poor little Ailisha had enough trouble when she see him as it was – this'd crown it. Maybe if he'd of made more effort to be a proper dad . . . What would Rosie say when she see him? Thinking about it, didn't look like sympathy'd do him no good at all. But it'd still be nice to see her. One thing she never was, was boring.

The club was always crowded at Sunday lunchtimes, mostly with men who preferred roast beef sandwiches with mustard to their wives' grilled chicken and steamed vegetables. Jack would probably be here himself, if Elizabeth hadn't beaten him to it. Rumour had it that it was all on again with the lout; perhaps Rosie had an announcement to make. Not that it would last. Each time she'd lived with someone, they'd ended up back on the street pretty smartish, clutching their little holdalls and looking bereft. But it would bring some interest to what had been, so far, a thoroughly dull month. She felt a hand on her shoulder, and turned.

'Hello, Lisbeth. This is Alex Tolliver. Alex, Elizabeth Small.'

Good grief. So the news had come in person, and very personable he was, too. Slow smile. Great eyes. Nice pair of shoulders. Pity about the clothes, but Rosie would see to all that, and for now they at least seemed to fit. Extremely well. Rosie raised her eyebrows, one of her more annoying knowing grins on her face.

'Yes, all right, I'm surprised,' admitted Elizabeth. 'I'm sorry, nice to meet you, Alex. I would say I've heard so much about you but that wouldn't be true, I'm afraid. Rosie keeps her affairs pretty close to her chest.'

'Best place for them,' said Rosie, sitting down and indicating that Alex should do the same. He moved stiffly round the table: rather Byronic.

'I thought a bottle of St Emilion would go nicely with our sandwiches.' Elizabeth gestured at the hovering waiter. 'Is that all right for everyone?'

'Didn't realize there was a particular wine that went with sandwiches,' said Alex, dead-pan. 'Is it white or red?' Did he genuinely not know?

'Red,' Elizabeth told him. 'If we have the beef, red seems the obvious choice.'

'And God forbid our Elizabeth should make anything but the obvious choice.' Rosie certainly was on form. 'I want *foie gras*, anyway,' she added.

'You know how they get it?' asked Alex. 'Didn't realize you'd go for that.'

'If you'd thought about it, babe, you would.' They both smiled. Curiouser and curiouser.

'Couple of beef for me, then,' he said. 'To go with the wine. No, make that three.'

The wine arrived first. Elizabeth watched as Alex sipped it, but he didn't seem either to be overly impressed or unduly repulsed. His ignorance must have been a joke.

'So tell me everything, since Rosie never will. How long ago did you two meet?'

'Two months? Something like that. Two or three months.'

'And where was—'

'Oh pack it in, Lisbeth, he doesn't want cross examining.'

'Are you quite sure about that?' she said. He really was very attractive, if you liked them ungroomed. She crossed her legs, so her skirt rode up a fraction of an inch. Alex didn't display a great deal of interest. Unusual in any man, even in one who was being chewed up by Rosie.

'I get enough of that at home,' he said. *At home?* Damn Rosie's reticence.

'Are you trying to suggest I'm a hanging judge?' said Rosie. Alex laughed, and rubbed his thigh. Elizabeth felt like a wallflower at a ball. Distinctly B list.

'You should hear what Jack calls you,' she said.

'I can imagine.' Rosie picked up her wine glass, and held it against her cheek. 'But I bet he doesn't say all he's thinking.' Ouch. That was entirely called for, although it smarted. For the life of her, Elizabeth would never quite grasp what it was they all saw in Rosie Spence. Alex looked at that enigma as though he didn't think she was one, smiling with the left side of his mouth. Then he glanced over at Elizabeth, catching her eye with a brief, intense gaze. She coughed, and sipped her wine, which made her cough again. Feeling a complete fool, she took her handkerchief from her bag, and held it to her lips. 'Very Victorian heroine,' Rosie commented. 'When did the consumption kick in?'

'A week last Thursday,' said Elizabeth, just managing to get her breath back. 'Oh good, here's our lunch.'

*   *   *

Dear God, he ate like a navvy: great wolfing bites, chewing only enough to ensure that the pieces were possible to swallow. Typically, Rosie ignored her knife and fork, sticking her fingers into the goose liver and sucking them, tearing at her bread and playing with it, holding lettuce leaves between her thumb and forefinger as she talked, then absent-mindedly popping them into her mouth. It ought to have looked common, but somehow it didn't; the male crew on the next table was covertly watching with something other than disapproval in their eyes. However, when they looked at Alex, it was in apparent astonishment that he should be at a table with Rosie and Elizabeth. Women wouldn't see it that way; they'd find something raw in Alex's bloody enjoyment of the rare beef, and would want to insist that Rosie use a bloody fork.

'Did I tell you,' said Elizabeth, desperate to keep her mind from the movements of Alex's wide throat, 'the coroner actually returned a verdict of accidental drowning?'

'In the bath in a private hospital,' Rosie said to Alex, pausing to lick the dressing from a slice of tomato. 'Elizabeth was hoping for a lack of care verdict, to go for negligence.'

'It used to be common,' said Alex, swallowing. 'My great-grandmother died like that, as late as 1959. Before that, lots of people did, especially kids and old people. That's why hospital baths are so heavily supervised these days.' He crammed more sandwich into his mouth.

'It's very educational, going out with you,' said Rosie. She smiled, pushed her plate away and examined her fingers.

Elizabeth couldn't believe it at first. Rosie held out her sticky hand, without saying a word; Alex picked up his napkin, dipped the end of it in his water glass, and wiped her fingers clean. Extraordinary. What was he, her servant? And yet, Elizabeth felt as though she had wandered into someone else's bedroom, and accidentally seen them making love. Her face was hot. She abandoned the remains of her sandwich, and stood up.

'I'm just off to the loo,' she said.

'Thanks for sharing,' said Rosie. But she was still looking at

Alex. He kissed her hand. Then he turned to Elizabeth and grinned. He was challenging her, the presumptuous yob. The trouble was, she hadn't an inkling of how she ought to respond.

Done a wrong'un, there. Ordinary, Darren would of been a bit careful in here what he said bout birds blokes had been with, but he was too fucked off to bother. Sides, might as well take advantage – everyone knew Ben was like a brother. Weren't easy down the yard even, with him out of action. Forms and that . . . Be back fore long. Weren't like he was crippled.

Knackered. Five days of meets since Ben, and that pub just weren't letting go. Not like Freddy to sell him a pup, even one from the same litter, but he was making it crystal how Charlie weren't going to be done, either meaning of the word. No matter who it cost. And *someone* had to be seen to pay, some way. Whatever way was taking miles too long. Freddy might well be having a scout round for that someone, but . . . Go round see Mum in a minute – get a decent Sunday dinner, gravy and all. Doubt she'd do a proper afters though, not the way things was.

'There you go, Spence.'

'What? Sorry, mate – miles away. Cheers.' He threw half the brandy down his neck. One result – he was getting a lot of freeman's over this. But like that cunt of an old man taught him, right from when he was brung down the club to drink Coke and take shots on the bar billiards for the blokes, *Always get in one more round than the other fella, then no one can talk about you.* And he was right. Them drinks would have to be paid for, sooner or later.

'Choker about Benny.'

'He'll be okay. Doc says it's mostly cosmic.' He'd make a move soon. The blokes meant well, but they was doing his head in. So was this place. Used to be a good little boozer, fore they done it up – could be anyfuckingwhere now. Pretend beams, and Tom's missus into one if you spilt anything on her flash curved bar. He was fed up with hisself, simple as that.

It was like he'd been living in his own head long with The Lion and Ben and Freddy and Charlie, all of them in there, with the rest of The Mice knocking at the door, and there just weren't enough room. There didn't seem to be nothing outside his head, nowhere he could let all the shit out. If he did, anything might happen.

'How's your Rosie doing? Told she's seeing some big cunt. Must put your mind at rest.'

'He's big, yeah.' Fuck off. Every nobody so interested in Ro now. Even that Patterson boy Sam'd been asking round bout her, giving hisself a profile he'd never dare have normal. Freddy said he'd come up all jittery, asked him if she was seeing the social worker. Not proached Darren, though, lucky for Patterson. Nose ointment, what's it have to do with him? With any of them. Darren just wanted to see her face, be sure in his own head she was really all right. Then perhaps there'd be some room in there what'd let him see stuff outside. Time out. Like when he went fishing, and everything else went away. Some blokes made out they went fishing to think, but Darren knew better'n that. Fishing was there so's you didn't have to think. Perhaps he ought to get hisself indoors after dinner, put one together and try and get some kip.

Or perhaps he'd just have a look in at Ben.

'God, come in, Daz, if you're coming.' But she kissed him and give a little smile.

'Where's he?'

'Bathroom. You sitting down, or what?'

Bit much, still being in your dressing gowned at six o'clock of a Sunday. Perhaps she'd been in the bath – doubt there was a shower in this pit. He picked up a serviette off the floor. Someone, must be Alex, had drew a picture on it, of a tall stacked bird with a big nose. You could tell she was posh, but he couldn't of said why. There was a bubble coming out her mouth, with words in it, smudged where it had got a bit wet.

'D'you want this?' He felt like screwing it up, but he just waved it at Rosie.

'Thanks, yeah, I'm going to keep it.' She opened her bag, what was the side of her chair, and leaned forward to put out her fag. When she sat back up straight, her bare leg was sticking out of where the material joined. Held out her hand for the picture – he nearly dropped it where he was more looking at her bag. Could member their old man saying *Cover up, love – you're too big to sit like that now*, but she'd never took no notice, not even when she was five. She was lifting up her leg now, looking at it. Stroll on. Good job it was only him in the room. Probably make no difference if there was half a dozen blokes getting an eyeful, she'd still of done it. Any higher and they'd of been able to see what they specially shouldn't.

'How are you doing, Darren?' Alex had come in, and was stood there in just a pair of jeans, with his hair all wet, holding a right tired-looking towel up to his chest. What's the matter – didn't he want Darren to see his tits? Rosie put her leg down, but she still never covered it up. Alex grabbed a tee-shirt from the top of the telly, put it on like Nan used to put her swimming costume on at Southend, trying to hide behind the towel. Darren catched a look at something on his chest. Red scars. The bloke been around a blade, or what? Recent, and all. Darren would of tried to get a better view, but Alex's nan must of taught him as good as theirn had. 'How's Ben?'

'Got some infection thing, but he'll be sweet. D'you want to put the kettle on?'

'What sort of infection?' He started rubbing his head with the towel.

'Some ear thing.' What, he have the ear thing and all? Gone deaf all of a sudden, so he never heard bout the tea. Nana done that sometimes.

'Are you sure your doctor knows what he's doing?'

'What are you, some sort of cunt? We wouldn't let Ben see just any old person. Cunt.'

Alex stopped drying his hair and looked at Darren. He had

one of his Rosie things in his eyes. Darren weren't in the mood for this – if the cunt started getting stroppy, he'd have to sort him out, and that'd be right bad far as Rosie was concerned.

'Put the kettle on, babe. For me,' said Rosie, all quiet. For a minute, Darren thought she was talking to him, but she weren't. She put out her hand and touched Alex on the leg, like she used to do to calm Shandy down. She was the only one what could do that. Alex put his hand on hern, then went off to the kitchen. Sorted. Rosie stared after him. She never said nothing.

Hard to member things, sometimes. You got pictures in your head what you couldn't join up to no words, so you never knew where they was from, sept they must be from a long time ago. It was dark as a nigger's arse, and most probably Darren shouldn't of been sitting on his tod in Barmy Park. Not when there weren't enough light to make out the flowers, not the way things was, but he never felt like going the pub, or home, or anywhere. He just wanted to sit and member things, get hold of some of them pictures, make them mean something. If you couldn't put your life together, there was sod-all point in having one. It was his birthday next week, and Rosie hadn't membered. She must have pictures of her own, birthday cakes and booze-ups and that, but none of them had his name put on them. His girl could be right good on birthdays and all. That was one picture what did have words to go with it – a St Christopher, gold, when he was going off to Spain with that Angie one. *Here are, darling. Happy birthday and stay safe for me, okay?* From a proper shop, up West. Darren put his hand over it. Hadn't never took it off.

'Oy!'

Darren's hand went from his chain to his inside pocket in two seconds flat.

'You see a skinny bloke, leather jacket, about? Supposed to meet me on this bench.'

Just a nother druggy what needed to learn some manners.

But Darren weren't bout to waste his time learning him. He looked, right deliberate, at the bench he was on, and then to his left over to the middle one and the one on the far side. All empty sept for him.

'I'm the only one here, and I ain't skinny, know what I mean?'

The druggy fucked off, disappearing into the dark like he'd been just in Darren's imagination. From somewhere near the library, a voice shouted *Ponce!* but he ignored it.

It was bitter. He lit a fag to warm hisself up, like he was a wino. That was one of his pictures – some poor old soak shivering over a roll-up, what he was having trouble keeping alight cos it'd started to spit. When was that? A nother picture – Mum crying, her dressing gowned all open. But that weren't just once, was it? She'd got big by then, but Darren thought he could see her when she was more slimmer, crying and screaming, dressed more proper. Must of been bout the old man, but he couldn't hear no words, just see the redness of her face, and the way crying made her eyes all small. And loads of pictures of his Rosie laughing – all different heights, all different hairstyles, all different types of clothes. What was so funny, that many times? And then there was the one with her face smashed in. Didn't need no words for that one. He'd killed the cunt. Must of been fifteen year ago. He was getting old. Even Jill'd been gone for ever, years now. Took too much with her and all. *You straighten out, maybe you'll see me again.* Never happened, though – even the picture in his head was all ripped. Rosie'd right liked Jill, used to joke she was too good for him. Yonks ago. Perhaps he should shack up with a nice bird, have a kid. That'd please Mum, anyway. But nice birds never grew on trees. And be truthful, he never really liked them all that nice.

Rosie stepped back, and heard a sharp intake of breath as her foot came down on the pervert's. Serve him right, whoever he was, being stupid enough to feel her up on a tube that wasn't even that crowded. God knows why she didn't just go back home; there were plenty of dangers outside of the ones created by her brother's chosen career. But it was a pity the gorillas didn't travel in the same carriage as Rosie, they'd be even more effective than a kitten heel against unwanted attention. And hadn't that woman next to her ever heard of deodorant? Maybe it would be worth owning a little car after all, even living in London; Rosie must ask Daz about it sometime. A more pressing concern was a new ladies' front for underneath her pleading gown: in choosing her original one, she'd gone for the optional lace, and that had been a mistake. The woman with inadequate hygiene pressed the button to open the doors; automatically, Rosie went to follow her out, just remembering in time that she still had to go on to Alex's. Her toes felt really pinched, and she had six more minutes of standing. But at least going home to someone meant you could get a massage. Yeah, there'd been quite a few mistakes along the way; the trick was to move on, to ditch the lace, to tighten and tighten your grip. Puritan plain, that was what she wanted. And for no one to be able to judge what was underneath that front.

'I love your feet.'

Rosie watched as Alex rubbed oil between her toes. Every touch was as though an electric wire joined her feet to her . . . *why* was there no word for the female *bits* that wasn't clinical or coy or more appropriate to the pub than to sex? Even as Alex's serious concentration made her shudder with tiny shocks, she was forced to behave, inside her head, like a repressed virgin with a part whose name she dare not think.

'I can pick things up with them,' she told him. 'Including men, evidently.'

Alex laughed.

'I've not heard that one before.' He kissed her sole, ran his tongue over her heel. It seemed that this was the most important thing in his life, to service her feet, to ensure that no part of them was neglected, that no millimetre remained unkissed.

Pressing her foot into the side of his face, he smeared oil over his cheek. She could feel the bristles of his beard growth against her slippery skin, sand under the sea. 'I could do this for hours.'

'Do it for hours.'

It was . . .

no question

Jesus

      Never . . .

So

              Oh, Christ.

'I love you, Rosie.' Alex sat on the floor at her feet, his arm heavy on her knees.

He'd only said that once before. Rosie thought that this time, there was no ambiguity; she knew he was in love with her. Every time she'd made him roll over, every trick she'd had him perform, every way he'd offered himself, had let her know that. And she wanted his devotion; it had been long in coming. But she didn't want to look too closely at whatever she was supposed to feel about him.

Don't you want to make love to me?

I want to know what you want, in terms of sex. That's what's important to me.

Kissing her, stroking her, gentle and sweet. Or kissing her, stroking her, with such ferocity that she felt he'd have to fuck her or implode. But gentle or passionate, he'd break away.

And yet he offered her the best of himself.

Do you want to see my portfolio?

Spread out on the floor, a carpet of his sketches, pictures that told his life. Although none of Louise, his look assured her. But there were other women: the tiny Japanese girl at her easel; a wide-shouldered black woman, please God too beautiful to exist outside of the sketch; a much older white woman, painting her toenails (the aunt?). Alex was nothing if not eclectic.

He'd stood at one edge of the carpet, Rosie at the other. He wasn't smiling. She was, but only inside her head. He held out his arms to her: an invitation. Slowly, she skirted the pictures, moving around their edges. But never looking down. *Please, Rosie. For me.* It was crueller by far to keep walking, relentlessly yet casually avoiding their touch. Rosie reached him.

Think I can't?

I don't know.

She laughed then, and stepped back. Her heel caught the very tip of the long hair of the Japanese, just splitting the ends. And she knew it hurt, and that he needed more. For her to go deeper than the deepest oceans.

Clear them away, Alex.

It wasn't that she really wanted it straight, but she didn't want Alex actively not to want to make love. The few times they had, it felt more as though they were making a concession. A brief concession. And Rosie wasn't sure to what. If she were back in her own place it would be easier, but here, anything she felt had to take on board the narrow little flat, the cheap red wine, the proximity of the Centre. Sometimes, it seemed as though Alex's home was just another office that they didn't have room for in that depressing building. And if she could be happy here, what the hell did that say about her? She might just as well take a legal aid post and be done. Wear her hair short (no fuss), buy serviceable shoes (or rather, shoes that no one in their right mind would want to service), and spend her free time volunteering down the Centre. Why not go the whole hog and get fat, and if Daz or someone said anything about it, she could quote from *Fat is a Feminist Issue*. Either that, or she could go mad like the luscious Louise, so that Alex could make a better job of saving the person he loved, this time around.

'I love you, Rosie.'

'Do you, now?'

'Lager, cheers.' He'd thought he'd known why Rosie had asked him round Alex's, but there was nothing. Sweet fuck all. Being offered a drink never counted. When she'd opened the door, she was wearing a dress what he'd never see afore – tight, red, long, and shoes what no sensible person would try and stand up in, let alone walk around. So he was sure he had it right. They'd be going out to a flash restaurant. When he see Alex, in jeans and a jumper what looked like his nan had knitted him, he even thought that it might be just the two of them. Blinding. But all he got was did he want a lager or a poxy red wine. Not even a bag of smoky bacon. Bitch. 'Your lipstick's smudged, doll.' Weren't really, but it give him time to get over it, Alex fetching the lager and Rosie going the bathroom to check. Straight away and all, like he'd known she would. Vain little cow.

Cheap lager in a yellow can, with big crosses on it. For indoors, Darren always brought bottled now, and Rosie did and all, specially for him. Not here, though.

'Do I get a drink, or what?' Rosie'd put more lipstick on, like the more there was, the less chance there'd be she really would smudge it. It was more redder than the ones she wore normal, most likely to go with the dress. Darren couldn't see why she'd tarted herself up, if they weren't going nowhere.

'Sorry, love. Wine?'

'Yeah. And can I have it in—'

'The blue glass. I know.'

Well cosy. She have her own plate here with her name writ on it and all? Rosie moved a big pile of them beigey-coloured folders off the table, stuffed them in her briefcase, what looked right strange gainst her posh outfit, and settled herself down. Alex give her the wine – in the *blue* glass – opened hisself a can, and sat on the floor by Rosie's chair.

'Sure you're wearing enough shit on your nails, girl?' Darren give her a meaningful.

'Leave it out, Daz, Alex likes it. And so do I.' She smiled, the tart. Give him likes it, in a minute. Have her dying her hair blonde next. No he wouldn't, not if he wanted to live. 'Anyway, I asked you here for a reason,' she carried on, ignoring Darren's evils.

'Yeah?' Keep it casual. Little tease. They *was* going out.

'Mm. I want to get back to normal. Is that realistic? I've stayed nearly two weeks now.'

'Was going to say bout that.' It felt true. He had been going to say, he was sure he had. Wanted her safe, but couldn't see Alex was necessary now. No, Darren was certain he weren't. Pretty certain. All them meets meant The Lion was prepared to listen, spite what happened. And doing Ben ought to keep them sweet for a while. Pretty certain. 'I reckon you can come home.' He took a few gulps of the rubbish lager. See how cosy they'd be when Ro was back where she belonged. Rosie put her hand on Alex's shoulder.

'Fine,' she said. 'I'll stay tonight and maybe tomorrow, then I'll go. All right, babe?'

Alex twisted his head, looked up at her. Darren couldn't see his eyes. Just hope it was the right thing. Couldn't think of a good way round, not one what'd solve it in one hit.

A couple of cans in, they did bring out some peanuts and cheese and biscuits. Knock yourself out, sweetheart. Like being at a party for Biafrans. Weren't even real butter for the biscuits. Darren felt like skinning up, but he didn't want to go through that shit with Rosie again. Come to something, when you couldn't have what you wanted the day you was thirty-eight.

'Got anything sweet?' Wouldn't be no cake, though.

'Yeah we have, as it happens. Alex, do you want to get the doughnuts?'

Fair enough. He loved doughnuts. Specially the ones with jam in them. Alex heaved hisself up, and Rosie smiled at Darren.

'Here, angel, do you remember that time in Wessex Street when Mum made that bread pudding that came out like a brick—'

'Solid. And the old man was putting in that path . . .' They both laughed. 'Bet it's still there – any money. Oh, cheers, mate.' Yeah, they was the ones with jam. She must of got them for him. He could see how she forgot his birthday and all, what with one thing and a nother. Even Mum'd only brought a small card, what weren't like her at all. The bigger the card, the more she loved you. And if it had glitter on it and all that, you was right onside with her. 'Upset Mum though, it did. Right cunt, weren't he?' He picked up a doughnut and bit into it. Handsome. Minded him of after school when Rosie was little, only then she'd lick the jam out of both of theirn, and he'd have to eat the rest.

'Who's this?' said Alex.

'Our dad.'

'Thought he wasn't around?'

'No, he left Mum when I was about . . . what would I have been, Daz? Nine?'

'Bout that. Fucked off over the river with some tart.'

'Don't you ever see him?' Alex grabbed a doughnut. Rosie tapped his arm, to say she wanted a bit. He held the doughnut out, and she took a bite, what left sugar on her chin. Alex wiped it off with his thumb. Lipstick on his doughnut. Yeah, very cosy.

'No, neither of us do. It'd be too disloyal to Mum, apart from anything else,' said Rosie, with her mouth full. Mum wouldn't like that, tell her that much for nothing.

'What was he like?' Alex stuffed most of the doughnut in his gob.

'Like I said, mate – a cunt. Flash bleeder, always suited and booted. Well clever, though – knew all about history and that, done the crossword in five seconds flat. Good snooker player, cards and all.' What's he telling Alex all this for? He never talked about the old man, not hardly even to Rosie. 'She looks a lot like him.' Did and all, specially around the eyes and nose. Darren'd always hated his own eyes, what got crusty if he was knackered, and what didn't seem to have no lashes, less you got right up close to the mirror.

'In The Mice, they used to call him Cliff the Book,' said Rosie.

'Why, because he had one?'

Cheeky fucking cunt! Rosie creased up, but Darren weren't having that.

'What's the matter – you think if you ain't got exams it makes you some sort of thicko?'

'No, it was just a joke.' Alex held up his hands. 'All I meant was, it doesn't seem to me like books would be all that valuable there. Why should they be?'

'Look, mate, make jokes like that and it makes you look like a cunt, know what I mean?'

Alex took a long swig of his beer.

'Look, Darren,' he said, 'don't keep calling me a cunt, especially in my own flat. Okay?'

'Don't act like one, then.' Cheeky *cunt*.

'No, I mean it. I really don't want to fall out with you about this, but it's getting to me.'

They was both looking at him, steady. What was going on, here? What was that Alex doing, fronting him like that? And Rosie saying sod all. Was the cunt the fucking word police now? What's he think it was here – just ask for respect and you get it? Had to be earned. You never got it just by being able to wipe sugar off of Rosie's face, and give her a pacific glass, and make her laugh at what she shouldn't of laughed at.

'What if I don't give a monkey's?'

'Then I'm really sorry, but you won't be welcome here. And that's not what I want.'

Why'd Darren be bothered bout coming to this poxy hole, anyway? He took a fag out the packet, and tapped it gainst his hand. If he made Alex right, he'd lost. But if he called him a cunt and decked him, Rosie wouldn't never let it go. And he could do without getting into a fight – could have him, no question, but Alex was big and might get a couple in hisself. Specially if them red marks *was* scars. Darren didn't need to walk round looking like he'd been slapped, not with the way things was. Must of took something, for Alex to say that. And it'd take something, for Darren to hold out his hand.

He held out his hand.

Alex shook it and smiled. Be fair, it was a proper smile, not a cocky grin sort of deal.

'Thanks. Appreciate it. Right. Anyone need a drink?'

'I bet the birthday boy needs one,' said Rosie.

Connie knew that Alex was angry with her, but she'd diagnosed the client as schizophrenic because there was no more accurate label. That meant, of course, the Centre would lose to St Clements, and Alex made it clear he thought the loss a moral injustice. He fumbled with a matchbox, sending the matches flying.

'Planning to set the place alight?' she asked. He didn't even smile. Although smiles always alter a face, they transformed Alex's: his normal expression was almost sullen, the flesh skulking around his jowls, but when he smiled, his skin sprang back against his cheekbones, dimples appearing, taking years off him. Connie had always rather fancied Alex, but it must be exhausting to go out with someone so relentless. He had no truck with compromise. If she had to make a professional judgement, she'd say that he exhibited a mild form of manic behaviour, arising from an addiction to adrenaline. A compulsive personality.

He stood, smoking furiously, tapping the butterfly poster with his free hand.

'You just decide what someone's like, give them a label,' he said eventually, his deep voice raising in pitch, 'and then construct a whole set of consequences. You can't do that, Connie. People have reasons for behaving in certain ways that might have nothing to do with what we have access to.' He scratched at the poster with his nail. 'Sometimes,' he added, slowly, 'you have to make leaps of faith, if you want to be any use.'

'Lighten up, Alex. Come for a drink, talk it over.'

'I'm sorry, but I couldn't handle that tonight. It'd choke me.' Moving away from the poster, running his hand through his

unruly hair. 'I can't anyway, I'm meeting a friend. And I promise
you, you wouldn't like each other.'

As usual, his own constructed consequences were the only
just ones.

Chapter Eight

It was the difference between the West End and a grotty pub theatre, between having a whole wardrobe at your disposal, and making do with one suitcase, a quick-change artist on the road. Rosie wanted to change slowly tonight, leaving Alex naked face-down on the living room floor, his hands tethered behind his back, as she tried out and discarded various dresses and shoes in her warm solitary bedroom. She rolled her stockings on, taking minutes over what should take seconds. He wouldn't move without explicit permission, he was way too proud. Yet she was never quite sure how far he would go, wasn't even sure how far she'd go herself. Maybe further than he thought he could handle in one direction, and not as far as he seemed to think he wanted in another. They needed something to intimate unendurable pain; she'd have to raise the question of a code word. Soon, anyway. And that would be to go way further than a man offering his body to be walked on, it would be to give a name to what they did. To what they were. No going back. What about when the relationship was over, what happened then? Just see herself down The Mice or at the club, saying *Nice to meet you. By the way, I'm into . . .*

What would be the point, anyway? Ridiculous.

Crush them all like
    ants.

So glad to be back in her own place. She reached into the wardrobe for her cream Versace. Last time she'd worn that had been at Randa's party, just before she'd met Alex, where she'd nearly gone home with that gorgeous black barrister. Until he

spoiled it, the way men always managed to. *I'll make you feel
like no one ever has.* Yeah, right. You could almost feel sorry
for them. No, not the Versace; she slung it on the bed. Maybe
that little suede thing Ben picked up for her on his travels. Daz
had gone into one, *What d'you think she is, a tart?* but Rosie
loved it. So soft, the skin of a baby animal, its hide having
had no time to toughen up. Edmund, her Mr Transitional Man,
had really liked that dress; when he stopped saying it looked
stunning she'd kicked him into touch. He'd cried then, but who
could tell if that was an act or even relief? She hadn't been
about to let him stay around for her to find out. Not a prayer.

'Turn over.' Rosie pressed her foot into the side of Alex's face.
   Not an easy move, with his hands tied together, but he
managed to twist his body round, and even smiled when finally
he was on his back.
   'You look wonderful.'
   'And you look seriously uncomfortable.'
   'I am. But I like you making that effort for me.'
   'For you?' She'd done this for her.
   'You wouldn't look like that for just any old body.' There
wasn't even the smallest trace of an upward inflection in his
voice.
   'Fancy yourself, don't you?'
   'No, but you fancy me.' He laughed.
   'Do I now?'
   'Course you do.' Alex looked her over, slowly, still smiling;
Rosie shook her head. She'd have to get a proper collection of
stuff; shoes and leather straps and cock rings weren't going
to be enough, not for much longer. Rosie always prided herself
on her professionalism, no matter what she did.
   'Alex, you know when you went to that whore? Did she
specialize at all? I mean, was she . . .' *say it* '. . . any kind of
Dominatrix?'
   'God, no.' Alex laughed. 'She was this bored pro who charged
tourists well over the odds. Sexual tourists, you know.

Specialized in extortion, if she specialized in anything. I suppose that was humiliation, if you think about it . . . and what happened, or what didn't happen, was humiliating, no question.'

'Not a problem you seem to be having at the moment.' Rosie brought up her leg, pressing her toe down on Alex's cock. 'Why did you go to her?'

'Do we have to talk about that now?'

Rosie increased the pressure, her red metal heel brushing his balls.

'I want to talk about it,' she said. Snookered.

'Okay. I thought . . . because my wife . . . Christ, I don't know why. Wish I hadn't, to be honest. It just made things worse.' He wasn't smiling now, but he still had a hard-on. Rosie didn't know whether that entirely pleased her. Was talking about it more of a turn-on than trying to do it had been? Or was it the mention of that bloody word, *wife*? 'Can't even remember her face, not that it matters,' he said. 'I was glad she was plumpish, because of how painfully thin Louise had got, I do remember that. But it didn't help, in the end.'

'Are you glad I'm fat, then?' She jabbed at the top of his thigh, and at Louise's name.

'Don't be . . . how are you fat? Might as well say I'm short.'

'Just checking.' She bent over him. 'Like to make sure I'm nobody's antidote to anything.' Twisting one of his nipples, making him wince, almost secure of her pleasure again.

'You're just you.' His voice deeply affectionate.

'Bless,' she said, making it sound sarcastic. But meaning it, just a bit. 'Over by the far wall, Alex.' He raised his eyebrows, as if to say *how?* but almost at once he began to wriggle towards the wall, pulling up his knees to avoid the little table, pushing himself across with his feet. Looked like the carpet was scraping his arms. At least he wouldn't get scabies, the way he might well have done had they still been at his place. No amount of Shake 'n' Vac could help that sad old excuse for a Wilton.

'This all right?'

'Yeah, stay there.' Steadying herself with the tips of her fingers against the wall, Rosie stepped up on to his chest. He exhaled. 'Hurts more, does it, when I've not got a chair?'

'Jesus. Yeah, and those shoes . . .'

'Nice, aren't they? That's what you were going to say, wasn't it?'

'Yeah.'

'Say it, then.' My God, he was beautiful, under her pressure.

'They're . . . really nice.'

'And I'm sure you were going to thank me for wearing them.'

'Yeah . . . I mean, thank you,' he said. She moved, fractionally. Alex cried out. His arms, taking her weight and his own, must be crushed. But he kept his eyes open, looking up at her with admiration. 'Christ, I can't breathe.'

'It's the Alexander technique, remember?'

'Bitch.'

'What was that you called me?'

'Bitch.' Softly, under what breath he had left.

'You ain't seen nothing yet, babe.'

He closed his eyes.

'Tea, boys?' Sue come in, carrying a silver tray. Darren could of cheerfully knocked it flying. Much as he liked seeing her normal, this was all he needed, with him trying to get out of Freddy sactly what the *Once and for all* meet with Bow was, and why Darren weren't being included in it. Rosie'd been back home a couple of days now – Darren needed to know the score, if she really was safe. It was his responsibility. But spite that, what'd he been told? Evidently, someone'd been putting theirself around more than they normally done, being more visible, and it'd give Freddy an idea. Rung a bell, but Darren couldn't put his finger on it. And that's all the info he was getting, and now he had to drink it down with his tea, like a good boy. But give Sue that, she always done things nice. Proper china pot, cups and saucers with gold round the edges, milk in a nice little jug. Mum'd like a set like that. Rosie said they was common, but she had some front, with her mugs with sheep and things on them, and milk from the carton.

'Thanks, love. We've about finished here.' Freddy shot a look at Darren. What's he think he was? Like he'd ever say nothing front of Freddy's missus. Biscuits on a plate, even. Right nice. Not a bad looker, neither, and a good little mum.

'You all right, Sue?' Weren't her fault she come in at the sact wrong time.

'Yeah, you know. He keeps me busy.' Nodding at her old man, laughing, showing her teeth all white. 'Always keeps us all busy, don't he?' Little wink at Darren, what Freddy never see. She was righter than she most likely knew. Old-fashioned right good girl.

'Kids okay?'

'Oh they're fine, yeah. Jason's still a bit of a sod, then boys his age are, aren't they? But Mandy's doing really well at Senior's, won some speaking competition for the whole of Tower Hamlets. And you know Jackie – she don't change much, bless her. Have a biscuit – or I've got some fruitcake if you'd prefer? My mum made it, drowned it in brandy, crafty moo. She's meant to be off the booze but you can't blame her, can you? You got to have some fun in this life.'

Lucky bastard.

The colours always got to him, after all them years. Something bout a fire, even one what farted evil-smelling black smoke from the plastic. And when the red copper started to glow sort of greeny-gold, it was like someone turned on a light in his head, filling it up. Right hard work, but for a few minutes you could afford to just watch the colours, where it always felt like autumn, with the light on in your head to help you see. Magic. You lit a fag, but what normal was a glow in the dark was like nothing. Taking the piss. And the damage it could do was nothing to what the fire could of, and not just cos of the fumes, neither.

Weren't sactly how he'd of thought he'd spend his life, with scrap supporting the real stuff. When he was at school, all he'd thought bout what to do after was he had to have dough. No matter what. Weren't much to choose tween him and Ro on that one. But what d'he have, when it come down to it? Fire might be beautiful, but end of the day, he was still burning the shit off the metal hisself at this age. Only a littl'un, tonight. Didn't want no casual about. Be strictly truthful, this burn was a risk he never really needed to take – should of waited till next week, when there'd of been more gear. Not that much more, had to be said, what with recycling and plastic guttering and all that. Fucking conversationists. But he wanted some time on his own, cos it looked like tonight Freddy was *finally* offering the landlord a final solution. Hadn't been anything this heavy for a good few year – not what dragged on and on and on, so's it got in the way of their normal rounds. Up and down the Mile End Road like some postman, nearly getting a knife off that spade . . . now he was being scluded. He could get why – him or even Rosie might well be the assurance policy. If Freddy fucked up, that could mean dropping Ro in it. And he'd kill the cunt.

Fucking kill him.

She'd looked well when he'd picked her up to take her back to her flat. *Rosie Rosie* – one of the old man's lame jokes. Limped, most of them did, with both feet. But that one sort of fitted, when Rosie weren't all pale with great big shadows under her eyes. Trouble was, everywhere that Rosie went, her lamb was sure to go. He limped with both feet, and all. Arm round her shoulders, like she was coming out of hospital, carrying her suitcase, keep asking her if she was all right. And she loved it, making out like he was getting on her wick, but giving him them special little smiles, all excited. What'd he got? Access to gear, maybe. Do-gooder doing Ro some good in the pharmaceuticals. That'd be a grin. Whatever it was, Darren reckoned he never kept it between his legs. Must be his *brains*.

Birds was a mystery, that way. Always had been. When he was bout thirteen, there'd been that skinny bird. What was her name? Sally, something like that. Followed him round for months. In the end, he'd give in, took her the pictures, even got a bit of tit – what there was to get, which was nothing at all, but still. Then the next week, she'd asked Ben out, just like that. When Ben'd said *What about Spence?* she was meant to have come out with some shit bout him being too hard. What was that to do with? *Sandra*, that was it – Sandra Griffiths. Ben went for it and all, the Jewbag. Said he had her but Darren never believed him.

Rosie'd been a nightmare when he first starting taking birds out. *Daz's got a girlfriend, Daz's got a girlfriend . . .* on and on in her horrible singing voice, right down the street. *Give 'em the old Razzle Dazzle . . .* Crime gainst music, her voice. When he looked into the fire, it was like he could still see her, skipping after him with her hair all flying around and her socks falling down. That's one thing what'd changed – she was always maculate now, even in jeans. Could take her anywhere.

Not that he'd of brung her here – she hated turnip country. Said it was a known fact all axe-murderers lived there, or had holiday cottages there, any rate. Ever since she was little – *No, don't want to, Dad. It's full of dead things and buzzy things.* She'd always wanted to go the sea, Southend for the machines or Leigh for cockles, but Darren'd always right liked the country. All that space for your head. Even now, with only the fire and that starting to be stared out, you could see from the blackness how much space there was. If he ever had a kid, he'd like to live on a farm or something. Have a couple of dogs, and some horses. Always fancied having a go at riding one. Rosie said they was smelly things what bit just for the sake of it, and lived stood in their own shit. She might hate all that housework stuff, but you'd never catch her with muddy boots. He chucked his fag at a piece of metal, and chewed his lip.

If Freddy ballsed up, and made his girl look any less maculate, Darren'd finish him. He meant it. Untangling his gloves, he stood up and tested the fire with his foot. Weren't no doubt now in his mind that The Lion wouldn't let it go till someone was paying, official. Playing noughts and crosses with the boys weren't their style no more, not less they couldn't get that payment. And if it went wrong, and Rosie . . . Spite that at times he felt like throttling her hisself, she was special. Class. No one was going to take that away from her.

Black, on white. Red, leaving trails of itself, animating the game, amalgamating it with all others. And that black, on white, where white should have had the advantage and didn't. Pawn into Queen.

'Oh God, Rosie . . .'

She could see he was having difficulty holding it together. Should she get down?

'No.' The adrenaline hit was incredible; who'd have thought that one little word could give you such a buzz? No. Suffer, go on, take it, if you think you're hard enough. She laughed. 'Too much, is it?' She screwed her heel into his nipple.

'N . . . no.' It ended in a groan, making it a long word, multi-syllabled. He got full marks for it, and cried out again.

'What about now?' Catching his chest hairs in the metal tip.

'No.' Through set teeth. There were tears in his eyes but she knew he wasn't about to cry. Tears poured instead through his skin, fear making him sweat. Slippery and acrid with fear, he was; Rosie's foot slid down his body, leaving a bloody print. 'No,' he whispered.

But no sometimes does mean yes.

'Cope with it this time, and I'll think about giving you a code word for the future.' Finally saying it, as the only player with any chance, as the only authority capable of scoring, it wasn't difficult after all. It felt wonderful. No, more than that; it felt *right*.

Freedom.

And when eventually, she'd taken the black from the white

and lowered herself on to his tongue, she placed her hands on his chest and dug her nails into his wounds. Blood on blood.

This was what she was meant to do.

Alex got into bed beside her, slipping his arm under her shoulders. She curled into him, tracing the marks on his chest with her fingers. Until a couple of days ago, there hadn't been a man in her bed for a long time, maybe a year, and although it was a king-size it felt small, cramped. Hadn't felt like that in Alex's place, even though his bed was barely a double. She couldn't get used to the invasion here. Rosie concentrated on breathing slowly, trying to make herself relax.

'All right, love?' he said, doing his mind-reading trick. Ought to be in the bloody circus.

'Yeah.' Rosie propped herself on one elbow, reached for her water, and nearly choked. Shit. Co-ordinate breathing and drinking; should be simple enough, millions managed it.

'Careful.' He put the glass back, patted her shoulder, and shuffled down the bed, pulling her into him again so she was lying across his chest. 'I love you,' he said.

His hope was palpable but how could she reply? *Love*. Sure, she wanted him: he was the most sexually exciting man she'd ever met, despite the problems (or because of them?). And even though it was still weird to have him here, it was good to feel his arms around her, and the little kisses in her hair. But love? It didn't get said easily, not by Rosie. Only to two other men, in fact, not counting family; it always meant giving too much of yourself away. The first one had been so long ago, she could hardly remember why she'd bothered. Scottie was a different deal, but at the end of the day she'd had to leave him, too. He'd thought he wanted her because she was, well, how she was, and then spent the next three years trying to make her into something else. Male logic. Yeah good one, Scottie. No amount of imaginative sex, flashy holidays and always remembering her dress size at birthdays and Christmas could make up for wanting to turn her into a Stepford wife. *Golem*.

'It's all right, I don't need you to say anything.' Definitely the circus.

'You do make a difference to me,' she conceded. And that was hard enough.

'I know.' Arrogant sod. But he squeezed her, as though pleased she'd admitted something. 'You make a massive difference to me as well, Rosie. I was a real mess when I met you. Couldn't see how I was ever going to sleep with another woman. I had some problems with that before I got married but afterwards . . . You've woken up that side of me again. I even notice other women more.'

What? Bastard. That's great, another bloke who thinks with his dick, and it's all down to her. Marvellous. Suppose he wants to make love to them, and get abused by her. The best of both worlds. Eating his cake and having it.

'Oh, that's good.'

'Don't be like that, they all suffer in comparison. Have to really, they're not you.' He took her hand, and pressed it into a bruise on his stomach. 'I'm having much less of a problem with what I am sexually, relative to you.' His face was serious. 'All I want to ask, and I'm only asking, I'm not making any demands, is you don't do this, what we do, with anyone else.'

'But it's okay to do other things? Sleep with other men?'

Rosie heard him breathe out, through his nose.

'I didn't say that, I can't stand the thought of it. But the thought of you doing what you do to me to someone else is even worse. Or mixed up with it or something. Sorry, this is coming out bollocks. But you know what I mean.'

'Do I?' Of course she did. He was asking to be the only one in her life capable of giving her what she needed. Funnily enough, it hadn't occurred to her that she might need any other at the moment. Not that she was about to tell Alex that. He might think she was caught. He might go so far as to think she was in love with him. Gently, Alex pulled her up, so that he could reach her face. He kissed her.

'What are the marks on the tops of your legs from?' he said.

'Accident.' Jesus. He'd waited what, more than a fortnight to ask that?

'No they're not.' He touched them. 'They're all different. I think they happened over a period of time.'

'It's vile.' Cut, cut, cut. But only where it wouldn't show. Cut herself out of this place; make room for the new stuff coming in. Slice, slice, slice.

'Tell me.' It didn't sound like a request.

Shit, she'd never even told Scottie. Haltingly, she formed the narrative for Alex: the 'A' level years, the first year at Queen Mary, how she used to cut her own flesh. Knives, scissors, broken cups. Until one day, with a piece of glass in her hand, she'd seen herself in a mirror: confident, clever, in control. How could she explain her inside urge to that reflection? She'd thought, right, I won't do this any more, I'm going to pretend to be that person in the mirror, to be normal. Never happened again, although the desire had taken years to disappear beneath the carapace. Rosie's words felt sharp in her mouth now, as though they could leave her tongue gashed, damaged. She found it difficult to face Alex, yet she steadied her gaze against his.

'I went on a course about it,' he said, pressing his nails into her scars. 'A lot of users are self-harmers. The course material claimed it was to block out the pain in their lives.'

'I do like a nice bit of psychobabble, me.' She wanted to spit blood. 'I did it, babe, because I wanted to feel something. So it's the opposite of your *course material*. I was on automatic pilot for so long, so bloody determined to have more than my mum had, nothing else mattered. And I still had to fit in, so I spent any free time getting stoned or drunk or fucking. Then I took up cutting.' She'd never articulated that before, not even to herself.

He moved his hand from her scars to her face, running his thumb along her mouth.

'When I was a kid,' he said, 'if an adult, especially a woman, bested me and there was nothing I could do about it, I used to get a shiver run through me. Even if I knew it wasn't fair, and that I was in the right, I still . . .'

'Three Blind Mice.' Rosie nipped his thumb, hard.

'Ow! What?'

'Your code words. They can be Three Blind Mice. Now make love to me.'

He did, and it was better, but there was still something he wore like a condom, a barrier between them that simply didn't exist when she caused him pain.

Beep, beep bloody beep. Alarm. No, she was back home; her alarm was set to Radio 2. Alex's pager. He sat up and fumbled for the intrusive box. Little brother.

She put her hand on the warm sheet where he'd been lying. What was the time? Christ, five-and-twenty past four. It had better be an emergency, an OD at least. If it was just one of those whinging junkies looking for a bit of succour, then surely they could get lost. Five-and-twenty past four. Rosie closed her eyes, trying to get back off, but her toes were clenched as she waited for Alex to announce he was going to do his Florence Nightingale bit. She'd had to go out herself yesterday night, down to the nick, but that was a nice little earner, worth the cost of sleep. Even worth being trailed there by the gorillas, as though her movements were illegal. The risks in his job brought bloody low rewards.

He came back into the bedroom, and pulled on his underpants and jeans, looking round for his tee-shirt.

'God,' he said, but quietly, as though not to disturb her if she were asleep. Some chance, with him lumbering around like a fairy elephant. She sat up. 'You awake, love? Someone's turned up out of his head. Really bad. They should have sent him down the hospital, he shouldn't be anywhere near the Centre in that state. But it's—'

'So you have to go running.' She shrugged on her dressing gown. Alex sat on the bed, and started to put on his socks; Rosie tried to wrench the duvet from under his bum.

'When *I* run, it's because I really have to,' he said. 'Just because he should have better help doesn't mean I should give him none at all.' He got up and took his carrier from the embroidered chair, rummaged through it with a cigarette between his lips, checking for God knows what file or form or letter. 'See you here tonight, about nine?' he mumbled.

'Taking a lot for granted.' Rosie stretched to reach the lighter for him. Christ, it was freezing in here.

'It's probably still better if you're not on your own here any more than we can help.' That wasn't the same as saying he wanted to be with her, though, was it? He kissed her on the cheek. 'I've got to go. If you need me—'

'I can page you.'

'Yeah, you can.' Bastard wasn't rising to it. Might as well get up herself, pull out the laptop; have to get those new Woolf rules sorted if she was going to help William with his Civil. There'd be room in the bags under her eyes for souvenirs, but if she dropped a Temmy now she'd be sparko till the afternoon, and she couldn't afford to take the morning off.

'Where's he, then?'

'At the Centre. What's happened?'

'Nothing bad. I was just sort of passing.'

'At seven in the morning?' Been to see a mouse about a lion, more like.

Daz looked awful: his lizard eyes appeared to be bleeding into his skull, and he was so drawn that Rosie doubted he'd slept at all. Yeah, she could smell the charcoaly dampness that followed a burn. *Dirty Dick from Hackney Wick*. If she knew her brother, he'd have had a line or several, to look that dreadful.

'It's sorted, Ro – I just had the call. What I mean is, it nearly is – you ain't got nothing more to worry about. And no one's been hurt. We'll leave you with just the one minder for a couple or three week to be safe, maybe a month, but other than that, sorted.'

'No one's been *hurt*? She was younger than me, Daz. Imagine burning to death.'

'She weren't meant to be there.' He bent to pick up her mug from the floor.

'How the hell do you know?' She glared at him. 'Anyway, that hardly makes it better, does it? Oh it's okay, I wasn't meant to be here. Bit warm for the time of year.' Sorted. Without anyone else being hurt. What did that mean? Gorillas for another month; she knew how Princess Diana must have felt. It meant it'd take a while to arrange. No one hurt; not knife-edge justice, but a gentler, respectable avenging. A set-up, it must be. Water and stones. It would take time to make a case. 'Sorted how, exactly?' she asked. Curt.

'That's all I know, doll.'

'Well, you might as well be off, then. Stick that mug in the kitchen on your way out.' She sat on the settee, pulled her Powerbook towards the edge of the coffee table. All you know, yeah right. And if it was *sorted*, she'd had all that fear, for this. A reckless waste of adrenaline. Please God, let it at least be a villain, someone who should be going down for something, if not this. She wondered which brief they were using, what the cost would be.

'Got time for a spliff, sort of celebration?'

She caught his gaze and held it, drawing it deep into her.

'I never get stoned when I'm working,' she said.

Thank God Alex was here; Jeni hadn't been coping terribly well on her own. She didn't remember Sam Patterson from before of course, but she knew the type. Dysfunctional family. In and out of trouble since his early teens. Latent amphetamine problem, that didn't look terribly latent at the moment. What Alex would call a speed-freak. Bit of a maverick, Alex. Jeni couldn't always approve of his methods and decisions, and there'd been talk of disciplinary action, but he got results. And there was something sad about him, like he desperately needed to be loved. The stubble was thick on his face this morning, as though he didn't matter to himself anymore. People said he'd had a tragic marriage; Jeni had always been good with those in pain. And she'd always liked older men.

'What's she still doing here, guy? We don't need her, you know me, I'm on the level. Shit, man, she's freaking me out. She looks like my nan, but with a young face – too weird.'

Alex turned to Jeni. He shrugged.

'How about going next door, getting us all some tea?' he said.

He had a kettle. Sam shouldn't have been there in the first place; Jeni had put herself at risk, paging Alex for him. Maverick.

'I can make some here.'

'No, I don't think so.' They both looked at Sam, who was trembling so violently that he hardly seemed capable of drinking tea. A vile smell came from his too-thin body: curry scented with urine. Alex spoke again, firmly. 'Two sugars, thanks. Three for Sam. Now, what's all this with the bad speed . . . Close the door will you, Jeni?'

It wasn't that she minded making the tea; she could see that the lad was in a real state, and Alex knew what he was doing. He didn't mean to be hurtful, they'd always got on very well. It was surprising there weren't rumours, in fact. Jeni hoped Sam wasn't continuing to insult her in her absence; that would put Alex in a terribly difficult position. It was a good thing, she supposed, to be so dedicated to your job, but it could make anyone who got in the way feel as though they'd done just that. And she knew perfectly well how many sugars he liked.

She took her time over the tea. And knocked on the office door before going in. Alex was sitting on the edge of his desk, his hand on the young man's shoulder. Sam covered his face with a scarf, noisily gulping mucus.

'You're all right, mate,' Alex soothed him. 'Come on, it'll be all right. We'll get you back in here, I promise. Nice group like before, little rest. No point in having friends in high places if they can't pull strings for you, is there?'

Sam coughed, which might have been his way of laughing.
'He hasn't been referred, Alex . . .'

'So I'll get him referred.' If she hadn't known him so well,
Jeni would have said the look he gave her was distinctly nasty.

'What's she mean, man? Is there a problem with it?' Sam
uncovered his face and wiped his snotty nose on his scarf.

'No, you know what women are like, mate. Like a real good
fuss.' Alex checked his watch. 'You put your feet up in here
for an hour or two. Have to kick you out about eight, I'll want
to ring my girlfriend, let her know I'm all right, seeing as I
left in the middle of the night. Like I said, women love to fuss,
especially my Rosie.'

'Yeah?' Sam's head shot up. 'She worries?'

'Fusses, anyway. Then I'll start ringing round for you. Is that
okay?'

Men. A woman would never take so much upon herself, and
simply assume that anything she did was bound to be right.

Chapter Nine

The City pub was half empty. Mostly couples, drinking Chardonnay at the pseudo-rustic tables, eating food they'd appropriated from their grandparents: pints of unshelled prawns in beer glasses, bangers and mash, egg and chips. Five years ago they'd have thought food like that was *a hoot, darling*, although they'd have been quick enough to nosh down paella or cassoulet on holiday, or chopped herring in a deli. *Authentic*, that would have been. Rosie wouldn't eat here if she were paid, not in this or any other universe. Alex laughed and rubbed her shoulder.

'I'll just get some whelks and a doorstop of bread, then.'

'Whelks? Are you sure?'

'Joking, love. Not like you not to pick it up. I'll get chips.'

Rosie smiled. He was right, should have seen that one. Practically had bells on it. Alex ordered from the bluff bloke, handing over a twenty. Landlord, she'd lay money. Looked like he was a bit too keen on his own food; probably called it *grub*. When the landlord came back with the change he winked and handed it to Rosie rather than Alex. Without thinking, Rosie took it.

'Got to look after the lady,' he said, winking again.

'You don't know the half of it, mate,' said Alex. The landlord chuckled away, although he couldn't possibly have cottoned on. Rosie passed the money to Alex, and they sat at the nearest table.

'Suppose it sounded innocuous to him,' said Rosie, picking up her glass.

'It was.' Alex gazed at his pint, then looked up and winked. Rosie leaned over to kiss him. 'Although dressed like that, he'd have to wonder,' he added.

'Excuse me, this jacket's a Gaultier.' Rosie unzipped it as she spoke, enjoying the feel of brand new PVC under her fingers. Alex adjusted his carrier on the seat next to him. There was even a hole in the bottom of this one; how he didn't lose all his papers was a miracle. For his birthday, Rosie was definitely going to get him a briefcase. Gucci.

'What've you been up to today?' he asked.

'Our office manager's on a major clear-out. There's files from years ago, literally, not closed because there's stuff on them like who does the fiver on a client account belong to? I kid you not, it's chaos. So at lunchtime I slipped out, bought this,' she shrugged off her jacket, 'and had a wander into a travel agent's. I've been thinking about booking my summer holiday . . .'

'Nowhere too expensive, I hope. I can't afford it.'

Who said anything about him coming?

'I did see one, in the Dominican Republic. I thought that'd be right up my street.'

'How much will that cost?' Alex fell in as Rosie shook her head, and he laughed.

'That makes the score even, I reckon,' she said. 'Anyway, what sort of day you had?'

'Not great. There was one I couldn't get on my crossword, really annoyed me. Then Sam Patterson turned up again, still in a state. Can't get out of him what's wrong. And I'm having big-time trouble getting him a referral.'

'Why's it so important?' She knew the Pattersons, they'd lived in Pemell House all her life. Wasters. Though Sam, the youngest, was a poor little beggar, with his shakes and his starvation cheapness.

'I've always had a bit of a soft spot for him. He keeps on trying, has done for three years, since he was seventeen. Shouldn't be talking about this, really.'

'No.' She studied her cigarette packet. So much for having some time out. Alex could never leave it behind, never. Rosie's work was merely her enabler, the background supplier of what was real; Alex's defined him. He lived his job as much as Daz did. 'Tell you what, why don't you not talk about it?' she suggested.

From the spiel that followed, Alex clearly didn't intend to take her advice. Finally, the landlord put a basket of chips on the table; Rosie was half surprised they didn't come in newspaper. Alex stuffed a handful into his mouth. Least it shut him up.

'Give us one.'

'You always do that! Why don't you ever want your own?'

'Getting your own's not the same, they never taste as nice. Ai, that's hot.'

'Serves you right.' Alex blew on a chip, bit it and put the other half in her mouth. Okay, maybe she could forgive his obsessive need to help the disadvantaged. This was what mattered: sitting in some horrible pub, knowing that Alex despised it as much as she did, and being fed chips. Jesus, she even quite missed him when he wasn't around. At least for now, their lives seemed to mesh. She couldn't legislate for him meeting someone whose life was less compromised in his terms, or who was into the idea of marriage and kids, or who could simply fall in love with him and with the force of that lead him away. But at this moment, she knew he belonged to her. 'What?' he said.

'Nothing. I was just thinking I'm glad I met you.'

'That's almost a proposal of marriage, coming from you!'

'Don't push it, babe. Give us another chip.'

'If you give me your shoe.' He waved a chip in front of her face.

'Now?' Rosie looked around the pub; no way giving Alex a shoe would go unnoticed. She pushed one off with the toe of the other and held it out, over the table. 'Chip first.'

Alex made the exchange, with exaggerated courtesy. From

his inside pocket, he brought out a pen. He turned the leather over in his hands, speculatively, and paying no attention to the curious looks of the punters, began to draw on the sole.

'That cost a lot of money,' Rosie said.

'Mm. Good.' Absently.

Rosie picked another chip out of the basket and waited.

It took fifteen minutes, but it was worth it.

'Here.' He kissed the shoe and gave it back to her. At the next table, a woman tutted. Rosie hadn't known people really did that. She smiled at the woman, turning the sole upwards.

He'd drawn a rambling rose, twisted round the trunk of a solid tree.

'An oak?'

'Yeah, you townie.'

She slipped it back on to her foot. It felt like stroking herself.

'Instead of getting a cab back, shall we stroll over to the tube?' she said.

He'd thought she might have had him with her, but she never. Mum'd be right disappointed with that. There weren't no winning for Darren on this one. He was getting fed up with being poked at for information and all. How did he know if Alex was good looking, or what he took home, or if Rosie was happy? Had to hold his hands up and say Ro seemed to like him a lot, but he couldn't say no more'n that. Mum'd even asked if Darren thought they was likely to get married. Said he couldn't see Rosie marrying nobody, but how the fuck did he know? Said fuck and all, and got his legs slapped for it.

'You here, then?' said Rosie.

'No, it's me twin brother,' said Darren.

'One's enough.' She took off her coat and slung it over the back of the settee. 'That's cold out there. Any tea in the pot, Mum?'

'Just made fresh. No young man again?' She done one of her faces, and Rosie bent over the table, poured herself tea.

Darren was gagging for a proper drink hisself, and he'd lay money his girl was and all, but if Mum made tea, you drank it. Simple as that. Rosie took a swig standing up, and then stuck the cup on the floor. 'Careful!' Mum said.

'Yeah, I am being.' She sat on the settee.

'Biscuit?'

'No thanks. I've not long had my tea.' Looking at Darren. Yeah, sure. Rosie never eat this early. Wouldn't kill her to have a custard cream or something – save a row, what he could well do without. All week, felt he was taking punishment for it being sorted. Stroll on.

'You're not slimming?' Mum grabbed herself a biscuit and stuffed it in her mouth, chewing loud like she never did, like she was shouting at Rosie for not having one, but without using no words. Darren took a chocolate finger, dunked it in his tea. Rosie just sat there and smiled. Mum snatched a nother loud fig roll. 'There's not a peck on her, is there, Darren?'

Shit. Bound to say the wrong thing here, one way or a nother.

'No – but it's up to her, ain't it?'

'Likes them skinny, does he, this Alex?'

'Oh for God's sake, Mum, I'm not skinny. I just don't fancy a bloody biscuit.'

'That's enough of that, my girl. You only had to say. Bli, if I said black was white, you'd say it was navy blue.'

She wouldn't never learn, that was Rosie's trouble. Always rise to it, right from small. And it weren't fair to upset Mum for no reason, specially not when she was still wild over Ben. Specially when it was Darren she was wild with, out of some female tuition.

'What's the news then, Mum?' he said, but he should of got it in quicker.

'What do I do, to get news? See your nan today – when was the last time you two did?'

'Yesterday,' said Darren. 'Took her one of Sue's mum's cakes.'

'Crawler,' Rosie whispered.

'She never said. Got round to ringing Auntie Mim – says they've give her a false leg.'

'Wow, she'd be great in a magician's act,' said Rosie. 'Wouldn't even have to bother sawing her in half. Here, Mum, that what you mean by saying she's your half-sister?'

'Rosie Violet Spence! Can't believe I gave birth to such a wicked little moo.' But she never said it serious. Rosie laughed, took her feet off the floor and tucked them under herself. 'Feet, madam.'

'I'm going in a minute anyway, I told you I could only pop in. There's someone waiting for me outside, isn't there, Daz?' Said in a purposely false sweet voice. Yeah, he was still well in trouble for not splaining bout they'd picked a ringer. But she'd of worked it out. 'I've got to get back up the office. We've got some new evidence coming in on one of our biggest cases, so I'll be there till midnight, I reckon.'

'That's your look-out, you can still take your shoes off.'

'But I said, I'm going in a minute.'

'I don't care – take them off, please.'

'Telling me you want me to go now?'

What was happening here? Even for Rosie, this was a bit much. It was Mum's settee – not hern. Them shoes fucked up everything she put them on. Records, lino, Blondie posters. And Mum was into one. Well bad. Rosie never even looked up for a fight – she was just sat there, sort of smiling. But not sactly. More like she was smiling inside her head, and only a bit of it showed on the outside. He couldn't call this one.

'Come on, sweetheart – Mum's only saying. Lot of dough, that settee was.'

'I know, I paid for half of it.'

'What's that supposed to mean?' said Mum. 'That you can come in here and do what you like with it? Indian giver now, are you?'

'No, I was just replying to Daz, nothing to do with my feet.' She weren't moving, sept to lean forward and pick up her tea. .

Must be stone cold. She swallowed it, and balanced the cup on the arm of the settee.

'So give it best and put them down.'

'Okay.' Rosie uncurled her legs, right slow, stretched out one of them. There was ink or something on the bottom of her shoe, all smudged in. She stood up. 'I'll be off, then. I'll try and call in on Nana tomorrow, or if not, the next day.' She blew a kiss at Darren, then bent to kiss Mum – who let her. And if Rosie weren't going to pay for this, he knew who'd have to.

Being naked always meant stripping your self bare. Rosie wasn't embarrassed by taking off her clothes, but there were so many consequences, so many flesh-eating parasites waiting to nibble through to your insides, that she never removed everything without a sense of the risk. And just when she was beginning to feel that the risk might be negligible, Alex went and proved her original theory. Of course. Bastard.

They were in her bed, Alex gently kissing her shoulders and arms, Rosie occasionally moving a hand across the expanse of his scarred back. He flinched whenever she touched a particularly tender mark, but she wasn't going for serious hurt, just a lazy reminder of how they'd spent the previous couple of hours. She was in some discomfort herself; the result of constantly looking down from heels was a pain in the neck. Although that was one self-inflicted injury she had no intention of fighting against. Her thoughts began to drift to the Hopkins case. Have a stunning result there, if they really could establish precedent. Mustn't let her relationship with Alex blunt her concentration; she was leaving that bit earlier most days, bringing less work home. Not good signs. She felt Alex's breath, warm on her arm, and stretched.

'I'm not going to say this often, Rosie, I don't want to devalue it, but . . .' Alex spoke with his lips against her skin, muffling his voice '. . . I adore you.' He pressed his face into her shoulder, then looked at her, waiting. Rosie knew that wasn't merely a

conventional form; he thought he was prostrating himself
beneath her. No admonition to tread softly. Real courage. She
stroked his hair, not sure what to say, even what to feel.

'Do you, now?'

'Yeah, I do. Not because you're perfect. You're not.' He shook
his head. 'But because you think so much of yourself.'

Bloody cheek! She struggled to get up, but his weight had
her pinned.

'So my self-adoration leads to your adoring, does it?'

'I didn't mean that. Come on, love, you're being deliberately
obtuse.' Alex released her, and they both sat up; he reached
for her cigarettes, but lit only one, passing hers over cold. She
took the lighter from his hand and sparked it, not looking at
him.

She wanted to ask where he saw those imperfections: in her
slowly aging, softening body, in whatever he thought he could
see beyond that? In the smallness of her breasts, the breasts
he still couldn't bring himself to touch, in the heart beneath?
In the scars on her thighs, in what had caused them? But no
way was she going to voice any of that, not while she was
naked, in bed, no escape. Doubtless, her self-doubt would
weaken his adoration. Why did he have to say the first part,
if he was only going to follow it up with the second? She'd
been proved right yet again: men were there to mess with your
head, and the best chance they had was if you were naked. In
the raw.

'What did I do wrong? I can tell I've done something, but
I can't think what.'

'Nothing.' She drew up her knees under the duvet, hugging
them with one arm.

'Am I supposed to be able to read your mind now?'

*Powers failing you, are they? They'll chuck you out of the
circus.*

'Just leave it, Alex, will you? There's nothing the matter. Be
told.'

'That's just it, I'm not being told, am I? About anything at all. Look, this isn't going to work if every time I do something you don't like, you just go in on yourself.'

'I'm not.' Burrow, burrow. Right through the flesh if you could.

'For God's sake, woman, I'm not an idiot. Was it because I said you weren't perfect?'

'No. Of course I'm not perfect, no one is.' She didn't need him to think she was perfect, it really wasn't that; but if he could assert that she wasn't, in the middle of saying something so major, then how deep *were* the imperfections, to him? And if she explained, she'd be exposed: the opposite of thinking a lot of herself. He had her in a corner. That was the feeling she hated most in this world.

'I think you're really exciting, you know that. What do you want me to say? I'm proud to be with you. But you're the most infuriating woman I've ever met. No one stands a chance with you, do they? One cock-up, and you're bolting the door. You can be such a hard bitch.' He threw back the duvet. 'I'm going for a piss.'

Rosie looked down at her nakedness. She was nearly thirty-three, what could she expect? She was wearing her whole life on her bones. Every man, every drink, every night of working until she couldn't keep her eyes open, every row, every cigarette; all the everies covered her, dimpling her thighs, roughening her elbows, wearing her out, little by little. It was the same for everyone, of course, and she knew that most of the time she looked pretty damn good, but nevertheless, there her life was, in her body. And all the everies were in her mind, too; what could she expect, at nearly thirty-three? She carried her whole life around with her in her head, and some of it didn't look too attractive now. There were no moisturisers, no dyes, to help with that. No matter how much money you had, or who was prepared to pay, everyone was basically fucked when it came to looking good inside their mind.

Alex came back into the bedroom, and sat on the edge of the bed, put out his cigarette.

'I didn't mean to upset you,' he said. 'Things come out wrong sometimes, with me. But you've got to be straight here, Rosie, else how are we ever going to work it out?'

'You're a clumsy bastard.'

'I know. But I do love you.'

'Even though I'm a hard bitch?'

'Maybe because you're a hard bitch.' His beautiful, brief smile. 'Sometimes that's a definite advantage, anyway. I know that's what you want, that you enjoy it. It's really important to me, I couldn't have predicted how important.' Alex scratched his chin. 'Some days, even at work, I just can't get it out of my head.'

Rosie searched his eyes; how far did he mean that?

'It's just . . . you've got this way of getting to me,' she said. 'I'm not used to it.'

'I get to you, do I?' he said, reaching for her. He was grinning now; not cockily, but like he was really delighted. She let him hug her, and even gave him a quick squeeze back.

'Don't get carried away, Alex, I didn't say . . .'

'Didn't you?'

'Cheeky sod! You'll pay for that one, sooner or later.' She pulled his chest hair.

'I don't doubt it for a minute,' he said, laughing.

But she played back that conversation a couple of days later. Don't kid yourself: in the end, it was always the woman who paid. Mum had drummed that into her from the time she was nine, and at that age, the only posh job Rosie could think of (except for being a teacher, yuk) was the law. She hadn't known any grown-ups, not even men, with a job like that. Not much later she had realized for herself that no matter how many times you were able to hand the bill to someone else, no matter how carefully you became the kind of woman who rarely had to put her hand in her purse unless she chose to, you'd always have to settle sometime. As soon as she opened the door, she had a feeling this was it. Pay-back time.

Alex looked terrible: he hadn't shaved, the creases around his eyes seemed gouged into his flesh, and he'd definitely been nowhere near a comb. He ran his hands through his hair, as though conscious of what a scruff he was, but he couldn't seem to say anything.

'What the hell's wrong with you? Babe? What's the matter?'

'Uh . . . Rosie . . . I'm not . . . I'm not going to be able to come round for a few days.'

What was going on, here? Last night, Alex had left a message on her mobile to say he couldn't make it because of an emergency at work; didn't seem important, as the mix-up with the VO meant Rosie hadn't got back from Colchester until half-eight, and she'd scrounged supper and a bed at Randa's place. But more nights? Alex wasn't the Centre's only line manager.

'Why not?' Keep your voice even, girl.

'Stuff going on at work. Sorry, I know this is bollocks but I can't do anything about it. I haven't slept at all.'

'So I see.'

'I will explain. But I haven't got time now. I just thought I should tell you, face-to-face.'

'Tell me what?'

'That I can't see you for a while.'

'Does your governor know?'

'My . . . ? No. Can you tell him for me? There can't be much risk, can there? You're down to one minder . . . God, can't believe I can just say that so casually. But you said there's nothing to worry about now. There's not, is there?' Looking distracted rather than concerned.

'Not much, no.' Unsuccessfully, she tried to wrest his gaze from the wall above her head. Alex had never understood the situation. Now it was as though he didn't care.

'I'll give you a ring in a couple of days, is that okay?' he said. What, he couldn't even ring before then? There was something very funny here. Rosie wasn't her brother's sister for nothing: she could smell trouble. She had to be on her guard.

'Whatever. See you around, then.'

'Yeah. Soon, I hope. Are you sure you'll be all right?'

'Always am. 'Bye, Alex. Be lucky.'

He did look down at her for a moment then, as though wondering what to do. Clumsily, he kissed her on the cheek, and
turned to leave. He hadn't even bothered to take off his coat.

She heard the door close. Well, that was that. She looked
at her watch: ten past eight. Way, way over the yard arm, and
clearly, she wouldn't be able to focus on that possible unlawful
imprisonment, even for the sake of Freddy's associate. There
was a bottle of Glenmorangie in the drinks cupboard; Rosie
poured herself a large shot, put on a CD, and curled up in the
armchair, her feet under her. Flesh against cold leather.

Perhaps it didn't matter what had gone wrong. The fact was,
something had, something that made Alex look like a tramp,
that left her alone with a single malt and Diana Ross. She'd
begun to expect too much, that was her trouble; for once, she'd
been unable to harden her heart. A memory of something read
long ago crept up on her mind: *I could have loved him.*

Yeah, she could have done. If she could have loved, it would
have been Alex Tolliver.

Her throat felt tight. She swallowed a mouthful of her drink.
It went down into the hard place inside her stomach and stayed
there, making no difference. The shame of it. So much for making
connections; you thought there was something real, maybe even
profound, between you, and all the time the other was looking
for a way out. What she didn't understand was why Alex had
made her believe he loved her. That was, well, it was sadistic.
And she had believed him. Not that she'd thought he'd love her
for ever (no one really did for ever, except as a trope) but she'd
thought he'd meant for more than a few weeks. Maybe he'd
heard the rumours about Bow; *Love alters . . .* except that she
hadn't altered. Alex had always known what her client base
was, right from their first conversation. And that inaugural visit
to The Mice: *you can protect them from the one thing they're
really scared of;* was that overt admission frightening him now?

Yet Rosie didn't think the fire was the issue, not really. A catalyst at most, and if Alex had convinced himself that was more than an excuse, then he was deluded. It had always seemed to Rosie that Alex didn't exist when he wasn't with her, but of course he must, with his own, second, thoughts, with the betrayals that make up most men's lives. *Don't put all your eggs in one basket.* Although between her (please God) welded-on coil and his reluctance to make love, eggs weren't the issue either. He'd worn the Ben stuff, and Daz playing gangsters, hadn't even pressed her on why, which wasn't like him at all. No, he'd probably decided it'd got too heavy; probably sensed she could have loved him, and had panicked. Rosie had seen Daz do that with lots of women. She was buggered if she'd cry. Or do anything at all.

Just sit here until she felt better, sipping malt, letting that sweet voice wash it through her.

She stroked her arm. Outside, cats began a fight, their awful screeching interfering with the music. Maybe they were courting; who could tell the difference, with cats?

All she had to do was get through this one night. Then she'd be fine.

Belly dancer. Pretty. My granddaughter – yes, yes. Not right, am I? Know that. Pretty girl. My daughter. No, Pat was never a pretty girl, not like . . . Rosie. Yes, Rosie. Rosie and Darren. But this lady is grown up. Rosie? Got all her exams, now she's on the telly. Ain't it marvellous. Nice cup of tea. Where's your shoes? Your feet'll get cold.

'D'you fancy a nice cup of tea?'

'I'll do it, Nan. I've got some Black Magic here, and some smoked salmon, look. Shall I make you a little sandwich?'

'Lovely. Your day off, is it?'

'No, a long lunch hour. I've been meaning to come for days, but you know how it is.'

'Where's Darren?'

'You saw him a little while ago, Nana. Remember? He said he brought you cake.'

'Naughty boy. Full of brandy, that was.'

'Nice, was it?'

'Oh yes, dear, lovely. But he's a naughty boy, trying to get his nana tiddly.'

Better now. This was Rosie, and they were going to have a nice little sandwich, and tea, and Black Magic. I've been dreaming, again. Not nice, my dreams. You want to get hold of yourself, Violet, that's what you want to do. Any fool could see this was Rosie. Looks just like her dad, but with hair like me. Used to have. Everyone says so. Mary, Mary.

'There you go then, Nan. Careful, that tea's hot.'

'Wouldn't be very nice cold, would it?' Made her laugh. She was always laughing, when she was a little girl. 'Are you dancing, today?'

'Yeah, Nana, that's right. Can't stay long as it happens, I've got to get to rehearsals.'

'You work too hard.'

'Tell me about it!'

'Are you married, dear?'

'Married? No. What makes you say that?'

What makes me say that? Say what? Got it wrong again. Back of the class. Everyone over the horse except Violet Clarke. Boy's shoes. Kicking them against the wall, trying to spoil them. Mummy was very cross. Violet said a wicked thing – *Go and boil your head, your eyes ain't done!* Mummy cried. When I started work, I made my first hat for her. She cried again. Clever, I was, with my hands – no back of the class when I started work.

'Nan? You still with us?'

'No, I've moved to Spain. Nice bit of salmon, Mary.'

'Rosie. I'm Rosie.'

'I know that. You're courting, aren't you? Pat told me. Does he love you, dear? Is he what you want?' Wrong, wrong, wrong. Poor pretty was spoiling her eyes. 'Don't cry, chicken. Not one of them worth it.'

*   *   *

Taking it right slow, he sat up in bed. Yesterday, he'd even got up for half-hour, and he hadn't wanted to throw up at all, so things must be getting sorted with his ear. Taking its time – been weeks now. Three weeks? Four? Lost all track. Face was still right sore, though, and it itched real bad, but Doc reckoned that was a good sign. Might be, but he weren't the one having to lie on his hands not to rip the thing to shreds. Better off sitting up for a bit, and waiting for Mum to bring something what could be kept down.

Fancied a bagel yesterday, he had – first thing he'd really wanted since it happened. But then Mum'd told him that Blooms had closed down, and she'd have to go up Tesco to get anything even halfway decent. Put him right off. Closed. All them years of hearing he was getting tall, all them years of hot bread of a Sunday, gone. Told Spence, and he put it down to all the fucking Pakis what was opening shops round there, selling curry sandwiches. Ben liked a good Indian, but that weren't the point. Restaurants was one thing, but taking away shops what'd always been there, taking the bread out of English people's mouths, well, that was bang out-of-order. Perhaps he'd ask Mum for some tomato soup, if the Pakis could manage to sell that. He weren't struck on any other flavour, but tomato was all right, if it was Heinz.

Rosie'd got him a massive box of them Thorntons chocolates. Spence'd brung them over. Be nice for when he could fancy them. And a card and all, with a picture on the front of what looked like a load of fog. She liked all that art stuff. Inside, she'd put *Don't worry, Ben: a stitch in time saves nine! Thinking of you. Love, Rosie xxx* Sharp. Always had been. Used to be right annoying when she was a kid, but she sort of grew into herself. Not just in her ways, neither, but in her looks. Before she went away to the university, it was skirts up her arse, fishnets, even pink hair, one time. But after she got her qualifications, she was the business – and she knew it. Funny enough, she weren't so up herself as what she'd been when she got her exams at school.

Ben felt for his fags, but it'd be stupid to light one. Might even pack up, this rate. Had a go at smoking yesterday, but he'd only had one drag fore he knew it was a right bad idea. Have to have them there though, in case. Fiddling with the packet was least something to do with his hands – awkward, otherwise, in his mum's house and his guts still not too clever. But his right hand did go down to his cock. Queasy or not, he had a bit of an hard-on.

Could remember the first time Rosie had give him a boner, not counting when any bird within ten yards had, even the teenage ones. Shit, she'd been a cow. Spence'd go mental at her, with her coming in off her face at three in the morning covered in love bites, but she'd just wrap him up in words. One night she'd rolled in like normal, and Spence'd asked her who she'd been with. All right, he'd asked her nasty, but still. She got an envelope out her bag and threw it at him. *Here are, read that if you're so keen to know. It's a love letter, in case you don't realize.* Ben'd hated her for that, for a good while.

But after she'd done her university, there was that party for her at Pat's place, and she'd come in looking so horny it weren't true. Ben could still remember what she had on. Plain black dress, tight, bit above the knee, hair up, gold sovereign, suede shoes, sharp. She'd spotted him, give him a massive smile, and come over and kissed him on the cheek, asking him how he was doing. He could smell her perfume, not like a chemist's, but like some sort of flowers. That done it – he'd had to pull his jumper down over his cock. Not that it had a chance, he weren't stupid. Obvious what was on her life plans. Once she had what she wanted and no one couldn't stop her, she was blinding. And now no one stopped her, not ever.

He had a proper hard-on, now. Give it a few pulls, but then took his hand away. That'd be all he needed, for his mum to burst in, or for his guts to let him down. He looked up at the ceiling. Knew it so well now it was like his long-lost brother. Even spot the wrinkles, if you looked hard enough. Fitting on the light was called a rose. Would be, wouldn't it, when he was trying to think about something else. Trouble was, weren't much else to think about. He hoped she was all right. Spence said they'd found a ringer who'd hold his hands up to the blaze. Said if it all went sweet, Rosie weren't in no more trouble provided she kept her nose out. Said least the big geezer was good for distracting her. Probably hypnotized her with long words out of books. But life had to be lived, not read about. And if Spence was getting all matey with the cunt, he might end up trusting him that bit too far. Not that Ben'd say nothing, he weren't suicidal, but he'd feel a lot better if he could just see her for hisself.

She didn't know what she was doing here. Maybe she'd just turn round and walk away; she didn't have to knock, he'd never know. Some prat had smashed the bulb out at one end of the corridor; it was pretty dark to be standing here on her own. Better make a decision.

She'd told him to piss off when he'd rung. But there was something in his voice: desperation, maybe. Not that he'd begged, but the request sounded so urgent that as soon as she'd slammed down the 'phone, she'd changed her mind. Idiot. He probably wanted to tell her *face-to-face* that he didn't want to see her any more. But she was here now. Might as well knock.

'Rosie, it's . . . oh God.'

God what? Moves in mysterious ways?

She might as well have been a bailiff, to judge by Alex's expression. He still seemed worn out and stressed but at least he'd shaved, after a fashion, and was wearing clean clothes. Rosie had spent too long herself deciding what to wear; didn't want to seem to have dressed up, but couldn't pitch up looking like a slouch, either. In the end, she'd gone with her good Armani jeans, suede jacket, and knee-high boots. Not much of a heel.

'Uh . . . come in.' He made no attempt to kiss her.

'Thanks.' She followed him through the narrow hall to the living room. But something felt wrong, not the same. What was it? The smell, yes. The flat usually reeked of polish, but tonight it smelt like . . . like a laundry.

And that was why.

In the middle of the living room. An ironing board. Folded on an armchair, freshly pressed clothes. More clothes. Crumpled in a basket by the board. Things on hangers blocking the doorway to the kitchen.

'You taking in washing? Jesus, I know you earn a pittance, but this . . .' They were all women's clothes. All of them, as far as Rosie could see. A cotton blouse draped across the board, half ironed: arms and collar smooth, left breast pocket wrinkle-free, the rest waiting for attention. Alex had been pushing the iron into the creases of some other woman's clothes, creases made by someone else's body. Intimate, domestic act. 'What the hell . . . ?'

Alex unplugged the iron, and picked up the neat pile from the chair. He stood there, pathetic, then disappeared into the bedroom, returning empty-handed.

'I lost track of the time,' he said. 'I thought you weren't . . .'

So he'd been desperate to see her, then. God, she was a mug. That tremor in his voice, probably from too much bloody house-work.

'So what's with the Baths number? Or is this just another one of your hobbies?'

'Do you want a drink?'

'No, I don't want a drink. I want to know what I'm doing here.' She unzipped her bag. He passed her an ashtray.

'This isn't easy.'

She looked at him. Buggered if she'd ask him again.

'These clothes . . . Rosie, they belong to Louise. My wife.'

Chapter Ten

'So he walks in, and his flat's full of gear again – hi-fi, video, telly, the lot. Couldn't believe his fucking eyes, could he? Must of thought the geezer'd got religion, cos it was all the exact same stuff. And he never sussed it. Brains of a rocking horse.'

'How come it was the same stuff?' Mikey leaned across them to get a roll-mop.

'It was the same stuff, boy, cos we was the ones what took it in the first place. Cleaned him out. Then two month later, we put it back.'

Darren weren't saying nothing. Well childish, waste of time. What's the point of doing pretend jobs – there was enough to do, sorting this and that to make a few bob. Hadn't earned nothing serious in nine month, not out of the yard anyway. And Freddy had him collecting the Friday loan money door-to-door recent, like he was the tally man, cos people weren't paying otherwise. Lost a regular earner to that big firm, and all. Then yesterday, Charlie'd asked Darren if he'd knock out some smack. *Nice bit of bunce for your bin, easy money.* Stroll on. Felt more like smacking him one for idiotness. Spastic wanted to get in with the Soho racket now, spite that Freddy told him straight it was a nother league. Charlie thought the Boyds was the fucking Krays. Mrs Boyd, God rest her, should of drowned him at birth.

Picked up his pint, sat looking at it in his hand. Felt a bit off. Never helped, seeing that bird around again, what looked like Jill. *Goose walked over your grave.* See her from behind, and it was right hard not to put his hand out, touch her hair.

Hardly no one had hair that nice. Stupid bleeder he was, having a good old wallow down a memory lane what was always going to be closed in real life. But he was sick to death of now. Missed Rosie popping in here.

'You all right there, Spence?'

'Not so bad, mate. Yourself?'

That Alex was drawing her more to hisself, like he was saying he could give her stuff she couldn't get nowhere else, and she was believing it. Believing it. If she found out it was Sam Patterson going to take the rap, who was off talking to Alex all the time down the Centre, what'd she believe then? Straight away, she'd see. Spite that Freddy was making Patterson realize he never had no choices bout saying he done it, that never meant the social worker wouldn't fight in Patterson's corner. And that meant gainst The Mice. Gainst Darren. See how much she'd want to be with Alex then. And Ro weren't stupid, she'd know Patterson was why she weren't being hassled no more. Muscle watching her just at night now. Not counting *Alex*.

'One in there, boy?'

'Think I'm going to shoot off in a minute.'

Darren had to tell her bout her bloke's connection – it was, like, a sort of duty. Yeah it was handy, cos she'd leave the cunt, but it was still right. No, couldn't be bothered with his pint. Mikey'd said there was that film on telly, with that tall bird. Might give that a look instead.

'Your *wife*?'

Alex ran his hand over his face.

'Are you sure you don't want a drink?'

Rosie lit a cigarette. Her brain felt numb, as though it had already been drinking but had forgotten to send the signals to the rest of her body. She sat where the fresh ironing had been, feeling like a spare bit of skirt at a wedding; funny, she'd have expected that she would walk out, but her body and her brain really didn't seem to be connected at all. She couldn't even remember taking off her jacket, but there it was, on the arm of the chair.

'Wine,' she heard herself say.

Alex ducked under the clothes hanging in the doorway, to get to the kitchen. Cheap stuff, but not tacky: lemon blouse, soft green dress, black trousers. Tiny. Doll's clothes. Suddenly, size eight-to-ten seemed enormous; Rosie looked down at her thighs, and felt that they must belong to someone else, they were so huge. Her brain was wearing someone else's body. Alex came back into the room carrying two glasses of wine. Neither glass blue. His head brushed against a miniature skirt, sending it floating to the floor. He passed Rosie both glasses, and carefully hung the skirt back on the hanger. Was he doing it on purpose?

'I don't know where to start, really,' he said, taking his wine from her and sitting on the floor. Next to the ironing basket.

'Just start.' So I can get out of this, get on with my life.

'Right.' Alex took a deep breath. 'Four days ago, Louise turned up at the Centre.'

At the *Centre*? What, to dry out? Rosie held up her hand.

'Hold on a second, she's not here now, is she?' Taken in the poor little junkie, had he?

'No. God, no. She came to find me, to let me know she was all right.'

'Thoughtful of her.' What did *all right* mean? 'Couldn't she have sent you a postcard?' They're back together. Must be. Rosie took a gulp of her wine, seriously annoyed to find her hand shaking. Another thing her brain hadn't clued her up on.

'I . . . yeah, she could have done, I suppose. Old habits die hard.'

Well, clearly. Especially hard habits.

'Alex, I'm not being funny, but either you get to the point, or I leave now. Your call.'

His voice came out flat, like he'd been rehearsing how to say it, and hadn't settled on an interpretation. Rosie had heard

Miranda's voice get that anonymous quality many times when she was practising for a play in college.

'She wants us to try again,' he said.

'Right.' Get up and go. Now.

'No, I'm not going to get back with her. I'm with you, and even if I wasn't, I wouldn't.'

'I've heard it all, now. With me, are you?' She gave a sarky laugh. 'She either came back to say she was hunky dory, or to ask for another chance. Make your mind up.'

'She said it was to stop me worrying, then she said there was more to it. She sort of trapped me.'

'Thought you said she was insane?'

'She's better than she was. I imagined she'd been living rough, but she hadn't.' They looked at each other. Alex was in a lot of trouble; his eyes had tears in them, and he kept rubbing the back of his hand over his mouth. Rosie tried to take it all in, but whatever he said, there it was, the bloody ironing. How did she know it really was only four days ago that his wife had pitched up? What about all the times he'd supposedly stayed late seeing clients? What about that mercy dash in the middle of the night, who was that really to save? Anyway,

'Where is she?'

'In a B and B. The friend she was staying with moved away, and she didn't have anywhere to go. I'm just trying to help her get back on her feet.' Involuntarily, they both glanced down at Rosie's boots. She picked up her jacket and laid it across her lap. If she cried, she'd drown herself. 'Don't go,' he said. Low, hoarse.

'Why not? I hope you're not trying to say there's anything to stay for.'

'Rosie, please.' He pulled a hanky from his pocket, and blew his nose.

'What's the matter, babe? Not what you were expecting? Or wasn't I meant to find out?'

'I . . . what can I do?' Alex knelt in front of her chair.

So much for adoring her; so much for doing anything for her. Yeah, do anything so long as there was no one else to be doing it for instead. It all made sense now: why she was kept on the periphery of his life, why she'd never met any of his friends. He never even talked about them. Mentioned going for the odd drink after work, that's about it. And come to think of it, the names she had heard tended to be female. Maybe there was a whole string of them out there.

'Have you just got a general need to roll over for people, or what? How is that acceptable, exactly? What do you do, just tell me what you think I want to hear?'

'I'm shattered, I can't think straight. It was a real shock, her turning up like that. What I feel . . . felt for her is definitely in the past, I promise you that, but I couldn't have just thrown her on to the streets.'

'Especially not without nice clean clothes. Fuck off.'

'I was going to tell you. That's why I rang.'

'Is it, now? No, you're not on, babe.'

'It's not as though you offer anything even approaching commitment,' he burst out, his voice climbing too high. 'Not even provisionally. You can't claim you tell me everything I need to know, not even you can twist things that fucking much. For all I knew, you'd understand.'

'Well, I don't.' Rosie stood and put on her jacket. He thought the situations were *comparable*? 'And you know what's really sad? You've been such an idiot. You ask me round here, and all right, I tell you I won't come, but there had to be a chance I would. So what are you doing when I arrive? Her ironing. And frankly, babe, I don't think I'd want to be with someone that stupid.'

'No, I suppose you wouldn't.'

'Enjoy your housework.' She pointed to the basket. 'I'd do that cream one on a low setting if I were you. Synthetics can just shrivel right up.'

'Rosie . . .'

*   *   *

Darren sat staring at the crossbow on the back of the door. Lovely piece of work – you wouldn't get one like that now. His back was bothering him a bit. All this sitting. Getting a bit of a gut and all – nothing to speak of, but more'n he had a year ago. He could member the old man patting his own stomach, saying *Cost a lot of money that did, boy.* Might well of done, but it was funny how him and Rosie weren't never fat. Only bout three weeks to Christmas – that wouldn't help. Mum thought the idea was to buy up half Tescos, specially boxes of chocolates, and once you started . . . He was a bugger for peanuts and all. Then there was the fights to look forward to, with Mum going into one with Rosie where she wouldn't eat Christmas pudding and mince pies. Made her right, they was horrible, but couldn't she shove them down once a year?

Through the office window, see someone come into the yard. Yeah, it was her. Darren looked at his watch – only twenty minutes late. She picked her way round the pipes, pulling a face when she nearly got her foot caught on a roll of mesh. Weren't exactly dressed suitable.

Rosie come in, moved a pile of dirty books off the other chair and sat down, crossing her legs. He felt a bit funny bout the books, but she never even looked see what they was. Not like her to miss a trick. Didn't look too good – big bags under her eyes, few spots on her chin, and a lot of slap, covering up fuck knows what else. Hair looked all stiff and all, like she'd gone mental with the hairspray, and one of her nails was broke, bad. She just sat there, picking at her fingers. Darren felt in his jacket, began to put one together. Light, though – if Rosie was in a state, draw could give her the fear. He put in the roach, shook it down, sparked up.

'There are. Go easy. Nice bit of Rocky, that.'

'Mood I'm in I wouldn't care if it was shit home grown, long as it did something.' She dragged on the joint, held the smoke down for ages, then dragged again afore anything come out. The joint was half gone fore she handed it over. 'So why d'you summon me?'

'This ain't easy, girl.' Darren bit the inside of his cheek, stop the grin coming out. 'It's got percussions.' Rosie touched her spots. She never said nothing. 'Thing is, the fire,' Darren went on. 'Turns out, it was Sam Patterson.'

'Was it, now? Okay.' She nodded. 'You brought me out of the office to tell me that?'

'And . . . you ain't going to like this. But, Patterson's been going up the Centre for a while now, talking to your bloke. Sorry, doll.'

Rosie made a funny sound, a kind of pushed-out laugh.

'Daz, are you trying to tell me who I can see and who I can't? Because if you are, you've got another think coming. Just leave me out of this. I don't want to know.'

'Turn it in. All I meant was—'

'Not interested.' She was wild now, tapping her nails against his empty mug and shaking her head, just that tiny bit. He often thought she got that off someone, but he couldn't get the picture straight in his head of who it was. Half being careful crumbling dope into a joint and half keep on watching her, he had to stop hisself reaching over to hold her little hand. She'd call him a bastard, and pull away. But spite the temper she looked so . . . what's the word? Vul something. Vulble? Like all her nerves was on the outside, and anyone touching her even right soft would hurt so bad she'd scream. Was keep seeing the geezer so important to her?

'Since when d'you let any of them get one over on you?' he said. Rosie closed her eyes. When she opened them, it was like she'd been somewhere else. His heart turned over. She looked so sad.

'Are you going to light that, or what?'

'Since when d'you let any of them get one over on you?'

Rosie watched him crumble dope into the joint. She scratched at a paper cut on her hand. Once, to answer your question, sweetheart. She closed her eyes. *I've had enough of you now.* Or, to be strictly accurate, dozens of times, but only one man.

Sling your hook now.
You're spoiling yourself, you are, now.
I've had enough of you now.
Had enough of you.
Had enough.

Being sent to her room, making out she didn't care. Curling up on her bed with a book, to stop herself thinking about it. Until the day he took himself off, instead of sending her away. Never heard it again.

'Are you going to light that, or what?' she said. But that was just something to say, to stop Daz looking at her with pity. She kept opening her mouth, and words were coming out, but she wasn't listening to her own voice, to what either of them were saying. Sam Patterson. Oh shit. No. And Daz thought that meant he was going to get what he wanted. He'd never liked Alex. But of course, he had what he wanted, if he only knew it.

The hairdresser was a good idea, even if it had come from Daz. Garry had fitted her in with a seven o'clock, and pretty little Liz did the colour, her voice merging with the head massage, soothing, familiar. Cream leather trousers, her Gaultier jacket, the boots she'd bought with Randa. Nearly hadn't worn those; they'd been charged with something that had fizzled out without even a whimper. But she was damned if she'd let that bastard tell her what to wear. Least William's Civil had gone well: that supercilious Houton demanded costs, Rosie argued, and he then had to hear, *How can it be you to whom I award costs? Counsel, you have lost.* Only three hundred, but victory was the point. Stuffing the middle classes was what she needed right now.

She felt nervous in the cab. Ridiculous, but there it was. Probably still paranoid from the smoke. Hard to imagine what he'd look like. Hard to imagine how she'd react. She dug in her bag for her mirror, to touch up her lipstick. Squinted at her reflection, what she could see of it. Not too bad. A big improvement on the last couple of days, anyway.

He opened the door himself; she hadn't expected that. Oh, the poor bloke. The stitches were out, leaving puckered welts down his cheek. He'd lost weight too, and he hadn't had an ounce of spare on him in the first place. He smiled when he saw her, but it wasn't his old ferrety-faced grin. More of a skew-whiff attempt that came out like a grimace.

'All right, Ben?' She put her arms round his neck and hugged him, hard. Against her cheek, she could feel his scars.

'Blimey, think I'll get cut up every day, if that's what I get for it,' he said. Even his voice was different; his words came out tighter as though they too had been slashed and stitched back together. She tried to laugh, and kissed him lightly on the lips.

'You going to keep me out here smooching on the doorstep?'

'Depends if you're going to keep on with it indoors.'

'Don't push it.'

He led her down the hall into Cath's living room. She hadn't been here for years. It still smelt the same: chip fat and Lemon Pledge, with a hint of Femme. She settled into the armchair, watched Ben open the big, white cabinet and start fussing around with bottles and glasses. He gave her the good stuff, she noticed: Glenfiddich. With his back to her, she could see that his jeans were hanging off him; he didn't seem to have any sort of bum left at all. Bless him, putting the water in a little jug. He was like a boy on a first date, desperately trying to get it all perfect; her heart hurt for him, with his poor face and his bones all sticking out, but there was no way she was going to give him a pity fuck. Not even to spite Alex.

He sat on the settee opposite her, and picked up his B&H from the coffee table. She shook her head. From the way he put one in his mouth, careful to balance it, Rosie realized he was having a hard time moving his lips properly. Please, don't let him dribble his drink down his chin.

Rosie was wracking her brains for something to say, and Ben was just looking at her. With his marked-up face, if Rosie

hadn't known him, he'd have given her the creeps. But she
made herself look back at him: that was why she was here.
She had to believe that Sam Patterson was preventing her from
ending up like Ben. Yet even as she traced the scars with her
stare, she knew it wouldn't have happened. The landlord was
grieving, angry, bitter, but he wasn't likely to be kamikaze.
Down deep in her worst moments of fear, Rosie had never
really felt that the threat was fatal. Maybe Sam . . . just because
he looked as though he'd have a job striking a match, didn't
mean he hadn't done it. Guilty until proven innocent. No.

'I had your big law book.'

'What?' For a second, Rosie thought Ben's injuries had gone
to his head.

'You know, when you was at that law school place. You left
a big book at your mum's – I took it home. You'd written your
name in it, and scribbled things, and underlined stuff.'

'You took my book home? Why?'

'You'd written all over it.'

'Yeah, you said . . . oh, right. Long time ago, sweetie. Even
you were quite young then.' Shit, don't let him make a declaration.
Rosie remembered having Jimmy Oaks's history book in her bag
when she was about eleven. In her bedroom, with a chair pushed
against the door, she'd taken it out and traced his tiny writing
with her fingers. He was fifteen, and well out of her league. But
Ben must have been twenty-six when he'd done the same. And
to admit it now . . . 'Sorry, Ben, but don't go all nostalgic on
me. I don't do mushy stuff, you know that.'

'Yeah, think I'm getting a bit morbid, cooped up here for
weeks. Going back me own place the weekend. Maybe I'll go
down The Mice tomorrow, get back into it gradual.'

'Good idea.' She nearly offered to go with him, but she
couldn't. Thankfully, he didn't ask. He never had asked. 'Be a
doll and do us another little drink, will you?'

No note. Just the poem. Alex, of course. The words felt vaguely
familiar; Rosie counted the lines: fourteen, yes, a sonnet,

probably a Shakespeare sonnet. She went to the shelves, took down her Complete Shakespeare. Here you go, sonnet number 58, apparently. Must have taken some research; Alex wasn't even a fiction sort of person, let alone a poetry sort, much less a Shakespeare sort. Ossified by his Richard three, Henry seven, Henry eight. Her hulking Philistine. She read the poem again.

> That god forbid that made me first your slave
> I should in thought control your times of pleasure,
> Or at your hand th'account of hours to crave,
> Being your vassal bound to stay your leisure.
> O, let me suffer, being at your beck,
> Th'imprisoned absence of your liberty,
> And, patience-tame to sufferance, bide each check
> Without accusing you of injury.
> Be where you list, your charter is so strong
> That you yourself may privilege your time
> To what you will; to you it doth belong
> Yourself to pardon of self-doing crime.
> > I am to wait, though waiting so be hell,
> > Not blame your pleasure, be it ill or well.

Don't give me that.

A reversal of culpability: in whose eyes would the injury constitute an assault on his feelings? How could she exonerate herself, when the so-called crime had precedent only in his head? And who'd been bloody waiting; it was days since she'd seen Alex. The whole thing was an inversion, another case of a man offering something that was really about him. Not her, at all. In those terms, refusing to posit an accusation was in itself an accusation; he should be the defendant here. And if he were her vassal, he was that mad She-Bitch-From-Hell's vassal, too. Words were too easy for people like them. Yeah, he was great on the big gestures: *Walk all over me. I adore you. Let me suffer.* But when it came down to it, there was nothing to back them up. Words. Where were the things they stood for in all this?

Rosie threw the big cushion on to the floor, pulled off her shoes, and sat down. She read the poem again, then put it on the little table and lit a cigarette. Smoking way too much at the minute, and that morning's hangover was still hanging over. Nerves totally shot. Couldn't concentrate in the meeting this afternoon, when she'd been arguing that it should be she alone who took over on the Hopkins case; unsurprisingly, William hadn't seemed convinced. Yesterday, over two months after the event, Charlie Boyd had been questioned briefly and released. No charge, none pending. So far, it looked like Sam wasn't in the minds of the Old Bill, but that could only be a matter of more time. And now Sam's knight errant was trying to get back onside. It was too much to deal with; his coming here was one burden too many. The only thing it had going for it was the fact that if she saw Alex, Daz wouldn't be able to think he'd had anything to do with their breaking up.

The images you construct of people disobey you; not simply the people themselves, whose own idea of their reality stubbornly conflicts with yours, but even your dreams of them won't bloody stay put. In place of Alex as the one man capable of bridging the divide, Rosie now saw him as an emotional chancer. He'd squandered her image of him with that ironing; all that was left was her derisory *I was adored once, too.*

She wanted a drink, but it was way too much of an effort to go over to the cupboard. Or to put the telly on, or music, or dig out one of her old comfort-food books, *Brideshead Revisited* or *Little Women*. Too much of an effort to do anything except try not to think, and without the aid of any narcotics. And occasionally to glance at the sonnet.

The buzzer went. She got up, and crossed the room to the intercom; it occurred to her that the anxiety was gone, and she had to acknowledge that release had for her a proper name.

'Rosie, it's me. Can I come up? Just for five minutes.' Alex. Of course. Didn't usually bother with the entry-'phone; like most people she knew, he could get round it. Five minutes? Was that all he wanted of her? Great, just great. Although it wouldn't take that long to tell him he could sod off. Typical, giving her just enough time to digest her mail before pitching up. He'd probably rung Polly, to see what time she'd left. Efficient even in defeat. She checked her face in the hall mirror. A bit drawn, but okay. Pity about the work clothes, but at least he couldn't think she'd dressed especially for him.

He'd made an effort: the shave was as close as it ever got, he was clean, wearing his new black jeans, and carrying, instead of the usual Sainsbury's number, a plain blue plastic bag that probably contained chocolates and wine or some such corny offering. Rosie was annoyed with herself for being able to see how attractive he was. If he smiled and showed those bloody dimples, she'd have to kill him. Alex dropped his gaze, then looked straight at her. No, not this time, boy; you'll have to work harder than that. He put the bag next to the settee, and took off his coat. Then he was stuffed, because he usually hung it in the hall.

'Oh, give it here.' She slung it over the back of the settee, kicking the cushion and her shoes out of the way at the same time. 'Do you want a drink? I was about to have one anyway.'

'Thanks. Vodka would be great.'

She poured the drinks, gave Alex his (no lemon), and sat on the armchair. The poem was still lying on the table. Shit. Should have moved it. Alex continued to stand. He said nothing. She was buggered if she'd help. He swallowed his vodka, and put the glass on the table.

Then he took off his jumper.

And his tee-shirt.

He gave her one of his intense looks.

Rosie stared. What did he think he'd be getting here?

He bent down, unlaced his trainers, and took those off as well, and his socks.

Straightening, he began to unbutton his jeans.

'That's enough, Alex. Stop it right there.'

She could hardly believe what she was seeing. What the hell did he think he was doing? But there was a part of her that was excited by the gesture. Careful, she reminded herself, you know he's good at gestures. Alex did up his flies, and stood there for a second. Plan went wrong, did it, babe? But he picked up the bag he'd brought with him, and gave it to her. Then he knelt in front of her chair.

'I've got something special for you.'

Rosie opened the carrier. Candles, and matches. And a Paradiso bag. She emptied it all on to the floor. A cane. Two wristbands with pointed studs. And a collar. So this was the deal, was it? *Buy one.* She fingered one of the wristbands. Those studs were seriously sharp. There was something else, which had rolled under the larger bag. She felt for it. A plain gold band. Heavy, thick. Made to fit a man. It had to be his wedding ring.

'I messed up, big time, I know that. But I'm asking you to forgive me, Rosie. Please, just give me another chance. I'll do anything.'

She put the ring on to her thumb. It was still way too big.

'And bringing me a few toys is supposed to make it okay, is it? I don't think so, baby.' She crammed the rest of the stuff back into the carrier.

'I know. I just wanted to give you something, something you'd like, something you wouldn't get given by anyone else.'

'Where is she?' Rosie twisted the ring on her thumb, and tapped it against her teeth.

'Still in the B and B. But I know she has to find somewhere else.'

'And you have to help her.'

'No. Not if you don't want me to, no. I really couldn't have seen her on the streets, but she's clean, and got a bit of work, and—'

'That's really nice, Alex. Why don't we have a little chat about how well she's doing? I'd right like that.' Clean. So the visit to the Centre had been purely personal.

'I'm sorry, I was just trying to make you see what's important to me.' He looked hard at her. 'And that's you.'

'So she isn't?'

'She was, you know that. I thought she was the one, but
. . . bollocks, I'm doing it again, aren't I?'

'Oh, yeah.' Rosie watched as he took her cigarettes, lit one
and passed it to her. He was breathing heavily, she could hear
it, and see it in the way his chest moved. This was an invitation. Well, if that was what he thought he wanted. She drew
on the cigarette a couple of times, then ground the glow into
his nipple. He flinched, badly, but didn't draw away. And she
couldn't help getting some satisfaction when she noticed that
he was starting to get a hard-on. 'That means sod all,' she said.
'In fact, it's very far from all right.'

'All I'm asking is that you give me another chance.'

'No man can serve two mistresses, Alex. Read your Bible.'

'I realize that. And I promise you, I only want you. Anything
else seems absurd. I'll do anything to make you believe that.
Anything.'

'Anything. Like trawling through Shakespeare's love poems,
knowing you'd be bound to find something appropriate?' Still,
he did have the guts to nod, biding the check. And at least he
hadn't gone through some dreadful schmaltzy anthology.
'Anything? A divorce?'

'That goes without saying.' He was begging her with his
eyes, but what happened next time little Louise had a crisis?
Or some other woman whom he felt compelled to help? It was
bad enough that his job gave him opportunities to put his own
needs last, although she didn't think he was sad enough to
eroticize that, at least. But then, who knew? And of course
there was still Sam between them. She picked up her drink
and drained it.

'You can get us both a refill, while I think about it.' If she
let him back in now, could she ever trust him? Every time his
'phone or pager went, would she be thinking it was Louise,
summoning him to her helpless side. The bloody power of the

vulnerable. And who was paying for this B and B? Alex didn't have much money, but she was certain he had more than his *wife*. 'Does she know about me, Alex?'

He put her glass on the table, and hesitated before sitting at her feet.

'She . . . no.'

'Why not?'

'Look, there's too much I've been responsible for. If I present as someone who's in a good relationship, then that might send her . . .'

'So all this, the grand disrobing and the ring and the promises that you'll do anything, mean what? I'm so important to you, am I, that you keep me a bloody secret? I think you'd better get dressed.'

'I'll tell her.'

'Jesus, if you haven't already, what does that tell me? That if I turned you down, there was always her to go back to? Or were you planning to see us both?'

'No, of course not.'

'No, of course not. I thought I told you to get dressed.' Keeping her face impassive, Rosie looked on as Alex picked up his tee-shirt but continued to hold it against his chest. 'And take your shit with you and all,' she said at last, thrusting the bag at him. Alex's ring was still on her thumb; she slipped it off and flung it on to the carpet.

Briefly, Alex looked as though he might tell her to fuck off herself, but then he nodded. He put his tee-shirt on the table, pulled on his socks, picked his top up again, and dropped to his knees, looking for the ring. Rosie could see it, just in front of the table; evidently, he couldn't.

'All I do with you is mess up,' he said, towards the floor. 'Sometimes, I don't even know what it is I'm meant to have done. But it's all just words, Rosie. I mess up with words. Yeah, of course I should have told you about Louise . . .'

'Ironing isn't just words.'

'No, no it isn't. But that was just a really big mistake. I

mean, not just, it was. But everything else, I've . . . well, like you'd say, I've called it wrong.'

She saw him spot the ring.

He slid his hand across the carpet to retrieve it; quickly, Rosie stretched out her leg, covering the ring with the ball of her foot. He raised his head to look up into her face. She almost smiled. But.

'Did anyone know about me? Friends, people you work with, your family. Anyone.'

'I've occasionally mentioned in passing I've got a girlfriend. I know what it looks like on paper, but I wasn't keeping you a secret, I just don't talk about personal stuff much. When Louise went, it was all a bit public, so I'm careful now. We lost a lot of our friends because of the way she, you know.'

'But the truth of the matter is, most people didn't even know you were seeing anyone.'

'No, I suppose not.'

'Like to keep your options open, do you?'

Alex sat back on his heels, the bag beside him, his tee-shirt on his lap. His chest was faintly scarred, and his nipple was beginning to blister under the black residue of her cigarette. She twisted round to reach for her drink, and took a long swallow. Couldn't help wondering what those bruises on his thighs looked like now. Even though she was equally tempted calmly to say *Piss off*. And mean it.

'Rosie, the times I've spent with you, when it's good, are the best times I've ever had. Even thinking about you, never mind seeing you, are some of the best times I've had. I don't want anyone else. I know you find that hard to believe, but it's true. What I get from you, I've never had. With anybody.'

'But no one knows you had it with me. And what don't I know about you, babe? It's all part of the same thing.'

'No, it's not. I'll walk around in a tee-shirt saying *I love Rosie Spence* if it'll make you happy. But I can't change what's gone before. I wish I could, but I can't.'

The wedding ring felt hard; hard but small.

He'd still lied to her. He'd still rushed round after Louise the minute she cocked her tiny little finger. She couldn't run the risk of coming second to anyone, let alone his wife, even temporarily. It was too dangerous.

'I've got hold of something,' he said to her silence. 'I've been a bit slow with it, but I've got there in the end. As far as sex goes, I think it's a privilege to serve you like that. You can do anything you like to me, and I'll thank you.'

'Really?' Yeah, great on the big gestures.

'Really. I love it, because you do. I just want the chance to show you what you do to me. Should've stayed away probably, looked round for someone safer. But I couldn't, that's not what I want.' He shook his head. 'I can't go back to anything else now.'

Could she? Rosie looked down at Alex; he was good, but how good?

'Kiss my foot,' she said.

'Which . . . Rosie, which one?'

'I think you know that, don't you?'

He bent over her, and touched his lips to the hidden ring. 'I love you,' he said against the nylon. He raised his head.

'Who said anything about love?' Rosie folded her arms. Alex shrugged, helplessly.

'I'm not presuming anything here.' He stretched himself out at her feet, and turned over so that he was lying on his back. He must know she was on the verge of telling him to go; he'd left himself completely open to humiliation. Rosie looked down at him. He gave the briefest of acknowledgements, barely a flicker of his eyelids. But she understood.

As she pressed her foot into his face, she realized.

She was in love with him. And he probably knew it.

Chapter Eleven

She'd brought him, after all. And dressed him, to judge from the pristine chinos and leather jacket. Rather a nice Paul Smith shirt, too. Elizabeth hadn't seen Rosie in that frock before: soft green leather halter-neck (from Whistles?), with shoes the same colour. A pre-Christmas shopping trip, no doubt. Well, well, a kept man; she couldn't believe it had been an exchange of gifts. No wonder Rosie had been incommunicado for over a fortnight; they'd obviously been making up.

'Don't you both look fabulous.'

'That was the general idea, Lisbeth. Although it's a filthy night out there, doesn't look like we'll get a white Christmas. Perhaps you expected us to pitch up in jeans and anoraks?'

'Perish the thought. There's bubbly in the kitchen, Jack insisted, he has a vulgar streak a mile wide that man, or wine, or spirits at the bar. Another whim of my husband's, I'm afraid,' she added to Alex. 'But I expect you'd prefer a beer?'

'Why?' he said. It was becoming cumulatively clear what he and Rosie had in common.

'Why indeed. Well, if you would, there's some Grolsch in the fridge.'

'See you've hit the bottle already,' said Rosie. Elizabeth was about to protest, then she saw the joke and brought her hand up to her freshly dyed hair, feeling self-conscious. Alex laughed and made his way across the room, without staying to ask where the kitchen might be.

'So it's all back on, then?'

'Who said it was off?'

'Not you, that's for certain, but two or three weeks ago you looked like hell, darling. I think I'll check he's not trying to find a drink in the walk-in wardrobe or something.' She followed Alex out to the kitchen, where he was being talked at by Aimless Angus and his pal.

'Apparently Rosie Spence has arrived. He came in with her.' AA waved his champagne flute at Elizabeth. 'Might be my lucky night, tonight. You don't know her, do you, Geoffrey?'

'No.' The pal shook his head. 'Who is she?'

'More like *what* is she,' said AA. Elizabeth shrugged at Alex. But she had no intention of stopping this; she was having far too much fun. Alex poured two glasses of champagne. He wasn't going to let on, was he? Fabulous. 'Crumpet, that's what,' AA continued, 'bit on the thin side, no knockers to speak of, but what an arse. Knows how to move it, too. Once saw her leaning across the bar in the club, and was tempted to slip it to her then and there, from behind.' He mimed the action, bleating with laughter. 'Not exactly one of us, but that's entirely the point. Even makes up for the knockers.'

Alex turned round, slowly, and put his great paw on the buffoon's shoulder.

'Careful,' he said pleasantly, 'I don't want to have to take this outside.'

AA looked as shocked as his formless face would allow, and ushered the pal out of the room. Elizabeth went after them, smiling over her shoulder at Alex. He didn't return the smile.

William had pushed his way through the crowd, and was dutifully kissing Rosie's cheek. Elizabeth decided that Rosie needn't know how her honour had been defended.

'Was that your chap walked off just before?' asked William. 'I'd keep a closer eye on him than that, dear. He's positively animal.'

'What is it about parties that makes you give Billy Butlin a run for his money?' said Rosie. But she was pleased, any fool could see that. If there had been trouble in paradise a couple of weeks ago, it had certainly been worked through. Probably in bed. Disappointing, in a way; it wasn't often Elizabeth got a real chance to go Rosie baiting. The gallant reappeared then, carrying the two glasses of bubbly.

'William, this is Alex,' said Rosie. 'William's one of the senior partners in my firm.' They shook hands. Rosie took a cigarette from her tiny beaded bag, and waited; Alex dug into his pocket, produced a lighter, and held the flame out for her. Old-fashioned courtesy? Not if that lunch in the club was anything to go by. Elizabeth felt her stomach tighten.

'And what is Alex?' said William.

'Mine,' replied Rosie, complacently, and laughed.

'And apart from that, I work in drug rehab.'

'Ah, on the side of the underclass,' said William. 'You won't find many soul-mates amongst this company.'

'Isn't a question of sides. I don't have many well-off clients, sorry, *customers*, because we're a charitable institution. What about detox places like the Priory? Holiday homes for the rich and famous. And I bet a good few of the people here tonight'll be slipping off to do the odd line.' Again, he spoke pleasantly, but Elizabeth noticed that he straightened his shoulders, as though squaring up for a fight. Quite amusing, given William's predilections.

'Casting aspersions on my guests?' she said, lightly touching Alex's arm.

'Derrida talks about a Greek word that means both cure and poison,' William asserted pompously, pinching the bridge of his nose and blinking rapidly.

'*Pharmakon*, yeah,' said Alex. 'But it's obvious, one relative to the other, the only difference is of degree. It's disingenuous to make a big deal of it. Derrida's a tosser.' Extraordinary. How would he know about that? And Rosie was practically beaming, the lines round her eyes deepening as she looked at him. Just for a second, Elizabeth thought she glimpsed what it was men saw in her friend.

'What doesn't kill us makes us stronger,' Rosie said. Alex grinned.

'So this is the famous Alex.' Randa hoved into view, chiffon scarves trailing, carrying a tumbler of something-with-orange. 'I'm the BF. Not that you'd know that, given that I've never been allowed to clap eyes on you.' Ostentatiously, Randa looked Alex up and down. 'Do we think he'll do?' she said to Elizabeth. 'Walker or leading man?'

'In no universe is Alex anybody's walker,' said Rosie sharply, slipping her arm around his waist. It wasn't often one saw Rosie Spence protecting anybody. Not *pro bono*, anyway. She liked to say she was always keen to help those more fortunate than herself.

'Is Rosie bringing you to our weekend?' William asked Alex. 'I've just got hold of a modest retreat in rural Gloucestershire. We could talk some more about French philosophy.'

'Rosie won't go,' said Miranda. 'She wouldn't survive five minutes outside of walking distance of a Clinique counter and an Oddbins.'

'Damn straight.' Rosie put her hand on her bony little hip, looking for all the world like an expensive hooker. Time for a diversion. Elizabeth tapped Susie on the shoulder.

'What are we paying you for, darling? My neighbours' teenager,' she said to the others.

Susie came rushing back with a tray, like a dumpy serving wench (if serving wenches ever wore skirts that barely covered their bottoms). William and Randa helped themselves to asparagus rolls. A fearful waste; no doubt Randa would puke hers up later. Alex raised his eyebrows at Rosie. She nodded, scarcely perceptibly. He chose the smallest, neatest roll and held her glass while she ate. The girl began to walk away.

'Hang on,' said Rosie, licking her fingers and taking back her drink. Alex grabbed a handful of food for himself. It was like watching a dance: difficult to decide whether there were choreographed moves involved, or whether the dancers were merely in tune with one another.

'I'd like one,' said William. Rather wistfully. But whether he meant another roll or someone to choose one for him, Elizabeth couldn't tell.

The cab protected them, but it didn't do a lot for the poor cow on the pavement as it sped through one of the wider puddles. Rosie laughed.

'You're a nasty piece of work,' said Alex, squeezing her hand.

She looked out at the deceptive shine on the Bloomsbury streets, at chip wrappers and Coke cans made less incongruous, turned into distant boats in the yellow half-lit night. It was almost lovely.

'D'you reckon they'll notice we've left?' Alex asked, as they drove past Holborn tube.

'Yeah, no question. I'm usually one of the last to leave those things, and I'm usually well gone. Original good time girl, that's me. That's why I get invited.' Performing seal, balancing middle-class balls. Or sometimes kicking them. But surely it couldn't be long now before she got her career-defining case; then maybe she'd be the one throwing the fish. 'You had a few admirers tonight. Mind you, I'd've thrown a pink fit if any of them had tried anything.'

'They wouldn't have dared.' He brought her hand to his lips. 'Have we got any bread in? I quite fancy some toast.'

We? She had, yeah.

'We haven't got any white, you'll have to make do.'

Bastard was still grinning as they pulled up outside her building; he could bloody well pay, then. Rosie struggled with the door. Flinging it open at last, she exclaimed, loudly. She just couldn't resist. Especially knowing there were no minders to watch her movements, no one to report back to her brother. It was over; this was her first night of freedom.

'I used to love doing this as a kid!' Jumping out of the cab, kicking at the water, feeling thirty-three years of autumn leaves and summer beaches. No, come to think of it she hadn't done anything even remotely like that in the last twenty-five, but she ought to have done.

'Careful, love.' Alex got out of the other door, walking round the cab to the kerb, skirting the puddle.

'Why?' She splashed out the other side, and unlocked the security door.

Rosie squelched into the flat, taking off her coat. Alex hung his jacket in the hall; she switched on the small lamp in the living room.

'Christ, look at the state of me,' she said, putting Macy Gray on the CD player. 'Three hundred quid, and they get ruined first wear.' She turned, and raised her eyebrows. Was he following her drift? 'Look.'

'They're covered.' Alex bent to examine the foot she'd raised for inspection. 'Filthy.'

'Streets of London, babe.' Rubbing the sole on the carpet. 'I should move to suburbia.'

'Yeah, sure you should. Do you want me to get a cloth?'

'No.'

'If you take them off, I'll see what I can do.'

'No.' She smiled. Funny how smiling could be so catching.

Alex took a swig from the bottle of regular Coke that was now inevitably resident in her flat. He'd probably buy it with extra sugar, if you could get such a thing.

'Well, you're stuffed then, aren't you?' Wiping the back of his hand across his mouth.

'No.'

'No?'

'I seriously doubt it.'

'Rosie . . .'

'Mm?'

'What, you think you've got the right . . .'

'Don't you?'

Alex shook his head.

'Come and sit down,' he said.

'If they stay dirty, they'll stain,' she said, getting comfortable in the armchair, leaning back into it and crossing her legs.

'I know, love, but what's the alternative?'

'Now there's a question.' No question; he'd do it. He had that lazy look on his face, the one that said he'd do what she wanted, in his own time. But the point was, this was *her* time. For now. 'And I'm sure there must be an answer,' she added. 'You just need to find it, before I'm forced to throw them away. And my mum brought me up never to waste anything.'

'Sensible lady.' He crouched on the floor, and stroked her ankle.

'I'm clean, Alex. It isn't me that needs attention.' He'd do it, for sure. But even though she'd known he would, the knowledge hadn't prepared her for the feeling as he ran his tongue over the leather.

It might as well have been over her naked skin.

He'd killed her for love, that was his claim. Murder cases weren't within her usual remit, nor had this one come out of her standard client base, but William insisted she at least look at it. Rosie read the statement again: the man tortured his wife because she loved someone else. Tossing the file on to the little table, Rosie curled back into the settee, warming her fingers on her mug. She didn't want this case, didn't want the man to become 'the client', to become 'Richard'. Didn't want to defend violence as love, to delimit sexual feeling by isolating, privileging, possession. *Crime passionnel*; a misnomer. Passion shouldn't be criminalized, for God's sake, and torture shouldn't be excused by passion.

Rosie put down the mug, rubbed her feet. She scratched at the red polish on her toenails, watching it come off in little flakes; so what, Alex was working tonight. Maybe even seeing Sam. *Want, love, need*: the sexiest words in the language. And the most ambiguous. *Each man kills the thing he loves*; if that were true, what would be the point of the struggle to stay alive? She'd tell William to stick the bloody case.

Louise, Daz, Sam: a thin protective film preventing the final penetration of Rosie's pain into Alex's pain. And she didn't need to add this case to that film. It wasn't the same, it wasn't.

That wife didn't consent, and that husband didn't love. Nothing
freely given. Not the same thing at all. Although consent was
no defence in law: in the infamous Spanner case, defending
sado-masochism as consensual had been denied on the grounds
of *public policy*. Rosie even thought she remembered that one
of the defendants had been convicted solely for aiding and
abetting his own assault. Ben . . . Shit. Suddenly, Rosie had a
flashback to that open wound in his cheek, to his scarcely
conscious murmurs of pain. She picked more viciously at her
nail polish. No, Ben wasn't a sacrifice; Rosie and Alex would
have discovered what they were even without that trigger.
Surely they would. And she was buggered if she'd let what
they had be cheapened by defending its parodic manifestation.
The case wasn't winnable, anyway.

Mum'd brung out the table, and put a cloth on. He'd had to
find her a new dinner set and all – just for the geezer what
Rosie shouldn't of been seeing. Why was she still? The house
mostly smelled right good: cooking meat, and the onions in
the potatoes, and that spice Mum'd started sticking in her apple
pies, after she see it on that cooking programme. Darren couldn't
think of when the last time she'd done an apple pie for him
was. Fat cunt got the lot, though, didn't he? Not that he could
shout, but that weren't the point. Pity she done cabbage – even
the other smells couldn't of hidden that horrible stink. She took
her apron off, give it Darren. Underneath, she had on one of
them flowery things what looked like curtains, but she'd had
her hair done, put on the old lipstick. She wouldn't never make
someone off the telly, but she looked nice, like a proper mum.
 'Get us a little sherry, there's a good boy. And pop the wire-
less on, find us some music. If you turn a light on under the
blue pan, not too high, then that's that job jobbed.'
 Darren was only halfway down his bottle of lager when they
heard her key in the lock. She come in, leading Alex by his
hand. And she looked the best he'd seen her in weeks.
Well-smart trouser suit, sort of tight and not tight, make-up

just right, green shoes what he hadn't seen afore, and a big smile. Hadn't seen that much recent, neither.

'Nice to meet you, Mrs Spence.'

'Call me Pat, dear.' Her telephone voice. 'I was beginning to think Rosie'd made you up. When she was a little girl, she told her teacher she had an horse, what we kept in the back garden. And he believed her! I never knew till he asked me how it was. An horse in Wessex Street. Be truthful, it tickled me. She always was a good little fibber, butter wouldn't melt.'

'Mu-um.' But she was laughing. She'd smartened the boyfriend up – Darren weren't stupid, he could recognize Rosie's tastes. Lovely bit of leather, must of cost her a packet. What's she think she was doing? When there was loads of them what'd buy her what she wanted, and she'd never have to put her hand in her pocket. Darren'd get her gear, anything she fancied. But not for that Alex.

'There's some red in there.' Rosie give Mum a carrier. 'I did get some flowers and all, but I've managed to leave them indoors.' Talking too fast. 'What're we having?' She sat on the settee, and patted the cushions for Alex to sit next to her.

'Roast lamb. You like roast, Alex?'

'Yeah, I love it.'

'A big man needs his fuel.' Mum smiled and nodded, all pleased. 'Pity you can't talk her into eating more. And we've got smoked salmon for starters.'

Starters? Of a Friday? They never hardly even had starters on Sunday dinner, less Darren brung over a claw from the stall. Bleeding Christmas weren't for a few days yet.

'I'd have got you a black pepper grinder, if I'd known,' said Rosie.

'What's wrong with my pepper?'

Rosie wouldn't of got out of that one if it weren't for that Alex being here. But she'd brought Darren one of them grinders, one time, and he had to make her right. That sort of pepper was better with smoked salmon.

*   *   *

Could notice Rosie was making an effort – eat all her fish, and
took quite a bit of dinner. She put some beetroot on her plate,
and offered Alex the bowl. They was both trying not to laugh
– what was so funny bout beetroot? Only thing the boyfriend
never touched, as it goes. Mum was right on form – her lamb
come out handsome, so she was well happy with herself,
specially when Alex said it was sactly like he liked it. Any
further up her arsehole and he'd disappear.

'And we heard all this squeaking, coming from his room.
So I goes in there, and under his bed, guess what we found?
Go on, have a guess.'

'Mice?' said Alex.

'Oh no, I'd've died. No, kittens, family of kittens. Wild ones,
what d'you call them?'

'Feral?'

'That's it. He'd only picked them up somewhere. Been there
days. He'd been feeding them milk from one of them things
you get at school, in science. D'you remember that, Darren?'

Yeah, and he membered bout the old man chucking them
in the river, and all. Very fucking funny. Still made his gut
hurt to think bout it.

'Here, I got Ben and me tickets for York Hall – we ain't
been for ages.'

'He'll enjoy that. Mint sauce, Alex? Mind you, I always used
to like the boxing.'

Yeah, till Dad took you that schoolboys' match and you had
to be brung out in tears.

Alex took four more potatoes, more gravy. Where's he put
it all?

'When I was a girl, we used to go up York Hall every Friday
night for a bath.' Mum couldn't seem to shut up. Looking at
Alex, like she was letting just him in on something. Like Darren
and Rosie hadn't heard this stuff a million times. 'Used to get
a little sliver of carbolic, and a towel like a board. Could use
them to cover the pool for the boxing matches, they was that
hard. Then afterwards, for a ha'penny you could get an hot

Oxo. And if you was really flush, another ha'penny and you could have a slice of dry bread with it. Oh, it was really lovely.' She smiled, like she could member the sact taste that second, stead of the proper gravy.

'On Sunday afternoons, my aunt came round and she'd make us Bovril and toast,' said Alex. 'Same deal, really.'

Stroll on. If Mum said she liked shit and sugar, would he have to say he did, and all?

'That suit thing's all right, girl,' said Darren.

'Yeah, nice isn't it? Felt like splurging lately, now I feel free. I *minded* feeling trapped.' Must of meant bout not having no more minding, but she put her hand just for a second on that Alex's arm, stopping him from cutting up his meat. He looked up from his plate and smiled at her. It made Darren think there was always more going on with them than what he could make out. How much did Alex know? They both done words underneath their words, and only the ones what you could hear was meant for anyone but them. It was horrible.

The apple pie and custard was on the table when the bloke started to come unstuck.

'So how come you've never been married, Alex? Never found the right girl?' Mum was cutting him a massive slice of pie. He looked at Rosie, who was sort of froze, the smile on her face looking like she'd painted it on with her lipstick.

'I have been.' Dead calm. Mum never stopped cutting and dishing up the pie, but she weren't smiling. Married? Why hadn't Rosie never said nothing?

'He's been divorced going on three years,' said Rosie.

'What happened?'

'Mum!'

'She was mentally ill, Pat.' Bit less calm. Alex put a massive spoonful of pie in his gob, like to shut hisself up.

'Oh, suffered with her nerves, did she? Shame.' She eyeballed Alex. Obvious he had a job swallowing his mouthful, dropped his spoon in his bowl, what made the custard splash on the cloth. 'Children?' said Mum.

'It was never the right time.' He picked up his spoon again.

'Never is,' said Mum. 'If we all waited till the right time, human beings'd die out. Don't you like children?'

'Yeah I do, as it happens. Some of them, anyway.' He had a go at a laugh. Rosie'd gone bright red, and was shoving down custard like she was starved. Took no notice of her pie, though, like she never knew it was in her bowl.

'Well that's good.' Mum started on her afters, looking a bit more normal. 'We all make mistakes when we're young, don't we? Nobody's perfect – I always say it'd be a boring world if we was. Their dad and me split up over twenty years ago.' This was a turn up. Rosie stopped stuffing her face, and looked at Mum. They both picked up their wine at the same time – Rosie lifted hern out to Mum, like she was giving a toast at a wedding. Mum smiled and done it back. Something'd happened here, but Darren was fucked if he knew what. And even more weirder,

'Anyway,' said Alex, 'I'm happy now, and that's the main thing, isn't it?' Just like that. Like Mum'd give a monkey's if he was happy, long as Rosie was.

'Course it is,' said Mum.

All Darren could think of was to ask if there was any more custard.

And Rosie was happy with that Alex – least, she was today. Darren could notice that, the way her face had been all lit up through most of dinner. It was like something had happened in her head, what wouldn't stay inside, and leaked out through her eyes. No matter what Darren done for her, he never made that happen. Not never. His heart went all funny. If this carried on, she'd marry Alex just to keep whatever it was that come out of her. Thing was, couldn't blame her.

When Mum took Rosie off to do the washing-up, Darren thought he might get a chance to get one in, do a bit of damage. Then Alex told him fore Darren could say nothing, that his missus'd been stunning but he should of seen well afore he did it weren't no good. Be fair, Darren couldn't say he hadn't never made a wrong call on a bird hisself. Percy Edwards he weren't.

'I do know Rosie's special, Darren.' All serious. Darren felt a lump come in his throat. Swallowed it down with his brandy. Caught him unexpected, way Alex sounded like he meant it. But shouldn't of been surprised when the cunt went on to spoil hisself after that. Social workers always had to do it.

'Heard you got a boy keeps coming round your work,' Darren said, casual like.

'All the time.' Helping hisself to more brandy.

'No, I mean a pacific boy . . .'

'Sorry, I can't talk about anyone specific. Client confidentiality.'

Just you wait till Patterson gets picked up. And he will, make no mistake. All we're waiting on is time. But maybe even that never meant the geezer wouldn't marry his Rosie.

Rosie was lying on her living-room floor, with her head in Alex's lap, the dust from the carpet tickling her nose. They were both barely on the right side of not being pissed. She held her hands across her stomach; it was swelling by the second. Too many potatoes. Alex stroked her hair, and smiled down at her; he'd made tea, which they'd left cooling too much on the little table, and they were listening to The Beautiful South. Rosie grinned.

'Never occurred to me you'd admit to being married,' she said.

'It's best your mum knows. What would it look like if it came out in a year's time? She'd think we'd been lying to her.' He dragged on his cigarette, and put it between her lips.

'It's all wet! What did we call that at school? Bumming it, that's right.' A year's time; was he really thinking so far ahead? Would he still be, once he knew?

'I don't even want to see the connotations of that,' he said, laughing. Oh God, he was so relaxed. Over the past couple of weeks, underneath her pleasure, she'd waited for Alex to discover Sam Patterson's blame, to transfer it to her. *Liar, liar, the pub's on fire.* Sam could steal it all away. Alex touched her face and reached for her tea. 'Want this?' He steadied her as she propped herself on one elbow and took the mug.

'Alex, you moron, that's yours. Yuk.'

'Sorry, love.' He lifted his mug out of her hand and gave her the other one. 'The only dicey bit tonight was admitting about . . . Louise's mental state.'

'My family don't believe in mental illness. They think that sort of belief's optional, like with God.' There you go, she could have a conversation that included the midget's name, no danger. She put her mug back on the table, turned to kiss him, lightly, passed back the end of the cigarette. 'Like being behind the bikesheds this, isn't it?'

'I was never behind the bikesheds with someone like you, Rosie.'

'I'm not sure I was a girl like me, back then.' If she wasn't careful, she'd end up giving away too much here. But it was so nice just to do nothing with someone, and feel good about it. Not to have to sparkle and watch every word. Not to have to perform for a mean crowd. Not to feel judged. She could put her head into the lion's mouth or not, as she chose: it was her call. As long as she didn't get too comfortable with that, maybe it would be all right. Maybe.

'Your mum wants you to have kids, doesn't she?'

'Yeah, before it's too late, she'd say. I know this sounds awful, but I can't, I just don't want a, what would you say? A half-caste, I suppose.' A child with a name, but no place; it verged on child abuse. She watched Alex nod, thoughtfully, and gulp noisily at his tea.

'Cold. Bollocks. I really wanted kids once, but . . . Philip Larkin territory. And see, I do know more than one poem.' He pinched her cheek. She willed herself to smile. *Don't mind, don't mind.* He's just talking about the past, that's all; we've all got baggage. 'Haven't you ever got close to getting married?' he asked, pulling her back down into his lap.

'I was engaged once, but he turned out to be just like the others. Controlling.'

'Yeah, well I can see why that didn't work out.' Alex laughed.

'Shame really, it was a lovely ring.' *No one will ever love you like I do;* the kind of remark that sounds like a romantic, passionate thing to say, and is really an insult. She'd handed the ring back to him. His good-looking face closed over, making him look like a waxwork of some long-dead movie star.

No one will ever love you like I do.

God, I hope not!

Brilliant exit line, if she said so herself. And if she'd cried (well, all right, she had), it had been later, where he couldn't see. Hard, even when you were the one doing the killing, to accept that love dies. To see it turned into a waxwork. And to think that maybe, you wouldn't ever love again. But people do, of course. Even the most cynical of them. Even her. If she hadn't met Alex, there would have been someone else, sometime. But she was quite sure that there would never, if she'd waited her whole life, have been anyone she could have loved in just this way. If she stopped loving him, there would no replacement. Maybe something quieter, safer, but nothing that could make her feel like this. And that thought made her vulnerable.

'You won't be getting anything like that from me. Big diamonds or whatever,' said Alex.

'Emeralds, actually. No, I know.' She raised her eyebrows, asking him the question.

'So what is it you want from me, then?' He watched her continue to look up at him. 'You want me to offer myself, don't you? Well, I do.' Nodding. 'I've never met anyone before who I believed would be capable of just taking that from me. Thought it'd be like they were doing it just to please me, or like I was coercing them. An invitation's different. I'd only ever give that to you. Ever.' He stroked her ear-lobe. She felt as though her ears were hot, burning hot; wanted to bite his lips until they bled, to stop him saying this stuff she so wanted to hear. If he left her, his words would still exist between them, the definition of regret. 'More or less as soon as I met you,' he went on, 'I really wanted to please *you*. Sexually. *Really* wanted to. I've never had that feeling so strongly before, not with anybody.' Until they bled. 'God, I really love you, Rosie, so much.'

'I . . . know you do.'

He rang to say he was on his way back. There was panic in his voice as he claimed to love her; sounded very different when he'd said so the night before. Kept her voice neutral, *I'll see you in a bit, then*. She knew what to do; if he couldn't cope, he'd had it. *Cut off your nose to spite your face*. But Mum didn't realize the most important thing wasn't how you felt about another person: it was whether you could trust, and then live with, how they manifested their feelings for you. What was the point, if he couldn't take everything she needed him to take? Their relationship would just end up in the London Dungeons, which she wasn't planning to visit. Ever.

She was glad now to have this time on her own, but she kept the reason turning over. *Is Ally there?* A female voice, more girl's than woman's: small, fey, high. Rosie had held the 'phone out to Alex, its cord freak-show umbilical. Then. Then he went. *This is the last time, Rosie. I promise. Don't be like that, please, love. It's been so good between us lately.* Except that I've stayed away from your place. Except I've carefully not asked. Except every time you come here, I'm relieved you're not lying to me, for that night at least. And now the munchkin had her number; her voice had been inside Rosie, literally inside. Nothing could make that not true. Okay, babe, one last time; that's the only chance I'll ever give you. That's my promise.

Rosie poured her new Lime Essence into the bath, watching the green oil swallow the water. She slipped off her dressing gown, tested the bath with her toes. Too hot. Just a splash of cold. The warmth settled her as she relaxed into it. She loved a bath; not for getting clean, that's why she had a power shower, but for soaking in her thoughts. Different when she was a kid. Nan had a thing for Dettol: a capful in every bath, another in the final hair rinse. And she always seemed to be around on bath night. To this day, neither Rosie nor Darren would have Dettol in their flats. Mustn't spend too long in here tonight; she had a lot to do before Alex arrived. Had to polish her old snakeskin boots, check the wristbands, test the cane, get out the candles. And the collar. *Caveat emptor.* Careful what you wish for, Alex.

She glanced round the flat when the doorbell went, and switched off the lamp so that the only light in the living room came from the dozen candles. Brighter than she'd anticipated. Slowly, she put out her cigarette and took a sip from her wine. The bell went again. Patience, boy.

'Come in.'

'God, Rosie . . .' He stared at her, and she laughed.

'Close the door, you're letting in a draught.' As he came into the living room, Rosie put her foot on the little table, her heel clicking against its glass top. 'Been having fun, babe?'

'No. I—'

'Later. There's an open bottle of wine next to the CD. I'd pour myself some, if I were you. And you can press Play while you're there.'

Even by candlelight, Rosie could see that Alex was shaking, his face shiny with fear or excitement. He drained his glass, and sent Lou Reed's gravelly drawl into the room: a gift from Alex, after their first real date; a missing part of her education, he'd said.

'You look . . .'

'Yeah, I expect I do. Get undressed.'

'What?'

'Do you want me to have to repeat myself?'

'No. Sorry, love.' He began to pull off his clothes. She tapped her foot on the table.

'Not exactly Speedy Gonzales, are you? Pass me a candle.'
'What?'

'Have you been on the stupid pills while you were out? A
candle. Long, thin thing made of wax, flame at the top.' She
saw Alex look round, as though trying to discover where he
might find such a thing. He was naked now, the whiteness of
his skin shadowed by the flames. On top of the telly, Rosie
had put her double candlestick; he went to pick it up. 'I don't
need the holder, babe, just a candle.' Awkwardly, Alex detached
one of the candles, and passed it to her, careful not to get wax
on his hands. Pointless precaution, my darling, but no, I don't
want you doing it to yourself. 'Now kneel, and if you say
What? I really will think something happened to your brain
out there.' He knelt by the table, clearly tensing his shoulders.
'What's the matter, feeling a bit apprehensive? You've taken
worse than this.'

Drip, drip, drip. Creating shapes across his shoulders.
Noticing, slightly detached, that wherever wax had already
been, another splash made him gasp. The candle was burning
uneven in her hand; mustn't let it spill on to her, that would
be undignified. She thrust it at him.

'Get rid of that,' she said. 'I want a new one.'

Wax, on his shoulders, chest, stomach, balls. Red, where she'd
peeled some of it off, just to see what would happen. Scratches
from her studded wristbands, where she'd caressed her work.
Get me a drink, baby, and she could cover his back. *Put the
CD to the beginning*, and there were the soles of his feet. As
a little girl, she'd loved her kaleidoscope; now she had a living
one. Turn the screw, and make a new pattern. Just because she
could. For the sake of it.

She took the cane from the shelf under the table. Ran it
gently over his erection. Then.

His voice was louder, for a moment, than the music.

Vicious.

And the pattern changed. Shifting colours. But better than

her childhood toy, because with every turn, the textures shifted too, sliding from wax to skin to blood.

It isn't only women that bleed.

'Bitch. You've got no right . . .'

'So?'

'God, you bitch.'

'I think you mean thank you, don't you?'

'I . . . yeah. Thank you. I love you.'

'Lie down again.' Using his face, she stepped on to his chest. Snakes so dangerous that they can kill after death. Biting in, filling his body with their poison. Double venom.

'Shit. Can't breathe.'

'Good.' Constricting him. 'You've got code words. Three . . . what is it? Three . . . little words. Telling me you need to use them?'

'No . . . agh.'

'Problems?' She rested her toe on his cheek.

'I'd . . . rather have you . . . tread on my . . . face, than get . . . a blow job . . . from anyone else.' The final 's' came out sibilant, as though she had punctured him. As though he were transmogrifying into a snake himself.

'I should bloody well think so! Am I supposed to be pleased by that?'

'No. No, course not. Sorry . . . talking bollocks.'

'So it's not true?'

'No. I mean, of course it's true . . . God, Rosie . . .'

'Because I demand fidelity, babe. You have to want only me.'

'That's . . . easy.'

'You sure about that?'

'Agh . . . shit. Yeah, yeah course I am.'

'And you have to want me as I am. And take whatever it is I want you to.'

'I'll . . . do my best to take it.'

'Maybe that won't be good enough.'

Under her feet, slithering but sure, the whole of her past

registered. All present and correct. Flesh and fowl and good
red herring, swallowed whole. Every pair of shoes she'd owned.
Every pain. All he'd made her feel, all she'd felt. Every code
word, every book that cost her too much. The mistakes she
hadn't been allowed to make; the ones she'd wrested from the
grasp of her policing mind. The manacles. The scars they left.
From this day forth.

'Just like the movies.'

'What sort of movies have you been watching, love?' They
were curled up together on the settee, smoking, framed by
convention. Rosie traced the wax on his chest; must really
hurt, when she pulled it away from the hairs. Like a plaster,
but worse. Pity about the collar, but it hadn't felt right. There
was always next time. Or the time after. 'We really must set
up a camera sometime, that'd be amazing,' Alex said. 'Before
we met, if I tried to put real people even in my fantasies about
this, it didn't work.' He kissed her. 'You're the only one I could
surrender control to.'

'Yeah,' she said. She stroked his arm and smiled. The point
wasn't so much pain *per se*, but how much he could take. For
her.

'That feels nice.' He touched her hand. 'I think I need to
thank you properly. I love all of it. This side, and the making
love, and everything. In the past, well, it was difficult although
I had a good time then, too, but it was different. It wasn't
anything like so exciting, and . . . intimate, as what we've got.
Even with Louise at the start, I loved being inside her, and
when she sucked my cock it felt like she wanted to eat me,
but—'

'Jesus, Alex, don't you ever learn?' Rosie pulled away, drew
hard on the last of her cigarette and ground it out. The stupid,
stupid bastard. What did he think tonight had been about?
Exorcizing the demon of Louise. Supposedly. Oh God, it was
as though because of what they did, there were no boundaries
left. It amounted to a kind of mental cruelty; Rosie had become

a role, a function, able to bear anything he needed to offload. She didn't doubt that what he'd been trying to say was that the present was better than the past, but the result was yet another pain for her list. And there was nothing under her feet but the cushions of the settee.

'Rosie, don't—'

'How am I going to like listening . . . Would you? I can't believe you sometimes. It's like you do it deliberately. And in case you've forgotten, you were with your bloody wife tonight, paying her bills with God knows what money, while I was getting everything ready. Bastard.'

Alex moved to the edge of the settee, and rested his face in his hands.

'I'm so sorry,' he said through his fingers. 'I was trying to tell you how happy I am.'

By making me unhappy.

'Fucked that up then, didn't you?'

'No question. God, the last thing I want to do is hurt you. I love you so much.'

'So you keep saying. Too easy.' And you're telling me more lies. You might love the rest, but you don't love making love. Not to me, anyway. You don't. You loved being inside her, but not me. So what else isn't true? With what we do, there has to be truth, Alex. And you continually deny that. As though she'd spoken aloud, he shook his head and stood, fetched the bottle, drinking straight from it. Rosie swung her legs down, and held out her hand; he gave her the wine. She raised it to her lips, took a long swallow. 'What happened, Alex?'

'I gave her a cheque from my deposit account, for a room she's found.' He sat on the armchair. 'That's the lot, she's cleared me out now.'

'You've been paying for the B and B, haven't you?'

'Yeah.' He looked at her. 'Darren's right, I'm a cunt. But I told her I want a divorce, and the two hundred quid was the last thing she'd get from me.'

'What did she say?'

'What you'd expect. Well, what I'd expect. Hysterics for ten minutes, then nothing. Calmed right down and apologized, said she'd be fine.'

'Right.' Clever. She was no slouch, then. 'How come she rang here?'

'Me. I messed up again. She kept turning up, and I told her it wasn't a good idea to see each other, even as friends. So she started pestering the people I work with. Then when you nipped out the other day, I rang the B and B from here, to tell her I'd met someone else, and—'

'She did 1471.' Bad, bad call. In every sense.

Rosie picked up the cold stump of a candle that was lying on the carpet, turned it over in her fingers. She knew that she'd remember his words for a long time, whenever they did make love, whenever she put her lips to his cock. And she'd remember the lie. The well-intentioned lie, sugaring the poison. If they were to stand any kind of chance, he'd actively have to prove himself in more ways than being able to handle being her kaleidoscope. To submit is a verb. Suddenly, Rosie realized that meant words were never easy, even for people like them.

'Okay, this is the score,' she said. 'Either you cut off all contact with Louise, now, and get the divorce entirely through a solicitor, or you can forget about us. Believe me, I mean it.'

Alex scratched at a strand of wax on his thigh.

'She's no threat to you, you know. She couldn't ever be,' he said.

'Did I say she was? But I'm not going to have this. It's like she's got some control over our relationship, and that's not on. Not acceptable.'

'In any universe, I know.' He smiled. Rosie was taken aback. She'd have expected a bit of protest, or at least more grovelling. Not smiles. 'That all seems fair enough, Rosie. Course it does. It's not like I ever want to see her again. It's been over

for a long time, since well before we split up. I'm sorry, love,
I'll make it up to you for being an idiot.'

'Yeah, you can try.' She wondered if he knew what it cost
her to say that. And to smile.

Chapter Twelve

Ben see them come in, even though he was at the other end of the bar and the place was heaving. Always was, Christmas Eve. Alex had his hand on Rosie's shoulder, like he was trying to stop her disappearing in the crowd – as if she could ever get lost in here. They pushed their way past the pool table, her getting little pecks every five seconds, and him having a few blokes shake his hand. Like they just got engaged or something.

'Happy birthday, darling.' Ben stood up, kissed her on the mouth. Not proper, but enough that the boyfriend would notice. Sweet as. Fuck him. Ben had special privileges now. 'You all right, mate?' Stuck out his hand – had to make the effort.

'Yeah, fine. You seem as though you're doing okay.'

Ben touched his face, looking at Rosie. Ailisha'd screamed when she see him. Tricia'd said it was just she weren't used to him, but he never thought so.

'Sorted. Back to normal, nearly.'

'From Tom.' Spence come over with a tray. Bottle of champagne, four glasses, and nuts in a bowl. 'Said to wish you many happy returns.' He bunged the tray down on the table, and pulled Rosie into a massive hug. 'Happy birthday, girl. Many of them.'

'I've had a fair few already, thanks. Think I'll stop at this one.'

Spence poured the champagne one handed, like a waiter in some flash gaff. Always been good at that stuff, he had. Same as his old man, who used to say the family had small pockets and big tastes. Bigger pockets these days anyway, and their arms was always long enough.

'To Rosie,' said Spence, holding up his glass. She smiled, and held hern up and all.

'And merry Christmas,' she said.

Ben thought about the card in his pocket. He'd signed it *Lots of love*, and put five kisses. Would she think he was a soppy sod? She was laughing at something Spence'd said, her free hand on that Alex's leg. Alex put his hand over hern, and leant forward to top up her glass. What if Ben got the card out, and she laughed at him?

'What you got me, then?' she said to Spence.

'You can have it tomorrow, it's joined up with your Christmas.' He winked, and put his hand in his jacket, then took it out with nothing in it.

'Daz, don't be a git.' She slid her hand out from under Alex's, and pulled her hair away from her face, making out she was angry with him. Spence felt in his jacket again, and brung out a jeweller's box. She snatched at it like a big kid, and opened the lid. 'It's lovely,' she said, all quiet. She slipped off the diamond what she was wearing, and put Spence's ring on instead.

'Well, I know you like old stuff. Weren't being tight – new stuff would of been cheaper. Freddy said it was Victorian, or something.'

'Yeah, it is. Look, Alex, garnets. And little seed pearls.' She held out her hand for the boyfriend to see. Interesting one. Ben weren't exactly convinced Alex was all that pleased about it. 'Perfect fit. I don't know what to say, Daz.'

'Not like you.' But he couldn't keep the grin off of his face. Rosie kissed him. 'What else you had?' he said.

'Mum got me make-up. And supposedly Nan bought me some Black Magic, but Mum must have got them, and all. My best mate gave me a book I was after. Oh, and William at work made the whole office chip in for a Harrods voucher, so's he didn't have to think about it. Might give it back to him on his birthday.'

Spence looked at Alex. Neither of them said nothing. Alex grabbed an handful of peanuts. Ben felt a bit sorry for him. Was about to say to him should they have a real drink, when Little Les come up behind Spence, and put one of his mitts on his shoulder. Spence turned round, quick, his hand on his inside pocket.

'Fucking hell, mate – leave it out, will you?'

'Sorry, Spence, wanted a quick word, about Patterson. Small little problem with a detail.'

'Not now. It's my Rosie's birthday, and she's off out to eat soon. Catch me later.'

'Many happy returns, Rosie love.' Les never seemed to notice Spence was pissed off. 'Can I get you all a drink?'

Alex was twisting the ring on Rosie's finger. He weren't happy, neither.

'Not for me, mate,' he said.

'Les, this is Alex *Tolliver*. Rosie's bloke,' said Ben. For a split second, Spence and Rosie, what looked so different, could of been twins. Identical evils.

He better leave the card where it was.

The cab pulled away from the restaurant, but Alex rapped on the partition for it to stop.

'No, we're going to mine for once, love,' he told Rosie. 'I've got something for you.' Rosie felt her heart literally miss a beat, but she got a grip: must *not* turn Alex's flat into her private chamber of horrors. It was Alex's space his wife had invaded, not Rosie's. Don't confuse the two.

'You didn't eat much for you, babe,' she said, trying for nonchalance.

'Tell you the truth, I've been a bit nervous about your present.' He slid his arm across her shoulders. 'Didn't spoil it, did it?'

'No, I thought it was a bit disappointing, didn't you? Still, least it was on expenses.'

'I really want you to wake up at mine for Christmas as well, especially as I have to work it.' Did he? It had all been a bit sudden. Rosie was determined not to ruin her birthday with paranoia, but if she ever found out that Alex wasn't at work tomorrow, or even that Louise had pitched up there, that'd be it.

'Better make it worth my while then, hadn't you?'

'I always try,' Alex said, and kissed her cheek.

She hadn't really expected to see any evidence of women's clothing in the flat, but couldn't stop herself having a quick check as she took off her coat. Nothing. But there wouldn't be, would there? He'd hardly make the same mistake twice. Alex was faffing about with the tape deck, kept changing his mind about what to play.

'Do you want a drink?'

'I'm not bothered.' She sat on the arm of her chair, yawning, and flexed her fingers, the light catching her ring. 'Shall I just have a nice little nap while I wait?'

He opened a can; Rosie watched his thick neck move as he swallowed.

'Are you having a nice birthday?' he asked.

'So far. Mind you, not much of it left.' She glanced at her watch. Alex smiled.

'All right, I get the point. Just wait there a second.' He left the room. Rosie brushed at a crease in her skirt, fiddled with her necklace. What was he doing, weaving her a jumper?

The living-room door opened. Alex had a wrapped present under his arm. There was only one thing it could be; only one thing it was ever going to be.

'It's not much I know, but I got my cousin to frame it and yes, I told him who it was for, and that I was seeing you. I said you were brilliant, as it happens. I've been working at this for weeks, on and off, whenever I've had a spare half hour. Usually when I've been picking my gear up. I—'

'Alex, can't I just open it?' Rosie stood and held out her hands.

'I'm quite proud of it,' he said. 'But I wasn't sure . . . that sort of thing's so personal.' He came further into the room, and handed her the package. 'I love you. Happy birthday.'

Rosie stroked the wrapping paper. Only it wasn't. It was artist's paper, washed over with water colours, red and green and gold. Nice touch, babe. The present was quite heavy but not very big, less than A3. Rosie smiled at Alex and tore at the wrap, allowing it to land in shreds on the floor.

Then she looked at the picture.

The Three Blind Mice.

Except that the people weren't.

In charcoal grey, there was Daz, amphibious but smiling, talking to a hippo dressed as Tom at the bar; a stoat (Ben? Yeah, it must be), his coat perfectly smooth, stood waiting, a pool cue in his paws. Various gorillas in suits held pints, their huge hairy hands decorated with jewellery, and a few female rodents sipped at coloured drinks or laughed, showing their sharp little teeth. But the picture was set up so that gradually your eye was directed to the table in the furthest corner, where a leonine figure with a scarred muzzle was lighting the cigarette of a black panther, golden eyed, her expression between a smile and a snarl.

It was beautiful, and it made her laugh. She held it at arm's length. The glass made it seem as though you were looking at the punters through a window. She felt like a voyeur, even as she examined herself.

'It's terrific. You must know it is.'

'What do you reckon to us?' Alex said, clearly relieved.

'We look pretty bloody good. In fact, we come off best, don't we? Not that I'm arguing with that. There must be hours and hours of work here.' Carefully, she laid the picture on the floor between them. Alex moved nearer; they each stood staring down, as though Alex had put a mirror to Rosie's window view, she thought, so he saw what she saw, upside down.

'Thank you, babe. I love it.' She nudged the frame with her

toe, and took his hand, making an arch across the pub. His arm, her shirt, marble-white, shadowing the figures.

'I wanted to show you how much I think of you.'

She stepped closer to him and kissed him, hard.

The glass held for a second, then
    cracked.

She felt him shudder, but he didn't break their kiss, slipping his tongue into her mouth and pulling her tighter into him.

It was so close.

She'd so nearly told him she loved him.

They drove through the persistent dire weather; the last few days of the year seemed as though they were being drizzled away. Oddly enough, the first time Rosie had seen Soho she'd been with Daz then too, when he'd refused to take her to a strip-joint. Still hadn't been to one, come to think of it, but she didn't feel like suggesting they did. A café would do. Anywhere outside of their indigenous habitat, in their life-long paranoid tradition of having family discussions where Mum couldn't possibly overhear. Rosie had an hour yet before she had to meet Randa at Jimmy's, and she wasn't taking Daz in there, for him to call the waiters *Zorba*. Once they'd managed to park, they half-heartedly scanned the street for a likely place.

'Might as well try here,' he said, 'I'm getting slowly drownded. Thinks it's a bit poncy though, don't it? Ain't one thing nor a nother.'

She made him right, it thought it was in France. In the summer, no doubt, it'd be full of tourists, half-pissed men with hopeful erections, but today, in a midwinter that didn't even have the heart to be bleak, solitary Suits had *Yep, Yep*, urgent conversations with their mobiles, and sales shoppers delayed their guilty journeys home by staring into the dregs of their cappuccinos. If they couldn't afford it, what were they doing pretending they could make the grade?

'She can't stay at yours, Daz. Mum had a fit at me.' Rosie poked her spoon into her espresso, then clinked it against her

brandy glass. Some recess this was. 'Don't know how she got
the idea in her head. Wasn't you, was it? I tried to tell her.'

Come stay with me, Nana.

Oh no, dear – you'll be too busy with your dancing.

Mum, then. You know, your daughter.

*Course I know. Bad child. She tried to poison me, two
Wednesdays on the trot. And she brings men home, great hairy
things they are, sitting round the bath in the nuddy. Your
grandad wouldn't like that.*

At least let Darren stay there with you.

*He's too much for me now, Mary. I can't cope with a four-
year-old at my age. Lost the pussywillow, I did. I shall like it
in his flat, shan't I? Make a nice change for me.*

She just wouldn't be told, and what right did they have to
force her? It'd be days before her place dried out; if they tried
to get her in anywhere on a temporary basis, they'd have Social
Services sticking their beaks in quicker than you could say
mad old bat.

'Notice the whole joint reeked of Dettol?' said Daz. 'She must
of poured all the bottle in to go with how much water was
coming out.' They both made retching noises, and laughed.
Nan had flooded out her bathroom properly this time; it had
almost brought down the living-room ceiling. They'd finally
got her to agree to go to Mum's for tonight, but Nana had her
stubborn head on: there was no way she'd stay longer, and
she seemed to think going to Daz's would be a treat. Mum
would have to go round there all day every day; Nan would
never know where she was. Rosie watched, slightly sickened,
as Daz ripped his Danish apart. She shook her head at his offer
of a bite, pushing away the plate he was holding out to her.
He shrugged and stuffed as much as he could into his mouth
at once. Didn't he know how many calories were in a Danish?
'This is mental, darling,' he said through the pastry, then swallowed. 'We're kidding ourselves.' Yeah, but then they always
did. Like with the pawning of Nan's good ring, the aborted
purchase of Mum's place, the way they didn't contact their

father when Rosie qualified. Each time, the two of them had absconded for a private conference. And each time, 'Ain't up to us. Sup to Mum.'

'I know. And I think she'll let her, save Nan getting too distressed.' All the thinking, planning, persuading. Probably came to a year of their lives so far, only for that. Sup to Mum. 'Aren't you worried about her being there?' It'd doubtless mean a gorilla, just when she thought they'd finished with all that. Nan would probably think he was one of Mum's great hairy men, and call the Old Bill. 'Where will you go, Mum's?'

'Oh yeah,' he looked his disbelief. 'Have me wearing a vest by end of the week – between that and her going on about the state of me gaff. No, do me head in, that would.'

'Ben's?'

'Thought I could stay with you.'

Just lying there on the floor it was, like she never cared about it no more. Darren see it when he went to chuck that fucking paper. He picked it up, made it jingle about, had a look at the charms. Soldier, little book, cross, heart, the shoe. He could member when she got it, for her birthday that time and then the first charms on Christmas. Mum'd brought the bracelet, and Nana'd got that flower. First Christmas without the old man. The shoe Darren'd give her, for a sort of joke when she got her lawyer exams. That emerald thing'd been from Scottie. But mostly they was from Nan. From when she could still pick stuff out. He put the bracelet on the little table, laid down and pulled up the covers. Not sactly comfy – weren't like her settee was material, even.

He could hear their voices in the next room, but not what they was saying – he was well worried bout what else he might hear. No, she'd know it would barrass him too bad. Make him feel queasy, and all. And it still stunk in here from the take-out. Rank and greasy. Funny how things what could smell so handsome when you was just bout eat them, reeked so bad after you'd finished. Same things and all. Same smell,

but with the looking forward to gone all sour. Chinese –
Darren'd sprung for it. Rushed him nearly fifty notes, thieving
Chinky gits. Just for her to eat like it was poison. Have to
watch it, she would – getting a bit more thin round her wrists
and places. Not that he'd never say nothing bout it to her.
Not like *him*.

'That skirt your mum got you's a bit big, isn't it?' he'd said.

'All right to skin up?' Darren'd put in, quick. Not to help
him, but so's she never felt bad. 'This ain't tied to his job, is
it?' See Rosie look over at Alex. He lifted up his shoulders
much as to say it was down to her. But he weren't none too
pleased.

'Not tonight, Daz. Why don't you have a brandy?'

'Cos I fancy a spliff.'

'Then go see Ben or something.' She tried to soften up her
words with one of her smiles. 'I'll sort the sounds, what's
anyone want?'

'The Police.' 'Dusty.' They looked at each other, then at Rosie.

'That settles it, Cowboy Junkies do you? Anyone want that
drink?'

When Rosie settled back down on her cushion with a massive
scotch and that horrible whiny music on too loud, Darren
thought he might try again for a smoke. But then he thought
better of it – no sense in winding her up for the sake of it.
She curled her legs under herself, runching that new long skirt
all up. No tights – not something she'd leave off normal, less
it was the middle of summer. Might of got them wet outdoors,
not bothered putting new ones on. Hair sort of looser and all,
more soft, like the damp'd washed out the hairspray. She looked
different, like one of them arty birds or something. Get chilly,
sat there like that.

'Better not leave it too late – got to get down the yard by
seven.' Stuck sitting up till they went abed.

'Are you going over yours tomorrow, see Nan?'

'Don't know. Got a right full one, might have to knock Nana
on the head.'

'That's a bit extreme,' said Alex, giving a laugh. Cunt. Rosie laughed and all.

'No, she'd clip him round the earhole, he tried anything with her,' she said. 'You had permanently red ears at one time, didn't you, sweetheart? And I had a permanently red bum.'

'Well I don't know, do I?' Alex took a mouthful his drink. 'All the arcane stuff goes on round here, might be an old ritual for all I know.' Fishing. That's what he was doing. He must take Darren for a right muppet. Alex stood up, went to where his carrier was leaning gainst the wall, took out a paper. 'Talking of East End rituals, seen this in the *Standard*?' He give it Rosie. 'Page five. Seems they're appealing again for witnesses to that arson back in the autumn. The Red Lion. Think they must have a lead. Well, blatantly, or they wouldn't be stirring it up.' Rosie never opened it. Put it down the side of her.

'You know I have to get *The Times*,' she said. She touched the paper. 'Today's, is it? Caught yourself up on your cross-words, then?' Playing with her bracelet. Darren wanted to say *Read it out!* but he couldn't show no interest. Though Alex weren't looking at him, obvious who this shit was for. What'd the geezer heard, or thought he'd sussed? Paper was sat on the floor next to a half-full carton of chow mein what Rosie must of forgot to take out. Darren's stomach felt heavy, like he'd been trying to eat the paper and all by mistake. Rotting away his guts.

'Couple of clues I couldn't get,' said Alex. 'But I reckon I will.'

'I'm sure. Need another drink? Daz?'

Darren might not get the *Standard*, but he knew the cunt's game. Trouble was, had to look like he never. Patterson might of said something. Maybe Rosie'd even told him. And Darren couldn't make out to hisself that the bloke was stupid, neither, else Ro wouldn't be seeing him, would she? Guts was so full now, he needed a pony – but if he left the room, it'd look well funny. Have to cork it.

'Why don't you have that joint, Darren?' said Alex. 'I don't mind if Rosie doesn't.'

'No, brandy'll do me. Got to get me head down soon.' Stroll on.

'Perhaps you ought to go home tonight. What with Daz in the living-room.'

'Yeah, I've got a bit of a cold anyway, don't want you to get it.' Absently, he stroked her leg and sneezed. He'd agreed just that bit too quickly there. And what cold? First she'd heard of it. But at least he hadn't gone back to the paper. Oh Christ, what had Alex got hold of? Was this what she'd been dreading right from early December, since Daz had told her who they were holding responsible? A late Christmas present, long anticipated. Don't accept it, give it back.

'She rang again, Alex. Daz was here.'

'Great.' He sighed. 'What did she say?'

'The usual. Asked for *Ally*, asked me to get you to call her. Yeah, right. Mind you, I suppose I didn't have to tell you.' She felt she didn't have quite enough oxygen, and made herself yawn. 'But I did, I always do. She got what she wanted.'

'No she didn't. I'm not going to ring her back.'

But she'll be able to get you at home. You, your *Standard*s, that voice. The holy trinity.

As he left, he kissed her forehead.

It wasn't the sex, Daz had scuppered that one for the next couple of nights anyway, but Alex hadn't even told her he loved her since the grand gesture of her birthday. Perhaps he didn't, outside of those gestures. And which of them had he been fronting out tonight? Almost going too far, just holding off. Controlled. But not by Rosie. So then by Sam, or by Louise? Without Alex's noisy, familiar breathing beside her, Rosie could hear the flat sound of her place, and underneath, that fidgeting about next door. She didn't want to miss Alex too much; didn't want to offer him that much. And how did she know that home was where he'd really gone?

Perhaps from now on she'd have her most intense conversations with the girlish, disembodied voice that had forced itself into her life. A voice whose significance Rosie couldn't gauge; a cypher she couldn't crack. She'd like to change her number, but *Never let them know they've got to you, girl.* In her dreams, the voice acquired a body, a face, a set of physical gestures; not always the same from night to night, but inevitably invested with the illusions that a past (your own or someone you love's) too easily acquires. She was sure Alex would have sketches and photos of Louise, but Rosie would cut out her tongue and eat it before she asked to see them, and anyway, she didn't think she could bear to look. Funny how someone that tiny could feel way too heavy to handle. Demeaning to be so wound up about another woman; demeaned the one thing she couldn't afford to be. It made a nonsense of everything that had made so much sense. But at the end of the day, here she was, alone.

Except for Louise.

Shulde aulde acquaintance be forgot; perhaps it didn't mean if they were, perhaps it was a question. Rosie had always hated New Year's Eve: the pathetic, desperate kisses of acquaintance terrified of being alone or sober, for that one night of the year at least. Terrified of being forgot. Dreadful evening, despite Randa's best efforts at compulsory fun. Coming home to the same message on the answerphone that Mum left every year. Alex drunk, after hours of determinedly keeping a toe on the moral high ground while all around them the other guests hadn't given a toss where it began or ended. Rosie actively forgetting his interest in the paper. The New Year had happened without them, some time when they were in the cab home. What a waste of the Prada waiting list. And great, five minutes after they got back, Daz pitched up. His party had been a wash-out, too.

So Alex and Daz got the vodka out.

Not that it was an alliance; Rosie felt like banging their heads together. Maybe if she'd been as pissed as they were she

wouldn't have thought anything of it, but a headache had kept
her relatively sober, and now she sat next to Alex on the settee,
sipping tea while they gulped at the voddy. Daz never could
hold his booze, and Alex now seemed to have decided to get
totally off his face.

'The gov'ment wants to up that whatsname. Ban over drugs,'
said Daz, emphasizing the last three words by thumping the
arm of his chair. 'We was saying that tonight. Not draw or
nothing, that's all a load of fucking shit, but crack and that.
Them Rasta cunts sell it outside the Juniors, they do. You seen
them, with them plaits and woolly hats? Got nits, well-known
fact.'

'You should know,' said Rosie.

'Ban over drugs?' said Alex, imitating his inflection.

'Yeah. It might even put you out of work, mate.'

'Bollocks. Government campaigns are insanely, *insanely*
expensive, and they don't work.' He assumed a right-on voice.
'Just say no, kids.' Shaking his head. 'Look, right, look, users
have to get their money from somewhere. Makes perfect sense.
Every actual pound spent on actual treatment for users, on
detox and rehab, saves about three quid in reduced crime costs.'

'How d'you know?' said Daz.

'Believe it or *believe it not*, a government-funded study.' Alex
laughed through his teeth and sloshed more vodka into their
glasses.

'But that might put *her* out of work, if there weren't no
crime. Thought of that?'

'Would it, love?' Into her face. Rosie turned her head. She
just wanted to take a Temmy, lie down, and make it be
tomorrow. But she didn't want to leave them together. 'Anyone
got a fag?' Alex whispered in her ear. She gave him one, which
he dropped under the table; at least he hadn't lit it. 'What's
the matter?' he said, leaning into her.

'Bit of a head, that's all. I've taken some Nurofen.' She pushed
him away. Christ, he was heavy. 'And I'm knackered.'

'Anyway, she's very good at what she does.' Alex grabbed

her knee. 'Very good. All the people were running round like she's the bee's pyjamas tonight. Which she is.'

'Think I know that a bit more'n you.'

'I'm not being funny but will both of you shut up?' said Rosie. 'You're doing my head in, the pair of you.'

'Yeah, mate, how much d'you know about what she does?'

'Daz, watch it, I mean it.' Jesus, this was all she needed. Not now, not tonight.

'I know what she does.' Alex nodded, vigorously.

'Great, so we all know what I do. Now it's time for bed, I think, don't you?'

'It's re . . .' Daz tapped his fingers against his mouth. 'No, hang on, I fucking know this.' He pushed himself to the back of the chair. 'Re-cid-ism. Redicidism.' Shit. Of all the times for Daz to be colouring inside the margins. Alex took Rosie's hand.

'Recidivism?' he said. 'I don't know that you should say that about her, really.' For a drunk person, his voice sounded firm. Oh, Christ. She was going to leave home.

'She don't mind.' Daz looked surprised. 'Why'd she mind that?' He struggled to get out of the chair. Shit, no. No. 'Going for a slash,' he said. Thank you, God.

Alex put his arms round Rosie, his lips against her ear. He started to sing, half under his breath; she thought he was trying to be romantic. Then she made out the words.

You changed your life, darling, but you forgot to change your mind.

Rosie rested her elbows on the low work surface, her head in her hands. Pair of kids. No, that wasn't fair; it was just that they were trying to occupy the same space, and finding it crowded. Although if Daz didn't go home soon, Rosie might have to drown herself. And why on earth had Alex decided to stay over? Too drunk to consider leaving, probably. At least they were both asleep now; she'd left Alex snuffling to himself, and she could hear Daz's snoring from here. Five o'clock. They'd both go mad at her if they knew she'd got dressed again, run to the twenty-four hour for more milk. Now she'd over-filled the kettle, and it was taking ages. It'd be so good when she could get back to work.

The kitchen door opened. Rosie didn't lift her head.

'You okay?' said Alex softly, closing the door behind him. Sounded like he'd slept most of it off, although she wouldn't want to light a match around the fumes he'd brought in.

'Yeah. You want tea?'

Alex leaned over her, kissed the back of her neck. Then he ran his hand over her bum, not in the familiar gesture, but speculatively. Unusual. Rosie stayed where she was, waiting to see what he'd do next. He put his hands on the work surface, so that she was between his arms, and pressed himself into her, bending his knees. There was a faint indignity about it, with her head practically level with her arse. If she hadn't been wearing shoes, she'd have been too short to feel his erection against her bum.

'I'm sorry, baby,' he said. His voice choked, as though he might cry.

'What for?' She tried to stand up straight, but he pushed her head down, not aggressively, firmly, until she had to fold her arms into a pillow to be at all comfortable. What the hell was going on here?

'I'm really sorry.' He kept her pinned with one arm, pushing up her skirt with his free hand. This wasn't Alex's style.

'Shh. Daz's next door, remember.'

'Yeah.' But he continued to raise her skirt. 'But I have to, my love.'

Have to what? Before she had a chance to answer herself, Alex had wrenched down her briefs over her hold-ups, imprisoned her again and shoved his fingers inside her.

'Alex!' But although she was almost angry, she was wet.

'I'm sorry.' He took out his fingers to open his jeans. 'Sorry.'

'For Christ's sake, he'll hear.'

And he entered her.

She struggled, but he wouldn't let her go and she didn't really want him to.

'Just have to know,' he whispered as he thrust into her, 'what they're wanking over. All the tossers at the parties. Just need to feel you come on my cock. You never have, have you?' No. And with Alex, she didn't bother to fake it; there were too many ways she could make him make her come for faking to be other than a travesty. 'God. Never been this hard inside anybody. Even though I've been drinking. Oh God. I'm sorry, baby.'

'Be quiet. You'll pay for this, boy,' she said. She knew it was the right thing to say. And despite the fact that she was moving with him now, she meant it.

'Yeah, anything. Just let me make you come.'

And by degrees, she almost forgot about the next room, almost forgot about the strangeness of him, and, eventually, let him make her come, biting her own lips to stop herself crying out.

They faced each other afterwards, both a little out of breath.

'What was that all about?' said Rosie. There was a soft thumping inside her head; not like the earlier headache, but more as though something was trying to get out. She listened to it, feeling as if she were hearing someone else's blood course through her. Alex's eyes welled up. Had he really upset himself so much?

'Did I force you?' Speaking low.

'No. Well, sort of. But you'd have stopped if I'd seriously wanted you to.' She touched his face. 'I promise you, babe, you would.'

'Would I?' A few tears spilled over.

'Yeah. Anyway, it's given me loads of ammunition.' She wiped his tears with her thumb, the uneasy sounds in her head fading. Alex tried to smile. Then he sank to the floor, kneeling at her feet as his sperm trickled out of her.

'I'm sorry.' He bent to kiss her shoes, the floor in front of them, sat back on his heels.

Rosie kneeled next to him, stroked his hair. He closed his eyes, pressed his head into her hand the way he always did, making soft sounds between pleasure and pain. Christ, he thought he'd done something awful, that she was absolving him. It wasn't awful at all, just a surprise. She could have done without the proximity of her brother, but they were adults. Perhaps it had come out of all manner of dark shadows but it was light here, safe, warm. And then Rosie thought she knew.

'I'm not her,' she said.

'I know that, God you don't think . . .'

'No, I don't.' And funnily enough, she didn't; Alex wasn't enacting some fantasy here, with Rosie cast as the mad rejecting wife. It wasn't to do, even in an anti-fantasy of her own, with him loving being inside Louise but not Rosie. She'd meant something sadder and more vague than that. 'Look at me, babe. That's it. We might not have the world's most conventional relationship but it *is* a relationship. And that means there's room for all kinds of sex in it. Our biggest buzz is probably always going to be to do with Dom—'

Gently, briefly, he touched her mouth with two fingers.

'I'm not too sure I'm happy with labels,' he said.

'Don't care what you call it, precious. I just care about doing it.'

'Yeah, so do I.' He nodded. 'Big time. Sometimes, I can't believe it's happened to me. I feel . . . lucky.'

'I know, and I'm glad. But it doesn't mean that it has to be like that every time, that you can't ask for other stuff. Or me. I'm not saying I won't then use it against you, but only sexually, babe. Not in any other way.'

Alex held her.

'You can be such a bitch,' he said, after a few minutes. 'But sometimes, you're just not. It's not that I think it's all going to be okay now, but I feel like it's got to be better.'

'Yeah. And like I said, it never hurts to get extra ammo.'

'Never hurts you, anyway.' This time she thought he did smile, that she could feel it against her cheek.

'Alex, I have to ask you something.' She pulled away slightly, so she could see his face. If she was going to brave this one, she had to do it properly. 'Why do you never touch me here?' She took his hand and placed it on her breast. Her heart was hammering, he must be able to feel it. But she had to do this. Alex left his hand there for a second, then moved it to her leg.

Even now he couldn't bear to touch her breast.

She felt a complete idiot. He could touch her scars, kiss them, run his tongue along them, but he couldn't stand to touch her breast.

'It's not what you think,' he said.

'And what's that, exactly?' Forcing herself to keep her eyes on his face.

'Well, I don't know. But you won't have it right.' He rubbed her thigh. 'I think you're totally gorgeous. Every bit of you. But . . .' Always a but with Alex. 'You won't like this.' He looked away. A poor little victory.

'No.'

'I haven't got a thing about big tits, you know. I don't think you'd look better if you had more, they're fine, it's not about that.'

'What is it about, then?'

'What it is, I'm frightened, Rosie. It's like, *there* you're too young to be touched. Like a teenager. Sometimes, I can't even look at you there, naked. It does repel me to be honest, because it makes me feel like a pervert. I haven't got a thing about teenage girls, far from it, but it seems to me if I played with you there, it would be like I did have. Can you understand that?'

'No.' *Rejection.* She could be spiteful here, say it was okay practically to rape her in front of her brother was it, so long as he didn't sully himself by touching her tits? But she didn't. She felt too humiliated, as though Alex had tethered her wrists and stomped all over her. And there was no buzz for her in her own submission.

'I've always felt like that, even though I've nearly always been with small-breasted women. Not that I've had hordes of girlfriends, as you know.' *What about Louise?* But you can't ask questions like that when you're bound and gagged. 'Rosie? Say something, please.'

'Nothing to say.' Her voice phlegmy. She repelled him.

'Do I satisfy you? Sexually?'

Rosie was taken aback. How the hell could she answer that one? Of course he did: there was no greater sexual thrill than having someone you loved, respected, desired, even liked for Christ's sake, lie down for you to walk over. But he was saying yet again that she wasn't perfect. And with the weight of that pressing into her (almost breastless) chest, how could she admit that she'd never before known such sexual satisfaction, liberation? Increasingly, it seemed to her that there was a big difference between people who borrowed from the edge to spice up their domestic sex lives, and people like Rosie, like Alex, whose sexuality was uncovered in its use. But it made you so very vulnerable; in chaining another, you chained yourself.

'Because,' he added into her silence, 'all I know is that I ought to be under your feet. It's . . . because of what I saw when I was growing up, I've always felt sex was dirty or wrong. Even the desire for it made me feel a bastard. That sort of got proved along the way.' With the oblique reference to his wife, he shot Rosie a nervous glance. 'And it's like, being under your feet makes it cleaner. Does that make sense? That's where I should be, it's a privilege. I don't say that often, because it's not easy to say. It'd kill me if that wasn't enough for you.'

She looked at him; his eyes had tears in them again.

'It is,' she said. 'But that doesn't mean you don't hurt me, Alex.'

'No,' he said. 'It seems to mean I do.'

'And that wasn't easy for me to say.'

Chapter Thirteen

Good-looking bird, bit younger'n Rosie. Smiling in most of the
pictures. Sort of plump, not bad legs, really nice tits. Too much
slap, but she weren't no tart, by the looks of her. And one of
her as a kid, fat and all serious with them horrible plaits mums
used to make their girls have. Rosie wouldn't never let Mum
do them. Didn't see them much now – must be out of fashion.
One with a little boy and a baby, by the swings in Barmy Park.
Her kids, most likely. Darren felt a bit funny, choked up and
sort of hot. Never thought, when Nana give him the cardboard
envelope, it might have stuff like this in it. Was keeping it in
the bottom of her bag – evidently come through the door, back
when she was stopping at his. Opened it, she had. Right handy
being senile. *Look at the pretty.* Now he couldn't stop looking.
He pushed the photos away cross the table, but careful, so's
not to mess them up. Never took a mastermind to know she
was the landlord's dead sister. It was like them appeals off the
telly, where famous people tried to get you to give money by
showing you pictures of starving wogs. Must think it was taking
too long, backing the Old Bill. A reminder. The more pictures,
the bigger amount of holding Patterson's hands up. And be
fair, they was a week into January now, what must make it
least seven weeks since the *once and for all* meet. Trouble was,
the druggy was so out-of-it, they was still having a job getting
him to get his story straight. His being a fucked-up nothing
was what made him a good ringer, but it made him a dodgy
one, and all. Darren leaned over, picked up one of the photos
again. Looking at the paper in this one, laughing at something

in it, sitting on an old flowery settee. *Paper.* Was they stupid,
or what? Thanks, Alex, mate. What'd he said that time? Paper
was appealing for witnesses? So that's what Darren'd find them
– miles better'n an appeal off the telly. A witness. Most likely
Freddy'd of had to come round to that, but Darren'd got there
quicker – Billericay boy give it him on a plate. Finished their
crossword. Whatever they'd been doing in the kitchen New
Year's, what they'd made him listen to, this nearly made up
for it. Darren put the photo down. Yeah, nice looker. Had been,
anyway. Couldn't help from seeing at the end of the day,
weren't no one's confession that was the deal.

He must know how it was, man, Alex always knew everything. Freaky. But Sam weren't sure what he'd told him before
and shit. Wasted, man – scrambled eggs for brains. Alex said
he'd be all right in the head, and Alex knew what he was on
about, but he weren't looking after him, despite what he'd
promised. Used to think if he had an old man, he'd of liked
him to be like Alex. His brothers'd piss theirselves, but Sam
never wanted Alex thinking bad of him, only maybe it didn't
matter now. No referral. Promised him seven, eight weeks ago.
Seven, eight weeks of wondering if what the Boyds said might
be true. Couldn't sort it out in his head, everything gone
wrong. That bird died – if Sam done it, then he killed her. A
murderer. Alex even told him he shouldn't keep turning up
at the Centre at all hours. When Alex looked at him, used to
believe like someone cared. Not like the God Squad, but like
– sounded like a poofy thing, only it weren't – like he could
understand what was in your head, and not make you feel
bad about it. Even if you made a tit out of yourself, crying
and shit, even when you couldn't deal with it and had to have
something, he weren't just disappointed with you. You never
felt his bollockings was going to last. And Alex was sorted,
guy. Really had his shit together. Head straight, all that. But
it was true about him and Rosie Spence, everyone said so,
even Alex now. Oh, man. She was a scary lady. Must've turned

Alex against Sam. Alex said he'd be all right, but he weren't, and it weren't easy to keep what happened in your head, not when it was like a tea-strainer. Rosie Spence'd got to Alex's soul. Every night, Sam dreamt about the fire, big fired-up dreams. Maybe didn't matter about the referral, not if he'd done what they said. The Boyds made him say it over and over and over and over to them. *I-knew-The-Lion-owed-Charlie-money-and-I-did-it-off-my-own-back-so's-I-could-get-in-with-The-Mice.* Why'd he want to get in with them? Always thought them mice looked like rats. But they was telling him how he done it, and it was easy to get confused. Easy to get wasted, too. When a butterfly flapped its wings near Charlie Boyd, he pulled the frigging things off. Alex told Sam he couldn't've done it, but that might just be to get him more confused. Rosie Spence might've told Alex to do that. And if Alex never believed he hadn't done it, there weren't no way Sam could believe it himself.

'I don't believe he fucking did it, Rosie, not for a second. You should see the state of the poor kid. He doesn't even know himself what's true.' Alex stood by the window, lighting a cigarette, his hand shaking.

'But—'

'No, I don't want to hear *buts*. He's just some pathetic little druggy as far as . . . whoever is concerned. Dispensable. Disposable. All the other fucking words beginning with *dis*. No one has any responsibility, do they? Not in your world. It's always down to someone else. Fuck it, if he goes down for this, it'll be the end of him. Don't you care?'

'Of course I—'

'You know what? Darren was right New Year's Eve, even though he didn't mean to be. It's all fucking corrupt.' He moved towards the door, and began to hit it, softly, rhythmically, with the side of his fist. 'A young woman *died* in there. I can't stop thinking about it. I thought I didn't have a problem with what you do, and your world. Well, no, I knew I did, but it didn't

seem that different from things I have to do. But I'm beginning to think I was wrong.'

Rosie felt at a severe disadvantage, sitting down. She got
up, and went over to Alex, attempting to stroke his arm.

'Don't,' he said.

'Look, Alex, this has got nothing to do with me. I haven't
even got any bloody idea whether he did it. Maybe he didn't,
but it'd never stand up.'

'Who did do it?' Alex grabbed her hand and held it. 'Come
on, who did it?'

'I don't know.'

'Sam keeps on about Charlie Boyd. Your fucking Charlie
Boyd did it himself, didn't he?'

'I said, I don't know. And he's not *mine*.' She wrenched her
hand away.

'No? But that's why you were being minded, wasn't it? That
fire had to do with one of them down your pub, and you were
what? The consolation prize? Bet Darren knows.'

'You can't ask him. Not that he'd tell you if he did.'

'Honour amongst arsonists. Great philosophy.'

He went to the table and tossed his cigarette into the ashtray.
There was ash on her carpet, where he'd just let it fall as he
smoked. He lit another. Rosie was faint with a rush of oxygen
to her brain; she tried to slow her breathing. Shit. *Shit*. There
was no way she could get out of this one, and yet she wasn't
guilty. Since when had being Darren Spence's sister been a
crime? Like Alex said, a woman died in there. Christ, didn't
he remember what had happened to Ben? That could have been
her. It was like being in a thriller with no denouement, a film
on an eternal loop, taking them back to where they'd started.
She'd had a bitch of a day, hadn't got home until nearly nine,
there'd been three messages from Louise, and now this. And
she couldn't even mention the calls: *quid pro quo*, Louise for
Sam. It was tempting to tell Alex to get lost, but if she did,
he'd see it as an admission. '*Snot fair*. She could almost imagine
being reduced to the state where she'd tried to follow Daz and

Ben around, whinging about not being allowed to play out with them, or whatever dead cool things they got to do.

'Do you want a drink?' she said, against his bitter smoking silence.

'That's right, your answer to everything.' He licked his thumb and forefinger, pinched out his cigarette; his expression cooled into contempt.

Rosie followed him back over to the window, and took hold of his arms.

'I understand you being upset about Sam,' she said, not letting him drop his gaze. 'Like I said, maybe he didn't do it. Okay, but neither did I. Yeah, of course you're right, I was being minded because they thought someone . . . and you know what it was like for us.'

'No, I never did know, that's the point. You never told me anything, and I was stupid enough to let that be.' Alex pulled one arm free, rubbed his hand across his mouth, leaving a slight black residue. 'I actually believed you'd tell me when you trusted me enough, as long as I trusted you.' He laughed. 'There's been bits and pieces coming out for a while, muddled crap about lions and fucking mice and fires. But today he said he'd set light to The Red Lion to get in with Charlie Boyd, though he couldn't remember properly. Then I saw what the truth was.'

'Which is what, exactly?'

'Don't give me that bollocks. He's being forced to take the blame. Simple.'

'Not by Daz, that's for sure. Jesus, if it went wrong . . . he's had one stretch and he couldn't handle that.' Rosie crossed to the settee, perched on the edge of it. 'What did you do with the cigarettes? Oh it's all right, they're here.' Neither of them said anything for several minutes, until Rosie couldn't stand it any longer. Fight or flight. 'So what's all this about?'

'You know full well what it's fucking about.'

'No, Alex, I don't, as it goes. Are you after an abject confession of responsibility, or what?' She crossed her legs and

watched the lengthening ash of her cigarette, wondering if it
would fall. Christ, it was just possible that she was being outed
here, and she couldn't see any way of protecting herself.

Alex moved to the armchair and sat down, heavily. He
gestured for the cigarette packet.

'You don't do abject, as you'd say.' He sparked the lighter,
looking into the flame for three or four seconds before holding
it to his cigarette. 'I want . . . a concession, I suppose. I want
you to see we're all culpable here. You, me, Darren, Charlie
Boyd, even Sam. I hate everyone over this, fucking everyone.
That girl was only in her twenties.'

'You hate me?' She felt sick.

'You *knew* the Old Bill would get Sam, didn't you? I'm
assuming that's foregone? You knew, and you didn't tell me.
Didn't even tell me why you were in danger, I only started to
work it out after Christmas. I hate everyone, Rosie. Including
me.'

How could he hate her?

'I'm going to have that bloody drink, even if you're not.
Self-righteous . . .' She fought the tears in her voice and won.
Looked round for the ashtray, just making it in time. She
rummaged in the back of the cupboard for the sticky remains
of a bottle of Wild Turkey, and poured a huge measure. If he
cast her in the role of irresponsible lush, she'd bloody well
give him a great performance. He'd surpassed himself this time.
What did he expect? She couldn't have told him, even if she'd
explicitly been told herself, which she hadn't; that would have
been to choose. Impossible. Her lives duelling, probably until
the bloody death. That was no choice. Rosie felt for Sam, but
he wasn't down to her. Freddy would never let Charlie suffer
for this: if someone didn't get put away, they were all up for
grabs. The consolation of their philosophy.

'Rosie, can I change my mind? About the drink?'

'Evidently.' She splashed some bourbon into another glass,
and put it on the table. 'What are you going to do?' Moving
to stand behind the settee, both hands around her own glass.

'What can I do? I tell you one thing, I'll stand as a character witness if it comes to it.'

'It won't help. Even if you're right, he won't dare plead anything but guilty in court, not without protection.' She hadn't meant to say that much. They looked at each other. Oh God, Alex wasn't being self-righteous: this was old-fashioned principle. Wrong-headed, sure, but there were worse sins. 'I'm sorry,' Rosie said.

'Are you?' He didn't look angry now, only strained.

'Yeah. Even if he did do it, he's just a fall guy. Your butterfly.' She walked slowly around the settee, hesitating before sitting down. 'I couldn't have done anything different, Alex.'

'Maybe not.' He reached for his drink. 'But maybe I could have. Couldn't even get him that referral, could I? Maybe I should have tried your methods and paid for one.' Giving her a sideways glance. 'Whether he goes down or not, he'll be using on-and-off his whole life. I've been surprised before, but I'm certain this time.' He coughed. 'You know what's really terrible? I'm more frustrated about me not being able to do anything than about what using does to him.' Swallowed half his Wild Turkey, and coughed again. 'Shit. I just, I really hate that you're messed up in . . . I do know you're a good lawyer. But sometimes, I wish what you did was more . . . that you could choose a bit differently.'

'Pays for what I am, sweetheart.'

'That's part of the problem.' He levered himself to his feet, and came to sit beside her. 'I really like what you are, most of the time. But there's a massive price-tag attached. Sam . . .'

'Yeah.' She took his hand. It felt hot. At this moment, she didn't want him to lie down for her. She just wanted to make it all right for him. 'So what now, babe?'

'*Babe*. You know, I love it when you call me things like that, but it doesn't mean anything, does it? Me, Darren, the bloke in the newsagents. It's not just for me.'

'It all depends on what's behind it, *babe*. What's that got to do with anything?'

'It's all got to do with it,' he said, quietly. Rosie felt the panic rise again, but she forced herself to stay silent. This was it. The first time in her adult life that she was going to sit it out. Whatever happened. This was the one man it was *possibly* worth risking rejection for. Alex twisted Daz's ring on her finger; she felt sweat gather underneath the band, her skin speaking for her. Then he lifted her damp hand to his cheek, rubbing it against his stubble. 'I don't want to lose you,' he said. 'But you've got to understand this isn't easy for me. I've been driving myself mad thinking one thing then another about you relative to this. And about me. Then today when Sam . . . I wanted to make you see that everything we are has consequences. It was like, it was hitting me for the first time. Properly hitting me, does that make sense? Not just what you are, but relative to me, as well. My decisions aren't that much different, not really.' His voice bitter again. 'But I get to play the good guy.'

Rosie knew she was in trouble here; not because she thought Alex would leave, but because suddenly she knew he wouldn't. This was a new deal: someone who laid out the problems, admitted their own liability, yet didn't let you off your bid. He expected her to understand that for him, his hatred joined them as much as his love for her did. How the hell was she supposed to call this one? No, she knew the answer. Straight. If she had the guts.

'I don't think you just play the good guy, precious, I think you have a bloody good crack at *being* it. I'm not like that, but I admire it.'

'Thought I was a self-righteous bastard?' Alex smiled, faintly.

'Yeah, that too, sometimes. But it goes with the territory, doesn't it? Anyway, that's part of what you've got me for, to stop you getting too up yourself.'

'I've got you then, have I?' He rubbed her thigh. She leaned over his arm to get her glass from the table. 'You're stalling, Rosie.'

'Yeah.' She sipped at the bourbon. 'We could be a disaster, we both know that. But I can't see any alternative.'

'I just want to hear it,' Alex said. Gently, he held her chin, turning her face towards him. 'I've waited a fuck of a long time.'

'What if I can't?' Her throat was dry. *Seem calm, seem calm.*

'What if you won't. Nothing. But I'll be disappointed, big time. That's not emotional blackmail, I'm just being honest. And yeah, I know there's bound to be a price, there always is, with you. But it's worth it, to me.'

Rosie called it; this might be the biggest mistake of her life, but she was going to play.

'Okay,' she said. 'I love you.' It felt less like a bid than like her own plea. She heard Alex exhale; must have been holding his breath. 'Don't pretend you didn't know,' she added. 'But it doesn't solve anything, does it?'

'No. I'm still really glad, though. And I do know I'll have to get an injunction out on Louise, somehow. I'll find the money, I promise. And for the divorce.'

Quid pro quo.

She thought he was going to kiss her, but he didn't. Love couldn't cancel hate.

The feel of avocado as she slipped it, ripe and greasy, from its skin; extra virgin olive oil leaving its filmy release on her fingers; black pepper clinging to the green flesh, to the oil. Rosie didn't do cooking, but she loved the physicality of preparing certain foods. Certain expensive foods. Part of her was always aware that she never knew the exact price of out-of-season vegetables and exotic seasonings; she got a conscious buzz out of her ignorance, of piling the stuff into her basket on what William would call a whim of appetite or desire. Once, visiting Janey in Sheffield, she'd gone into Morrison's, where beans could be bought for a couple of pence and where yogurt was considered extravagant. *I favour a plain biscuit* where they couldn't buy fancy. The anxious faces in the queue, searching for change in tatty old purses; the bodies, carrying around years of chips and making do, lardy and coarsened beyond all reason. No, that was the point: they couldn't get beyond the reason. Rosie had felt stomach-churning disgust as well as pity, and whenever she remembered it now, out shopping, she always threw in a couple of things she didn't even want, just to show herself that she could. *Damn right.*

She was putting this meal together for Alex. A gesture, a symbol of their new togetherness, of openness. The past week or so had been difficult, with each of them trying not to mention Sam. He was always there, buried under every conversation, but at least they were attempting a life apart from him. And so Rosie had decided to offer the meal. What a nice domestic scene it must make: the woman in the kitchen, her hands slippery with food, the man in the living room, choosing the music, pouring the drinks. She'd even hoovered. Rosie smiled to herself. Domestic. Yeah, right. You want domestic, go marry a cook. She had other fish to fry.

The plate looked just that tad crammed; Rosie took off a slice of avocado, popped it into her mouth. Much better. Green, brown, white, red. Just remove one fragment of truffle. Perfect. On a side plate she'd put great chunks of fresh buttered bread. She licked her fingers, then rinsed them under the tap, careful not to splash her dress. Her mum would have been wearing an apron, one of those stupid things that stopped at the waist, that she'd been making since the fifties. Rosie had one somewhere that Mum or Nan had given her one time, but she'd rather cook naked than wear it. Sometimes, what you saw was what you got.

'It's ready, babe.'

'Great, I'm starving.' Alex looked up from the piles of CDs he'd made next to the player.

Rosie carried the plates over to the little table.

'Move that, sweetheart.' She touched the gateleg with her foot.

'You want me to move the table?'

'Well done, Einstein. Just put it up against the settee.'

'We're not sitting on the settee then?'

'You're really getting the hang of this. Be up to that million before you know it, and you'll still have all your lives.'

Alex grinned, one of his slightly cocky numbers, and got up to push the table to where she wanted it. She put the plates on the floor, inside the oblong marked by four round indents. A virtual table.

'No cutlery?' he said.

'No.'

'Looks lovely.'

'I took a lot of trouble.'

'You mean you peeled things and cut up cheese?'

'Cheeky sod, I steamed the asparagus. I'd watch it, if I were you.'

'No you wouldn't.' He walked carefully round the marked-out space, and put his hands on her waist. She let him kiss her, then stepped back.

'I thought you were starving?' she said.

'Yeah, I am.'

'Looks like it. You haven't even tried to touch the food.'

'Didn't think I was supposed to.' He looked down at her, that smile back in place, provocative. She stroked his face, lightly.

'Really calling them, aren't you?' She moved through the invisible barrier, standing close to the plates. 'How hungry?'

'Very.' He held her gaze.

'My mum always told me the way to a man's heart was through his stomach.'

'I don't think this was what she had in mind, was it?'

'And what's this?'

'You tell me.'

A fortune squandered underneath her shoe.

'Still hungry?'

Alex nodded, his expression serious now.

'So eat.'

He dropped to his hands and knees, and looked up at her. Then he did start to eat, an animal at its bowl. No, not an animal: a big, beautiful man on his knees, foraging for the flattened morsels as though they were the greatest delicacy he could imagine. Nourishing her. The world could have straight sex, and welcome. She kept very still, watching his tongue as it licked the pulp from her heel.

'Bread?'

He paused, and nodded.

'But I don't want to fall over, do I?' she said. 'And I don't want to get the carpet dirty.'

Christ, he was good. From the methodical, efficient way he solved the problem, you'd think he'd been in training all his life. He started on the bread with her clean foot in his hair; she was buggered if she'd make this easy for him. Food was meant to be savoured. She'd never bought that eat to live stuff. And clearly, her Alex didn't, either.

He was coming a fucking fixture, following around after Rosie like a ginormous puppy. She was still well into him, and all – Darren could make that out from the way she was always touching him. Not soppy or nothing – that weren't her style – but the hand on his arm, or touching his cheek, just quick, so's most people wouldn't of noticed nothing much. Not easy to tell if the nail from the news'd be put in Alex's coffin or Darren's. Felt like months since New Year's stead of weeks, and it'd been murder. Or worser, like torture. Darren couldn't get out his head bout, bout, blank it. *What the eye don't see.* He never heard nothing from her kitchen, that weren't what'd happened. Couldn't be. Just wished he could stop thinking. Specially when he see them. Not that they see him tonight, walking straight past like Darren was any old cunt in an Armani suit.

'All right, Al boy? You looking after this one for us?' Tom was pulling Alex's pint afore he even asked for it.

'You think she needs it, then?' Saucy git.

'When I ain't around, maybe,' said Darren. They both turned round slow, and neither of them could be arsed to smile at him. But Darren still let Rosie kiss him on the cheek. 'What you two up to?'

'We're off to see Mum,' said Rosie, 'and I don't know about
you, but I find it way easier after a drink. Anyway, I've had
a total bitch of a day, did you hear?'

'Yeah. But he'll be out in three – a result if you think bout
what could of happened.'

'Shall we sit down?' Alex said, squeezing Rosie's arm. 'She's
dead on her feet.' Rosie smiled at Alex. If Darren would of said
that, he'd of been told to keep his nose out. He wished Ben
would get a move on, even up the fight. But it weren't a fight.
Or if it was, it was like that one where the English bloke made
mincemeat of the American, and then it was said like it was
a draw. The only thing was, she'd always be his sister, but she
weren't going to stay with no geezer for ever. No way. So
perhaps it was a draw, if you looked at it like that. Alex might
of took her more away than what she was, but she'd always
be back. She belonged round here.

Looked a bit knackered tonight, she did – but sort of glowing.
Minded him of a length of copper at the start of a burn, where
the colours was changing while you watched, but you couldn't
see a straight difference between one and the next. He'd have
to tell her – she could well of heard it by the time they left
the pub anyway. And Darren wanted it to be him what said,
even if that was a bit evil. But he'd more or less warned her
she couldn't carry on with Alex. Where the hell was Ben? Must
of got involved. Darren'd've made a proper time, if he'd of
known Rosie'd be here. He felt in his pocket for his fags. Most
likely left them on the bar.

'Got a straight, darling?'

She slid the packet cross the table. Little hands, she had.
See the veins in them, like you could in the old man's. Rosie
always said her hands was ten years older than what she was.
Ring looked good. Fucking nail varnish, though – that white
stuff what made out like it weren't meant to show, but it was.
Specially gainst some cunt's jeans.

'Mum says you've taken Tom's niece out a couple of times.'

'You seen her?' Make the effort. 'She's a sort, mate,' he said to Alex. 'Legs up to her bum, right sweet smile. But you can't shit on your own doorstep, know what I mean?'

'She's too young for you, anyway,' said Rosie. Cheeky bitch. But she had a point. Sometimes, it was hard to member he'd be forty in two years. Birds like Di might look the business, but they never had enough of a clue about bed, or what he was on about, or what was important. And he never wanted to look like a sad old git. 'Aesthetic sense versus sexual sense,' Rosie said to Alex, who laughed. Sounded like a load of Double Dutch to Darren. Way she looked over told him she knew it, and all. If she weren't careful, he'd almost enjoy giving her the news.

'Resulting in sensory deprivation?' Alex come back with, well cocky. Most likely making out he understood what she meant.

'Hardly,' she said.

'Swallowed a couple of fucking dictionaries, have you?' asked Darren, nasty.

'Sorry, sweetie. Take no notice of us.' Hand on Alex's leg – again. Blank out them sounds. Blank them. Most probably an argument – they'd knew he was in there. She wouldn't never make him listen to what it sounded like she was making him listen to. Couldn't hardly stand it. Noises, with the wrong pictures joined up to them. Don't look, then.

'I need a word, Ro,' Darren said, giving her a meaningful.

'Sure. Go on, then.'

'No, a *word*.'

'Stop playing silly buggers, just say it.' She run her hands through her hair.

No choices, then. He looked at Alex.

'Sorry, mate, thought it'd be better coming from Rosie, cos I know you're volved with him. They've picked him up on a charge. Sam Patterson.'

Rosie leaned her elbow on the table, and put her forehead in her hand.

Alex was staring at him. Not like he was going to go into

one, but like, like Darren was the lowest form of life. Weren't him what picked out Patterson – stupid little druggy shouldn't of made hisself so obvious, nosing bout all over, with his questions bout Rosie. No one would of thought of him otherwise.

'What time was this?' said Alex, not bothering to blink.

'Safternoon, I think.'

'I've got to go. I'm sorry, love,' Alex said to Rosie. She just nodded, what was right odd. 'Don't worry.' He stood up, then bent to kiss her on the top of her head.

'I'll go home,' she said. 'Come over or ring me, yeah? Hang on a sec.' She felt about in her bag, brung out her keys, and got two off the ring. 'Here, babe, take my spares. Keep them.'

He was pissing off and she was giving him her keys?

'Thanks. Really, thanks.' He touched the side of her face with the back of his hand, grabbed his leather and that fucking carrier and left. Rosie downed her wine.

'Have to get the scum off the streets, don't we?' she said. 'Can't have the general public in any danger.'

'What about that Alex?'

'D'you know what, Daz? I love him. Dangerous enough for you?' And she got up.

Stop her. Stop her. Stop her.

'Have a nother drink with me, girl.'

'No thanks. I'm going home to wait for him.'

She never even turned round to say goodbye.

Chapter Fourteen

That half-asleep state, not with dreams but where hallucinations suffuse reality, making you start, minute by minute, into terrified wakefulness, immediately drifting again. But this time, as she sat up in bed, she found Alex getting in beside her.

'What's the time?'

'Gone four. Go back to sleep.'

'I wasn't, not really.' She rubbed his naked shoulder, and he kissed her hand.

'He's been charged, love. They let me see him, and they've got him a brief of course. He's in a real state.' He pulled her into him, and hugged her. 'I couldn't do a thing, Rosie. I felt . . .' His words became a mumble, as though he were falling asleep.

'You want to talk about it tomorrow?'

'No.' He hugged her harder. 'I mean, no, I want to tell you now. Not that there's much to say. There's a witness, apparently. Convenient, don't you think? Sam's so confused, he thinks that means he definitely did it.' He let her go. 'Your fags here?' Rosie reached across him to switch on the bedside lamp, shielding her eyes against its harsh glare, and felt for the packet underneath her book. 'Thanks.' He dragged so deeply that the end of the cigarette glowered. 'And I'm a right bastard, because all I wanted to do was get home to you.'

She stroked his neck. *Home*.

'Fraternizing with the enemy,' she said.

'No, I didn't mean that. I meant . . . I wanted to get out of the smell of piss, and having to deal with that poor kid, and just be held. Do you love me?'

'Yeah, you know I do.' She moved her hand to his chest, dropping hot ash on to his stomach. Alex flinched. 'Sorry.'

'That's okay.' He balanced the shell ashtray on his legs. 'I keep seeing his face, love. But that's no use to him, is it? My nice liberal pity. I'm here, in a comfy bed with a beautiful woman, feeling sorry for some druggy who hasn't got a chance . . . great.' He brought his fist down into the mattress, upsetting the ashtray. 'Bollocks.'

'Don't worry, I'll sort it.' Rosie lifted the edge of the duvet and shook the ash back into the shell. Then she rubbed at the black mark, shuddering at the dry-slimy feel on her fingers.

'Had to happen.' He sounded close to tears. 'Look, I know it's a lot to ask, but can't you help him, in some way? As a lawyer.' Playing with the ashy mark, staring down at it.

'I haven't taken from the duty list for four years. Anyway, you said he's got a brief.' She felt as though she was offering up Sam herself. 'He'll get legal aid, babe. Even the Maxwells did, you know. It's a Criminal case.'

'Yeah, it is,' he agreed, with too much feeling, turning to look at her. 'But what representation will he get, realistically? It's all so much bollocks.'

'I can't, Alex. You know that.'

'Yeah, I can see that.' He nodded. 'No, I can.'

She wanted to tell him she knew in her heart that Sam hadn't done it, but in no universe was that possible. Instead, she put out her cigarette, took his from his mouth and crushed that out too, and began to make love to him.

She knew he'd far rather have had her help.

And she also knew he wasn't going to ask again for it.

'Don't.' He pushed her away. Of course he did. The last thing he'd want was sex; close his eyes, he'd probably see Sam. But he wasn't the only one in this bed. He wasn't the only one affected by it all.

'I just wanted to make you feel better.' Or make herself feel better.

'It won't. God. I think I make it pretty clear about me, especially relative to when I can and can't have sex.' He rubbed his chest, hard. 'I've practically given you an instruction manual, for Christ's sake. But you ignore it, everybody always does. I shouldn't have to tell you this. There's no value in you giving me what I want if I have to tell you what it is. You of all people should know that.'

And that meant, did it, that his needs had to be paramount? When their needs collided, his had to flatten hers. Oh shit, no. Not another Scottie. Always the woman who paid. The way Alex drew his mental pictures of the past, she could never have such a firm profile; Rosie wasn't used to losing, nor to an opponent embalmed and safely entombed in before.

'I suppose *Louise* was bloody telepathic, was she?'

'In the beginning she was, always got me right, for years.'

'So you never get it wrong with me?' Bastard.

'Of course I do, but that's not the point.' He ran his hand over his face. 'I'm sorry, I was just hurt, I didn't mean that about Louise.'

'No?' But Rosie was sure he had. Perhaps she had some telepathic powers after all.

'No. Give me a cuddle, love. Please. That's what I want more than anything in the world right at this moment.'

Rosie held him. But he'd had to tell her to, and her arms were rigid with jealousy and pain. It took until daylight for her to forgive him for her failures.

She'd thought she wasn't interested in statement clothing; of course, all clothes created an identity, but she'd liked the idea that what she was came out of a statement that was ambiguous. Now she wanted the iconography, a symbolic confirmation. As she left Ben's place, she checked her watch. Just time to get back across town before the late-night shops in Soho closed.

Rosie hadn't intended to visit Ben yet. She had PMT from

hell, had eaten an entire bar of Fry's Chocolate Cream and a
KitKat. Then she'd managed to sound like a Magistrates' Court
hack, calling the judge *Your Worship* instead of *Your Honour*;
what had she been thinking, after years of getting it right? And
Alex had left a message on the mobile to say he was working
late. Sod her chargeable hours, she was always well ahead of
the game, anyway. All Rosie wanted to do was to leave early,
have a long bath with an early Iris Murdoch, a serious scotch,
and find some trash to watch on telly. Maybe drop a Temazepam,
and get a proper sleep for once. But she didn't fancy being on
her own. Louise was bound to have rung. Worse, she might
ring tonight. Rosie certainly wasn't going anywhere near the
pub; she was avoiding Daz, unless there was no other way. And
she couldn't face the club. *Your Worship*. God.

Funny thing about your mates: they were the ones you least
wanted when you were having a bad day. Or maybe other
people didn't feel like that, maybe those networks of sisters
she'd read so much about were reality for some women. When
Rosie was on form, she loved boozing with Elizabeth, or shopping with Randa, or gossiping for hours on the 'phone with
Janey. But when she was feeling like hell, she didn't want them
to see. Daz managed to be one of the boys, always had been.
But it occurred to Rosie now, as she scanned the street for a
taxi, that she'd never been one of the girls. Not inside. You
had to believe it for it to be true. A cab drew up at the corner.
Rosie got in, still not sure where she was going. The driver
half turned his head; she saw a deep scar along the side of
his face. Might as well pretend to be one of the lads, then.
She had nowhere else to go, and she had a promise to herself
to keep, for Alex.

Ben stood in front of the mirror. Like being in one of them
Fun Houses at the fair – except this weren't no fun. And when
he left the bathroom, he wouldn't be leaving his reflection
behind and walking out with a normal face. This *was* his normal
face, only except for it weren't normal. Doc said the scars

would fade, gradual, but he'd stay all puckered up. First of all he couldn't look at hisself, but now he looked all the time. Getting on for three month now – hard to believe that. Good job he weren't never no oil painting. But perhaps that made it worse. Always done all right with birds, specially tall ones with big tits for some reason. But he had to face the fact that that weren't going to be the case no more. Face the fact. Fucking face was the fact, weren't it? He looked like a cunt. Funny thing was, he looked like what he weren't and all, like an hard case. And it weren't being an hard case what got him like this. He touched the scars. Felt horrible, they did, like he was growing extra skin, with lumps underneath it. Him and Spence had took the piss something chronic out of Paul Campbell for his acne at school, even now he was called Crater Face. Ben'd swap, no danger. They'd call him something soon, if they never already. Kept thinking he'd ask Spence, but something stopped him. And the stupid sod was too soft-hearted just to come out with it. He was unless Ben pissed him off, anyway, and he was getting a lot of rope with Spence at the minute. That made him feel funny, and all. Like even his life weren't normal. Like he was a cripple.

The doorbell. Most probably Spence, seeing if he wanted to go The Mice. Taking for knocking for him, he had, like they was ten again. Only now there was no one to ask if Ben was allowed out. Should of been. Should be someone to say *Don't stay out too late, boy* or even stop him from going. When Tricia got knocked up, she never wanted nothing much more to do with him. Sept for dough. Thought it was meant to be the bloke what run off. At this rate, him and Spence'd end up two lonely old gits, off down The Mice every night with no one giving a toss if they got off their heads. Spence never even had the excuse of a knackered face.

'Rosie!' The last person he expected.

'That's my name, don't wear it out,' she said, in an on-purpose kid's voice. Just like years ago, only then it hadn't been for a joke. She give him the bottle she was holding.

Glenmorangie. She could be a right good girl sometimes.

His place was a mess. If he'd of known, he'd of had a bit of a tidy round. He picked yesterday's *Mirror* off the settee, and a couple of empty cans off the floor. She was here. *Rosie*.

'Don't worry about it, I've seen worse,' she said. 'I'm not stopping, just thought I'd pop in, see how you were.' But she'd never popped in round his flat before. Rosie sat where the paper had been, her legs crossed, one of her shoes dangling from her foot. That was another thing what reminded him of when she was a teenager, but he couldn't work out if it was on purpose this time. 'So how's it going then, Ben?'

'Okay. Still get me bad days. Keep thinking perhaps I'm always . . . like there's never going to be a day I forget what I look like.' She'd have the answer. He'd been thinking how to find out, and then like magic she shows up. He wished he'd thought to sit next to her, would of been easier than facing. But he liked looking at her. 'Rosie, what do they call me?'

She never made out for one second like she didn't know what he was on about.

'Frankenstein,' she said. Looked right at him. 'Franky. Won't be long before they're calling you it to your face.' And she never even stuttered over that word. Face.

Frankenstein. Funny thing was, it was Rosie, years back, what'd told him that weren't the name of the monster, it was the name of the scientist geezer what made him.

'Ignorant sods,' he said, and give a laugh. She caught on and grinned back.

'It's bound to look worse to you, darling. Everyone else'll get used to it much quicker.'

'But what about people who don't know me?'

'People?' Raised her eyebrows. Should of known she'd know.

'Yeah, all right, birds. Women.'

'You're not going to buy it if I tell you it's personality that counts, are you?' She had the front to laugh. Ben hoped she never noticed his boner. Better change the subject.

'Good about Sam Patterson finally, ain't it?'

She pulled her hair away from her face. Just stared. Felt like for ever.

'Why?' she said, after a lot of for evers. Ben knew something was going wrong here.

'Cos of you, and me, and Spence . . .'

'So that makes it good?'

'I never said—'

'Yeah, you did.' She uncrossed her legs and put her shoe back on proper.

'Sorry, Rosie – I never meant to upset you.'

'That's not the point. Jesus.'

Ben felt like his back was against the wall. She had him slammed there, not just with one of her looks, but with something what was behind her words. He could hear it, but he couldn't suss it, like a tune going round in your head what you couldn't quite catch hold of.

'Sorry,' he said again. His hand went to his face – couldn't help it.

'Everyone knows Sam couldn't have done it,' Rosie said. Ben never answered. He knew that for briefs, even for Rosie, there was a massive difference between knowing a thing and being told it straight out. 'A good legal could maybe get him out of this, even now,' she added.

'Yeah?' What the hell's she mean by that? She was looking at him cold, nothing give away in her eyes. Ben fiddled with the cushion aside of him. 'What's Spence say?'

'Haven't seen him.'

Why not? Ben had what he'd wanted for a fuck of a long time – Rosie Spence in his flat, all on her own, to hisself. But at this second, he wished she was a million miles away.

'Straight up, darling, don't know nothing for definite. You know they tell me sod all.'

'*Et tu, Brute.*' She stood up. 'I'm off. Sorry, Ben, but don't be too surprised if they can't make it stick, that's all I'm saying. Don't forget where the burden of proof lies. He might even get proper protection.'

Ben stood up and all. He weren't too sure whether to kiss her, but then he thought better not. She was into one – quiet, but pretty definite. Her coming here weren't magic at all.

'Thanks for the scotch.'

'Pleasure.' Never sounded like it. Then she put her hand on his cheek. He kept right still. Thought for a split second she was going to slap him, but she smiled and kissed him, or sort of, on the corner of his mouth. 'Maybe I'll see you around, sweetie.'

He couldn't work out why, but that was the most horrible thing she'd said to him in years.

She stared at the full-length mirror. Incredible. Not a stranger, but herself transformed. Even her eyes were different, her pupils dilated so far in anticipation that her irises seemed black, and although it might be a trick of the mood or of the light, they shone with what looked like madness. She put her hands on her hips, thrust one leg forward through the split in the skirt. It made her laugh, that she'd created an image of what she was about to do. Clichéd, but made new because she wasn't some pro, or a young babe playing at the look, or someone who'd been practising for years; she was making a declaration, using the available symbols, of what had grown up between her and Alex. The general to represent the specific. And she looked great.

Rosie walked over to the dressing table. The PVC swished as she moved, a faint echo of her intent. From a drawer, she took out a whip, and loaded her other new toys and those Alex had bought after that ironing into a leather Gladstone bag. She'd worn PVC before of course, but never this thin, this shiny, this purposive. Tightening one of the buckles on her top, she went back to the mirror and fastened the wristbands.

It was the boots that transformed the clothes, from play to the real thing. She watched their reflection as she turned her foot to the side. Seven-and-a-half-inch heels. Black patent. High on the ankle. Functional. Boots made to walk on other than pavement. Dominatrix boots. She held the whip against her leg, posing. And she laughed again.

'Alex?' She opened the door a crack and called through.

'Yes, love?'

'There's a bath run for you. Go and get in it. You can add more hot if you need to.' Quickly, she shut the door, before Alex came into the hall. Five minutes. She'd give him that to get undressed and into the bath. But that was the end of her concessions.

The bird weren't bad looking – bit hard faced and more skinny than what he liked, but she weren't no dog. *Fur coat, no knickers* – well, weren't like he sactly objected to that.

'What can I do you for, darling?' he said, giving her the smile.

'You're Spence, ain't you?' Swollen mouth. Hard to say if she'd had a slap, or a touch of the tar brush. He looked her over, purposely slow.

'Yeah, that's me. Why, what you heard?'

She pulled up a chair and sat close to him. He could smell her perfume, cheap stuff, piled on. Bad sign. Birds should know about all that. Spite that the pub was right quiet tonight, could smell the interest of the nosy gits and all, waiting to see what Spence'd do bout some bird they didn't know. Fore long, it'd be like the place'd been heaving at the time.

'Heard all kinds of things, believe you me,' she said. 'Buy a girl a drink?'

This never smelt right to Darren, even despite that her perfume filled up his nose. It was like she'd done it deliberate after all – making her the only thing he could concentrate on. But he went the bar, waved away the new little barmaid, got the Governor over.

'See the bottle blonde sitting where I was?' Darren said. 'Oy – not too obvious.'

'Wearing the rabbit? Everybody see her, mate.'

'Any idea? And do us a vodka and orange and a pint.'

Tom set the tap going, and turned to the optics.

'Knocks about with one of them nutty Pattersons,' he said. 'Not Sam, one of the older brothers.' He looked back at Darren without no spression on his face. Darren nodded.

'Owe you one.'

The bottle blonde was smoking a fag, one of them all-white mint things you never hardly saw no more. She was leaving a load of pink lipstick on the butt. When he put their drinks down on the table, she crossed her legs, letting her skirt ride up. She think he was simple?

'So why'd'you come here? I know I'm an handsome bastard, but it weren't that, was it?'

'Hadn't seen you, had I? Not properly. But now I have—'

'Do us a favour, darling – cut the shit. If you've come with a message, spit it out. Ain't got all night.'

'Funny – seemed to me like you was on your own, and all settled in.' Had to give her that – she weren't slow. But then, neither was Darren. He took a pull on his pint and waited. She eyed him, then spoke again, firm. 'You're letting them believe it's Sam.'

'Far as I'm concerned, it was.' Stroll on – sending birds to do a man's job. Or perhaps she'd just come off her own back, feeling sorry for her bloke's little brother. Either way, it was a waste of time. Them Pattersons weren't no threat. She, or someone, was just chancing their arm.

'Thanks for your concerns. Though I'd love to know why you don't give a shit?'

'Conflict of interests.' He loved that – *conflict of interests.* Rosie used it all the time, but this tart weren't to know that. She looked bit confused, but weren't bout to admit it. Good girl. If it weren't for who she was, Darren might be tempted here.

'Yeah, his brothers weren't never in your gang in the play-ground, was they?'

'Playground's that bit bigger, these days.' Too big sometimes. 'And be truthful, the gang ain't mine. Want a nother drink?'

She picked up her glass, what she hadn't touched, and shook her head. He had a funny feeling she liked him, when she never expected to. But she must be well into that Patterson, to come in here looking. And part from anything else, Darren didn't need no more strife at the minute. Pity. There was a spark in them eyes you never see that often. Bottle – what had nothing to do with her hair colour. The sort of front Rosie had too much of – this was just an hint of that, but still. What'd she thought was going to happen? Perhaps she'd reckoned it was even worth fucking him, to get him onside. Yeah, right pity. But on the other hand, if she'd of done it just for someone else, because she loved someone else, that was a bit sick.

'Listen, I feel sorry for Sam,' he said, when he never meant to. But it was true – he did feel for the poor kid. She smiled at him, sort of sad, over the top of her drink.

'Yeah, daresay you do,' she said. 'Perhaps you all do, even that . . . But no one's going to do nothing about him, are they?' Her face, what'd seemed so hard at first, looked sort of blurry now. Under the slap, he could notice lines – not big wrinkles or nothing, but soft little cracks in the skin. When he thought about it afterward, he couldn't think what made him do it, but at the time, something about the way her hardness melted down forced him to want to explain hisself.

'Years ago, me old man was on strike from his work,' he said, feeling like he should of started with once upon a time. 'So they went round the factories collecting for their fund thing.'

'Like for the miners?' She leant more forwards.

'Sort of. But a lot of the blokes was geezers with families, so they was claiming and all.'

'Dole?'

'Yeah. But then somebody shopped them, told the dole bout the collections.' He waited, see if she could get it. She pushed her hair off her face, like she was doing a Rory Bremner on Rosie. Spooked him a bit, it did.

'One of their own, I suppose?'

'Yeah.' Right pity she was spoken for, and by a Patterson. 'A fucking Jehovah's Witness, what'd got on a guilt trip. Had to leave the manor. Nearly had him bad, they did, when they found out.'

'More'n if it'd been nothing to do with them.'

'Yeah.' He swallowed half his pint and watched her face get back hard, like when metal cooled down and went into a nother shape.

'Thanks for the Jackanory,' she said. 'I'd better nip the loo, before I throw up in here.'

She opened the bathroom door without knocking. Alex looked round.

'God,' he whispered. The flannel glued to his hand and his chest.

Rosie stood in the doorway for a moment, then came into the room and closed the door. She dropped her bag beside the bath.

'I hope you're getting clean for me, boy.'

The flannel didn't move.

'Are you deaf?' She rapped the rim of the bath with the handle of her whip.

'No. Sorry.' He couldn't seem to look away, but he began to rub the flannel, slowly, over his body. Rosie leaned her back against the door, watching. There was a faint buzzing in her ears, and her head felt as though someone were pressing hard into her temples. He was such a big man to look this vulnerable, this exposed. She moved to sit on the lid of the toilet. Crossing her legs, she tapped the whip softly against her stockinged thigh, and then against her boot. Alex continued to wash, methodically, the order of which parts he cleaned dictated by the ritual of years. 'Where did you—'

'Never mind that. And don't splash me, all right? Just wash.'

He finished his bath and pulled out the plug. The water began to drain away, but still he sat there, shivering slightly.

'You can dry yourself now,' she said, polite, formal. She even got up to pass him a towel. 'I'm very thoughtful, aren't I?'

'Yeah. Thank you.' He stepped out on to the mat, and towelled himself, carefully.

'Use my body moisturiser. No, not the vanilla one. The Elizabeth Arden.' She doubted he'd used such a thing in his life. He plastered on too much, his skin visibly slippery. 'Are the curtains drawn in the living room?'

'Yeah.'

'Good. Get the big mirror out of the bedroom, and take it in there.'

He hesitated for a second, then left the bathroom. Rosie heard the bedroom door open, and saw him carry the mirror into the hall. She picked up her bag, followed him into the living room, the height of her heels dictating a slow, heavy-footed pace, tilting her body forwards.

'By that wall, I think. Yeah, that's right.' Rosie unsnapped the clasp of the Gladstone and took out a new restraint. 'Turn around.'

Do it.

The mirror.

Rosie on his skin, his blood	'I love you, Rosie.'
'Who do you belong to?'	'You.'
Every turn a rose	'I love you.'
Rosie on his blood, his skin	'I love you.'
'What do you say?'	'Thank you.'
Rosie's arm raised	'I love you.'
to bring the whip down on him	'Thank you.'

And his bitten-back screams, Rosie's soundtrack.

And Rosie's balance, her triumph.

Standing on his fear, his horror.

She was writing him, creating his terror out of nothing, the blank pages easier and easier to fill. A slip of her pen, and she could kill him off. But it suited her to keep alive his inarticulate pain, with the language she was becoming more fluent in, page by page.

Draw this, you bastard.

Draw this, my love.

The pen is mightier than the crayon.

A tongue clamp. He tried to beg her to take it off, his voice swollen with grief.

'Not unless you speak clearly.'

And then the moment she'd had planned. She removed the clamps, stepped from his body, let the whip drop.

The Collar.

I always told you to be careful, Alex. You bought this. Now I'm going to use it.

He'd admitted he belonged to her. Now she'd take him up on that.

'You want to come, boy?'

'Yeah. God, yeah. Please, Rosie.'

'Where?' She kicked him in the ribs.

'Your . . . boot. Over your boot.'

'How much can you take for me, if I let you do it?'

'I . . . don't know.'

'Everything I can do?'

'God . . . I'll try. Please.'

'Whose are you?' She buckled the collar, tight, about his neck.

'Yours.'

'Whose?'

'Yours.'

'Whose? Who do you belong to?'

'. . . Rosie Spence.'

'You're amazing.' Alex took a huge mouthful of pasta, and wiped his bread around the rim of his bowl.

'Because I know how to open cartons of sauce?' Idly, Rosie twisted a few strands of tagliatelle around her fork.

'Jars of Dolmio, anyone can do, but cartons of fresh stuff . . .' He laughed. 'No, because you did that tonight without any thought about me. It was like I was just an accessory. And I hated you for it.'

Rosie smiled, but she wasn't too sure what she felt here. *Hate.* She was hearing that from him these days almost as much as she was hearing love. And hate is the stronger word. But then, she didn't want him to react less violently, did she? No point in adoration if it was come by through being adorable. Any woman could get that, if she chose. She put her bowl on the pile of magazines, and lit a cigarette. He'd nearly finished, anyway. Alex swapped their bowls and ate the rest of her pasta in a couple of bites. She pulled her dressing gown more closely around her. That felt a bit chilly now.

'You loved it, didn't you?' He shook a cigarette from her packet. She nearly said, *What, the pasta?* but thought better of it. Her skin felt hot on the inside, despite visible gooseflesh, and her brain itched. She knew she was getting ratty, and she also knew that wasn't on. Adrenaline come-down. Same as with any upper, there was a price.

'Yeah. You want some more Coke?'

'No, I'll get us some wine out, if that's okay.'

'I'll do it.' She was restless. Anything was preferable to just sitting.

The cork splintered into the wine, of course it did. Rosie couldn't help thinking back to when she was sixteen, seventeen, and the best nights of her life had been followed by depression and paranoia. She'd seen it happen to Daz, too, on a bigger scale. Dance all night, and be messed up all the next day. Or in Daz's case, burn all night, when he'd loved the fires and there'd still been plenty to burn. Clockwork toys, wound up and run down. But kids didn't have those any more. Maybe it was more like being one of Daz's fires, from sparking to blazing, glowing to cold. The journey to ashes. A little death. She began fishing the tiny flecks of cork out of her glass, then gave up and sipped the gritty wine. Her cigarette had burned down in the ashtray; couldn't be bothered to light another. She rubbed her aching neck.

'What's the matter?'

'Nothing. Just drained.'

'Yeah, me too.' He smiled, fondly. 'It was relentless, but it was the most exciting thing I think I've ever seen, what I did see of it. Wish I could keep my eyes open all the time, but I just can't. God, Rosie. That was the most honest sexual experience of my life. Felt so right, like that's what I should be doing. From your point of view, it must have been amazing.'

'It was.' It had been. She struggled to get back at least a little of the glow.

'Come on, love, what's up?'

'I feel like one of your junkies.'

'Come-down.'

'Yeah.' Sod him. Trust him to understand, when it would have been easy to jump down his throat for getting it wrong.

'I feel really relaxed, even though I'm still in agony. Like I've had a massage or something. But when it was happening, I thought I might pass out from fear. You didn't give a stuff about that, did you? That's what I like about you, relative to this. You just get more and more ruthless. Like you're totally inhabiting yourself. I have to spend so much energy on not using the code words, you wouldn't believe.'

'Yeah, I would,' she said. But he didn't appear to be listening.

'Part of me feels excited when it's happening, then there's usually a shift to where I want it to stop. Though not this time, funnily enough. But when it does stop, I'm disappointed. It's weird. And then when I think about it afterwards, all I want is to be able to see it, and I get so excited by it that . . . weird. If I know it's going to happen, I feel this mixture of dreading it and wanting it more than I've wanted anything. Does that make sense?' He moved to the edge of the settee and reached for her hand. She gave it to him for a second, but it was too awkward, she had to stretch her arm too far, so she squeezed his hand and pulled hers away.

'It's different for me,' she said. 'I do monitor it, but there's a sense of being out of control at the same time.' A threat more real than apparent; unwillingly, it occurred to her that it was the opposite in kind of the fear they'd had waiting for a Sam Patterson to save them.

'Why didn't I meet you when I was twenty?' Grinning.

'Because I'd have only been nine, and that would've made you a pervert.'

'Anyway, maybe neither of us would have coped with this much younger.'

'Not at nine.' She ran her thumbnail over her lips. Would he really have wanted to have met her before? Not to have had his relationship with Louise? Before was a big place. Somewhere her brother romanticized. Somewhere she'd tried to leave. The place that mapped now, no matter what you did to cover your tracks. Not so much remembrance of things past, as remembrance for things future.

'And we wouldn't be who we are now if we'd met earlier, would we?' he said. 'I don't know, maybe that would have been better.' He laughed, but Rosie felt it as an attack.

'You wouldn't have got married,' she said, quickly.

'I might have married you.'

'You know I'm not the marrying kind, babe.'

'Not even if I promised to *Love, honour and obey*?' They looked at each other. For an instant, she was turned on again. But many a jest spoken in pretended truth.

'That might just have made me change my mind.' She flashed him a smile, to show she was in on the joke. But Alex didn't smile back. He came over to her chair, sat on the arm; she felt the weight of him as the chair sagged in his favour. He twisted his body so that he could see her, and the weight increased.

'Rosie, wouldn't you ever marry me?'

'You're married already.'

'Not for long, if Simon's as good as you say.'

'He is,' she said. Don't do this, baby. Not now. Not until she's really gone. And maybe not then. Shit, this is *me* you're talking to; you know what I am. 'He certainly costs enough. Well, not us, obviously, but as a rule—'

'You don't want to answer, do you?'

'No.' She held up her glass. The chair evened as he stood. Rosie put out her cigarette. She felt sure he wasn't going to leave this one alone. And to be fair, why should he? But she wasn't deeply inclined to be fair at the moment.

'There you go.' He gave her the refilled glass and sat on the settee, but as near to the chair as he could manage. 'I think I'm the marrying kind,' he said. 'Don't worry, I'm not trying to pressure you. I'm just saying, so as you know. It doesn't have to make any sort of difference.' He rubbed his hand across his mouth.

'Is that why you got married before? Because you're the type?'

'Not really. I'd never met anyone like her, and I was desperate not to lose her.' *Never met anyone like her.* He'd said that about Rosie, once. 'She only had to walk into a room, and I got a hard-on,' he continued. 'I'm not usually like that, not even when I was much younger. And when she played her violin, God, it was the sexiest thing in the world to me then. I don't even like classical, but I loved that. I drew her doing it, loads of times, but I couldn't get the movement, I'm not good enough. And of course, I couldn't show the music. Should have filmed her really, but I never did. Don't get cross with me, love. It was a long time ago.'

Before was something you could never compete with, because it couldn't be tested now. It was now that was measured against whatever you told yourself about before. Rosie felt a cold, strangling fist around her heart. She'd thought that only happened in novels. But novelists must get their material from somewhere. Or maybe it was the other way round, and this was a conditioned response. She'd read it, and replicated it.

'I wanted to look after her, as well,' Alex went on. Relentless. Ruthless. 'She seemed fragile even then, though she was impressive at the same time. I'll never feel . . . don't take this the wrong way, but I'll never feel like that again. Not so sure of anything. I was wrong about her, of course I was. Big time.

But . . .' He finished his wine, and poured some more. 'Aren't you ever going to say anything?'

'Nothing to say. Go on.'

'There's no more, really. Just, I didn't know how wrong I'd been until I met you. I knew I didn't want her back like she was when she left, but I compared everyone I met to how she'd been when I first knew her. You were the only one I couldn't do that with. Not that anyone else was like her, but you were so . . . you were *too* different. Are you cross?'

No. The fist had got so tight that she was numb. Protecting herself, like she always did. Or the hundreds of novels she'd read were protecting her. She shook her head, curled her feet under her, making herself as small as possible.

'What about you with that bloke you nearly married? What was it there?' He looked genuinely interested. Didn't it bother him at all?

'He was drop-dead gorgeous, and just that little bit dangerous,' she answered, carefully. 'Bloody idiot, I was. And he was a male version of me, working-class boy made good.' Her tone was deliberately ironic. She stopped to think. 'It was the best sex I'd ever had,' she added. Rosie knew she was being a bitch. It had been true, back then, but did Alex need to know that? 'And he was seriously bright, without having had it all handed to him.'

'Yeah, the middle classes are trained from birth, so a lot of us look bright even when we're not really. Not me, obviously.' He laughed. Rosie wanted to slap him.

'I *hate* that romantic vision of . . . of how brilliant someone could be if they're given a go, just because they're quick,' she said. 'Being seriously bright is different, whatever the class.'

'I know.'

'Do you?' She was trembling. A stupid over-reaction. 'You remind me of Daz, in a way. You both see certain people, especially certain women . . . oh, all those women who were *total stars* with you, Alex. You see them in a sort of rosy light.'

'No pun intended.' Alex smiled, too indulgently. He really didn't seem at all pissed off.

'Yeah, very amusing. Anyway, I thought he and I had this recognition. But blood will out, and all that.' She closed her eyes, her irritation suddenly spent. Scottie. And it was Alex who was making her see Scottie more clearly than she had in a long time. The sweetest smile in the history of the universe, with that hint of wickedness. His smiling attempt systematically to crush the life out of her. No, she'd never marry. Christ, not novels now, magazines. Her heart suddenly felt less numb, but she wasn't sure whether it hurt.

'What are you thinking?'

'Just remembering.' Rosie opened her eyes. 'I don't think about him often. Hardly ever. I don't think about any of them.'

'There's been a lot?'

'Yeah. But only one I'd have married.' That was way, way below the belt. Alex winced, making no effort to hide his feelings. Wounded. If he hadn't minded about Scottie, clearly he did now.

'Did what happened put you off?' His voice a bit unsteady.

'I don't think I was really the type before him, I just didn't see it.' Offer him that; it was the least she could do.

'But when you said yes, he must have been the happiest bloke around.' Was this about her, or about Louise? 'Yeah,' he nodded, slowly, 'it makes sense that you didn't see it. Like we didn't see the thing with us. Without you, I'd probably never have done it, no matter how far my fantasies went.' Alex had recovered, or at least looked as though he had. He slipped off the settee and came to kneel in front of her chair. She put her hand on his head, stroked his hair. The fist further loosened its grasp, but she didn't feel pain, only affection. And tiredness.

'I doubt I'd marry you,' she said. 'But I do love you, very much.'

He rested his head in her lap.

'And you never can tell,' he said into the folds of her dressing gown.

*   *   *

Tried ringing her place, but she weren't there and her mobile
was off. No prizes for guessing where she was, then. No one'd
get the car or the twenty grand just for knowing she was round
at his. Fucking Simese twins. And Darren had a funny feeling
it was going to get more worser, once he did get hold of her.
Seemed as though Patterson weren't pushing her and Alex a
part like he should of done. More locked them together with
her keys. And if Ben was right bout her fishing round at his
a week or so back, that weren't good news. Darren drummed
his hand on the 'phone, wondering what was best. Allergic to
The Mice these days she was, and all – some of them was
saying that tonight. That wanker'd turned her gainst them, with
his pictures and crosswords and that. You could notice even
Freddy thought so. Way she'd looked at Darren yesterday . . .
Bet she never eat them chocolate cherries, and that right good
bottle'd be rotting in her rack. He looked at his watch. No,
weren't even worth ringing Alex's to check – this time of night,
he'd be well unlucky if they weren't in.

'You again? Jesus, Daz, why don't you just propose to us and
be done?' They never knew, then. Darren followed Rosie down
the hall – them shiny trousers she had was a bit tight round
the arse just for sitting about, and she had her shoes on. Maybe
they'd been out somewhere. Pity he was going to mess up their
night, if she'd been having a good time. But it weren't his
fault. Alex was sat in a dressing gowned, sparking a fag. Ro
might of been out with her mates, not with him. 'Social call,
is it?' Rosie sat on the arm of Alex's chair.

'No, not sactly.' He stuck his hands in his pockets, played
about with his change.

'Oh sit down, for God's sake.'

'No, I'm all right.' Never noticed that picture of a plate of
food afore.

'Do you want something, Darren? Tea, beer? There's some
Coke here.' Sounded more like Alex was offering arsenic.

'No, I'm all right. Look, there's something I got to tell you.'

'We guessed that, given the time.' Rosie put her hand on Alex's shoulder.

'You ain't going to like it.' He got his fags out his jacket. Violin one was gone, though.

'No,' said Alex.

'It's bout Sam Patterson.'

Rosie pulled her hair off her face and give him the look. Alex stared at the end of his straight like it was going to tell him the score.

'What about him?' he said.

'Couple of hour ago, it was. Don't go mental, right? He . . .' Darren was having a job with his lighter. 'He tried to top hisself.'

Now they was both doing the look. Tried to get the words in the right order, bout the trial date being set for April the first like some sort of sick joke, bout the transfer to Wandsworth, and mostly bout the kid being okay. Not the full shilling, but alive. The words kept getting stuck in his throat, and the pair of them stood up, come close to him, like they was all going to play one of them kids' games where you go round in a circle, holding hands. Sept that they weren't holding his hand, just pulling them words out of him, one by one, stead of in the whole sense. Then giving him some of them back. And more.

Go? When he'd come here special to tell them, so's they never had to hear it from no one else? There's gratitude. Umpteenth time of making hisself into the one what got shot for saying. Always the way. Always. It weren't like he'd had to, was it? But it meant he'd had it. And now he was being blown out.

Sling your hook, boy – you ain't necessary.

And that look on the old man's face when he said it. Darren see the tart behind him, all messy red hair and red lips and great big talons. She'd put her arm round the cunt, right skinny and white on his great fat gut. Minded him of a snake.

Could have put it a bit nicer than that, Cliff.

Didn't need her to stick up for him.

Their house, and all. Wessex Street. Mum's house.

So he'd fucked off. Next day, so'd the old man.

Tried staring now at the pictures on the wall, get the past out of his head. But couldn't see the present was all that much better.

'Sam'll be okay,' he said to Rosie.

'Yeah.'

Chapter Fifteen

'I know it's not my fault. That's what you want me to say, isn't it? And I know it's not your fault, either. But I know all that in my head, and I've still got this feeling here,' he thumped his chest, 'that it's got a lot to do with both of us.'

Rosie tried, really hard, not to mind Alex saying that. She was going to have to understand this one, as far as she could. He was furious, and anything she said would look like self-justification, even if she were only attempting to justify Alex to himself. The whole thing was muddled up inside him; at this moment, they were bound together not by matching rings or solemn vows, not by his collar, but by his guilt on both their behalfs. She kept stroking, kept kissing, but only his shoulder. He'd have to feel her support. That was all she could do.

He hadn't said much when they'd decided to come back here last night, except that he could see why she wanted to. Not that it could be much protection; the Centre had her number now as well as his. But this morning, it was as though the words had to be let out or they'd poison his blood-stream.

'What are you going to do?'

'I'll have to try to see him. I've still got my contacts from probation. Or maybe I can see him as his counsellor, even though I'm not. I can't think straight.'

'Today?'

'No, not today. There's nothing I can do about him at the moment, I'm in no fit state. I'd be a liability.' The anger fell from his face with the admission. He ran his hand over his mouth. 'Bollocks,' he said, softly. They looked at each other.

'You okay, poppet?' Rosie attempted a smile. He smiled back, faintly.

'Let's chuck a sickie.'

She nodded. There was no question about this one: Alex needed her. And to be truthful, she needed him. Jesus, it was a few short steps from love to need, even if you'd nailed your feet to the floor.

'I'll tell my secretary to . . . no I won't,' she said. 'They can bloody well manage. I'll just say I'm with you.'

'Thanks, love.' Alex touched her face. 'I just want to spend a day with you. Get drunk, have fun. We could get right away, go south of the river. I opened the bathroom window when I went for a piss. Going to be a lovely day, almost feels like spring.'

Rosie followed him into the living-room, and stood behind him, her arms around his thick waist, her forehead resting under his shoulder-blades, while he made his call.

'Jeni? Sorry to ring you so early. It's me. Listen, I won't be in today. We're sick of everything, we just need to get away . . . What? No, me and Rosie. I'll see you tomorrow.'

Alex was right, it was a beautiful day; cold but bright, what her mum would call fresh. A false spring, three even four weeks before the real one, that made you feel you wanted to make plans, despite another part of you that suspected it would be grey and horrible tomorrow, overcasting today's optimism. They'd got on the first bus that came along, got off at a cafe for Alex to have a quick breakfast, and then caught another bus that took them to London Bridge.

'I'm definitely with Sam Johnson,' said Rosie, taking Alex's hand as they crossed the river. Hardly dousing the thing in petrol, but maybe holding a candle to it.

'What? Oh, your *tired of London, tired of life* thing. How much of London do you ever see? The East End, Soho, your office, the courts. And the shops up West.'

'Yeah, but look at what I could see, if I wanted to.'

Alex looked.

'It's brilliant, isn't it?' he said. 'It's got to be the most romantic city in the world.'

'Yeah.' She pulled at his arm to make him stop, and kissed him. For once, there was no carrier-bag-briefcase to get in the way.

'Public displays of affection, without any alcohol?'

'Well, I'm on me 'olidays, sir.'

'Talking of alcohol, it's nearly eleven o'clock. We should find a pub.'

They walked past Southwark Cathedral and alongside a development to a pub Alex vaguely remembered; looked a bit touristy but it was on the river, right next to a boat.

'Replica of *The Golden Hinde*. Drake's ship. Seems tiny, doesn't it?' he said.

She contemplated the little boat. Ship. Bet it was covered in mildew or barnacles.

'Go on then, you're dying to tell me.'

'I think it was originally called something else.' Alex grinned. 'The Pelican? Yeah, I'm sure that's right. The Queen went aboard at Deptford, that must be why it's here, because it's so close. The biggest thing about it is that it circumnavigated the world.'

'Completely?'

He ignored her.

'Anyway, Drake was in all these amazing situations, robbing the Spanish blind and covering himself in glory, but he died of dysentery of all things, off Porto Bello.'

'Road?' That was quite interesting.

'No.' He looked at her with mock pity.

'Well, I'm not a boy,' she said, pushing open the door.

'Shame it's not Walter Raleigh's ship, really.'

'That's a thought. God, it's flash in here.'

'How much d'you reckon it'll be for a pint and a wine?' said Alex. 'We could have the one, then grab a bus to the Elephant or somewhere, do the crossword in one of the pubs there.'

'Oh Christ, this bit's non-smoking.' She pointed to a laminated sign on a table.

'Non-smiling too, by the looks of it. Do you think there's a sign about that? *Anybody smiling must sit in the darkest corner.* And I think laughing's probably banned altogether.'

Rosie broke the ban.

'I'll get these,' she said. 'You find us a seat in the civilized bit.'

When she got to the table with their drinks, he took them from her, put them down, pulled out a chair. She sat and smiled. A leather jacket doesn't feel anything like carpet.

Time out of time. Pretending that they were like any other couple playing hooky from their satisfactory everyday lives. Imagining that there were no obstacles to being straight-forwardly pleased to be together. On paper, as Alex might say, that's what they were: passion, emotion, intellect coming together in a way that seemed to defy dichotomies. A para-digm. And sitting here, sipping warm red wine and watching Alex's right arm move his pint to his mouth, the arm so big that his bicep merged into his forearm, Rosie could almost believe that they could take this feeling back with them. Rosie-and-Alex. Not Rosie, Alex and a burning pub. Not Rosie, Alex and a game of Chinese Whispers. No bloody damage.

'Last time I was in here was with a graphic designer called Camilla, believe it or not. Some double-barrelled surname,' said Alex.

'Oh yeah? So you bring me somewhere you've taken some other woman?' So much for it being just the two of them.

'I've only just remembered. She was after me, but I wasn't that interested. Ten years earlier I might have been, but if I'd slept with her after we'd come here, it would only have been because she could draw. I mean yeah, she looked great, but that's not enough.'

'Alex, I don't think I especially want to hear about how great she was and why you didn't sleep with her.' Her voice hard.

'Sorry, love, I was just thinking aloud. It's not important at all. Do me one favour, will you? Just for today, if I say something stupid, call me a cunt and leave it at that. I'll pay later, but not today.'

Rosie eyed him. Then she nodded. Outsiders would never understand, but he needed more affectionate leeway than most people, because he spent so much of his time laying out their courage with his body. No, with his mind. His guts, her garters. She could defer retribution.

'Cunt,' she said.

After that first pub, the day started to take on the soft edges of a fantasy, a daydream. A session. The Elephant and Castle provided them with a proper pub (with the imaginative name of The Elephant and Castle), complete with sticky tables and cigarette burns in the carpet.

'Darts player's favourite drink? Six.'

'Double!' They shouted together, making themselves and the nearby punters crack up.

'Maybe he nearly failed to make that movie?'

'An anagram. Give us the pen.'

'Cheat! You're looking ahead.'

'What have we got? F something I something N something something something.'

'You're bloody illiterate.'

They sat with their arms touching, partly because they needed to be close together in order for them both to be able to see the crossword, but also just for the sake of it. Rosie could feel his warmth through her mohair, although he was wearing a tee-shirt and no jumper in bloody February; one glimpse of the sun, and he was well carried away, even down to body heat. She occasionally kissed Alex's shoulder, casually, and he sometimes picked up her hand and rubbed it against his cheek, as though he hardly noticed what he was doing.

'Not bad, twenty-five minutes,' he said. 'I can't do it much quicker on my own.'

'Don't come it.' But the arrogant git knew she liked it.

'I used to play a bit of chess as well, especially at Enfield,'

Alex said. 'I wasn't bad. You know I used to make those crappy
little films? Well, when I was about thirty-five, I made one
about cerebral games. Images of the insides of people's heads
when they were playing.'

'Very deep, man.' Rosie made a peace sign.

'Yeah, think I thought I was the straight Derek Jarman.
Anyway, I entered a national competition with it, made the
finals as it happens and there was this public screening thing.
Only five films out of something like five hundred.' He was
looking at the table rather than at Rosie. 'But no one I knew
came. Not one person.' He must mean Louise.

'I would have,' said Rosie. And she meant it; it wasn't point-
scoring against his ex-wife. Or not just that. 'Even though I
hate surrealist shit,' she added, and laughed.

'Yeah, I know. The other parents all came, but you know.'
He didn't correct his slip.

'I love you,' Rosie said out of nowhere, surprising herself.
Alex grinned.

'Yeah, I know. I love you.'

'Horrible in here though, isn't it? Reminds me of the club
my dad used to belong to. I only got to go there once or twice,
but he used to take Daz a lot before they'd let him in The
Mice. In training, I suppose.'

'My dad never goes to pubs or clubs,' said Alex, doodling
a bottle on the edge of the crossword. Rosie waited. Then, sod
it, she had to make him tell her, here if not in the everyday.
Rosie-and-Alex.

'What about your mum?'

Alex spoke carefully, as though keeping his words within
the legal measure.

'No need. Drip, drip, drip. Do you know what I mean? And
all the bridge parties, and I think the lovers' flats. Or maybe
hotels, I don't fucking know. I never said anything about them
to my dad. In my madder moments, I sometimes think that's
why I got you, because it was somehow the right thing to do.
God, she's a really bitter woman.'

'I'm sorry, precious.' Rosie rested her palm on his cheek.

'Do you know one of things I love with us?' he said. 'You touch me.'

It made her heart hurt. She stroked his face.

'Shall we move on?' she said. 'Before we drown in all this schmaltz.'

'Okay.' He smiled. Yeah, she'd made a good call. 'What about Clapham? I know a pub on the North Side, and then we could walk across the Common.'

'A proper walk? Me?'

'Why not? It's no distance. We could have an adventure.'

Rosie considered her boots. Pretty high, but quite comfortable. And she did have her warm coat with her.

'Yeah, why not?'

They got off the bus in Clapham High Street, and turned down a road that ran alongside a big stretch of grass. That must be it.

'Here we are. The Windmill,' said Alex. 'I used to come here years ago when I worked in Putney, but it's gone a bit more upmarket since then.' It was a big pub, clearly aimed at the eating rather than the drinking crowd. A menu announced nearly fancy food at just over usual pub prices. But it hadn't been blanded out into a corporate identity, not like The Mice, and the Australian barman was friendly and efficient, with no stake in the place. 'Think I'll have a pint of Young's Special, seeing as we're on an adventure. Haven't had that for . . . ten years?'

'Okay. Well, in that case, I'll have Tia Maria and Diet Coke. It's disgusting, but it's what girls used to drink when I was a teenager. Or, no I know, brandy and Babycham. That was our special occasion drink at university. Expensive, but you only needed three.'

'Don't blame me if you're sick.'

'I won't be.' She paid with a twenty, checking that she had plenty of cash left in her purse. 'Yum, taste that.'

'*Yum?* What sort of word's "yum"?'

'I think I've regressed. Shall we sit down?' They found a table in the high-ceilinged back room, crowded only by the smells of other people's lunches. 'We ought to eat again at some point. But not here. Maybe a bit later on?'

'There's a lot of little restaurant thingies along Lavender Hill. We could try there.'

'Yeah, I'm easy.'

'Not usually.'

'So make the most of it.' She gave him her hand across the table, and he laughed.

'Will you marry me?' he said. 'We're on an adventure, remember.' He couldn't mean it, or if he did, he must have known what she'd have to say.

'No,' Rosie said. He shook his head almost simultaneously with the word. Yet perhaps she wasn't as predictable as all that. 'Or maybe yes,' she added. Alex watched her eyes. He's looking to see if I'm joking, she thought.

'Really?'

'No, of course not really.' She made a face at him.

'That's what I thought.' He ran his thumb over her knuckles. 'Okay then, let's move in together. We hardly ever spend a night apart anyway. Come on, I dare you. Double dare you.'

Rosie, Alex and the damage all in one place? Nuclear missiles round the door instead of flowers. But there was something that appealed. A small, soft place underneath her skin wanted her to agree. Nothing to do with her mind.

'Only if you move in with me.'

Alex increased the pressure on her hand, digging at a scratch with his thumbnail.

'I'd have to tell them at work, there's my flat, so you'd better be serious,' he said at last.

'I'll think about it,' she said, shrugging. Yeah, as it happens, she would. He was right, they'd given up all pretence that they each spent some nights alone; trouble was, he'd see their living together as commitment, not merely convenience. And that was dangerous.

'We could get a different place, together. No ghosts.' He looked confident.

'No, I'm not ready for that. But . . . maybe I won't rule it out altogether.'

They smiled at each other, a pair of village idiots.

'You'll think about it properly?'

'No more talking, babe. *Sub judice.*'

'You know I'm going to hold you to it?'

'Yeah. Do us a favour, get us a wine. I don't think I can finish this.'

Clapham Common didn't seem too stupidly big for a walk, not even to Rosie. More of a stroll. A lot of people clearly felt the same way, many of them young mothers with pushchairs. Please God, don't let Alex start asking whether she'd reconsider having a baby; just calling him a cunt wouldn't come close on that one. God must have been bothering to listen that day, because Alex seemed scarcely to see the kids. He loped along, an arm thrown across her shoulders, his odd, lopsided stride more obvious, yet somehow less embarrassing, than it was on a crowded street.

'Slow down, babe, it's not a race.' She was so unfit, she was getting a stitch.

'How do you know? I might have decided we were having a race, and just not told you.'

'Then you have to let me win, or I'll sulk and be a pain in the bum for the rest of the day.' She put her hand on her side. Shit, she'd have to get Randa back to salsa classes.

'You're always a pain in the bum. I bet you were the kind of kid who turned the board over if she was losing at Monopoly.'

'Didn't play Monopoly. Anyway, Daz did that, threw the draughts everywhere and accidentally-on-purpose knocked the cards flying. I just won.' She ducked out from under his arm, and moved round to block his path. 'Kiss me.'

'Why?' He looked down at her, pretending indifference.

'Because if this is a romantic walk, I want the full monty.'
She could almost believe that she meant it. 'If it was summer,
and the vans were about, I'd want an ice-cream.'

'Is that right? Shared between us, I suppose.' He tucked a
strand of her hair behind her ear. She shook it free.

'Of course. But I'd get the flake.' She put her arms round
his neck. 'Go on, kiss me.'

He kissed her, and they heard a ferocious shout of *No!* Rosie
pulled away. Was there some by-law that said No Snogging?
'This is a cycle path!' A very peculiar bloke on a bike shot
past them, all skinny thighs and weird calf muscles that stuck
out sideways.

'Wanker!' Rosie yelled after him. 'Jesus, I really have
regressed.'

'I like it. Makes a change.'

The wind was getting up now, blowing Rosie's hair into
tangles, and making her face ache. She'd look a right dog if
they stayed out much longer.

'Come on, I thought this was a race?' she said.

On Lavender Hill, they found, between the sad-looking elec-
trical shops and the seedy pubs and the trendy bars, a promising
restaurant. Small. The woodwork painted bright green. Its
owners seemed to think this was a village.

'What's the time?' She hadn't left her watch off for years.

'Ten past three. They're still serving, look.'

'Open all day, I imagine.' She pushed open the door. 'Order
us some wine, will you? I must just pop to the loo.'

Her luck was holding; she managed a spectacular Agincourt
moment with her hair, and had remembered to put her make-
up in her bag. She smiled at herself in the mirror. Not bad.
Even looked quite healthy. Must be the exercise.

'Great. Thanks.' Rosie slid into the seat opposite Alex, and
picked up the glass of wine he'd poured for her.

'Food sounds good.' Passing her the hand-written menu.
'What's a green platter?'

'*Greek* platter, you moron. Hummous, olives, pitta bread, artichokes, stuff like that.'

'I want that, then. And then steak in hot pepper sauce. And chips, I want chips.'

'Can I have some of your starter? Then I can order the goat's cheese starter for my main. Or maybe the chicken salad.' The salad. Fewer calories probably, even though it was a main course. But it didn't say how the chicken was cooked. Oh, sod it. Anything she ate today was in the land through the back of the wardrobe: it didn't count.

By the time the food arrived, they needed another bottle of wine. Alex was putting it away like he'd just come back from Saudi Arabia, and she wasn't doing too badly herself. She couldn't even tell whether she was drunk, which was rarely a sign that she wasn't.

'What's that?' Alex held out the fruit he'd just bitten. 'A prune?'

'Sun-dried tomato.' Rosie took it from him and popped it into her mouth.

'Are you sure?'

'Positive.'

'Not a prune, then?'

'No. Definitely not a prune.'

'Tasted like a prune.'

'Well, it bloody well wasn't. It's a tomato. Be told.'

She watched as he dug into the food with his fingers; she'd not seen him do that before. His fingers looked huge against the delicate bits of vegetables and bread; he smeared sour cream over the plate, chasing an olive. Weirdly sexy. Briefly, she wished they were at home, but then she realized that she was having fun, being out, on the adventure. Bloody hell. Fun.

'Do you want the other prune? I'm not too excited by them.'

'Yeah, okay.' She chewed the tomato, and licked her fingers. Then she lit a cigarette, drawing heavily on it a couple of times. 'Sorry, you haven't finished.'

He looked up from his plate.

'That's . . .'

She smiled at him.

'That's what?' Resting her elbow on the table, her cigarette hovering above the plate.

'That's okay.'

'No, I wouldn't hear of it. I'd better put it out.'

He laughed.

'Don't you think?' she added.

And crushed the cigarette into the remains of his hummous.

'God, you bitch.'

'Now I've gone to the trouble of putting it out, you'd better eat up, hadn't you?'

Without a pause, he started again on his food, wiping up the ashy hummous with a piece of pitta. Rosie watched as he lifted his hand to his mouth; she was turned on, amused, repulsed. Proprietorial.

With his arm curled round to shield it from her, as though preventing her from copying his work, Alex sketched something on to the serviette, his tongue between his teeth, humming an unrecognizable song in the back of his throat.

'Show, Alex!'

'No. You can wait till it's finished.' He didn't look up. 'I'll have you know I turned down a post-grad place at RCA, so you can just wait your turn.'

Under the table, she stamped her foot. Alex laughed, but still kept his eyes on his task. Seemed to take hours.

'There you are,' he said eventually, pushing the serviette across to her.

It was a cartoon in black ink of a woman (who looked a bit like Rosie) with one booted leg placed on the chest of a naked man (who looked a bit like Alex); underneath, he'd scrawled *Trophy Hunter*. Rosie smiled.

'It's great.'

'That's what I think, that's why I did it. It's the best thing that's ever happened to me. Can't always handle it but it's

always there, never goes away, and just now it seems like it's
all I want.' He picked up her hand and kissed the sketch.

'Can I have it?'

'Sure. All our stuff'll probably be in the same place soon,
anyway. I know, you don't want to talk about it, but I wanted
to say it. I liked saying it.'

She'd liked him saying it, too. Funny. She knew there'd be
problems, there were always, always, always problems with her
and Alex, but it seemed worthwhile trying to find at least some
solutions. In real time. They'd have to wait until the injunction was in place, to stop the Poison Dwarf coming anywhere
near them, but Rosie was pretty sure this was what she wanted.
As sure as she ever got, anyway. And that was the best she
could hope for.

'Do you want afters? Or shall we go? We could get the over-
land to Waterloo and, what am I saying? Oh yeah, then take
a stroll and catch the District all the way back. Or do you
want to get the bus again and stop on the way?'

Alex stroked the inside of her wrist.

'You just keep me hanging on,' he said. 'Bus. I can get a lot
more pissed if I really try. Anyway, it'll be rush hour. Let's
have ice-cream. Sorry it's not from a van. Then get the train
to Waterloo and then find a nice pub. We can look at Eurostar,
too. I like that. It's so pointy.'

'Pointy. Okay, my little anorak, we can look at the pointy
train if you want. And it'd be nice to look at the bridges all
lit up, too.'

'Can I ask you something? Before I agree to share my ice-
cream with you?'

'I guess so.' Shit, what was coming now?

'I know you love me, I know that.' He gave her one of his
twisted smiles; she wasn't sure if this was maudlin self-pity or
cheerful acknowledgement. 'But do you love me most? Most
ever?'

'Oh come on, you're hardly short on, what's the word? Self-
belief. You don't ask questions like that if you expect the

answer to be no.' She really didn't want to answer this. Of course, she could come out with stuff about being a different person from when she was younger, about that being one of many reasons why love wasn't comparable, quantifiable. But she knew she was being asked something historical here; not in terms of the future, but out of what Alex hadn't got from his past. And it would take guts to answer, because she also knew that she could never be sure enough of how he felt to ask the question of him. Of anyone.

'No, tell me. Please. I'll even let you choose the flavour. They've got lemon curd.'

'Lemon curd? All right.' She patted his arm, trying to gain some thinking time. Go with the truth, but keep it light. 'Yeah, go on then. I love you most.' Not blindly, the way she had Scottie in the beginning, but with the lights on. Because he needed it most.

He smiled again, a massive smile, all the way up to his eyes.

'Yeah?' he said. She shrugged, but it was too late. He was happy. 'Yeah,' he said.

That night, he slept curled at her feet; she slept better than she had in weeks.

Darren sat across from Ben in the curry house, trying not to look at that fucked-up face when he was eating. He knew that was horrible, but he couldn't help hisself. Lamb vindaloo didn't go down too well if you was forced to look at lumps of meat on your best mate's boat. Ben knew, and all, and Darren felt well bad bout that. Noticed Ben was eating with his head right down near his plate, resting his cheek on his hand. If Cath could of seen him, she'd have a go bout elbows on the table, cos she wouldn't of known what Darren knew. Ben'd never let her see that.

'What's yourn like? All right?' Darren felt he had to make the effort, make out like he never cared bout eating with Ben, even when Ben knew he did.

'Blinding.' He looked up, and there was all sweat on his nose and over his cheek and his scars. Bite-your-bum cheese always done that to him, and all. But he used to have two cheeks.

'I ain't all that hungry meself. Went a bit mental with the bhajis. Handsome, they was.'

'Yeah, greedy cunt.' Ben had a try at a laugh. 'As it goes, I've about had enough and all.' He put down his spoon. 'Want another beer? Oy, mate – two more Kingfishers over here.'

'Speak slow, he don't hardly understand English, that one. Ignorant bastard. Think they'd make the effort, wouldn't you?'

'Two . . . King . . . fishers.'

'Gone right downhill in here, it has,' Darren said. He pushed his plate away.

The beers come eventual. Ben done half his in one second flat.

'Forgot to say . . .' Too casual. Darren tuned in proper. 'See Charlie Boyd yesterday. At mine. Popped in, see how I was doing. Thing is, mate – he asked about if your Rosie knows Patterson's brief. Don't think Freddy knew he come.'

'Fucking great.' What's going on now? 'Forgot to say, did you?'

'Just waited for a good time.' Ben done the rest of his beer. 'Think he was only poking about – fact, I'm sure he was. But he asked if she was still seeing that Alex.'

'You say?'

'No. Didn't know what, you know, you'd want me, you know.'

'Yeah, you done the right thing.' That Alex. Must have a dick the size of a python. Don't think about that. Now he was getting pictures in his head like a porn film. King Dong. Don't listen. Blank it. He wanted to think Rosie weren't like that, but she most likely was. And she always seemed so different from other birds. Betraying, *betraying* little tart. Why was what the big cunt wanted more important than what Darren needed her to do? More and more, it got worser. And it was him she'd come crying to when she fucked the bloke off out of it. Perhaps he wouldn't be around, this time. Perhaps he'd let her be by her own, see what it felt like.

'You all right, Spence?'

'Yeah. I just don't like her getting volved in what don't concern her. Ain't she had enough grief over this? You member. You ought to know.'

'You ain't wrong.' Ben went for Darren's lighter. 'Charlie even offered me dough, compensation. Told him to stick it. Tricia'd go mental if she knew I turned down a monkey.'

'She's all right. Here, Franky . . . Benny . . .'

'It's okay, I know.'

'Right.' He done it on purpose, and Ben would of known that. 'Listen, do us a favour. If my girl or that Billericay Dicky come sniffing bout again, keep schtum, yeah? No letting her get round you. I ain't being funny, but I know what you're like with her.'

'No, I ain't silly.' Ben went a bit red. Well weird, way them scars stayed the same.

'Ain't saying that. But watch yourself. Ro gets into one, we'll all be in trouble. She wouldn't never be no grass, but she's so into that Alex . . . Just watch it.'

Ben broke off a bit of nam and stuffed it in his gob. He kept on smoking, like he never knew he was eating at the same time. Mum'd slap his hand for that. So would Cath.

'You know her better'n me,' Ben said with his mouth full and smoke coming out and all.

Thing is, ain't too sure any of us knows her, not really, not inside, where it matters. Gets me in the gut, but there most likely ain't ever going to be no septions to that. Not even me.

'Nurofen, grapefruit juice, tea, toast.'

'Sod off.'

'You've got to get up, love. Come on, take the Nurofen first.'

'Bastard.' Rosie sat up, and held her hand out for the tablets and juice. 'Do I look like a hag?' She ran her finger underneath her eyes; hadn't bothered to take off her make-up last night.

'Only a trainee one.' Alex put the rest of her breakfast on

the cabinet, sat on the edge of the bed, stroked her leg through the duvet. 'You'll be fine when you've had a shower.'

'How are you feeling?'

'Not too bad. Bit dizzy. But thanks for yesterday, I had a really nice day. Can't believe I actually forgot about him for hours at a time. Feel a bit bad about that now.'

'You needed it, babe. Time out. Pass my tea. Thanks. And . . .'

'No, you can't have a cigarette until you've eaten your toast.'

'Oh, I get it. This is what it's going to be like, is it?'

He grinned. She'd pleased him, saying that. Must be the hangover, making her come on all benevolent. She was about to say more, when the telephone went. Seven o'clock in the bloody morning. If that was Louise, she'd kill her.

'Shall I get that?' said Alex.

He stumbled out of the room, and Rosie took a couple of bites of her toast, then lit a cigarette. She could do compromise with the best of them. Alex was taking ages. 'Phone wasn't for her, then. Probably was that bitch. Still, she'd have to pack it in soon, go back to Lilliput or wherever she came from. Better get up in a second, jump in that shower. Couldn't even remember properly what she had to do today.

'Rosie?' Alex came back into the bedroom, ruffling his hair. 'That was Louise.'

'So what's new?' She poked at a blob of butter on her toast, spilling ash on to the plate.

'Said she'd tried to get hold of me yesterday. She's saying she's lost her violin.'

'And that has what to do with you, exactly?' Rosie felt her heart speed up.

'Nothing. That's the point, isn't it? I can't get rid of the woman. Do you know what? I loved her so, so much, and now every time I hear her voice I just think bollocks, Rosie's going to love this.' He sat down heavily on the bed.

Every time, no matter what it was he was saying about Louise, he had to remind Rosie that he'd loved her. She knew that, for Christ's sake.

'Simon's injunction'll sort her.'

'Will it? I'm glad you're so sure about that, because I'm not. She was raving on about you, as well.' He picked up a slice of her toast and bit into it. 'This is all I need. I've got to try to see Sam today.'

'So see him. Jesus. Why are you making such a big deal about this? You worried about her bloody fiddle or something?'

'No, course I'm not. I don't believe for one second it's gone anywhere, and even if it has, it's not my problem. But it's just one thing after another.' He hit himself on the forehead. 'Now I bet you're cross with me, going to have a major sulk.' Alex was spoiling for this one. Rosie could suddenly see it. He was far from stupid, he must know exactly what he'd said to upset her; he was looking for something else to feel bad about, something that wasn't to do with having taken a day off before seeing Sam. Something that wasn't to do with having woken up happy. And she knew she was mixed up in his feelings about all of that.

'I'm not cross,' she said. 'Not that much, anyway. I think you're a destructive sod, but I don't feel like playing.' She laughed. 'It'd be like fiddling while Rome burned. Anyway, I don't do sulking.'

'What do you call it, then?'

'Sod off, Alex. I'm doing my best here.'

'I know you are.' He nodded. 'I'm sorry. No one can do anything right with me at the moment, not for long, not even you.'

Rosie willed herself not to let that get to her. Let it go, girl. Just let it go.

'You use the bathroom first,' she said. 'Then you can get off.'

'Thanks. Do you know what? I don't think I'm suited to this job.'

'Sounds a bit self-pitying to me.'

'Probably. That doesn't mean it's not true, though, does it?'

'No, it doesn't. And there's no point in me telling you how good you are at it, because you know that, and it's not necessarily the same thing. But you can't decide anything now.'

'Yeah, I know. But I could fancy doing something with less stress and more money. You know, no Sams.' He put his arms round her, held her for a second. Then he stood up. 'I'll ring you at work, let you know what I'm doing.'

'If you need a clean towel . . . sorry, I'm going mad. You know where they are.'

'Bit late for company manners, isn't it?' He managed a brief smile.

She'd get it out of him, out of one of them. It was something she could hold in reserve, to offer to Alex if that seemed right. More importantly, it would give her the psychological authority to do something concrete for him. Might not do any ultimate good, but she had to try. Just resolutions weren't the point. Rosie's was a cobbled-together life, a practical and moral making-do, and it wasn't enough any more; she wanted this chance to make an emotional rather than a pragmatic choice. But oh God, what was she forsaking?

The yard was almost in darkness, the only light coming from the office. It was creepy enough in these railway arches when the yard was properly lit, but now it was positively tomb-like. Rosie tucked her hair down inside the collar of her jacket, and put her hands on the back of her neck; she'd done that from a teenager, ever since Daz told her there were bats here at night, that got caught up in people's hair. Protected species. What kind of sicko would want to protect flying vermin? Might be rats, too; she wished she were wearing boots. Flicking her hair out of her collar, she opened the office door. They were sitting either side of the desk, drinking tea and smoking a spliff.

'Hello, darling,' said Daz. 'What you doing here?'

'Have the chair,' Ben said, as he stood up.

'No thanks. I've come for answers, boys.' She folded her arms. 'I'll get straight to the point. If Charlie Boyd wanted you or one of your associates to collect a debt for him at The Red Lion, isn't it a striking coincidence that the same pub was subsequently burned out by a source unconnected to him?' Speaking calmly. 'If Sam Patterson committed the arson, and without having any authorization from Charlie Boyd to do so, why was Freddy Boyd prepared to lend you his employees to watch my flat?'

'I do enough for him,' Daz said, shrugging.

'Why was Charlie questioned so long after the event? Why was it merely a formality?'

'He never done it, I spose.' Tapping Ben's arm. Ben pulled on the joint, gave it to him.

'Why has the witness not come forward until now? You can't seriously attest he was intimidated by an underweight addict.'

'Patterson's brothers—'

'Are just bigger addicts, of longer standing. In your language,' she paused for effect, 'the witness is schneid.' Rosie looked at Ben. Ten to one Daz hadn't let on. 'Sam Patterson attempted suicide.' She held Ben's shocked gaze. 'Sorry, Ben. But tell me.'

'I don't know.'

'Tell me.'

'She's got the right.' Ben turned to face Daz.

'Why? She knows what she knows.'

'I need to hear the truth,' said Rosie. 'Explicitly.'

'Why, planning on going as his brief, are you?' said Daz, in his best sarky manner. Rosie sat on the edge of the desk, and took a mouthful of Daz's tea; it was disgusting, he took sugar, but her mouth was so dry, had been all day.

'Alex's moving in with me,' she said, scissoring her fingers to say she wanted the spliff.

'You what?' Daz's eyes grew more lizard-like, able to stare hard without blinking.

'Yeah, soon. So now you know why it's all so important to us.' She toked on the joint.

'I hope you'll be very happy,' Ben claimed. But his voice

was flat. He looked into his mug. Oh well, he'd get over it. Right now, she was more concerned about Alex.

'I think you're mental,' said Daz. 'But it's your life.'

'He's what I want, sweetheart.' With that, she realized how true it was. 'Accept it.'

'Have to, won't I?' Daz nodded, slowly. 'But I don't have to like it. While it lasts.'

'It might just, this time. He's different. *We're* different. Can't you understand that?'

'I can,' said Ben. 'He's a lucky bastard.' He put down his tea, then picked it up again. 'I'm going to say, Spence.'

'No you're not, cunt.' Daz rose slowly to his feet.

'I am. I can't . . . I don't know why, meself. But I am.'

'I'm telling you nicely, don't.'

Ben came round to stand in front of Rosie. She waited to hear what she'd long known.

'No, Patterson never done it,' Ben said. He was breathing loudly, through his mouth. Rosie held her own breath tight inside, as though she were afraid Ben would take her share, too. Jesus, what was Daz going to do?

'Stupid fucking cunt. That ain't going to make you no prettier, you know. And it ain't going to get her away from that Alex and on to you.'

'That's enough, Daz. I mean it.' Her voice low, careful, cold. Ben looked stricken, mortified. Rosie stroked his damaged cheek. 'Thanks, Ben,' she said. 'I've always known the score, don't worry.' She turned to Daz. 'Am I going to represent Sam? No, course I'm not. I wouldn't do that.' He watched her, his pale face reddening. 'But,' she went on, 'I know a man who would. Someone who'll keep me out of it. And you,' she touched his shoulder, 'forget it. I don't want Ben to hear any more about this.'

He stared her out. Or tried to. He dropped his gaze before she did, took up his stash box.

Rosie wondered how quickly Ben would forget.

*   *   *

She would more easily pick up a cab at King's Cross, and it was only five minutes or so from St Pancras. Although Rosie hated using her mobile in the street, she thought she'd better let Alex know she was on her way back. The way he was today, he'd be paranoid. As she pressed Home in the directory, she smiled to think how much he would despise someone he saw doing this; he called them the *I'm on the doorstep, I'm unlocking the door* people.

'Babe? Me. I'm just outside the yard. You got back okay then?'

'Yeah. You won't be long, will you?'

'No, coming now. If you want—'

'I just want to see you.'

'Yeah. Okay then, I'll be as quick as I can.'

Rosie felt as though she had a present for Alex, something he'd wanted badly from her. It could go horribly wrong, her ironic gift, but knowing that didn't make it less valuable; seemed to make it more so. In the kind of relationship they'd forged, trust was crucial. Even Rosie had to try to trust, to let Alex's values in alongside her own, to let Louise out. And he had to be able to trust her. Almost absolutely. Pain is a tool, in any of its manifestations: used as a standard for control in the world her brother inhabited; used as an expression of redemption in their love. She'd get Sam the best; Alex deserved her proof.

She turned up the collar of her jacket against the damp evening, and lengthened her step. Horrible, round here. William always said he didn't know how Rosie could bear to live in the East End, but she'd take that any day over the needle and fishnet culture of King's Cross. All the beggars, too; you never saw that, or hardly ever, in Whitechapel. The odd traditional wino, but not this, not the kids. Alex had once told her that when he first went into drug work, he used to come here, and think *opportunities*. But now, all he could see were opportunities that were never going to come about. He said they didn't get to the conception stage, so you couldn't even use an abortion analogy. When she was nine or ten, Daz had brought her here to look at the *prozzies*. He'd been fascinated by them, pointing out which ones were underage, which ones grandmothers. It was supposed to be some kind of dire warning, but somehow that got lost as they watched the faces out of the corners of their eyes, trying to see what made the prozzies do whatever it was they did. Rosie had known it had nothing to do with the women liking the men in the cars. And that had made her tummy feel funny. Still did, if she thought too hard about it.

The queue for taxis was long, but quick-moving. Rosie stepped from one foot to the other, in impatience, and because it was cold. She knew Alex would be pacing, getting up every five minutes to look out of the window, or cut up a lemon for his voddy, or to open a bottle of wine for her, or just to have a roam about the flat. When he was agitated, it was very physical, he couldn't keep the anxiety contained inside. It was hard to call what he'd be up for tonight; Sam would be uppermost in his mind, and maybe he'd want their mutual guilt ritualistically expunged. Or perhaps he'd simply want his hand held, literally or otherwise. She'd know when she saw him. Tonight, she wasn't going to push it; for the second time, what he wanted would come first. She could do compassionate. Even though she might continue to be implicated in his bloody guilt fantasies.

It was warm in the cab. Rosie relaxed her shoulders and looked out of the window; it was the inside of her own head that she saw. Daz had been diminished by saying what he had to Ben. Rosie felt ashamed of him, as though he were her son and had let her down by picking on a kid half his size. Pretty brave of Ben, though. Why had he confirmed it for her? It was as if he, too, saw it as a gift, something to give her on the announcement that Alex was moving in. A housewarming present. Or perhaps he gave it because he could.

'Cheers, mate. Keep the change.' Rosie slammed the door, and looked across the road, up at her flat. Alex was there, half turned away from the window, a glass in his hand. She raised her arm and gestured that he should pour her one. But he didn't see her. God, she hoped no one had noticed. Feeling a total idiot, she glanced both ways at the pavement as much as at the road, letting a Merc go before stepping out.

Then she heard it.

Christ!

A car.

What kind of moron?

She looked left.

Move.

Coming from nowhere.

Not right at her?

It . . .

Hated hospitals. She always did, and all. Wouldn't be none too pleased when she woke up and found herself in one. This was the same one Grandad had kicked it in. They'd all had to be tested for TB, he could member that. Where was the fucking doctor? Fucking Paki cunt, wouldn't tell them nothing. And Mum all white, not crying, not saying nothing. And Alex. Darren hadn't never seen a bloke so closed in on hisself. It was like he couldn't look at it, not at all. Made him right, it was more harder than anything to look at, but you had to. For her. She'd want to know, when she woke up, that they was all here, doing what they had to, finding out everything and all that. Just wished he could get that nursery rhyme out his head. *Ring around a Rosie, a pocket full of posies, a tissue, a tissue, we all fall down.* Went round and round, and all. Couldn't make it stop. *All fall down. Ring around a Rosie.* It was worser than anything, this waiting. Where was that doctor? Mum had hold of Alex's hand, but she looked like she never knew she did, and he looked like he never knew, neither.

Clock was doing his brain in. Think they'd have one of them ones what never made no noise. Like it was trying to keep in with his rhyme, clapping along with him like at Play School.

All – clap – *fall* – clap – *down*. Slow handclap at the boxing, where the ref give a bad result. Slower'n your heart, what tried to slow down to it. Clap-clap, clap-clap, clap-clap. And why'd they have to have it so hot? Fucking February, and it was more like summer in here. Most likely so's the germs had a right good chance of going home with the visitors. And the smell – like one of Nan's baths it was. How anyone could buy Dettol, he couldn't never see. Sort of smelt like sick. Rosie'd spew her guts when she woke up, smelling that stink.

'Mr Spence?'

'Yeah. What's the score?'

'Your sister's still unconscious, I'm afraid. We haven't got anything new to tell you at *clap* this *clap* stage *clap*.'

'But she'll be okay?' Get a grip, boy.

'We hope so. So much depends on the extent of her internal injuries.'

'Hope?' What did that mean?

'You can go in to see her if you'd like, but one at a time, please.'

'Why, if she's not awake? Can't sactly wear her out, can we?'

'No, but the nurse is trying to make her comfortable. Please, bear with us. Just go in, say hello. We don't know whether she can hear, but it can't hurt.'

'You want to get in there first, Mum?'

'Mm?' Mum sort of come to. She shook her head. 'Let Alex go,' she said.

'What?'

'She loves him, Darren. It's only right.'

She loves me, and all. He's been around five minutes . . . Then Alex looked up at him. He wouldn't ask, but there was some life come in his eyes, and Darren could really notice the poor sod didn't know what to do with hisself. And it was Alex what'd heard the massive noise, him what found her little body all smashed up at the knees and called the ambulance. Him what had called Darren.

'Yeah, all right. Go on, mate.'

'Thanks.' Alex got up awkward, like his feet was glued the carpet. 'Really appreciate it.' And he done a weird thing. Held his hand out. Darren shook it and, funny enough, meant it. Alex might be a cunt, but Mum was right, Rosie'd want him there. Him first. And if it got her better, that's what mattered. Darren sat in Alex's chair and Mum got hold of his hand, as if it weren't important whose it was she held, long as she did.

'She's my baby,' Mum said, in a voice what seemed too small for her body. 'My little Rosie. My Rose. That's why I called her that, you know. I come over all schmaltzy in the hospital, and your dad brought me a big bunch of roses. Red roses. They was called Christmas roses, if I remember right. I was going to call her Cheryl, but when I see them, I thought no, she's as perfect as one of them flowers. She was, and all. And it weren't a bad choice, cos she grew her thorns quick enough, didn't she? Little rot pot.'

'Yeah, you could say that. I member when she was born. Asked you to take her back, get us a dog instead.' They laughed a bit. 'Glad you never, though. She does my head in, but there ain't no one like her, is there? She's going to be all right, Mum – promise.'

'I know everyone thinks that about their kids, but she's special. I'm not saying she's my favourite, duck . . .'

'No, it's all right. Don't worry bout it.' He was all choked. Rosie was such a little mare, but you couldn't help yourself. If you could see it, you had to go with it. Not everybody could see it, but if you could, then there weren't no choice. It weren't nothing to do with her being or not being Mum's favourite, it was to do with her.

Clap-clap. Make it stop. You couldn't never think like the time was going normal, not with that clapping minding you every minute was only a second. Doing his heart in. Like time was fidgeting about, making you know it was there. Ants in its fucking pants. They was here much longer, he'd have to smash the bastard thing.

'D'you want me to get us a tea?' he said. Say yeah – anything to get shot of that time.

The big swing doors opened. Daz looked up. Alex and the doctor was back.

Daz was about to say to Mum to go in, but then he knew. *No*. Oh fuck, no. Not Rosie.

Alex's skin was gone all grey, and there weren't nobody home.

The doctor opened his mouth to speak, but Alex shook his head.

'She's dead, Daz. Rosie's just . . . dead.'

Chapter Sixteen

Rosie Spence
Sitting on the fence,
Got knocked down for
Forty pence.
No one cried
The day she died,
She was nobody's mother
And no man's bride.

He couldn't have heard that right; the little girls skipping to their rhyme couldn't have made up something so callous, surely? But if they hadn't, he had. He couldn't bear to stop and listen to the rhyme again; it was doubtful that listening would give him the truth, anyway. Trouble was, he couldn't forget it now, either. A stupid, pointless, inaccurate memorial, and he couldn't get it out of his mind.

Alex's hand closed round the keys in his pocket. His keys to Rosie's flat. He held on to their hardness, their permanence, hundreds of times a day. But as a talisman they were bollocks. There was nothing bad left to happen, except more and more and more time without her. Strictly speaking, he should give them to Rosie's mum or to Darren, but he couldn't. Right didn't come into it. If someone wanted the fucking things, they'd have to knock him out and take them from him by force. They were useless to him, but they were his.

If he'd had just a few more weeks with her, there might have been some small consolation: he could have been living amongst her stuff. It wouldn't have made him feel any better, that was unimaginable, but he could have slept in her bed, played her CDs, lived surrounded by her choices. His pain would have a setting that was hers. As it was, she'd left almost nothing at his flat, because they were there so rarely. Not even her smell, lingering on a towel or a sheet. If he'd only known, he wouldn't have washed them, would have made sure she'd kept a toothbrush there, some spare underwear, anything. All he had was one damaged picture, a gift in return for his gift of it. If it weren't for that, he thought he'd go mad. If it weren't for that proof, he'd have thought he'd made her up.

He didn't even have a photograph and he'd never been brave enough seriously to suggest filming them together. Why the hell not? Sketches, but even those didn't help much; he wasn't a good enough artist to show her like she actually was, and besides, she'd never seen his real attempts. They weren't invested with anything but his own bad opinion of them. She was barely present in them at all. If a stranger looked into the evidence of his recent life, they'd probably not realize that he had someone. And they wouldn't have the smallest chance of realizing it was Rosie, not in this or any other . . .

Alex had heard people say that when someone died, they kept seeing them in the street. Hadn't happened to him, and he knew it wasn't going to. It was impossible to imagine not seeing her again, but he wasn't going to conjure likenesses. He would always know before his brain could trick him, that others were not her. They wouldn't even be impostors. And although he envied those who did see fleeting versions of the person who had died, he thought that in the end, it meant their grief would pass. He couldn't envy them that, because it was all he had left of her.

Too often, he'd hated her, or nearly hated her. And that didn't go away, any more than the love went away. He hated her for leaving him. There'd been a few times, over the last couple of days, when he'd wanted to kill her for dying. That thought almost made him smile; it was so Rosie. She didn't do reasonable. Her legacy to him was her unreasonableness.

There was only one thing he could do for her now, when it had seemed there was the possibility of a lifetime of doing things for her. Or as much of a lifetime as he could think about. Some of which, lots of which, he wouldn't have wanted to do. Yet he'd have done them, most of them, because he'd have wanted to more than he'd not have wanted the tasks. But there was this one left, and he wanted that for himself, as well as for Rosie. Oh God, why had he kissed Louise back, when she'd first reappeared? Just once, from habit or history or shock, almost repulsive and immediately regretted, but why had he risked so very much for that nothing? He would make sure his divorce went ahead now, as quickly as possible. Otherwise, it would be a far greater betrayal: he'd be married to someone he no longer loved, when he felt in his heart that he belonged to Rosie. It would be as though his grief didn't possess him, and that he couldn't own it fully if others, including Louise, could see him as joined to anyone but his Rosie. He knew he'd be marrying death, but that was better than any other option.

He'd been walking without any clear idea of where he was going. But then he suddenly became aware that he was in Barmy Park. This was where she'd played as a child, venturing no further than that toy museum over the road from here. It must be strange, to have spent almost all of your life in the same few miles. She wouldn't have left. They wouldn't have moved to Hampstead or Hammersmith, much less away from London; he'd have had to be absorbed into her geography, and he'd never wanted that. But it would have happened. She'd have made spaces for him, given him a few yards just for himself, that he could choose, but she wouldn't have let either of them get away. A few days each year south of the river, drunk and happy. And that would have been almost unbearable, but it would have been just bearable enough.

An old man sat on the right-hand bench of three by a round flowerbed, chewing on a biscuit. Alex sat beside him, took out the keys and looked at them.

'Cheer up, son – might never happen.'

'No.' He glanced up at the little white flowers. Why were they called snowdrops, when there wasn't any snow? Maybe they weren't snowdrops at all.

'Woman is it? Wife? None of them worth it, lad. Take my advice – get yourself spruced up, have a shave, go out, find someone else before some other beggar gets her.'

'Plenty more fish in the sea?' It had been bad enough to lose a woman to madness. But this. There was no worse. None. And that would still be true if Louise had died. She had, in a way. If he lived to be as old as this bloke here, he'd never give anyone that advice. Because for him, it was never going to be true. How could it be?

'That's right.'

'Yeah. I've got to go now.' Before I kick your shrunken head in. And it's not your fault, and it'd be outrageous, but I really would, if I stayed here.

Drink didn't help, but when he found himself in the Roman Road, he went into The Beehive anyway. Didn't make things worse to have a shot of something inside you. He felt like ringing his mother, to say that after all these years he finally understood: it wasn't that you were trying to escape reality, just that it didn't matter enough to stay sober. Maybe he could even come to forgive her. Not that it seemed all that important to attempt reconciliation, but he couldn't recapture his long-held resistance. There wasn't any point. And there wasn't any room.

One of those background tapes was on in the pub. Alex braced himself; he knew that at least every second song would have words in it that were tough to hear. That was the point of pop music: your baby left you, or you were so happy together. He should know, he'd been listening to it for thirty years, more. And as he put away his first vodka, he was pitched straight into it: 'Ain't No Sunshine'. But he laughed. Michael Jackson, circa 1972; not a patch on the Sabuka version. That song had always reminded him of Rosie, anyway. When she wasn't there, the world had been that bit darker, that bit more lifeless. So the song couldn't affect him like he'd have thought it would; it wasn't applicable anymore. It really was funny. There was no possibility of her being about, was there? So there was no comparison to be made. She was always going to be gone. It was stupid to try to make some song mean the same as her being so gone.

Rosie had made him read *The Sound and the Fury*. He hadn't liked it. He thought the author was too in love with his tricks, and if Alex was going to read a novel at all, he wanted it to be straightforward. But Rosie had tried to persuade him that he was wrong, had read a bit of it out to him, where some bloke had gone on about *was* being the saddest word in the world. Alex hadn't seen it then but Rosie was right, it was amazing. He could only see that now, because he could feel it for himself. Rosie was what she was, a combination of continuous present and past tense for ever. And for Alex, *he was happy* had no present. Had been. Grammatical balls-ups. If it were true that you could experience nothing outside of language, then you had no access to an accurate representation of your past pleasure. God, he wanted so badly to tell Rosie that; she'd have loved pulling it apart. It was the sort of thing she liked to do.

He had another vodka, and then another; there was no reason not to. And all the time, he wanted her back, felt like screaming for her. But if he started, he was afraid he'd never stop, and the sound would blank out everything, even his pain. He couldn't handle the thought. His pain was Rosie, now.

It was her brother's idea that Alex went in the first car with the family. Chief mourners. Made them sound like a tribe. Alex panicked; his only suit was too tight, and anyway, it was grey. He could probably get one on the card, but he wasn't up to shopping. Drew might have one that would fit him, but he couldn't ring for the first time in three or four years and say out of the blue, *Hi, long time. Thing is, my girlfriend's just died, yeah, she might have been run over on purpose for all any of us knows, and I wondered if you had a dark suit I could borrow for her funeral.* It didn't read. But he couldn't let her down, she'd be furious. In the end, he settled on black jeans, black tee-shirt, leather jacket. That's what she liked him in. Or herself on. And no one commented. Darren looked terrible, despite the designer suit, but there was no way he could have looked anything else. His eyes were red, not only round the rims, but where his whites should be. Demonic. Or they would be, if there was any force coming from them.

'How's your mum?'

'Not great. Our dad's coming and all, she rung him. Never even knew she had the number. But he's in his own motor.'

'Right.' Alex was suddenly desperate to see the dad; he remembered Darren saying how much Rosie looked like their father, although you couldn't tell from that one blurred snapshot she had. But how could a resemblance be any good? It wasn't as though he *was* her.

'Just us in the car, and Mum – Nan's not up to it. Mum showed me your flowers. Nice.'

He couldn't have ordered a wreath. It would have seemed like a sick joke, sending flowers to his dead lover. So he'd sent a bunch to her mum. Not roses, though. Lilies.

'Had we better go?' Alex asked. 'The undertaker said . . .'

'Yeah, I spose. That's the thing, mate – don't seem to know what to do no more.'

'No. I know.'

'You and all?'

'Yeah. Doesn't seem to matter much, one way or the other.'

'No.' Darren held his gaze; there was no special pleading in the red eyes, no suggestion that they were in competition for who felt the most, or the least. Just the sense that he wanted to hold on to Alex's pain, to stare into it, lock it into his own. And Alex couldn't look away.

*   *   *

Nice service.

Lovely service.

It was a good service, don't you think?

She'd of liked that service.

Alex and Darren both burst out laughing. Everyone stared at them, shocked, appalled.

'She'd of loved all the crying, any rate,' said Darren.

'Yeah, but she'd have been so cross at not being around to see it,' said Alex.

It hadn't been a nice, lovely, good service. It was no service at all, to her. There'd been the obligatory half-arsed remarks by some vicar, and Elizabeth, Randa and the one from Sheffield, Janey, had all given tearful readings. They'd had to choose them, as Rosie hadn't made any plans for her funeral; she hadn't thought she did dying. Alex wanted to suggest Sonnet 58, but he couldn't have anyone else saying the words, saying they were his Rosie's slave. And could you be the slave of a dead woman? He wouldn't have wanted anyone else to read it and he couldn't have done it. Not unless he'd known that's what she wanted her slave to do. And she couldn't tell him now. So they'd had some bollocks instead, that at least made some sense: *And death shall have no dominion . . . Death lies on her like an untimely frost . . . Parting is all we know of heaven / And all we need of hell.* In the midst of life they were in death; perhaps the vicar knew what he was on about, after all. Neither Alex nor Darren had wanted to give the eulogy, so Ben had tried. But he hadn't got over what he felt, what any of them felt.

'She was a success, that's what Rosie was. We was all proud of her, round our way. And she was good friend to loads of us. She was loved, and we all feel for her mum, Pat, and her brother, Darren, and her boyfriend, Alex . . .'

He'd probably sweated over that speech, but he hadn't got close. And it was blatant that he knew it, too.

Alex hadn't been to an East End funeral before. The wreaths laid in the street for the neighbours to see sickened him. A parody of a wedding, with everyone coming out to see the bride's dress. Her name spelled out in pink roses. Rest In Peace in yellow carnations. A teddy bear, for God's sake, in more pink roses. Throw the bouquet, my love: I promise you, you won't want it.

She was there, of course. In a coffin chosen by her mother. No parent should ever have to do that for her child; Rosie's mother certainly should never have had to. It was white, over-elaborate, gold handled. Rosie would have had a fit, if she could have seen it. *And how, exactly, do you expect me to rest in that?* Then the long, slow drive to the City of London crematorium, waved off by the street, the older men removing their hats or bowing their heads as they passed. But although the chief mourners followed her as they always had, they'd return without her, as though they could really leave her behind.

They burned her. To the twenty-third psalm. Curtains closed around the coffin, and she was gone. Alex knew they didn't really burn her then and there; the urn Pat got back would probably contain bits of everyone who'd been cremated that day. But it felt like that's what they were doing. Rosie, who loved her CDs, was burned to the tuneless mumblings of the mourners. He should have offered her something better than this. He couldn't even sing.

She'd even hate this party, it was all wrong for her. And yet, they might as well eat and drink and be merry. Or sit in a corner and cry into their beer. Or go home, to be alone with their grief. None of it changed a thing. *Poppet, darling, sweetheart*; it was a wonder they didn't get diabetes. She'd been like that, the promiscuous whore. But maybe, if he thought about it enough, he'd be able to come up with one she'd used only to him. *Depends on what's behind it, babe.* Rosie's dad didn't come back to the house, but outside the crem, Alex had searched his features. Yeah, he had her eyes, but they didn't have the right person looking out of them. He called Alex *mate*.

'Son?' the father had said to Darren.

But Darren had turned away.

For once, Darren and Alex were in agreement: this man had left Rosie, of his own accord, where she had left them.

Rosie's mother wouldn't even look at him.

Fuck off, mate.

Pat hardly appeared at the party, staying in the kitchen, washing up glasses, making tea, getting bottle after bottle out of the cupboard. Darren had to be the host, checking that everyone had a scotch, a ham sandwich, a laugh.

'You all right, mate? Yeah, thanks, mate – preciate it. My mother made me a queer – if I send her the wool, will she make me one, and all? Yeah, cheers. She was, yeah. Bearing up, you know. She's in the kitchen – go say hello, but go careful.'

It was a bravura performance. Hardly knowing what he was doing, Alex grabbed a bottle of scotch and began to circle the room from the opposite direction.

'Thanks. Yeah, I was. I know you are, we all are. It was, yeah. I know she would.'

And whenever they caught one another's eye, they held the gaze for a split second. It felt as though they'd be doing this for ever, circling the room, filling glasses, checking in with each other's empty eyes. Still, there was no love lost between them.

Elizabeth, Randa and William stood in an expensive-smelling cluster by the window. Randa, in the centre, had on a black scarf, one of those floaty see-through things, making Alex think of the three witches. He felt proud of himself for that, wanted to tell Rosie. He'd always want to tell Rosie, wouldn't he? Elizabeth turned and saw him.

'Scotch?' he said.

'Thanks.' She held out her glass. 'Alex, I'm so sorry. We'll all feel it, terribly, but it must be worse for you.'

'Right. Yeah, thanks.' What the hell was he supposed to say to that? My life's just fallen apart, I don't see any possibility of ever putting it back together, of course it's worse for me than for you, far, far more so than you can imagine?

'I've known her since we were eighteen,' said Randa. 'We were at university together.'

'Yeah. Right.' He nearly added *Thanks*.

'The firm will miss her,' said William. 'She was unique. I doubt we'll find anyone else as good. Not without a long, hard search. The whole character of the firm will change.'

So fucking what? Alex wanted to punch him, self-serving prick. He moved away.

'Need a refill?' he said to Freddy. Sue's dress was too low-cut for a funeral. Not that Alex gave a toss, he thought it was quite funny, like she knew her tits were her best feature and couldn't bear not to put them on display. But it was the sort of mistake Rosie would never make; she'd never have come to a funeral in a short skirt to show off her legs, or something really tight to emphasize how slim she was. Although she would have worn beautiful shoes. He looked at Sue's cleavage. Thing was, he'd hurt his Rosie about something he didn't care about. Tits. You could get those anywhere, even at a funeral. He wished so much that he could touch Rosie's breasts just once, to take that hurt away.

'I'm sorry, darling,' Sue said. 'She was such a lovely girl.'

No, she wasn't. She was a bitch. Except when she wasn't.

'Don't know what I'll do without her,' said Freddy. Sue nudged him.

'Don't suppose he do, neither,' she said.

'We'll find out what happened, mate, don't you—' Freddy stopped as his wife elbowed him again. 'Sorry, bad time. But this ain't finished.'

Alex caught Darren's gaze.

Oh, it's finished all right. With the corruption of someone's soul. God, Alex would corrupt every conviction he'd had about Sam, if only he could revive her recidivism.

Ben sat next to that Janey, on hard chairs near the door. They were both wet-eyed. Janey touched Ben's scarred face; he pulled away from her hand. Alex vividly remembered the night it had happened, but what he remembered most clearly was not the blood, or the shock, or the fear for Rosie, but later, at his flat. The first time. When he'd said to her, *Walk all over me.* And the bitch had complied, like she was doing him a favour. Now she was walking all over the rest of his life. The fucking total bitch.

He made no sense to himself. Everything he wanted to do, everything he was prepared to endure, had nowhere to go. For so long, he'd protected himself, using the past to shore up a pointless present, never opening himself up too far when he could gesture to the early days with Louise and say *But I had that, nothing else will do.* And then Rosie decided she wanted him, and the past lost against her, crumbled into ruins. Now the future would always lose against her, too. There wouldn't be another release. By definition she was no protection, as Louise had been; Rosie couldn't protect him from Rosie.

Protection. *Bollocks!* She, they, had all their stuff at her flat, the whip and the crop and . . . everything. What was he supposed to do? Go there, hide it, protect her from her family, or her family from her, or whatever the hell that would be doing? What did she want from him? Now the funeral was over, they'd want to get in there, sort through her *effects.* Sort through her. Alex couldn't stand the thought of her being picked over, judged, by people who didn't have a chance of understanding. They thought they knew one person, and those things would show them what they'd believe was someone else. Especially Darren. Alex had never been comfortable with the way Darren had looked at Rosie, but if he saw her sexuality laid out, had to force it into bin bags for Oxfam, he'd implode. Would Rosie get a certain amount of satisfaction from that, and from the way it was affecting Alex just thinking about it? Or would she expect him to preserve how her family saw her, and not care either way for his dilemma. She loved him, she *had* loved him, he knew that. But she hadn't quite trusted him enough to give him the information to call this situation. Or had she? And now he understood how it must have felt when he told her she ignored his instruction manual; hers might have been less explicit, but he had been offered it to flick through and still he couldn't read it.

In the end, he went to the flat. He walked it, as he'd walked everywhere since she'd died (everywhere except to her cremation) and held on to the keys the whole way.

The first time he'd been back.

As he reached the building, he slowed up. How could he walk past the spot where the car had hit her? The keys dug into his palm as he forced himself on. If he looked at the pavement, he knew he'd see traces of her blood; not that there'd inevitably be any, but inevitably he'd see them. Alex let himself in through the security door, and ran up the stairs. Suddenly, being outside the flat was too much. He needed to be in there.

Everything was how he had left it: his half-drunk vodka (but with its slice of lemon turned mushy), the bottle of scotch and a waiting glass on the little table, an ashtray full of cigarette ends. Only that scream, that apparent explosion, were absent; he'd been afraid they'd be here too, with the bowl of cashews and the open TV page. He picked up the stale drink and downed it. Then he opened the scotch, and put the top to his nose. He could smell Rosie, some of her moods. A couple of mouthfuls straight from the bottle. A handful of nuts. His longing for her was so great that he picked up the paper, willing time back to halfway through last Thursday's *EastEnders*, so he'd still have that last sight of her alive ahead of him. She'd call him a sentimental moron for that, but he couldn't help himself. And maybe even Rosie would concede that there was nothing romantic about a crushed, bloody, broken near-corpse. But he'd give anything to have even the sight of that to come, the feel of her warm blood on his fingers as he stroked her hair, the rusty-oily smell of her last few minutes in the real world. Seeing her in the hospital didn't count. Watching her die . . . if it wasn't for those horrible machines, he wouldn't even have known she'd gone. Rosie could say what she fucking well liked . . .

Without really knowing what he was doing, Alex took her pen from the table, and put it in his pocket. It wasn't even a special pen, she'd just picked it up from Smith's or somewhere and didn't give a stuff about it, but he had to have it. He put the bottle top in with it, and a tissue that was screwed up on the armchair. Collecting shells on a beach; he'd only done that once, with his mum, before it had all started. But he'd seen other people do it. Random acts of acquisition. He grabbed the top CD from a pile, not even looking to see what it was, and a lipstick-stained butt from the ashtray. Then he got a hold of himself. If he took any more stuff, it'd never fit in his pocket, not with the folded-up bin bag as well.

He went into the bedroom. The drawers and cupboards were still all hers; he'd left some things here, but he hadn't even got round to organizing himself a drawer. On her embroidered chair was a tee-shirt belonging to him; there'd be a few of his clothes in the laundry basket, mixed up with her knickers, jeans, jumpers. Alex thought about it, but he decided he didn't want to sort them out; not that he couldn't bear to, but it was a tiny scrap of comfort, that jumbling of underwear, jeans. But their stuff? *I don't care what you call it, precious*. The labels had been right, though; she'd been right when she'd gone to use them. Labels of acts that after more than forty years had told him what his sexuality consisted in. He knew where she kept the toys, but should he go through the wardrobe, picking out certain of her clothes? The toys first.

Alex opened a drawer. There it all was, the restraints, the clamps, the cock rings, the whip. And his collar. He took it out, ran his thumb along the studs. Who did he belong to? A dead woman. And these things weren't toys, they were just pieces of metal and leather. He could hardly play with them by his own. Just a collection of expensive fetish stuff. You could buy them in any town more or less, if you had the bottle. He felt . . . stupid, that's what, standing there looking at a drawer full of things that would never be used on him again. How had he let them be used on him in the first place? On one level, it was easy to answer himself: because he'd wanted to offer himself to her, more than he'd ever wanted to offer himself to anybody. He wanted to please her, would have done almost anything to see that particular out-of-control flare in those eyes. But on another level, he had no answer, except to think that it seemed utterly pointless now, because she was gone. What he offered wasn't enough to keep her with him. The world got in the way. Maybe it had always been going to.

He took out the black plastic bag and chucked the stuff into it. He'd have to think later about what he'd do with it all. No point in keeping it, but there didn't seem any possibility that he'd be able to throw it away. When he opened the wardrobe door, her perfume seeped into the room. He didn't even know what it was called. She never wore much, but she put it on every day, and he wouldn't know the name if someone said it. He made himself reach into the wardrobe, run his hands along the fabric of her dresses, skirts, suits. So many clothes. There was a cupboardful too, and the other drawers, and the wooden trunk at the end of her bed. The suede dress. Last time he'd touched that, he'd felt her through it; now it was simply a length of hide, almost repellent. As quickly as he could, Alex grabbed anything he could find that was leather or PVC, even the skirts and trousers she wore as a matter of course, and crammed those into the bag with the rest of their things. Technically, he supposed it was stealing, but if he didn't know what to do with them, he couldn't believe that her family would.

The next day, he was back in her flat again. Darren had rung him up, actually rung him, to ask if he'd help sort through her things.

'What about your mum?'

'She don't want to do it. And I . . . look, mate, I'll be truthful here. I can't deal with it on me own.'

'There's her girlfriends?'

'I thought you'd fucking want the chance, you . . .'

'Yeah. No, I do. I'm sorry, I keep talking bollocks at the
moment.'

'I know what you mean.'

Alex wasn't an idiot; he knew Darren was no closer to
wanting to be his friend than he ever had been. But he also
knew that Darren was saying they were the only two who
could do this terrible thing. The only two. And that he'd had
to swallow his pride and make a choice. Alex had to be as big
as that, even if it was just for this one day.

They met on the street outside the building. Alex noticed
Darren averting his eyes from where he supposed he must
imagine the accident, or whatever it was, had happened. He
wasn't far out.

'Mum give me the key.'

'Right, right.'

'Look a right pair of cunts stood here.' He glanced at Alex.
'I never meant . . .'

'No, I know.' Alex stood aside for Darren to open the outer
door, and followed him up the stairs.

'I've never done this,' Darren said, as he put the key into
the lock. 'Not come in when she weren't about. Not even when
I stayed here that time.'

She's not at the shops, Darren. But he couldn't say it out
loud.

Alex had washed his glass, emptied the ashtray, but the
topless bottle of scotch remained on the table, next to the
nearly empty bowl of nuts.

'It's like that boat,' said Darren, almost whispering.

'The *Marie Celeste*? Yeah, I suppose.'

'Fucking hell, Al.' Darren lit a cigarette, passed the packet
to Alex, and they just stood there, smoking. They had no boxes
with them, no bags, Darren hadn't brought the lorry. What the
hell did they think they were going to do?

'Uh . . . what's the deal?' Alex said, eventually.

'Don't know.' Darren put his free hand in the pocket of his jeans. 'Mum said do the clothes, put them in piles of good stuff, stuff to chuck, and all that. And you'll have to have a look at her papers and computer, see what the score is there. Everything else – I don't know. It all goes to Mum in the will, sept for what friends want, at our . . .'

'Discretion.'

'Yeah. That means you and all. Take a few bits, you know.'

'Thanks. I will.' Alex felt like laughing.

'This is like when they send soldiers on a reccy, more'n anything else. Just seemed . . . I don't know.' His voice was choking in his throat.

'You just wanted to see it? Without her?' He spoke cautiously; when his dad, on the 'phone, tried to say he knew how he felt, Alex had slammed the receiver down. Dad hadn't even known her, for God's sake. He'd only known of her existence since Christmas. How could anyone know how anyone else felt?

'Yeah. Keep specting her to come in, tell us to get the fuck out of here.'

'And we'd say we thought we were doing the right thing, and she'd say, *Did you now?*'

'I keep doing that, and all. She keeps on saying things. I ain't mental, I don't mean I think I hear her, just . . .'

'Yeah.'

'I want it to stop.'

'So do I.' But he didn't think that either of them knew what it was they wanted to stop. Other than the fact of her being dead.

'With her gear, maybe a bird would be better. Don't know what's any good, d'you?'

'Not really.' But he knew he had to be in amongst her clothes again, smell that nameless perfume. 'We could make a start.'

'Yeah, okay.'

They went out to the hall, and into the bedroom.

'I ain't hardly been in here afore,' said Darren. Alex had to stop himself from shouting *I have! I have!* like a kid showing off.

'So what do you suggest?'

Darren opened the low cupboard.

'What's in here?' he said.

Her shoes. Was he completely stupid, or what? The most important symbol, the most important *thing*, and he'd forgotten to take them away. Those boots. Bollocks. Bollocks. Bollocks. It was because if he didn't know what to do with the other things, how on earth could he make a call on those? It was because he was stupid with grief. It was because he was a cunt.

'Fucking hell. Imelda whatsname.' Darren knelt on the floor in front of the cupboard, pulling out pair after pair of shoes, boots, sandals. The smell of her feet assaulted them, sweet, warm, fleshly. More than any other, this smell was Rosie, to Alex. And she still smelt alive. Occasionally, Darren tested a heel with his thumb, or ran a hand over the leather. Soon, they were surrounded by them; if he were to lie down, Alex felt as though he'd drown.

God, her shoes. Carefully, Alex knelt at the edge of the wave, picked up the green stiletto. He was overwhelmed by the need to kiss it, breathe through the insole, run his tongue over it. Quickly, he put it down. Where the hell were those boots? Darren was handling a sandal, one Alex had never seen Rosie wear. He wanted to scream at her brother, tell him to put it down, to piss off, to leave her shoes alone. Oh God. You could see, on some of them, the imprint of her foot. Shoes that lived, because you could see the shape of the owner's toes. But they'd never live any more, never grow, change, wear out, be replaced. Never walk through a puddle. Never walk over flesh.

He realized that Darren was crying. Not sobbing; loss was simply leaking from his eyes. Too big for him to contain.

'Stupid fucking shoes. She must of spent a fortune on them,' Darren said, his voice normal, despite the tears. 'Always told her she'd break her neck, one of these days.'

'It wasn't the shoes.'

'No, I know.' He was silent for a minute. Then, 'D'you think it was my fault?' he said.

Alex hadn't expected this, not at all.

'No,' he said. He didn't know whether it were true. Hit and run; could have been anything, any kind of corruption. Nobody saw. Nobody ever saw. Being with Rosie had taught him that. But he could blame Darren, himself, Rosie, Charlie, Sam, some stranger. He could blame worlds colliding, or go all mystical and Louise-like, and blame fate or karma. But he couldn't be bothered. All his energy was taken up with missing her.

'I tried so hard to find out,' said Darren.

'I guessed that. Nothing?'

'No. I want . . . I want someone to pay. Someone's fucking got to. Al, what did she look like? No, I know you said bout . . . I mean in the hospital, when she sactly died.'

'Exactly like she looked when you came in.'

'Like an angel.' Straight-faced.

'Well . . .' An *angel*? He knew Darren was stoned, but if he could call Rosie, alive or dead, an angel, he must be seriously off his head.

'How d'you give people what they deserve when you can't fucking know who's the cunt doing the deserving?'

'You'll find a way.' He was sure of that.

'Yeah, too right I will. You can depend on it, pal.' But he didn't sound angry, just bewildered. And still the tears came down his cheeks. He shook his head and reached further into the cupboard. 'What the . . .'

The boots.

Darren turned them over in his hands, as though he were an archeologist who'd just made an amazing discovery.

'You seen . . . ?'

'Mm.' He watched Darren seeing, really seeing the boots. Then Alex held out his hands; it was holding his hands up. 'Can I?'

Darren passed them over. He looked confused, even a bit scared.

Alex took the boots. He was shaking. Those boots had taken her further than he'd ever wanted her to go. They'd have taken her further still, had she not died. Would have taken him further still. He closed his eyes, then immediately opened them; he didn't want his private pictures played in front of Darren.

'Bit much, ain't they?' Darren said.

'Yeah.'

'She . . . No, don't matter.' Darren couldn't take his eyes off Alex. What the hell was going through his mind?

Alex pressed one of the heels into his chest, trying to make it look as though he were simply holding the boots close. Too late to pretend, anyway; Darren would either get it or he wouldn't.

'I want these. I mean, you said I could have something. How about these?'

'You want *them*? Why? You a bit funny, or what?'

'Like you said, they're larger than life. No one else'll want them.'

'Surprised she did. Yeah, take them. I never see her wear them, though. Must of been for a party or something.'

Further than he'd wanted her to go. Thank God.

It was two days later, no maybe three, when the shaking really started. For a week, on and off, Alex shook and shook. Cold all the time, even with the heating on. Some days, got so bad he could hardly light a fag. That's when he had cigarettes. He kept running out and not wanting to face the shops, so he had to roll up dog-ends. He couldn't remember where the Rizlas had come from, but he seemed to have lots of packets. Then he'd get brave, run down to the little shop on the corner, buy cigarettes, chocolate, lager, tea-bags, bread. When he ran out of marge, he ate his toast dry. Tea had been black for days. He couldn't add to his shopping list, because that would take him over his five items. It was important to do things in fives. Buy five things in the shop, and you might be able to eat something. Go to bed for five hours, and then you might sleep

for some of them. Watch five TV programmes, and for a couple
of minutes, you might get distracted. Wash your hands five
times, and you might stop biting at the side of your thumb
for long enough that it wasn't permanently sore. Play five
hymns in your head, and you might find your mantra or make
a better one.

Mine eyes have seen the

People kept ringing and ringing. But then he had a brilliant
idea and unplugged the 'phone. Work rang and rang; why
would he want to go in to work? When? Never. Or sometime.
Did it matter? Louise rang and rang. He told her, it wasn't her
he wanted to speak to; she wasn't Rosie. She cried. But he was
only telling the truth. Maybe when they were divorced, she
wouldn't keep ringing and ringing. And ringing and ringing
and ringing, and he could plug the 'phone back in. Dad rang,
but it was pointless talking to him, he hadn't known her. Pat
rang, but neither of them could speak for crying. No sense in
a conversation that had *Hello* and *Goodbye* but none of the
bits in between.

Glory of the coming of

He'd worked out why Rosie loved him. Because she knew
he needed love most. He needed it most. Not in an underdog
sort of way; she'd kick an underdog rather than stroke one.
And not because she was kind. But she just saw, with that
look of hers, that he needed to be loved, and he needed it to
be her. And she needed that from him, and it was easy to give
because it was her, even though he had to hate her as well,
some of the time.

The Lord He hath trampled

In a casual sort of way, he wondered if he'd stay for the
rest of his life in the flat, except for going to the shop. Suppose
the card would run out eventually. But not for a long time,
if he kept only buying five things. He couldn't pay it off, but
maybe they wouldn't make him, when they saw he'd only
been buying the essentials. Not like he'd gone out and bought
a CD player or a wide-screen television. He didn't need *stuff*;

he had the fucked-up picture in his bedroom, the black bag with their things in it under his bed. That was more than enough. Sometimes, when the shaking wasn't too bad, he wrote a word with her pen. Only one word, in case the pen ran out too quickly. Should be five words, but the risks outweighed the potential benefits in this instance. It wasn't always the same word, though. Sometimes, it was *Rosie*. Sometimes, *Spence*. Or *Shoe* or *Love* or *Death*. Depended how he felt. All short words.

Out the vintage where the

Her boots caused him a problem for a couple of days. It seemed right to him that he should make a shrine to her out of them, but it was hard to get his head around because she wasn't here, so what would he be making a shrine to? If she was never going to wear the boots again, was there any point in worshipping them? But then he saw *Songs of Praise* and (proving his five theory, validating his mantra) realized that her death made a shrine an even better idea than it would have been if she were still alive. Pity she couldn't see it, though. She'd love it, big time. He put the boots on top of the TV, because although he wanted distraction, he sort of didn't at the same time. Five times a day, he cleaned them with his tongue, and kissed them, and whispered her name to them. One day, the image of her wearing them was so strong that he had to masturbate, to come over them. But that made him cry, so he thought he wouldn't try that again for a while. He hoped she wouldn't mind.

It hurts, Rosie.

I know it hurts, babe, I know. It's all right. I promise you, it looks so good.

'Three Blind Mice!'

But she couldn't hear him. He knew she'd never ignore that if she could hear him. It was there to protect both of them. A good deal for her, even more than for him: she knew that having a code meant he wouldn't want to break into it. She just couldn't hear him, now he'd had to.

Grapes of wrath are stored

And then there was more ringing and ringing. Except it wasn't the 'phone, he'd seen to that. The doorbell. Alex shuffled to the door, putting a piece of Dairy Milk into his mouth.

Darren.

'Jesus, mate. You look like a fucking tramp.'

Couldn't look that bad. He'd had a bath every day. Rosie liked him to be clean. But Darren had probably had a bath every day too, and he looked like shit. Like he had no blood in his face, except in his eyes. Like he hadn't slept for a week. Like he didn't care about himself.

'What do you want?' He said it very politely.

'Me mum was worried about you. Sent me round. Be truthful, think she wanted me out the way. You going to let me in, or what?'

Alex wasn't too sure. Was he? He counted to five.

'Okay. Come in.'

'Look at this joint, Al.'

Alex looked. There were empty cans everywhere, and mugs of half-drunk black tea, and three overflowing ashtrays, and chocolate wrappers, and plates. He hadn't noticed.

'I'll clear up.'

'Just bung it all out the way. I'm going to put one together, and I don't want any shit about it.'

'Dope?'

'Yeah.'

Alex didn't care. Why would he? He carried the cans and things out to the kitchen, five at a time. When he'd finished, he got two fresh cans out of the fridge and gave one to Darren, who passed him a joint. He took a couple of hits, passed it back.

There's no pleasure now. Only pain.

He wasn't entirely convinced he hadn't said it aloud. But Darren didn't react, so perhaps he hadn't.

'How are you doing?' This time, he was pretty sure he'd spoken.

'How the fuck d'you think?'

Yeah, he must have done. Definitely. Darren wasn't the sort to ask philosophical questions. Although it was an interesting one.

'Badly.' Nicely ambiguous. Rosie would be pleased.

'You could say that. I can't handle it. And you can't, neither.'

'No.'

'How long you been doing that?'

'What?'

'Shaking like a . . .'

'Thing that shakes? Don't know. A week?'

'She . . . look, mate, she wouldn't want this. Don't give a monkey's meself – got me own shit to sort. But for her. We got to get you something. I'll take care of it.'

'Okay.' Alex didn't have any idea what Darren meant, but it seemed rude not to accept when someone said they'd take care of something for you. And when they said it was really for Rosie, there was no question of not accepting. 'Thanks. She'll be pleased.'

But he must have said something wrong, because tears came into Darren's red eyes.

'I keep doing that, and all,' Darren said.

Six weeks later, Alex was back at work. He'd thought he'd blown it, that they'd use it as an excuse to get rid of him, but in the event everyone had been nice to him, even the Board. It went on his record as nervous exhaustion. He had proper anti-depressants now, and the doctor tried to get him to go to *bereavement* counselling, but bollocks to that. He'd miss Rosie for the rest of his life; there was nothing anyone could say or make him say to change that. He was half of an equal and opposing pair; he'd never make full sense to himself again. You couldn't be a submissive without your Dominant. Call it whatever you liked, but the truth remained the same.

On Saturday, after a week at the Centre, Alex decided to start on his project. He'd been thinking about it ever since he'd returned from Pat's a month ago, but he wanted some semblance of the old routine before going out to buy the paint and brushes. Didn't want to make choices in the wilderness. At B&Q he found an amazing vermilion, a green, a sunshine yellow, and white with a hint of rose. That made him smile. He lugged the cans home on the bus. A woman sat next to him, asked him if he were doing a spot of decorating. He told her he was; it seemed easier than to explain.

Back at the flat, he brushed the bedroom ceiling. Then, standing on the chair from the kitchen, he marked out his design with a charcoal pencil. And he started to paint.

It took him all weekend, but it looked beautiful, even though he said so himself.

Roses. A ceiling full of roses.

Not a substitute.

The eternal submission of his life to her memory.

No more talking, babe.

Sub rosa.

Acknowledgements

I'd like to thank: Chris, whose ability simultaneously to offer space and support is so rare and valuable a gift. Who fixed my computer while ignoring my foul mouth and temper. Most importantly, he has never once counted the cost. Spell (then, now, always) and Michael, for their encouragement, suggestions and emotional ballast. Jerusalem, Spell. Our amazing Catherine, for her detailed legal advice and startlingly perceptive analysis. Dear Em and Dr Steve, for their enthusiasm and nit-picking, and for enduring drunken conversations about the themes. Patrick Walsh, my agent, Sally Abbey, my editor, and Sarah Shrubb, my copy-editor, for their faith and hard work. You have all improved this novel and I am grateful.

Special thanks to Jonathan Martin, who read and commented closely on each chapter as I wrote it, who took infinite pains with his criticism of subsequent drafts, and who discussed it all with me endlessly. Without his influence, I wouldn't have *Three Blind Mice* in any form; without his practical efforts, it would have remained in manuscript on my desk. Selflessly, he offered his talent, and in the process proved a true teacher. My biggest hope for this book is that it comes close to being what you always believed it could be.

Now you can order superb titles directly from Abacus